PRAISE FOR *TIGER MOON*

ALA/ALSC Batchelder Honor Book

Kirkus Reviews Best Book of 2008

★ "A distinguished book for older fairy-tale fans."
—*School Library Journal*, starred review

★ "Fast paced and exciting . . . wildly colorful . . .
beautiful language." —*Booklist*, starred review

ALSO BY ANTONIA MICHAELIS

Dragons of Darkness, translated by Anthea Bell

ANTONIA MICHAELIS

Tiger Moon

Translated from the German by
ANTHEA BELL

AMULET BOOKS
NEW YORK

PUBLISHER'S NOTE: This is a work of fiction. Names, characters, places, and incidents are either the product of the author's imagination or are used fictitiously, and any resemblance to actual persons, living or dead, business establishments, events, or locales is entirely coincidental.

The Library of Congress has cataloged the hardcover edition of this book as follows:
Michaelis, Antonia.
Tiger moon / by Antonia Michaelis ; translated from the German by Anthea Bell.
p. cm.
Summary: Sold to be the eighth wife of a rich and cruel merchant, Safia, also called Raka, tries to escape her fate by telling stories of Farhad the thief, his companion Nitish the white tiger, and their travels across India to retrieve a famous jewel that will save a kidnapped princess from becoming the bride of a demon king.
ISBN 978-0-8109-9481-2 (hardcover + jacket)
[1. Arranged marriage—Fiction. 2. Storytellers—Fiction. 3. Robbers and outlaws—Fiction. 4. Tigers—Fiction. 5. Princesses—Fiction. 6. India—Fiction.]
I. Bell, Anthea. II. Title.

PZ7.M5798274Tig 20008
[Fic]—dc22
2007022823

Paperback ISBN 978-0-8109-4499-2

First published by Loewe Verlag GmbH
Copyright © 2006 Loewe Verlag, Bindlach, Germany
First published in English in hardcover by Amulet Books in 2008
English translation copyright © 2008 Anthea Bell
The translation of this work was supported by a grant from the Goethe-Institute that is funded by the Ministry of Foreign Affairs.

Book design by Maria T. Middleton

Printed and bound in U.S.A.
10 9 8 7 6 5 4 3 2 1

Amulet Books are available at special discounts when purchased in quantity for premiums and promotions as well as fundraising or educational use. Special editions can also be created to specification. For details, contact specialmarkets@abramsbooks.com or the address below.

THE ART OF BOOKS SINCE 1949
115 West 18th Street
New York, NY 10011
www.abramsbooks.com

றோயீக்கு அவன்
பையனக்களுக்கும்
பெண்ககளுக்கும்

To Roy and his children

CONTENTS

ADVANCE WARNING

HOW DOES A STORY ABOUT INDIA BEGIN? Does it begin with the three great rivers—the Ganges, the Yamuna, the unseen Sarasvati pouring her dreaming waters down from the snowy mountains to the hot, dry plain?

Does it begin with the trinity of great gods, the Trimurti: Brahma, Shiva, and Vishnu, the Creator, the Preserver, and the Destroyer? Does it begin with those three making their way, armed with swords of wisdom, knowledge, and divine illogic, through the bewildering landscape of the last few thousand years?

Does it begin with the tiger roaming the jungle in the south? The cracked, scarred ground of the deserts in the north? The sultry air of temples and the cool shade of mosques? The upright military bearing of British churches? Or the vultures circling the Towers of Silence, where the Parsees lay their dead, not far from the pulsating, gaudy center of trade and commerce that is the port of Mumbai?

How does a story about India begin? With rain? Heat? Death? With the sacred white cows?

Does it begin with women winding white jasmine blossoms into garlands in the streets of Madras? Does it begin with fishermen freeing the glittering catch from their nets in Rameshvaram, at the farthest tip of India?

With children playing in the dirt of Calcutta, or holy sadhus greeting the dusty rays of the morning sun in Varanasi, their eyes turned inward and their thin hands held out?

Or does it begin quite differently—suddenly, abruptly, without warning?

Like life that is worth so little in India.

With a leap right into the midst of chaos. Yes, that's how it should begin.

SAFIA AND RAKA

Slowly the Indian wind in the air
heavily, lazily goes,
scents of spices it will bear,
while the sacred smoke it blows.

The Indian wind high over the land
roams wide, roams near and far,
burning as yellow as sun, as sand,
and as black as coal it will char.

The Indian wind in the streets won't wait;
it drives old stories on apace—
tales of life and love, of death and hate,
and fast, oh fast as you may chase
after the wind, I tell you true,
those tales are a danger, a danger to you.

O F COURSE THIS IS A COMPLETELY OUT-
landish story.

In India, all stories are outlandish, though only a few are *completely* outlandish.

Like life, this story begins and ends with a journey.

A journey through the desert.

One hot June day in the early twentieth century, the merchant Ahmed Mudhi and his men set out on the journey with which this story begins. Ahmed Mudhi was a prosperous man who liked to be called by the title of *Rajah*. He had many beautiful horses, and many (but not quite such a large number of) beautiful wives. The hair of his wives shone black as night, their eyes sparkled like stars, and the secret music of their silver anklets delighted Ahmed Mudhi's ears. But the whinnying of the black horses in his stables delighted him even more, until one day, as he traveled through the desert, he came upon the most beautiful woman he had ever seen. He found her by chance in a little village in the middle of nowhere, sitting under a date palm and dreaming. When she saw him looking at her, she cast down her unusually bright eyes, which Ahmed Mudhi took for a sign of modesty—and at that moment he would have given all his horses for her.

In the bargaining that followed, however, the price dropped a good deal lower, for the girl's father was poor, and glad that he wouldn't have to pay a dowry for his daughter, as was the custom.

The girl was called Safia, meaning *virtue*, and the Rajah thought it was a good name for her. She never once returned his glances, but Ahmed Mudhi's blood was surging with desire, and he knew he had fallen in love.

It was not love as celebrated in the romantic songs sung by the desert women. He was in love the way you fall in love with a beautiful ring, a pair of finely worked shoes, a silver necklace, an embroidered camel bag. The way you fall in love with something you must have at any price.

Ahmed Muhdi married the girl that same evening.

Although he was a devout Muslim, he bowed to the customs of his beautiful bride's family and went through a ceremony that was mainly Hindu. Not one of the women in his harem had been a Hindu—until now. But in the old days, when Muslims swept over the land of the desert in great waves to conquer it region by region, Muslim princes had married Hindu princesses.

So there was no obstacle to the marriage.

The girl's family belonged to a high caste. That didn't alter the fact that they were very poor. Indeed it probably made matters even worse, for it was almost impossible to find any of the daughters a bridegroom of equally high caste who would take her without a dowry.

To Safia's family, Ahmed Mudhi's proposal was like a sign from the gods, or, if not from the gods, at least it was a sign of improved financial circumstances.

Safia felt the cool silver of the wedding jewelry on her forehead. She looked at the Rajah and knew why these things were happening. She had heard many stories—too many. The Rajah would take her away with him, away from her dreams, the date palm, and her native land, because from this day on, she was his property. The borrowed jewelry weighed heavy on her head and shoulders—as if it would force her deep into the sand, all the way down to the center of the earth, where it would stifle her in the darkness.

She said nothing.

But Ahmed Mudhi did not get his heart's desire at once. That same night, urgent business summoned him back to the city. He left most of his men behind to escort his new jewel through the great expanses of the desert by slower, safer ways.

He spurred his horse on alone, looking forward to being united with his bride soon, in less dusty surroundings.

Safia's mother and her eight little brothers and sisters stood shyly in a row in front of what remained of the festivities—the discarded palm fronds, the fading garlands of flowers—and looked up at her as she mounted one of the Rajah's fine horses.

Her father placed his hands together in front of his breast and murmured a farewell blessing. He shed no tears. The dark skin around his eyes was as dry and wrinkled as the desert sand that ruled his life.

He had wept only twice in his life: once when he was born, and once when his best camel died. It was a long time since he had owned any camels. Life in its unpredictable course had deprived him of all his possessions.

When he saw his eldest daughter ride away, one of many

stones fell from his heart. He didn't love his daughter, but he was a man with a sense of responsibility. In the cool shade of the Rajah's garden, her rebellious heart would submit to a man's will at last, and the gods would forgive him for letting a Muslim have her.

He had no idea that he had pronounced a sentence of death on his daughter.

For no Indian likes to be cheated. And it was known, far beyond the bounds of his own city, that Ahmed Mudhi in particular didn't like to be deceived.

Rajah Ahmed Mudhi had bargained for a virgin. And only Safia knew that he wasn't getting one.

She tried to escape three times on the journey, but the men escorting her took good care not to lose their rajah's jewel. They had expected to have to defend his purchase against desert bandits, not against the iron will of the purchase itself.

At first they joked about Safia. Then they began to grumble, for she was clever, and once she almost succeeded in running away.

Finally, they put her on a horse in front of the strongest of them.

"That'll put an end to these stupid attempts to escape,"

said the men, and it did. Safia felt the sweat of the stocky little man behind her and smelled his greed. And she hated him. She hated him for seven days, although she knew it was unjust of her. He was only a servant: His spirit served the Rajah, and his body served nature.

He didn't touch her, but delivered her safely on the thirteenth day of their journey to the *haveli*, the Rajah's magnificent house. The busy life of the city of Jaisalmer teemed behind him as he bowed once more in the doorway and then closed the door.

Safia stood alone in the inner courtyard, which had a cool fountain playing merrily into a marble basin at its center. In the shade of the bougainvilleas—lush plants with bright pink flowers that clambered over the walls—a yellow canary sang in a cage of thin wooden bars. The slender trunk of a date palm rose in the middle of the garden, which was only one of many gardens here. Safia breathed in the silence and let her eyes wander. Her heart wanted to lie down and rest—make itself a bed in the green shade of the mango trees and listen to the sparkling of the sunlight in the fountain. But she called her heart to order. She must stay alert.

There's still today, she told herself. There's still this one chance.

9

When that chance was gone, she would submit to her fate, as the silver threads submitted to the intricate patterns embroidered on silks by the desert women.

She wished with all her might to succeed. The wall wasn't very high. Oh, how she wished not to be an obedient silken thread!

Tonight, when the Rajah summoned her, it would all be over. And the thread, her silver thread of life, would break. She knew that.

In the desert, rumors run over the hot sand faster than the wind.

The birds in the oases had long sung of Ahmed Mudhi's ungovernable temper, and by night the mirrors on the camel bags seemed to show the faces of two wives he had strangled some years ago in a fit of rage.

Safia had heard the desert scorpions, tails raised in the air, hissing a song of the Rajah's violent outbursts. Even the doves in their dovecote in this cool courtyard cooed verses about his jealousy.

Safia trembled when she thought of it.

And when she felt a cool hand on her shoulder, she was startled.

"Come with me," said the voice that belonged to the hand. A pleasant, gentle voice. At first she thought it was a woman's, but then she turned and looked into the face of a young man. A soft, almost childlike face.

"Come with me," he repeated quietly. "They've sent me to show you your apartments. The Rajah will not receive you tonight. He's unwell."

"Let's hope so," whispered Safia, but she whispered it so softly that the boy couldn't hear it, nor did he hear the relief beating in her heart.

She followed him into the dark of the house, trying out the word "apartments" in her mind. It felt cold, smooth, and clean, like a glass marble. She had never had a room of her own to sleep in before.

"My name is Lagan," said the boy. "Whenever you need something, you have only to call for Lagan."

"Lagan," she murmured. "*The Right Time*. A strange name."

The boy shrugged his shoulders. "They don't call me by it anyway. Here they call everyone by names that aren't their own. The women of the harem have sharp tongues."

Safia looked at him. "What do they call you?"

"Lalit," he replied softly, smiling. "*The Beautiful One*. They don't take me seriously."

She examined him. He was indeed beautiful, as beautiful as one of the stone statues adorning the inner courtyard.

His face was very regular, but it told her nothing. Yes, it would probably be hard to take him seriously. He seemed so childish. And he, too, she thought, was a servant. Nothing in his beautiful face belonged to himself.

She let her hand run along the balustrade as she followed him up the flight of steps, and she knew that she would miss the hot, grainy desert sand.

And so her brief life in the harem began.

It was some time before the Rajah could receive her.

No sooner was his urgent business behind the walls of Jaisalmer finished than a fever took hold of him and threw him on his richly embroidered bed.

So now he lay there burning, dreaming, and angry that he still couldn't touch the jewel he had brought home from his journey.

In his more lucid moments he had himself wrapped in soft blankets and sat in the little bay window of his bedroom looking out at one of the courtyards, where the beautiful girl from the desert sometimes dreamed beside the fountain. Just as she had been dreaming under the date palm in the oasis, he thought, in the place where he first met her. And he was consumed with longing for her, literally in a fever to feel her cool presence close to him. But his body refused to obey him, and Ahmed Mudhi had to wrap his soul in patience until the fever had died down.

Lalit had been in the Rajah's service for two years. He was very obedient, and he sent his wages home to his family every month.

Ahmed Mudhi had two chief wives and five lesser wives. They made the cool inner courtyards of the harem a landscape of glittering jewelry and shimmering silk, and in the course of time they had given him a great many children. The children grew and flourished like the fragrant jasmine in the courtyard gardens, and on many days Ahmed Mudhi played with them there in the dappled light and shade under the leaves of his mango trees.

13

Apart from Ahmed Mudhi himself, there was a small army of tailors, cooks, guards, and maidservants to look after the women. And during the last monsoon season but one, the Rajah, who prided himself on keeping a grand household, had also hired a young eunuch for the job of tending the doves and sweeping up dust in the inner rooms: Lalit with the beautiful, girlish face. Lalit divided his attention evenly between the doves and the dust, and he worked quietly and very conscientiously.

The women liked him, so they gave him a great many little errands to run for appropriate payment—and sometimes one of them would give him an even more generous payment for getting his doves to carry a love letter for her to a not entirely official lover in the city.

When he saw the Rajah's new, eighth wife, Lalit, too, was impressed by her beauty. It isn't true that eunuchs can't appreciate beautiful women, and Safia's beauty shone brighter than any he had ever seen.

But she was strange, too. She frightened him. He had heard the other servants talking about her, saying she was crazy.

She was different from all the women Lalit knew. She cast her eyes down like a timid girl, but when he met her gaze for the first time, those same eyes gave him a shock. There was a glow in them, and a hissing, like drops of water falling into fire. Her eyes were green as turquoise. He had never seen a woman with eyes the color of turquoise before.

She looked at her surroundings with those eyes like a small animal. Her glance moved back and forth, camouflaged by her lowered lids and long lashes. It was restless, hunted, sharp. She takes in everything, he thought: the tubs of palms in the courtyard, the shapes of shadows on the smooth stone paving, every door and every window.

She's planning her escape, he thought. He was to be proved right. Two weeks passed before she tried it one night.

But she didn't get far. Her hands were scratched by thorns when the guards brought her back, and the white teeth in her lovely mouth flashed fiercely. Lalit stood at the window of his little room, and though it was night, he could see that her green eyes were shining as if they had tears in them.

She had tried to climb the garden wall. And she'd almost succeeded. But from now on, they would watch her more closely. There'd be no second chance.

It was on the night of her one attempt to run away from the Rajah's house that she talked to Lalit at length for the first time. And it was on the same night that his life began to change.

Lalit had been lying awake for a long time, unable to sleep, and, in the end, he had risen from his bed to steal through the quiet courtyards. He heard the sleeping doves coo in their dreams, and he thought of the Rajah's eighth wife and her failed attempt to escape.

He couldn't help admitting that he was curious. Why had such a beauty tried to climb over the wall?

In the end, he summoned up all his courage, left his dreaming doves, and went up the stairs to her room.

He knocked on her door, very quietly.

"Come in," she said.

And there she was, sitting cross-legged on an embroidered cushion at the window, very still and very straight, looking out. She didn't even turn to him.

"I could see an oil lamp burning in your window," he said, blushing scarlet. "And I thought . . . I wanted to ask . . . to ask if you need anything."

She nodded. "Oh, there are a great many things I need," she replied. "But nothing you can bring me."

"Who knows?" he said gravely. "What do you need, for instance?"

She laughed. And finally she did turn around.

"The wind over the desert," she said. "The smell of an open fire. The course of the stars in the sky. Can you bring me any of these things?"

Lalit tried to think of a clever answer, but he couldn't come up with one in a hurry. So he shifted uneasily from foot to foot, looking at the little table in the corner of her chamber.

She had set up a kind of altar on it. He remembered how the other women had said she was a Hindu, not a Muslim, and he let his eyes wander over the tiny, brightly painted statuettes of gods arranged side by side.

They were all there: Shiva with the crescent moon in his hair; his wife, Parvati; Brahma with the four faces; and his wise bride, Sarasvati. Ganesh, the friendly elephant-headed god; Kali, goddess of anger; Hanuman, the monkey god; Lakshmi, goddess of prosperity, in her lotus blossom. And last of all Krishna, the flute-player.

No doubt she had been following his glance, for she looked at him and said, "You're a Hindu, too, aren't you?"

He nodded.

"I miss the stories here," she said. "The stories of the gods. There's no one here who knows them. The *Ramayana*, the *Mahabharata* . . . and all the muddled-up little tales of that great, intricate family."

She nodded to the figures of the gods, and it seemed strange for him to hear her talking about them. He wasn't sure whether you were allowed to speak of the gods like that, and what they would say if they heard you.

"Stories," she went on, "are an excellent way of escape."

She fell silent for a while, and he cautiously took a step closer to get a better look at her collection of gods. The little figures looked well worn, as if someone had picked them up and held them many, many times to ask their advice. The brightly colored paint was flaking off in some places, showing the plain, cheap wood underneath.

Stories are an excellent way of escape.

The words stood there in the room, hanging in the air around the figures of gods like a heavy cloud of vapor.

17

"What do you want to escape from?" he asked.

"Death," she said gravely, and again she looked out of the window, where Ahmed Mudhi's stone walls shrank the width of night to a dark rectangle.

"Death," repeated Lalit. "We can't escape death. We have to accept it when it comes."

"It all depends when that is."

"Oh," he quickly replied, "it's not up to us to decide when."

"Perhaps not," she said, "but it seems to be up to Ahmed Mudhi."

Lalit looked at her inquiringly, and although she was still gazing out into the darkness, she obviously felt his question in the stuffy air.

It was warm that night. The wind had died down, and it seemed as if whoever was responsible for the wind couldn't get it moving again.

"I'm going to die," she said with certainty. "When he summons me to him, he will kill me. He bargained for a virgin, and he was cheated. Everyone knows what he does to such women."

She looked at him, and her turquoise eyes flickered. "In India," she said, "there are too many names with too many meanings. Most of them are wrong. They call me Safia, *Virtue*.

But I am Shamin, *Fire*. They want me to be Satya, the *Truth*; Sadhana, *Reverence*; Sarala, the *Honorable*. But I am Sandhya, the *Dusk*; Sanvali, the *Twilight*; Sharvati, the *Night*.

"I am Shampa, the *Lightning*; Shalmali who lives on the silk tree; I am Shakuntala who was brought up by the birds. When I speak of myself, I am Raka, the *Full Moon*. That is who I was in the desert when they left me alone. If you call to me, call me by that name."

Lalit said nothing. He could still sense her turquoise eyes resting on him, and he had the feeling that she expected him to say something. But he kept silent.

There was nothing he could say.

"Perhaps I do need something after all," she said at last. "A story isn't a good story unless it has a good listener."

Raka stroked the god Ganesh's elephant trunk, and smiled again. "If you promise to listen to me, I'll tell you a story . . . Part of it every night. Will you listen?"

Lalit hesitated. Suppose he was found here? Was it allowed for him to sit with one of Ahmed Mudhi's wives by night, listening to her?

It wasn't forbidden. The twilight between the two of them sent a shiver down his back such as he had never known before. And he was still afraid of her eyes. But at the same time she fascinated him.

19

She stood up, and once again Lalit marveled at the grace of her figure. It wasn't surprising that Ahmed Mudhi wanted to possess her. But what Lalit saw in her eyes was at odds with Raka's charming appearance. Ahmed Mudhi, thought Lalit, couldn't have seen her eyes, or he wouldn't have dared to marry her.

She sat down in one corner of the broad windowsill, crossed her legs, and gestured to Lalit to sit opposite her.

"It can't hurt," she said, "to keep an eye on the night."

Lalit sat down, taking care not to touch her.

It struck him that he hadn't answered her question.

Not with words.

But the fact that he was sitting here at this moment was a promise to the Rajah's eighth wife that he, Lalit, would listen, as long and as often as she liked, every night while there was still time for it. The doves scratched his answer into the wood of their dovecotes with their dreaming claws, the cicadas chirped it into the night, and the leaves of the mango tree under the window rustled it in the green darkness.

And Safia—or Raka—could interpret such answers, just as she had interpreted the message of the scorpions in the desert foretelling her death. She cast her eyes down so as not to scorch her patient listener with the fire in them, and began her story.

காற்று

ᴛ̄ʰʳougʰ air

Tʜᴇ Bʟooᴅsᴛoɴᴇ

I DON'T HAVE TO TELL YOU THAT IN INDIA it's usual to live many times.

Our world is like a great, colorful board game: You rise and fall on it, depending how many points you collected in the last round you played.

Points for courage, points for loyalty, points for truthfulness.

In some rounds of the game you come into the world as a rat; in some as a wise man.

The gods themselves are born several times.

For instance, Vishnu appeared on earth seven times, but he did it under a different name every time.

At the time of this story he was called Krishna and was the god of love. He played his flute to beguile the girls herding cows on the barren pastures at the edge of the desert. That was a wonderful time, full of the fragrance of white jasmine and the scents of the night. The stone statues in the temples tell many tales of it.

But there is one tale the carved stone never tells—the story of how one day, in a palm grove south of Nowhere, Krishna became the father of a daughter.

After that the beautiful flute player disappeared, and his daughter grew up as an ordinary little girl in a family living in a village of mud huts and dust, where the sandy wind sang lullabies to her. Yet she knew, deep in her heart, that she was a princess.

One day she was playing at the side of a paddy field, feeding the birds, when the demon king Ravana looked out of a hedge and saw her.

His chief servant, Suryakanta, whose name means *Jewel*, was with him.

The presence of the demons made the birds nervous, and one of them pecked at the princess. With a cry, she withdrew her hand as a single thick drop of blood appeared on her forefinger.

In her sudden movement the princess turned to the hedge where Ravana and his servant were hiding. And no sooner had Ravana seen her beautiful face than he was lost: He fell in love with the child princess at once.

The blood flowed from her finger, but before it could fall to the ground, the drop became a red jewel the size of a pigeon's egg and began to glow with intense brightness.

And so Suryakanta, Ravana's greedy servant, fell in love, too. He fell passionately in love at first sight with the jewel.

However, before he could seize the precious stone, it fell into the green waters of the paddy field where the child princess had been playing. For a long time the jewel was lost among the green blades of rice growing in the water, until at last it was found by a farmer who exchanged it with a friend for a white cow. The friend in turn sold it to a traveling Frenchman, who later lost it to an Englishman in Paris—but that's another story. All I will say here is this: The precious stone disappeared for quite a long time, and only a great deal later did it reappear in India—at about the period when everything else in this story was taking place.

The years went by, and Krishna's daughter grew into a young woman. Her beauty, already great, increased until it was as radiant as the sun in the sky, and the demon king Ravana racked his brains to find a way to win her. For although she was living the life of an ordinary human being, her father, Krishna, secretly kept an eye on the princess.

23

At last, in a moment when she had fallen asleep unobserved under a date palm, dreaming of lands far to the south of Nowhere, Ravana's plan succeeded: His servant Suryakanta abducted her with the help of three white elephants, and the young princess was carried off to the overjoyed Ravana.

At this time, Ravana had made himself out to be human in order to enjoy many of the pleasant things that are denied to demons—fine clothes, the scent of almond oil in the water for his bath, soft carpets under his bare feet, and a good reputation. So when he wasn't lying in wait to abduct princesses, he was a rich merchant, and he hid the secrets of his true nature behind the secure walls of a fortified desert city.

Now Ravana, like every man in India when he plans to marry, wanted a god to predict the most favorable date for his wedding. He could hardly ask Krishna himself, and the four-faced Brahma happened to be busy somewhere else at the time, and so he chose Lord Shiva. Shiva set a date far enough away to give Krishna a chance to set his daughter free.

The princess had been abducted on the day after the full moon, and Shiva foretold that the next full moon would be the only lucky day for the demon king's wedding.

So Ravana had to wait a whole month before he could

marry his beautiful captive and unite her forever with himself and the demons' realm.

And within the space of a month, as Shiva knew—and so did the princess—all sorts of things might happen.

It would have been possible just to start one of those spectacular wars so common in the great days of Hinduism, with an army of gods and heroes fighting an army of demons. Krishna himself had once fought as counselor and charioteer in such an army.

But there was one problem: the British.

At the time of our story, the British were the colonial rulers of India, and they had brought new ways with them.

They had also brought something they called "progress." It meant that the country was moving away from its roots and looking toward an uncertain future. Those who wanted to be modern tried to act like the British. And the British lived a geometrical, well-ordered life full of important times of day.

People had stopped believing in magic and fairy tales. Although they might not like to hear it, the Hindu gods had shrunk.

And if no one believes in you anymore, you can't just go appearing wherever you like on earth.

Krishna and his cowherd's flute journeyed through the green water-meadows south of Nowhere for a long time, brooding. His daughter was living on earth as a human being, and Ravana, too, was making himself out to be a human at this time. In the end, Krishna had to admit that there was only one solution: He needed a *human* hero, a hero clever enough to outwit the demon king, strong enough to oppose him in battle, and noble enough to rescue the princess with her body and her morals intact.

But like people's belief in magic and fairy tales, heroes were few and far between in India at this time.

Krishna had a delicate chain with a small amulet on it made by the best silversmith in Madurai, and inside the amulet he placed a picture of his daughter (it was one of those modern sepia-tinted photographs).

Taking this chain, he stole into a sacred grove of trees by night and laid it in the heart of a lotus flower growing in a pool. The jewel caught the light of Raka, the full moon, and seemed to absorb it entirely—and from then on it shone with a soft and gentle glow.

Krishna's plan was simple and logical: The first man who visited the sacred grove to pray, and whose eye was keen enough to notice the details of holy Nature, would find the amulet. That man would be his hero.

And as soon as the hero closed his hand around the jewel, Krishna would appear and tell him what his mission was.

The sacred grove was one of the holiest and most ancient places of worship in India, so when Krishna saw it by daylight the next morning, he was more than annoyed to find that it now lay in the large garden of an English colonial villa. A fence separating the grounds of the villa from a paddy field ran to the left of the lotus pool.

Krishna ground his teeth, but he sat down and waited patiently for his hero.

The hero turned up around midday.

The sun was burning down on the fields, and Krishna wondered why the man was out and about in the murderous heat of the day, when every sensible person took shelter in the shade.

But the man had his reasons for leaving the nearby city of Madurai and crossing the open fields. He was only too happy not to meet anyone. His name was Farhad Kamal, he was about sixteen (he didn't know his exact age), and he pursued the reputable profession of thief and confidence trickster.

Farhad means *Happiness* and Kamal means *Lotus Blossom*, and up to this point in Farhad Kamal's life, he had not discovered what his life had to do with either of them. He had grown up in the streets of the temple city of Madurai and wasn't even sure of his caste, for he had no idea who his parents had been. He remembered his birth only dimly, and when he tried concentrating on the time immediately after it, he couldn't remember that well, either. So Farhad could only guess where he had come into the world, and he assumed that his surroundings at the time hadn't been very elegant.

Ever since he could remember, he had made his way through life more or less on his own, getting thoroughly knocked about in the process. He could neither read nor write, although he had an unerring command of the figures on the banknotes that he stole from people's pockets.

Sometimes he visited one of the great temples to pray to the gods, and as chance would have it, he usually came out again with a handful of coins from the plate left out for offerings. He had tried going into the new British church, too, but the donation boxes there were kept well locked, so he decided against converting to Christianity. The Muslims were clever and had driven him straight out of their mosque. So Farhad remained a Hindu out of what might be called his economic convictions, and on the whole he looked after himself successfully.

Anyone trying to describe Farhad Kamal in detail would have found it difficult. He took care to change his appearance so often that no one *could* describe him in detail. He was a master of disguise. Sometimes he had dark skin, sometimes his complexion was almost as pale as the faces of the British. Sometimes he had a long, wild mane of hair like an ascetic, sometimes his hair was oiled and short, sometimes he had a shaven head like a begging monk and no beard—and next day he might be sporting a dense stubble on his chin again. Sometimes he had a club foot with a makeshift bandage around it, sometimes he had several teeth missing—sometimes he had a few too many. For a while he had propelled himself through the bazaar on a board with wheels, pretending to be a cripple. It was one of the most strenuous periods of his life.

To his good friends, among whom he counted those rogues and vagabonds who would give him a meal, Farhad used to say, "You can see what a good Hindu I am. Like the gods, I have dozens of avatars; I take dozens of different shapes. And sometimes, when I'm picking a pocket, I have as many arms as the gods themselves."

There was just one thing that all the avatars of Farhad Kamal had in common: the wily and always slightly hunted expression in his eyes. It lingered in the tiny folds at the corners of his eyes, and you saw it only if you looked closely.

Walking across the fields on this particular day, Farhad wore his hair short and rather untidy, and his complexion

29

was pale brown. He was on his way to Mr. Basil Shaw's villa. Mr. Shaw had a pretty collection of antique china figurines in his sitting room, and Farhad's idea was to take a closer look at them—purely, of course, out of a keen interest in art history.

He was skirting the fence, looking for a place where he could slip through it, when he saw the silvery glow. It seemed to come out of Mr. Basil Shaw's lotus pool, and Farhad stopped and strained his eyes.

No, not out of the pool. The light was coming from one of the lotus flowers floating peacefully there in the sunlight. Farhad thought of Lakshmi, the goddess of wealth, who usually appeared in a lotus blossom, and his heart leaped up.

A little later, he found a gap in the fence and squeezed his thin frame through it like a stray cat. He kept under the cover of the sparsely planted trees growing around the pool, and the nearer he came to the water, the brighter shone the silver Something in the lotus flower, and the faster beat Farhad's heart.

Finally, with his bare toes touching the water, he crouched down and leaned far forward to reach the lotus flower . . . and his fingers met something cold and smooth. He lifted it from its bed of pink petals and held it up to the light. This was a wonderful find. In his hand lay a tiny, beautifully worked amulet of pure silver, with a chain also made of silver attached to it. His keen eyes assessed the value of the jewel, and his head sang for joy.

Who, wondered Farhad, hides a silver chain in a lotus blossom in the middle of a garden? And why?

He closed his fingers over the little amulet, looked carefully around him, and hastily rose to his feet. Never mind who had brought it here, or why—it was his now. He'd take a look at Mr. Shaw's porcelain some other time; now he must take his treasure to safety.

But he didn't get far.

Just as Farhad grasped the silver amulet in his fingers, a silent bolt of lightning struck the ground in front of him, and someone barred his way.

Farhad, not a notably courageous young man, was scared almost to death and staggered back. He shielded his eyes with his hand, because the bright apparition dazzled him, and he cowered like a dog caught doing something wrong.

Then he peered between his fingers and recognized the figure at once. He had often stood in front of the image of the flute-playing cowherd in the temple, waiting for an offering to find its way into his pocket when no one was looking.

"Lord . . . Lord Krishna," Farhad whispered, and he took another step back. He didn't let go of the amulet. A question shot through his mind: Had Krishna seen him steal it? Perhaps he was here just by chance . . .

"You have found the amulet," said the god, in a voice as gentle as the eyes of the white cattle that legend says he herded. "You are the chosen man."

"I'm the—what did you say?" stammered Farhad.

"The hero," Krishna went on. "The hero I need. The warrior I have chosen above all others to carry out the task that must be performed."

Farhad shook his head frantically. "Oh, no!" he responded in alarm. "There must be some mistake! I'm no hero, I'm most definitely no warrior. I can't fight, and I'm scared of everything! Of snakes, dogs, even the fish in this pool," he said untruthfully. "There's no way I can perform any kind of task!" Farhad had been stumbling farther and farther back as he spoke, and now one of his legs was in the pool up to the knee.

"Stand still and listen to me," said Krishna calmly.

Farhad nodded timidly, and sketched a humble bow. Fear of the god's anger had now taken powerful hold of him, and his knees were shaking in an unbecoming manner.

"Ravana," said Krishna, "has stolen my daughter away. You remember who Ravana is?"

"I-I-I think so," stammered Farhad. "The d-d-demon king. He carried Rama's wife Sita off to Ceylon once, didn't he? In the *Ramayana* legend? And you were Rama's charioteer and counselor, and helped t-t-to defeat his armies."

Krishna nodded. "That was long ago. At any rate, Ravana is now making himself out to be a merchant, and he lives in the city at the heart of the desert of Rajasthan." Lord Krishna rested his head on four of his hands and sighed. And then he told Farhad Kamal the whole story of the princess's misfortune. He told him about the date palm south of Nowhere, and Ravana's passionate love, and the abduction of the princess by his servant Suryakanta. "He is keeping the princess a prisoner in his house," he concluded. "And in exactly a month's time, when the moon is full again and the omens are good, he will marry her and take her away forever to his dark and evil realm."

"I-I-I'm very sorry to hear it," said Farhad, with his teeth chattering.

"But it won't happen," said Krishna. "Because you are going to rescue her."

Farhad stared at the god. "M-me?"

"Yes," said Krishna. "You. You were the one who found the amulet. You shall ride on a mount that goes faster than the clouds in the air, and I will make sure you don't lose your way. But you must do all the rest yourself. You have a month to reach the city in the heart of the desert and confront the

33

demon king. The wedding of my daughter and Ravana is to take place when the next full moon rises above the sand dunes. I'd advise you to set off at once. And take good care of the amulet. It will protect you."

"What do I get if I do this for you?" asked Farhad. Although so scared that he was still going hot and cold by turns, he had recovered his usual business acumen.

"If you succeed in rescuing the princess at the right time," Krishna gravely replied, "then in your next life, you will rise to a wonderful stage of being. You will be reborn as a wise and prosperous man. If you don't succeed . . ."

He paused. Farhad's fingers played nervously with the

 34 amulet.

"If you don't succeed," Krishna repeated, "you will be reborn as something low and disgusting. A worm, maybe. Or a woodlouse to be trodden underfoot by humans. And the cycle of your lives here on earth will be prolonged to infinity before you attain Nirvana."

He smiled.

Farhad went even paler than before.

"I wish you luck," said Krishna, and he put out an arm and passed three fingers over Farhad's forehead. Farhad sensed the divine sign that Krishna had painted there like a burning brand.

He saw the god smile his inscrutable smile once more, and then Krishna disappeared.

Farhad Kamal was left alone in the sacred grove in Mr. Basil Shaw's garden, alone with a silver amulet that bore all the gentle radiance of the full moon in it.

Farhad's knowledge of geography was confined to the immediate vicinity of his hometown of Madurai, and any notions he had of the location of the desert of Rajasthan were sketchy.

So he went back to the city and asked a *parota* seller where it lay.

The *parota* seller rolled up one of his paper-thin pancakes and thought.

"The desert of Rajasthan—the Thar Desert—is old and far away," he said. "I know that our land comes to an end somewhere south of here, at the sea, so the desert of Rajasthan can't be there. That means it must be to the north."

"How far to the north?" asked Farhad.

"On horseback, a dozen days and then another dozen," said the man who was buying the rolled-up *parota*. "Or maybe more."

Farhad sighed and watched hungrily as the man sat down at one of the old, low tables, and dipped his pancake

35

in red sauce so sharp that Farhad's eyes watered at the mere
sight of it.

"I don't have a horse," said Farhad, sitting down at the
table with the man.

"On foot it would surely take two months," said the man,
biting into his *parota*. Little crumbs of crisp dough clung to
the corners of his mouth, and when he swallowed Farhad
swallowed, too.

"I don't have two months to spare, either," he said. "I don't
even have enough money to buy a *parota*."

"If you think I'm inviting you to be my guest," said the
man, smiling, "you've come to the wrong place, my friend.
Look for a proper job and do something to earn your *parota*."

"I'm afraid I don't have time to look for a proper job," said
Farhad, surprised to find himself telling the truth for once.
"What I'm looking for is the city in the middle of the Thar
Desert. And I have to be there in exactly a month's time."

The man roared with laughter.

Farhad jumped up from the low table where he had been
sitting and left the place. As he did so, a *parota* found its way
off the stack the seller had been making and into his pocket.
Out in the street he began munching it rather unhappily.
He'd never found a way of making off with the sharp sauce,
so he usually lived on very dry food.

That evening, Farhad organized himself a bottle of the spirits distilled from all kinds of dubious odds and ends, and he sat down with it on the steps of a shrine by the roadside. The orange face of Hanuman the monkey god looked kindly at him from the shrine.

Above him, the full moon stood in the sky.

Farhad took out the amulet and looked thoughtfully at its radiance—like a second, smaller moon in his hand. What was he to do? He'd never been really sure of all that business about karma and reincarnation before. And now Krishna had not only proved that they existed, by appearing to him, he had also burdened him with an impossible task and condemned him never to escape the eternal cycle of rebirth and suffering. That was rather a lot all at once.

How would he ever rescue the princess if he couldn't even reach her in time?

Krishna had promised him a mount to ride that went faster than the clouds in the air. Of course, all the heroes in the world of Hindu legend rode animals of some kind. But where was he supposed to find this mount of his?

Krishna had promised to show him the way, but how was he to interpret Krishna's signs?

He had no idea what signs the gods gave. He wasn't even

sure whether clouds traveled through the sky quickly or slowly.
So the level in the bottle of spirits gradually went down, and
Farhad told his troubles to the monkey god Hanuman in his
little shrine.

"My life is forfeit," he whispered to Hanuman. "Even
worse, *all* my lives are forfeit. I'm going to be a worm, trodden
underfoot . . . a worm . . ."

Then his head sank against the iron grating around the
shrine, and a drop of spirits ran out of the corner of his mouth
and down his chin as he dozed off.

Just before he fell into a despairing sleep full of dreams,
he thought he saw Hanuman wink his left eye, as if trying to
tell him something. But he could have been wrong.

At that time, there was only a single road leading north from
Madurai. Farhad's sole companion on the road was his own
shadow as it clung to his bare feet in the bright morning sun.

He wore the silver amulet around his neck.

Soon after leaving Madurai, he came up against a British
police checkpoint.

Ever since the British had installed their queen as ruler
of India, replacing the British East India Company that
used to govern the country, they thought they had to set up
checkpoints everywhere.

As the police generally had some charge or other to bring against Farhad, he hurried off the road and turned left into the fields, where a narrow path wound its way past the green of the rice in the paddy fields and the red of the earth.

He was annoyed to find that the British had set up their checkpoint just where he needed to go, but at the same time he admired them in a way. They hadn't conquered India. They hadn't had to. Instead they had gradually infiltrated the country with their trading company. Yes, there had been fighting here and there. But by and large, not much trouble. One day India suddenly belonged to a British company, and as no country can belong to a company, the British Crown had simply taken it over in the name of justice and general political correctness.

It would be nice to know how to do a thing like that, thought Farhad. He'd have liked to learn from the British, who were masters of the art of acquiring valuable items by devious means.

But for now he struck out into other fields, the fields around Madurai and then the wild country beyond them. He had a feeling that the men at the checkpoint had seen him and might indeed have been watching him for quite some time, wondering where he was going. So Farhad chose ever smaller paths to get out of sight, always making sure to go in roughly the right direction.

Hadn't Krishna said he would show him the way? Farhad didn't think much of this promise when the path he was on began to lead slightly uphill. Then he saw, to his surprise, that for some time now he had been climbing old stone steps, always going up and never down. And they were getting steeper. On the bright side, the way ahead was clear, and it led north. Farhad didn't want to turn back and look for another path through the rocky, overgrown landscape.

Eventually, he had to admit to himself that he was climbing a mountain. By the time he reached the first viewing point, the countryside already lay some way below. He stopped and looked down.

"Going *over* a mountain to get somewhere," he said to himself out loud, "is what I call a rather stupid idea."

After the next flight of steps he added, "One of the stupidest ideas I ever heard of."

And after two more flights of steps, he told himself, "The British would never think of doing anything so stupid, which means they won't follow me, and I'm rid of them. So it is, after all, worth going the long way around."

Then he continued to climb up the rough-hewn stone slabs that looked old enough for the gods themselves to have made them . . . in a time when even gods didn't yet know how to build a proper flight of steps.

At the foot of the mountain, two men stationed at the British checkpoint shielded their eyes with their hands and focused their official gaze on the thin figure working its way up the steep and winding path.

"That's not him," said one to the other. "The man we're after is only disguised as an Indian. He really comes from England, same as us. Look at that fellow! Only an Indian would be crazy enough to climb such a steep mountain in heat like this. I'm telling you, that's one of the pilgrims who visit the holy man up there now and then. Did you hear the tales about him? They say he lives up there without food or water, drinking only the dew that falls on the leaves early in the morning."

The second man shrugged. "If they want to believe that, well and good. So our lad up there on the mountain is on his way to see the holy man. He's of no interest to us. He doesn't have the stone."

His companion nodded. "The stone is long gone. Whoever has it wouldn't hang around here. I'd have liked to see it, though. They say it's the shape of a huge drop of blood and it shines as brightly as the sun. The Indians tell amazing stories about it. The bloodstone, they call it . . ."

"Fairy tales," said the second man, putting a pinch of

chewing tobacco in his mouth. "It probably doesn't exist. Just a theft that the Indian merchants invented to keep us on our toes."

"Hmm," said the other man. "I wouldn't be so sure of that."

By this time, rivers of sweat were running down Farhad Kamal's back. He cursed quietly to himself because he'd forgotten to bring any water on this journey. His stomach felt as empty as a sack with nothing in it, and his legs were trembling with the effort of his climb.

At a place where the flight of steps wound its way up a particularly steep rock wall, the screeching of a group of monkeys tore him away from his dreams of cool water and white rice, and he stopped to watch them. They were chasing each other over the rocks, trying to catch one another's long tail amidst a great deal of jabbering. As Farhad tried to get his breath back, he looked enviously at the monkeys. How he would have liked to race up the mountain as they did, as if it were a level plain! How glad he would have been to take a shortcut up the rock face instead of toiling laboriously along the winding path! What wouldn't he have given for the agility of their long fingers and toes as they clung to invisible crevices in the rock!

Suddenly one of the monkeys left the rest of the group

and, without warning, raced toward Farhad. Farhad stood there in astonishment. Before he could react, the monkey reached out a long, thin arm to him—and snatched the silver chain from his neck.

Before Farhad could even blink, the animal let out a cry of triumph and shot away with its loot like lightning.

"Stop!" cried Farhad, waving his arms frantically. "No! Give me that chain back! Give me that chain back *at once!*"

The monkey jumped up on top of a rock, let out a whinnying sound like laughter, and bared its long yellow teeth.

Farhad approached the monkey, shouting, but the animal was not impressed. It took another leap and landed among its companions, who sniffed curiously at the strange glittering thing in its hand. As Farhad tried to reach his prey without falling down the side of the mountain, the monkeys seemed to be quarreling over possession of the chain. Obviously their pecking order held no clear rules for the acquisition of silver amulets.

In growing desperation, Farhad watched the animals tugging at the jewel and chattering angrily. First one and then another would get the upper hand and snatch the amulet.

He found a long stick by the side of the path and picked it up.

43

"You don't have the faintest inkling!" he shouted just for the sake of shouting. "The *Ramayana* tells us about an army of monkeys who helped Lord Rama to free his wife, Sita! But you bunch—you don't know anything about brave Hanuman, who reached Ceylon with a single leap! You're no help to anyone. All you can do is steal things, nothing else! Nothing!"

The monkeys looked at him as if his rage amused them. And for a moment, he had the feeling that one of them was winking at him—just the way the little orange statue of Hanuman had seemed to wink the night before. Strange.

Then it happened: One of the monkeys took advantage of the moment when all the others were staring at Farhad, snatched the amulet, and it broke in two.

Farhad cried out.

He grasped his stick more firmly, jumped up on the nearest rock, and began hitting out at them with his makeshift weapon. This time he did make contact with the monkeys.

Alarmed by the sudden attack, they ran away, jabbering angrily—and the one with the amulet dropped it. Farhad reached out and caught it just before it could fall away. Then he saw that it wasn't broken after all.

It had opened like a book.

Farhad looked at it with surprise. Until now he had been far too busy with other things to notice the tiny catch at the side of the amulet.

Inside was a miniature copy of a photograph. Farhad had to strain his eyes to see what it was, because the picture was indistinct, as if covered by a misty veil. But there was no doubt who it showed: The girl in the picture had long, smooth hair and big, dark eyes. She seemed to be looking out of the photo, returning Farhad's gaze.

So this was the princess, Krishna's daughter. Farhad imagined her sitting captive at this very moment in the dark apartments of the demon king Ravana, longing for daylight. In his mind's eye, he saw her going to the window, searching the desert with her lovely eyes for the hero who, she knew, would come to rescue her. The soft music of a sitar sounded in his ears, and a full moon rose before the picture in his mind, bathing the scene in an appropriate light . . .

No, he told himself. No hero would come to rescue the princess. She'd wait until the last moment, and she would wait in vain. Farhad's heart was heavy, almost as heavy as his weary legs when he began once again to climb. He might not have much in the way of morals, but like all Indians, he was sometimes sentimental about romantic stories.

For a moment he forgot that his real reason for wanting

to set the princess free was to save his own skin from Krishna's wrath.

He looked up from the path and saw the monkeys watching him from a little way off.

Once again, one of them seemed to wink.

Farhad reached the top of the mountain long after dusk had fallen.

The blue vapors of a warm, humid twilight lay over the land, and for the first time in his life, he saw just how endlessly far it stretched. A lake glittered in the distance down below, where a man was driving two white cows home.

46

Nearby, in the dying daylight, Farhad saw a ruined building—the fading light and crumbling stone were united in a lovely symbol of transience.

Then the sun sank slowly beneath the horizon, and soon only night was left. It suddenly turned very cold on top of the mountain. Farhad wrapped his arms around his thin body and decided to look in the ruin for a place where he could sleep. He cursed the bitterly cold wind sweeping over the grass and rocks on the mountaintop. Only a little while ago he had been relieved to feel cooler air. How quickly things changed when you were on the road!

In the sixteen years or so of his life, Farhad Kamal had

never been on a long journey before, and already he felt it was too much for him.

Suddenly Farhad noticed someone in the ruin. He was too tired and hungry to feel alarmed. The Someone was sitting on a carpet of grass in a room with no roof, feeding a little fire with sticks.

He was an old man, as thin as sandpaper and as wrinkled as the sacred temple elephants who would give anyone a blessing with their trunks for a few rupees. Apart from an orange cloth around his waist, he wore no clothes, and his hair was wild and gray with dust, hanging down to his shoulders.

"*Vanakam*. Welcome," said the old man, turning two astonishingly bright eyes on Farhad. They gleamed in the firelight like pebbles in a river. "Sit down by the fire with me."

Farhad placed the palms of his hands together in greeting, and squatted down opposite the old man.

"Many thanks, holy father," he said, for there was no mistaking that this was a holy man.

"What brings you here?" asked the old man, blowing on the flames. Farhad reached out his hands near the warmth.

"I met Lord Krishna," he said simply, "and I am very hungry and very thirsty."

The old man smiled and reached into a cloth bundle lying

beside him. Much to Farhad's surprise, he brought out a water-skin and three bananas. "Those who come to ask my advice," he said, still smiling, "bring all kinds of things that I don't need." He watched Farhad devouring the bananas and drinking the water, and finally he asked, "What did Krishna say?"

Farhad wondered why the holy man didn't doubt that he was speaking the truth. He acted as if people dropped in every evening to tell him they'd been talking to Krishna.

"Ravana has carried off his daughter," said Farhad. "Right now Ravana is living as a human being in a city in the middle of the Thar Desert, and he's going to marry Krishna's daughter at the next full moon."

48

It sounded slightly absurd.

But the old man only nodded. "Naturally," he said.

"Naturally?" asked Farhad crossly. "I don't see anything natural about it. I think Krishna might have looked after his own daughter a little better! And now *I'm* supposed to rescue her."

"You?" asked the old man, and Farhad, feeling slightly offended, said no more for a while.

"Last night," the old man went on, "Krishna himself appeared to me in a dream. He said Ravana had carried off his daughter. He showed me a picture of the demon king's terrible face, and my heart was in great fear. Then Krishna and the picture were gone. When I woke, I asked myself why I'd had that dream." He smiled a toothless smile. "And now I know. Krishna wanted to tell me you were coming."

"Hmm," said Farhad. In the first place, he didn't believe in dreams, and in the second place, he didn't think the old man was telling the truth. He himself often claimed to have had amazing prophetic dreams when he was trying to lure money out of someone's pocket. It was an old and very common trick.

"Even more common," said the old man, "is the gift of reading thoughts. Even if most men who are wise don't tell anyone they're doing it."

Farhad jumped and felt himself turn red. "And what are you doing up here, then?" he asked quickly, to change the subject.

49

"I live here," said the old man. "I meditate, I watch the clouds go by, and I talk to the gods. I've been sitting up here without food or water for seven times seven years. At dawn I drink the fresh dew from the leaves. The dew is full of mysteries . . ."

"How much longer are you going to sit up here?" asked Farhad, for something to say.

A slight smile came over the old man's sunburned face in the firelight, as it burned low. "Until the prophecy comes true," he replied, and there was considerable pride in his voice.

"What—what does the prophecy say?" asked Farhad, feeling rather lost.

"I don't know," said the old man.

"Hmm. I see," said Farhad. "But you're here because of the prophecy all the same?"

"Yes. I was given that task long ago in a temple at the foot of the mountain. Those who come up to visit me say there's no temple there now, only a British checkpoint. This ruin was once a stronghold. A long time ago, before the British even knew how to spell the word *tea*, the stronghold defended a realm that no longer exists. When my task up here is performed, the walls of the old stronghold will collapse at long last. And that's all I know."

"The way gods hand out their tasks doesn't seem quite fair," said Farhad. "I'd call it easier to sit up here staring at a few old walls than to ride into the middle of the desert and lose my life fighting the demon king."

"It all depends on your point of view," replied the old man gravely. "Some tasks call for patience, some for action. For tasks of patience, one needs an iron will. You, for instance, could never command your body to live on dew from the leaves, for your will is weak and your body greedy. For tasks of action, one needs trust."

"Trust?" asked Farhad doubtfully. "Why trust? Wouldn't

a good weapon be of more use, or a fast horse, or superhuman strength?"

The holy man tilted his head to one side and broke into a cackle of laughter as dry and cracked as his skin.

"None of that is any use," he said, "without trust. Even with a good weapon in your hand, you can hide in fear and trembling behind a melon stall. Even a fast horse can throw you off and land you in a stinking puddle behind the latrines of the British railroad stations. And even with superhuman strength, you can sink in an eddy while you're swimming and be washed up dead on the riverbank. No, trust is what you need."

Farhad squirmed uncomfortably.

Philosophy was a subject he had avoided as much as he could until then—and avoiding it isn't easy in India. Philosophy, thought Farhad, was a branch of knowledge offering very few financial incentives. Thinking too much about this, that, and the other never made you rich. It either got you thoroughly confused or put in prison.

"Trust in what?" he asked.

"Trust in yourself," said the holy man.

Farhad was about to say something in reply, but then the old man took Farhad's hands in his own, which were cold and rough. He held them for some time, silent and concentrating, as if he were listening to something inside himself.

"A long journey lies ahead of you," he whispered. "You will go through fire, through water, and through air on the wind. But Death stands at the end of the way."

"Death?" asked Farhad, horrified. "And—will I be reborn as something good or something bad?"

"Trust," whispered the old man, as if it were a prayer. "Trust."

Even more softly, he said, "When you reach Ravana's dungeon, you will meet his bodyguard, Suryakanta."

"Yes, I've heard of him," murmured Farhad, rather vaguely.

"There's an old story," whispered the holy man, "of how Ravana fell in love with the princess long ago. Few know the story today, but I learned it from my teacher in the temple long before I came to this mountain. On the day when Ravana first saw the princess, a drop of her blood turned into a jewel as big as a pigeon's egg and as beautiful as the sun. And ever since it took that shape, Suryakanta has been hunting for the stone. It bears the name of *bloodstone*, and it has been wandering through the world for a very long time, but Suryakanta has never been able to lay hands on it. Now and then the stone emerges in the possession of some rajah or adventurer, and then nothing is heard of it again for many, many years. It seems to exercise a mysterious power of attraction on all who see it, and many greedy men have owned it and lost it again. Anyone who brings Suryakanta that stone will gain admittance to Ravana's dungeon."

And the wise man smiled. "No bodyguard in this land is immune to a bribe," he said. "Not even a demon."

"Where—where's the stone now?" asked Farhad, holding his breath.

"Two travelers told me recently that it has disappeared from Madurai," said the old man.

"Madurai!" cried Farhad, leaping up. "But that's where I've come from! I've just missed it, so to speak!"

"Sit down. And give me a little time."

The holy man closed his eyes and, yet again, seemed to be listening to something inside himself.

Farhad was so impatient that it was difficult for him to breathe quietly, but he did his best not to disturb the holy man. If only he could find out where to look for the stone! For it seemed to him a far better idea to bribe Ravana's bodyguard than to face the demon himself in a fight. Perhaps Krishna's task wasn't as hopeless as he had thought . . .

And perhaps he, Farhad Kamal, really was the right man for it.

The holy man opened his eyes.

"Gaya," he said. "Go to Gaya, east of Varanasi, the city on the sacred Ganges River. You will find it there."

"How far is it to the sacred river?" asked Farhad.

"A long way," replied the old man. "Too far to think about it anymore tonight. Almost all India lies between this mountain and Gaya, and a great many dangers, too. But now let us sleep. It's late." He trod out the embers of the fire with his bare feet, and wrapped himself in his orange cloth.

Farhad made himself a bed on the bare ground and looked anxiously up at the sky, where an extravagant number of stars were moving on their courses through the night. If all those stars had turned to jewels, and if he'd managed to steal just one of them, that would have meant the end of all his troubles. But first he must set off for Gaya and find another precious stone. And still he didn't know how to get there in time.

Trust, he thought, trust in yourself?

The Night of the Rats

That night, the mountain shook.

The mountain was not a volcano, and it did not stand in a region where earthquakes were usual, yet all the same, the mountain shook.

The tremor came from deep below with a long rumbling sound, as if the mountain had to stretch and shake itself awake after a long sleep, ridding itself of something that had been living on it too long.

The monkeys sensed it before it came. They woke on their rocks, feeling uneasy, and began scurrying about on their long limbs without knowing what had disturbed their sleep.

The crickets chirped with a new note in their voices, and the rustling of the trees seemed to have lost the beat of its usual rhythm.

And Farhad Kamal, who was used to sensing danger, woke bathed in sweat and felt his nose twitch.

At first he thought he was lying by the roadside in Madurai and someone was about to go through his pockets. Then, for a moment, he thought it was a British police officer, and for some reason the man didn't approve of the place where he had chosen to sleep. And then Farhad Kamal sat up and realized that he wasn't in Madurai, but was on the grass carpet inside an ancient walled building.

Beside him lay the holy man, curled up in a ball to protect himself from the cold of the night. Farhad himself was freezing, but there was something else in the air as well. Something was wrong.

He stood up and went through the crumbling doorway of the ruin into the open. A strange silence lay over the mountain. All the living creatures around Farhad seemed to be holding their breath.

What was going to happen?

Farhad walked a few paces from the ruin, to the edge of a precipice. He couldn't see anything in the depths below but night.

And night was already beginning to fray at the edges, hesitantly giving birth to dawn—but it would be a little while yet before its first labor pains brought forth light.

Farhad stood quite still, feeling the cool wind on his cheeks and taking deep breaths of the night air. He had hoped that would calm him, but it didn't. Far from it: His sense of danger grew even greater. It swelled like a stream in spate, confusing Farhad, because there was really nothing in sight that his head thought dangerous. His heart, however, was singing of fear in his breast.

Soon after that, the mountain began to move.

It moved very slightly at first, and Farhad told himself he was just imagining it. But then the vibration beneath his feet grew stronger and stronger, and the ground reared and bucked like an obstinate donkey. Farhad had to cling to a tree to keep from being swept off his feet.

At the same time, a stronger wind had risen and was roaring around his ears, as if providing musical accompaniment to the show.

"Wake up!" Farhad shouted at the old man, and the wind tore the words from his mouth. "Wake up! There's an earthquake!"

The mountain uttered a deep roar.

Farhad's tree bent in the wind, and he clung fast to it. There was nothing beyond it but the precipice.

The holy man didn't seem to hear him, or perhaps he just preferred to stay in the remains of the old building. Either way, he did not come out.

Farhad saw the tall, roofless walls beginning to keel over before his eyes. It was too late to rescue the old man. First stone blocks came loose and fell, and then the entire wall just collapsed. Farhad saw it rush toward him.

He looked around quickly, but there was no escape. Behind him was the abyss. In seconds the avalanche of stones would bury him.

There was nothing he could do.

Trust, he heard the holy man's voice whisper. *Trust is what you need . . .*

Farhad turned and looked into the bottomless abyss. The wind was whirling a few leaves about down there.

You will go through fire, he heard the old man say, *through water, and . . . through air on the wind.*

Farhad closed his eyes. His knees were knocking the way they had when he met Lord Krishna. The first rock hit his shoulder.

He cried out, and at the same moment let himself fall forward into the wind.

It was only a single step he had to take. He was going to be smashed to pieces at the bottom of the ravine.

No, Farhad told himself as he fell. He was not going to be smashed to pieces. Courage might not be his strong point, but there was nothing else to do. He must at least *act* as if he were brave. And so he decided to heed the old man's words and trust the wind. He had closed his eyes tightly, and now he spread his arms out in search of help. All the belief Farhad could muster went into his prayer to the wind.

And the wind helped him.

The wind bore him up on its broad, unseen wings and carried him off and away with it, weightless, dreamless, unquestioning.

Behind him, Farhad heard the last of the ruinous old walls of the fortress fall, all that was left of a time when the people of India were strong and powerful, and English was a language of no importance.

The prophecy had been fulfilled: The old man on the mountain had performed his task.

And only now did Farhad Kamal begin to guess that *he* had been that task. The holy man had been placed there to tell *him* about trust. To give *him* water. To make prophecies to *him* about fire, water, and the wind. And the gemstone that would get him into the demon king's dungeon.

The wind carried Farhad as if he were a betel leaf.

He traveled light and fast. But where was the wind taking him? Dawn held Farhad in misty fingers, and after a while he saw the paddy fields below looking up at him with their watery eyes. Women were already on their way to work, their colorful saris bright among the awakening green like the tokens in a board game. Farhad thought he himself was on the board of a great, never-ending, unpredictable game. He was part of the game: He was a joker, and none of the normal rules applied to him.

For he was one who spoke with the wise and rode the wind.

He couldn't help laughing when he thought how little he resembled the Farhad Kamal he had been yesterday. Farhad Kamal was a master of the art of transformation, yet until now he had always stayed the same deep inside. Now, for the first time, he had the chance of transforming himself wholly. But he still wasn't sure if he wanted to.

Being a hero probably wasn't very comfortable.

The wind was in no hurry with Farhad. Sometimes it let him drop a little way through the air, and then he was afraid of falling. In his terror, he trembled and prayed. He vowed to be good and help the poor and needy—and anything else that occurred to him.

Then the wind laughed and caught him up again with its

long, invisible fingers, carrying him higher than before. And
Farhad felt relief pulsating through his veins like a wave of
warmth, and he forgot all about the poor and needy, until the
wind chuckled slyly again and acted as if it were about to let
him fall.

After a while, Farhad was so exhausted that he fell asleep
there on the wings of the wind. He slept a refreshing, light,
and dreamless sleep—a sleep as blue as air.

When he woke, he was alarmed to see the ground very close
now. In the distance rose the onion domes of a magnificent
palace, with the buildings of a city clustered around it like
weeds. But the wind was taking him straight to a little hill on
which Farhad saw the square outlines of temple buildings.

61

The next moment he was hovering among the trees that
lined the road to the temple. It must be a festival day, for the
road was full of people streaming toward the temple. A little
boy tilted his head back, looked up, and waved. Bewildered,
Farhad waved back.

None of the grown-ups noticed him.

A little later, the wind put Farhad Kamal, professional
thief and trickster, down in the middle of the crowd. Farhad
stumbled, and it took him some time to get used to moving
on his own feet again.

He had no time to decide which way to go. A throng of people simply swept him along with it. So he let himself drift with the crowd, wondering what this place was.

The only thing he knew for sure was that he was hungry. Morning had come and gone by now, and the sun stood high in the sky. There was a large black hole gaping wide in Farhad's stomach—a hole as empty as Nirvana.

The crowd carried Farhad along through a tall gateway covered with gaudily painted figures. It carried him to the first of the many courtyards of an extensive temple complex, and there it let him go. Farhad looked around and saw several stalls selling offerings: brown dishes made of pressed cashew leaves that were full of flowers, boiled rice, or sacred powder.

62

Farhad made himself small and slipped unnoticed under one of the stalls that had been cobbled together. Entirely by chance, two dishes of offerings made their way to him under this makeshift table, and though the sacred powder in one wasn't much use to him, the boiled rice in the other filled his stomach in a very agreeable way.

A supply of small metal figures of gods was waiting in a wooden box next to his folded legs. One of the figures moved and stretched its many arms. Farhad blinked in surprise. It was Krishna with his cowherd's flute.

"You're eating my offerings," said the little bronze god. "What's the idea?"

"I was hungry," replied Farhad. He picked up the figure and looked at it more closely. Indignantly, Krishna waved two of his arms about.

"Show some respect," he hissed. "Respect, that's what you lack. Do you know where you're going yet?"

"To Gaya," replied Farhad very quietly, worried the man selling offerings up above him could hear the divine dialogue going on below. "To find the bloodstone, and then I'm to use it to bribe Ravana's watchman."

"Excellent," said Krishna. "And have you found the mount you are to ride?"

Farhad shook his head, baffled. "I don't know where to look yet."

At this moment, an arm reached down and groped around in the crate of little gods.

"I'm sure I had another Krishna somewhere here," Farhad heard a voice say. "Where could it have gone?"

He quickly put the little bronze figure back in its place, and before Krishna could say another word, his metal manifestation had been sold.

Farhad's hand shot up to the table like a striking snake. It was only fair for the price of Krishna to find its way into his pockets (along with a few extra coins). After all, he was helping Krishna, so why wouldn't Krishna help him in turn for once?

Farhad was about to sneak away when he heard two women talking above him, and something deep inside told him to stay where he was a little longer, squatting in his uncomfortable position eavesdropping under the stall.

"I can't stand those rats in the eastern courtyard," one of the women was saying. "Sacred or not, even at a festival like this I can't stand them. But that tiger pacing up and down his island in the middle of the lake, oh, I like to watch him! It's good to know that although he's so close, he'll never hurt us."

64

"The tiger scares me," said the other woman. "Suppose he does swim across the pool of water after all and leaps on one of the pilgrims? There's hunger in his eyes and hatred in his white heart. He hates the guards and he hates the pilgrims—he hates all human beings because it was they who captured him long ago."

"Folk say he's a thousand and two years old," the first woman replied. "Not even an elephant can remember so far back. But anyway, he can't swim over here. Have you forgotten the old saying carved on the temple wall? *If the salty fluid of life touches the white tiger—the crystal-clear blood of the earth, the drops of death—then he will turn to stone—hard, cold stone.* So there you are—as soon as the tiger jumps into the water he'll turn to stone."

"Do you believe that story?" asked the second woman doubtfully.

"Of course," replied the first woman firmly. "After all, the tiger has lived for years without drinking water. Doesn't that surprise you? We *have* to believe in the gods, and we have to believe in their prophecies, too."

"Well, come along," said the other woman. "Let's go and offer the rats a little dish of milk. The god Ganesh, who goes riding mounted on a rat, will bring us luck one day. Or maybe one night . . ."

Farhad heard the women giggling before they disappeared into the milling throng.

His head was ringing. Where was this he'd ended up?

He had seen temple animals before. Back in the great temple of Madurai, he'd seen the chained elephant with its sad eyes constantly treading from one foot to the other. But sacred rats? And a tiger?

Have you found the mount you are to ride? he heard Lord Krishna asking in his head. Farhad's heart seemed to pump the wrong way with shock. His mount. Of course, he'd guessed it.

"Yes, I've found him," he whispered, "but how am I ever to tame him?"

A white tiger! Krishna might just as well have given him a bag of explosives as his companion. Or a British officer.

Trembling with fury and fear, Farhad crept out of hiding. "What's this supposed to be, Lord Krishna?" he whispered quietly. "A test? Another test, like riding here on the wind?"

As he walked through the temple courtyards, trying to calm his heart, Farhad kept his ears open, because if you keep your ears open you never need a map or guide. He realized, in astonishment, that the wind had carried him all the way to Mysore. Not that he had ever seen Mysore marked on a map, but if you kept your ears open in Madurai, you discovered that the two cities were at least several days' journey apart.

The temple where the wind had carried Farhad was dedicated to Durga, the angry goddess who rode a lion and stuck out her tongue to terrify her enemies.

"Round about here," an eager little boy told Farhad, "Durga conquered the buffalo demon Mahisha. Well—perhaps not right here in the temple. The guards at the entrance wouldn't have let the demon in, or Durga either. They don't like having to mop up too much blood."

Farhad nodded, and made off before the eager little boy could demand a couple of rupees for his information.

He was not particularly fond of Durga. She made his flesh creep, with the skulls she wore dangling from her belt and her angrily distorted features. He hoped he'd never meet her anywhere. The possibility of actually coming face-to-face with assorted deities all of a sudden, the way he'd met Krishna, was not exactly encouraging. Farhad pushed the thought and several fat women aside, and wriggled through the crowd into the next room in the temple.

He moved through the impenetrable darkness like a swimmer moving through water. No one who grew up in Madurai was going to lose his way in a temple—never mind how full of incense, how mazelike, how short of light it was. For a moment Farhad felt at home. Here and there, tiny oil lamps burned like eyes, and he greeted them as the guardian spirits of his childhood.

He nodded at the gaudy pictures telling the old legends; dipped his finger in the white, yellow, and red powder at the corners of the columns; and painted the signs of the gods on his forehead. And in the end, the familiar twilight of the temple interior brought him out in a courtyard with a rectangular pool of water in the middle of it.

Farhad stopped and blinked. For a few seconds, he'd forgotten why he was here. But now it came back to his mind with sudden force.

67

Or rather, with a furious snarl.

There stood the tiger in the middle of the large pool of water, on a tiny, walled island under a stone canopy.

His ears were laid back, his muscles tensed to leap—and his tail was lashing the dirty ground.

Farhad stumbled back. But then he saw that the other visitors to the temple were walking around the sides of the pool at their ease. Some were even standing on the shallow steps leading down to it, sprinkling the holy water of the temple on their heads.

Farhad also saw what had made the tiger so angry. A boy on the bank was busy throwing pebbles at the animal.

Was it true that the tiger would turn to stone the moment he jumped into the water? Was he really unable to harm anyone?

Farhad looked at the beast again, and then he realized how miserable he looked.

His coat was as white as the snow of the Himalayas, yes, but it was shaggy and had no luster. How dull the tiger's eyes were! He probably wouldn't have been able to swim across the pool even if he'd wanted to.

A wave of relief flooded through Farhad, and at the same moment, he wondered what use this worn-out old creature was supposed to be to him. Perhaps the white tiger had once been a mount for a hero to ride, but they'd kept him trapped here too long. He'd lost all his strength.

Farhad strolled along the rim of the pool and watched the tiger for a while. He walked up and down twice before he noticed something. Then he went all the way around the pool to make quite sure. Yes, there was no doubt about it: The tiger's eyes were following him. Of all the people walking near the water, the tiger had chosen to watch Farhad.

Farhad went up to the water and returned the animal's gaze. The tiger had blue eyes. Strange, uncanny eyes.

And with those eyes he spoke to Farhad.

"It's you," he said. Farhad jumped. "You're the hero."

Farhad looked around. Had the tiger really spoken to him? And if so, had anyone else heard it? No, everything was the same as before. The people by the water were bathing their feet, and the boy got tired of throwing pebbles and went away.

"I'm not a hero," said Farhad quietly, more to himself than anyone else.

He saw the tiger narrowing his eyes very slightly. "You're not?" he asked. "Then you must have stolen the amulet. You're wearing it around your neck."

Farhad put his hand to the amulet. He had mended the chain as best he could after the monkeys grabbed it.

"It's true, I did steal the amulet," he whispered. "I'm a thief, not a hero. But Krishna sent me on this journey. A journey to the desert of Thar. And I don't have much time."

"So it *is* you after all," said the tiger. His voice had a strangely soft sound, not like a tiger's at all. He sounded much more like a large, fat domestic cat. "You are the one I am to carry. You are going to set me free from this thrice-accursed pool of water."

"Is that so?" asked Farhad doubtfully. "How?"

"Am *I* the hero?" The tiger impatiently lashed his scruffy tail. "I can only leave if you free me. Think of something. You said you didn't have much time, so hurry up. I was—"

He turned around. And as soon as Farhad lost contact with those uncanny blue eyes, the tiger's voice stopped short. In fact he felt as if the tiger had never spoken to him at all.

Dazed, he stared at the black-and-white striped back that the tiger had turned to him. The cat was lying on his stone platform now, resting his big head on his paws, and seemed to be preparing to go to sleep.

Farhad blinked. Was he going crazy? The tiger's stripes blurred before his eyes and the world seemed to sway. Bewildered, Farhad shook himself. He had to get away from here if he was to clear his head.

He slowly walked back through the corridors and halls, concentrating on nothing but his own footsteps for a while, and at last the chaos in his mind died down. He passed a small temple to one side of the complex. It stood on the edge of a courtyard and was obviously not dedicated to the avenging goddess Durga. Ganesh the elephant-headed god looked down at Farhad from the roof of the temple, and he went closer. After all, thought Farhad, Ganesh was the god of clever thinking and ingenious ideas. Praying to him just might be a good idea. Also, unlike Durga, he was a distinctly friendly god.

Farhad went into the little temple, stepping over a threshold that came all the way up to his knees. Its height surprised him.

Then something small ran over his toes with cold feet, and the threshold didn't surprise him anymore. Suppressing a scream, he looked around.

Of course. The two women had been talking about the temple of the rats, and this was it. It had always surprised him that the god with the elephant's trunk chose to ride a rat.

But then why shouldn't an elephant ride a rat, if a cowardly thief and a scruffy old tiger were setting out together to rescue a princess? In India, anything has always been possible, and Farhad felt a bitter pleasure at having been born in this strangest of all lands.

He bent down to see the threshold in the doorway from the rats' point of view. Only then did he notice that it had tiny

71

iron spikes on top. It was a barrier that the rats couldn't pass, as water was for the tiger. They had a comfortable life scurrying around in their temple, but they could never leave it.

How strange, thought Farhad, that we have to imprison our gods . . .

And then another idea came into his mind.

He stood very still for some time, watching the rats and pursuing his idea.

The little creatures were drinking from their bowls of milk with tiny tongues, clambering around the statues of the gods, chasing each other all over the temple. One little statue of Ganesh wore two rats on its head like a strange kind of fur cap.

For a moment Farhad almost felt that Ganesh was watching him. Hadn't he just bowed his head a fraction of an inch?

But the god was motionless again. Had Farhad simply imagined that small nod? To be on the safe side, however, he nodded back at Ganesh, and smiled.

"I've thought of a way," he whispered. "A way for the tiger, a way for the rats, a way for me. Oh, yes, you bet I have."

Then he left Ganesh's temple, he left the temple precincts altogether, and set off into the city to stock up with funds for travel. And find a seller of sugarcane.

Farhad didn't return to the temple until evening. The stream of visitors had ebbed away; the colorful remains of the festival lay scattered on the ground. The temple looked exhausted.

Dusk was already falling around the trees on the hill, and the towers of the palace of Mysore behind Farhad glimmered only faintly in the twilight.

Soon night would throw her black silk sari over the land and its people, and then Farhad's time would come.

He hid by the outer gate of the temple precincts. It was closed now. And when the men on watch outside dozed off, Farhad threw a large bundle of sugarcane tied up with cord over the wall. After that he climbed a tree, and from the tree he got over the wall and opened the gate from inside—just a crack. He held his breath, fearing the gate would squeak . . . but no, it did as he wanted and was mute. The avenging goddess Durga and all her stone companions seemed to be deep in a dream.

Farhad hurried across the temple courtyard with his bundle under his arm as silently as if he were only a dream himself.

The rats were obviously surprised to have a visitor so late. Some of them were asleep at the feet of the gods, and Farhad saw their little noses twitching as they dreamed. Those who weren't sleeping began scurrying frantically around when he entered their temple.

"Hush," Farhad whispered to them. "Calm down. It's a beautiful moonlit night out there. I'm sure you never saw the moon shine so brightly . . ."

He knelt down and set to work on a piece of sugarcane with a knife. Then he inspected the results with satisfaction. One cane now led up to the high, spiky threshold of the temple on one side—and another led down on the other side. The rats couldn't have wished for an easier way out.

But obviously they didn't want a way out. They looked suspiciously at Farhad's structure and gathered in small groups as if to discuss the meaning of it.

Farhad could imagine the oldest rat saying, "What's that supposed to be? It's not exactly pretty. It doesn't look sacred, either."

"Perhaps we could eat it," another rat seemed to be suggesting. "But it's not in a very good position for that. Maybe we could pull it off the threshold?"

"Look, he's tied it in place," a third rat was saying indignantly. "How annoying!"

Farhad took a small piece of roasted meat out of his pocket and put it on top of the threshold, just where the two pieces of sugarcane met. Then he placed another piece of meat right outside the entrance. He saw the rats' noses twitching as they wondered if it was too dangerous to fetch the tidbit, or whether it was worth the risk.

Farhad left them alone to make up their minds. While the rats were presumably consulting behind his back, Farhad laid a trail of little pieces of meat right across the temple courtyard to the gateway. He worked fast and doggedly. But his labor paid off. When he finally turned around, he saw the first rats coming his way.

Farhad threw a few handfuls of rice into the courtyard, picked up his bundle of sugarcane and the rest of the cord, and stole farther into the temple precincts. It was so dark now that he had to feel his way along by the arms of the statues. Once he touched something soft and slippery, and withdrew his hand in alarm.

His fingers smelled of rancid fat.

Of course! He had touched one of the figures of Durga, the angry goddess. People tried to mollify her rage by throwing cool little balls of greasy ghee at her burning body, and the fat stuck there.

Farhad shook himself and wiped his hand on his old dhoti.

A little later, he reached the rectangular inner courtyard with the pool of water in it. The moon's reflection floated expectantly on the little ripples raised by the wind.

The tiger, wakeful and motionless, was crouching on the edge of his platform, watching Farhad, who acted as if he didn't notice the tiger's penetrating gaze. He had no time to feel frightened now.

Farhad laid the sugarcanes down side by side and began weaving the cord through them. He had practiced during the afternoon until he could make a reasonably good raft—but that had been on land.

Now everything depended on whether his raft would stay afloat on water.

His hands were trembling. He kept making mistakes, and then he had to undo the cord laboriously again. Sometimes he stopped to listen. Had the watchmen woken up? No, all was still quiet.

As soon as they woke, he'd have only a few moments to escape. The rats would distract the watchmen's attention, and of course they'd try to catch the sacred rodents. But that wouldn't take forever. Some time soon, the gates would be closed and locked again. And the guards would begin searching the temple for the intruder.

Although it was a cool night, sweat was streaming down Farhad's back. At last he had lashed the canes together, and for a moment he examined his raft.

It didn't inspire much confidence. More than anything

else, it looked like a heap of sugarcanes piled up at random, just lying around and waiting to have their sweet juice extracted in the brightly painted cane presses.

Farhad pulled the raft over to the edge of the pool and set it down on the water, where it lay lopsided. When he knelt on it, he was so surprised not to sink at once that he almost fell into the pool in sheer amazement.

He picked up the last long sugarcane and used it to punt the makeshift raft over to the stone island where the white tiger stood.

Only when he had almost reached the island did Farhad remember that this was a tiger he was planning to take onboard. A real live tiger. Old, scruffy, mangy, but still a tiger—a tiger with claws and teeth.

How could he be sure that the tiger really was afraid of water? And if so, was his fear greater than his wish to eat such a welcome snack as Farhad Kamal? Farhad had been thinking about the raft all day, and had given some thought to the rats as well. But not for a moment had he thought about the real aim of his plan.

The raft touched the stone platform, and rocked gently. However, it was still lying securely in the water.

Farhad looked up and into the tiger's blue eyes.

At that moment, he heard a shout from the entrance to the temple. The guards at the gate had woken up.

77

Later, Farhad wondered whether the whole of the rest of his journey had been decided in that split second. Or the whole of the rest of his existence.

He could have pushed the raft off again. He could have punted it back and run away. He'd still have had time. The watchmen were still busy catching the sacred rats. The tiger hadn't put his paws on the raft yet.

But Farhad didn't push off from the island.

He looked into the tiger's eyes and heard his words.

"Oh, wonderful!" said the tiger. "A thief as hero, a scruffy old tiger as his mount, and a heap of sugarcane for a boat." He put out one paw and cautiously touched the raft with his pink pads. The raft rocked.

"You can forget this whole idea," said the tiger, and Farhad saw his eyes widen. "I'm not coming with you. We'd sink. Without fail. Perhaps they haven't told you, but *if the salty fluid of life touches me—the crystal-clear blood of the earth, the drops of death—I'll turn to stone—hard, cold stone.* That's how the prophecy goes."

He stopped talking and went on looking at Farhad with his big eyes. And then Farhad realized that the white tiger was frightened.

Frightened to death, just like Farhad himself.

"Come on," he said. "Get on my raft. It's carried me, it'll

carry you, too. We must hurry! The guards could be here any moment, and that'll be the end of you and your freedom."

The tiger growled angrily, but Farhad knew that the anger wasn't for him but for the decision the animal had to make. He'd been waiting all his life for this moment, the arrival of the hero he was to carry—the moment when he would leave his cramped, undignified prison and prowl the land again.

Farhad listened intently in the darkness, but he couldn't hear footsteps approaching. Not yet.

"Oh, very well," said the tiger. "But move over to the very edge of the raft, please. If we're too close to each other, we'll tip over."

Farhad laughed nervously. "I wasn't going to get too close to you anyway," he said. "I may not be likely to turn to stone, but I'm definitely mortal. Particularly when I'm close to tigers."

"Ha, ha," said the tiger, flexing his muscles. The next moment, with a velvety soft leap, he landed beside Farhad on the raft. It rocked again, but held. The tiger looked anxiously at the little ripples lapping at the edge of the sugarcane, but none of them touched his white paws.

Farhad dipped his long cane in the water once more and began punting the unsteady raft back to the bank.

"Can you see the water?" the tiger asked when Farhad looked him in the eye. "Is it coming up here with us? Will it bite me?"

Farhad kept reassuring him that the water would obey the force of gravity and stay under the raft. The tiger wasn't convinced that the force of gravity worked by night as it did by day. Farhad did his best to act as if he were in the habit of punting wobbly rafts across pools of water. He fervently hoped the tiger didn't see his hands shaking. How long would it take the guards to catch the rats and then set out in search of the intruder who had set them free? Ten minutes? Two?

When they reached the stone steps going down to the pool, Farhad was as wet with sweat from the tension as if he'd swum across without any raft.

He jumped into the water, which was quite shallow here by the steps, and the tiger twitched nervously. "Don't worry," said Farhad. "I'll hold the raft while you jump ashore. Hurry up! There's no time to lose! But don't go thinking you'll be in charge once you're on land. Do you see my dhoti? It's soaked with water. I'll take it off and throw it at you if you run away. And I have very good aim."

That was a lie, but Farhad saw that the tiger wasn't going to put it to the test. He quietly growled in displeasure, and jumped on land.

Farhad took off his wet dhoti, rolled it up into a little bundle, and nodded to the tiger, who was standing by the pool of water, impatiently lashing his tail and waiting for him.

"Come on," whispered Farhad. "The guards are busy by the great gate. We'll go through the side entrance. As soon as I'm dry enough from running, you can carry me. That's how the prophecy goes, right? You're to be the mount that the hero rides."

"Stop showing off," said the tiger. "It was just luck that the raft didn't sink, not your skill."

Farhad stole cautiously toward the way out, and to his surprise the tiger trotted meekly along beside him. "Where are we going anyway?" he asked. "What's the aim of our journey?"

"Later," whispered Farhad. "For now we just have to get out of here."

A truly amazing sight met their eyes in the great courtyard. Thousands of rats scurrying about in the moonlight, their coats shining so they looked like a horde of giant beetles.

The watchmen had already closed the main gate again, but now the rats were climbing up the rough surface of the outside walls, disappearing the same way as Farhad had arrived. He hadn't expected that, and for a second he stopped,

81

placed his hands together, and bowed slightly in tribute to the clever rats.

The two watchmen had fetched a third guard from somewhere, and they were running about with large lengths of cloth, trying to catch the rats in them. It didn't look as if they were having much success.

Farhad was just feeling triumphant when the tiger shot past him like a white whirlwind. For a moment Farhad thought he was going to jump the wall, too, but then he saw that the tiger had no intention of running away. After two leaps he sat down and glanced around, and to Farhad's great surprise he looked guilty.

"Sorry," said the tiger's blue eyes. "It's my hunting instinct. The rats—I—well, I couldn't help it."

Farhad saw the great animal's forepaws twitching restlessly, and his tail lashing the ground more nervously than ever.

Farhad smiled, but then his expression suddenly changed.

"Look over there!" shouted one of the guards, forgetting about the rats. Now the other two had seen Farhad and the tiger, as well. One of the guards reached into a niche in the shadows where he had obviously left something useful: a rifle.

Farhad dropped his wet bundle of cloth, raced to the tiger, and swung himself up on the animal's back as if he'd never done anything else.

The tiger uttered a sound of alarm rather like an unsuccessful growl. But he stood up and began moving. Farhad clung to his shaggy coat and saw the guard load his rifle. The tiger was racing straight toward the marksman.

And just before he reached the guard, the tiger prepared to spring.

Farhad would never have thought there was such strength in the thin animal. His hind paws pushed off from the ground like two huge metal springs, springs that had been under extreme tension for years—and perhaps they had. Farhad clung on desperately and closed his eyes. He heard the men shouting angrily, and then a shot rang out.

But it didn't hit them. The tiger made a soft landing on the other side of the wall and bounded away, taking great leaps.

The world staggered past Farhad, a wild, disorganized spectacle, and he closed his eyes again.

After a while he realized that the tiger's leaps were slowing down and falling into a steady rhythm. He opened his eyes once more, and saw that the tiger had turned his head to face Farhad as he ran, which seemed to be rather a difficult thing

83

to do. But obviously Farhad could only hear his voice if they had eye contact.

"Could you kindly not hold on quite so tight?" asked the tiger. "You're pinching my left ear."

"Oh," said Farhad. "Sorry. By the way, my name is Farhad Kamal."

"Ah, you happy lotus blossom!" said the tiger.

"What about you?" asked Farhad, somewhat annoyed. "What's your name?"

"Nitish," replied the tiger with great dignity. "*Lord of the Right Way.*"

"Oh?" said Farhad. "But you still chase rats."

The Indian
Butcher's Stall

ALTHOUGH THE WHITE TIGER HAD SLOWED
down, his leaps were still as long as the bends in the
river and as high as the tops of the bamboos. Farhad saw
the earth glow red where Nitish's paws touched the ground,
and when his mighty tail swept across the fields, the rice,
maize, and banana plants snapped like blades of grass.

And with every step he took, the tiger seemed to
change. Farhad saw life gradually return to his white coat.
It grew smoother and thicker, gaining radiance until it was
as bright as the mountain snow that Farhad knew only from
pictures.

It was as if only a shadowy, unreal copy of the tiger had been waiting in the temple in Mysore. Now that he was free once again, Nitish became what he had been before his captivity: a young, strong beast of prey with deadly claws and an invincible bite—a creature fit for a true hero to ride.

Farhad held on to the tiger's fur and thanked heaven he had not met Nitish first as such a dangerous, terrifying big cat. If this supernatural creature had been waiting in the temple, he wouldn't have ventured within ten yards of that platform.

But Nitish still seemed to be afraid of water, if of nothing else. The tiger leaped over even the smallest trickle of water with such high, panicky bounds that Farhad's mind was set at rest. As immaculate as the tiger now looked from the outside, as confidently as he carried Farhad through the night, inside he was still afraid that a drop of water would turn him to stone.

At dawn, they stopped to rest under the spreading branches of a banyan tree, close to the cistern that provided a little village with water.

With a single graceful movement of one paw, Nitish caught a bird from up in the branches of the tree to satisfy his hunger, a black mynah with bright eyes. As he ate it, the tiger looked suspiciously at the cistern and moved a little closer to Farhad.

"It won't come out of there, will it?" he asked.

"The water? Not as far as I know."

"I was only thinking," said the tiger. "I thought it might be envious of me. Are you sure it doesn't eat birds?"

"Quite sure," Farhad nodded. "Water eats human beings, but not birds."

"Human beings?"

"Only when they're dead. We feed their ashes to it," said Farhad. "When we've found the jewel and left Gaya behind, we'll go on to Varanasi, where you'll see water eating the remains of human beings."

Nitish shook himself. "Oh, well, ashes," he said dismissively, then tore a wing off the bird, and ate it with relish. "Water must be very stupid to eat ashes. Tell me, my friend," he added with his mouth full, "how did you come to be given this task?"

"I climbed into a British garden," Farhad replied.

"You did *what?*" Nitish blinked in surprise.

"Yes, well," said Farhad, "I was trying to steal an amulet. A silver amulet. But it turned out not to be just any old amulet."

He sighed deeply when he thought of his fate, and then he told the tiger all that had happened since he, Farhad Kamal, master thief and professional con man, had met the god Krishna beside a lotus pool.

87

Nitish yawned from time to time and cleaned his paws
with his tongue.

"If you'll allow me," he said when Farhad had finished,
"let me sum this up. You have four problems. First: The
princess you're supposed to be rescuing is in the desert of
Thar, which is a long way off. Second: The jewel you need
for your task is in the city of Gaya, so you also have to go the
long way around. And third—" He stood up and stretched
as thoroughly as only cats can. "Third: You have short, weak
legs like all human beings. Climb on my back, human. With
a mount like me, three of your problems are as good as solved
already."

"So what's the fourth?" asked Farhad when he was upon
the tiger's back again.

"The fourth problem," replied Nitish, turning his large
black-and-white striped head to Farhad, "is yourself. You have
to be a hero to rescue the princess. And you're far from being
a hero yet. More than three times farther than the way from
here to the desert of Thar and back again."

If Farhad had ever gone to school, and if he'd had any idea
of geography, he would have been amazed to see how fast
the map moved away beneath them. It was as if the white
tiger only had to raise his mighty paws and someone gave

the earth a shove, sending it rolling on like a tremendous marble.

One of the most remarkable things was that no one saw them. They overtook carts, buffalo and oxen, and human beings. They passed huts and crossed bridges. Once Nitish even raced right through a crowd of people that had gathered in the road—and no one took any notice of them. For wherever they went, they were there so briefly that as soon as they arrived, they were gone again. And Farhad Kamal, who was a clever con man, thought to himself that this was the best trick anyone could play: deceiving people with their own blindness, fooling them with the truth.

The next time they stopped to rest, about the middle of the day, Farhad persuaded a blue-and-brown checked dhoti lying out in the sun to dry to come with him. He had been riding naked since he threw his own garment away in the temple. The cloth wound itself around his waist almost of its own free will. You could hardly have called it theft.

When night fell they slept side by side on the bare ground, but as neither Farhad nor the tiger had ever had a bed to call his own, they didn't mind.

On the second night after their flight from the temple, Farhad woke up, saw the gigantic, breathing mass of the tiger next to him, and felt frightened. The fact that the tiger's strides were as wide as clouds and he talked with his eyes didn't mean he might not suddenly take it into his head to eat his rider.

Farhad got up very quietly and crept into the nearest village, where he stole a waterproof bag made of goatskin, which he filled with water at a well. When he came back with this waterskin, the tiger woke up and blinked at Farhad with his blue eyes. The starlight shone in them, and to Farhad, it looked as sharp as the tiger's teeth. He clutched his waterskin in both hands and returned Nitish's gaze.

"Cowardly human," whispered the tiger with his uncanny blue eyes, uttering a soft, dangerous snarl. "Cowardly, cowardly little human."

Farhad Kamal knew he was a coward. "Better cowardly than dead," he said.

"*Sssss*," hissed Nitish. "And to think I'm carrying *you* all over India to rescue a princess! You!"

"Oh, do shut up, you great big blue-eyed cat," said Farhad, and he rolled over with his back to the tiger. But he took care to keep his waterskin within reach.

After that he always carried it slung over his shoulder by a strap, like a strange sort of weapon, and when night came he slept with the waterskin in his arms. Nitish growled whenever he heard the water sloshing around inside the goatskin bag, but he said no more about Farhad's cowardice.

The farther north they went, the drier it was. The monsoon seemed to be late in coming to this part of the country. The rivers had failed long ago, and Nitish crossed their dry beds with a kind of triumphant satisfaction.

"The water's gone away," he said, pleased. "It was too stupid to stand up to the sun."

"Without water there'd be no green trees with your lunch twittering in their branches," Farhad pointed out. "All living things, except you, have to drink."

"Even other tigers?" asked Nitish.

Farhad nodded.

That night Nitish's paws twitched in his sleep, and when he woke up, he gave Farhad a strange look. "I dreamed I was a perfectly ordinary tiger," he said. "Dirty yellow and thirsty. And I talked to the other tigers. It—it wasn't such a bad feeling."

He sounded surprised and almost sad. For a moment, Farhad felt something like affection for the great beast of prey. But as Farhad had never before felt affection for anyone, he didn't recognize the sensation in his heart and misinterpreted it as hunger.

"But you *aren't* an ordinary tiger," said Farhad. "You are Nitish, Lord of the Right Way. Let's get moving and look for something to eat."

They reached the city of Gaya on the fifth evening.

Farhad had been impatient to get there. His eyes were dry from the wind on the tiger's back, and his soul was dry from the barren, brown monotony of the thirsty fields.

And he also felt an urge to practice his profession. Like all who are good at their jobs, he was nothing without it—a cowardly little human, just as the tiger had said. His fingers twitched when he saw the first clouds of dust rising from the city, and his mind was already devising ways of purloining things he hadn't even set eyes on yet. What foreign riches would Gaya offer him? What glittering jewels? And what opportunities in a city where he didn't even have to disguise himself to go unrecognized . . . *One* jewel at least was just waiting for Farhad Kamal to take it.

"It's over there," he told Nitish. "The bloodstone lies hidden over there, beneath those clouds of dust."

The back of his neck tingled as he said the word "bloodstone." It was as if its name alone had a special kind of magic.

"I've heard of it," said Nitish. "There's said to be a curse on it."

"Even if there is," said Farhad, "I'm not afraid of any curse. What harm can a shiny stone do me?"

"They say," remarked the tiger, "that anyone who touches it will lose his life before the earth has gone once around the moon."

"That can't be right," said Farhad, "because the sun goes around the moon and the earth stands still."

Farhad and the tiger had both had about the same amount of education.

"Anyway, the stone brings death," said the tiger. "Death before a month is up. So people say."

"If I believed everything people say," Farhad told him, "I'd have my work cut out to fit it all into the twenty-three hours of every day."

"Twenty-six," murmured Nitish, with the air of a know-it-all. Then, with an angry snarl, he landed outside the first wooden huts of Gaya.

The huts had spread beyond the city walls like vines climbing over a fence, considerably enlarging the old city center. Now they were the first to greet the young stranger and his white tiger, for the tiger was going slowly enough to be seen for the first time. Farhad rode him into the city as proudly as a king on his horse. A crowd of children gathered and followed him, and the adults flinched aside in alarm as he passed by.

"That must be a true hero," said the old folk squatting in the dust outside their doors. "A hero riding a white tiger. The days of legends and old tales are coming back, and the British won't stay much longer."

"He doesn't look at all like a hero," said the young women, pulling their scarves over their faces when the stranger rode by. Not to protect themselves from the dust, and not to hide their beauty. Farhad knew they were hiding behind veils to preserve the *illusion* of beauty. The newcomer, who hadn't seen all those hooked noses and crooked teeth, could imagine them as perfect. He knew all about the tricks women played.

But none of them won the hero's heart with her beautiful, half-hidden gaze.

The hero's heart beat only for the bloodstone.

Like so much else, love had been a stranger to his heart until now. If you have to survive, you can't afford love.

Farhad and his tiger found a place to stay on the outskirts of the city. Heroes ought not to sleep on the bare ground, not when they're in cities. He promised to pay the next day, and decided to interpret the word "next" in rather a flexible sense.

After a good meal, which he also promised to pay for on the next day, Farhad set out in search of the bloodstone.

He was to find its trail where he least expected.

Farhad knew that in any city, all rumors inevitably come together at a certain point. So if you were looking for something, it was a good idea to locate that meeting place—then you'd be that much closer to whatever you were seeking.

He wandered aimlessly through Gaya for a while, with the tiger at his side like an overgrown dog. Walking through an Indian city with a white tiger attracted as much attention as doing a yoga headstand with a date palm under your arm. A crowd of children went along with Farhad, like a tail growing longer and longer, and in the end he was exhausted by all the curious looks turned on him. So he simply sat down on a low wall. The rumors could find their own way to him.

If he had thought more about where he was sitting, what happened next wouldn't have happened at all. And then he would never have found the trail of the bloodstone.

For the wall on which Farhad sat down was part of a large marketplace, and of all the parts of that marketplace, Farhad had chosen the one where the butchers had their stalls.

Sides of meat hung from huge hooks, headless chickens lay on tables, legs of butchered animals were everywhere—

and a black cloud of flies hovered over everything, buzzing greedily.

Farhad hoped the children would leave him alone now, but they didn't mind the blood on the butchers' stalls or the flies buzzing around them. They waited expectantly a little way off, apparently hoping that Farhad and his white tiger would put on some kind of fascinating show for them.

And that was exactly what they soon did, because Nitish picked up the scent of the meat. And he was hungry. He hadn't caught a bird yet today, and he had looked disapprovingly at Farhad's own meal of rice. Now his nose was twitching. And while Farhad tried to listen to what passersby were saying as he waited for the children's patience to wear thin, the tiger's tail began thumping restlessly on the blood-spattered ground at the side of the marketplace.

Some of the butchers stared at him distrustfully.

"Don't worry!" Farhad called to them. "He won't hurt you. And he can't kill those animals of yours because they're already dead and hanging from those hooks!"

The butchers laughed.

"The blood on the stone steps of your market," Farhad told them, "reminds me of something . . . now I wonder what it was . . ."

One of the men wiped his hands on the smeared lunghi

that he wore around his waist. "Sure you can't remember?" he asked softly, coming a little closer.

"No idea," said Farhad, secretly glad to have found someone stupid enough to fall for his trick. "Blood . . . stone . . . Can *you* think what it might remind me of?"

The man leaned forward and looked all around him. His face wore a knowing grin, and Farhad knew he'd hooked him. The more knowingly a man grinned, the readier he was to fall for a ruse.

"The bloodstone," whispered the man. "A jewel. But it brings bad luck. They say that the servant of Ravana the demon king has been after the bloodstone ever since he first set eyes on it."

"Really?" whispered Farhad. "Why, yes, I believe I did once hear something about that stone. Tell me, what does it look like?"

"Bright," whispered the man. "Bright as the sun and red as the princess's blood that it sprang from. And I swear it's at least as big as my thumb!"

Farhad looked impressed, though he hoped the stone wasn't quite as crooked and ugly as the man's thumb. "You seem to know a lot about it," he said in a low, confidential tone. "You don't have it hidden in your lunghi there, do you? How else would you know all those details?"

The man spread his hands as if to avert bad luck. "I wouldn't touch it! Never. Not even if it came as a gift! A stone born of blood, with a demon after it! Oh, no! But . . ." And now he lowered his voice even further. "They say it's been in this city for a while. It came from Madurai, where it lay sleeping for some time. And apparently it's now in the hands of . . . By the way, where's your tiger?"

Farhad looked up. The place where Nitish had been lying a moment ago was empty.

"Damn," he muttered.

He climbed up on the wall where he had been sitting, stood on tiptoe, and searched the market for a patch of white fur with black stripes on it.

"There!" cried the butcher who had been talking to him. "Here he comes! Look at that!"

And Farhad looked.

Nitish came racing across the market to him, and he wasn't on his own.

There was half a goat in his mouth.

"Oh, no," said Farhad.

The butcher jumped aside as the great beast of prey reached Farhad and put the goat down beside him.

"You were right," his blue eyes told Farhad as he licked the juices of the meat off his lips. "Stealing isn't difficult. I stole this on the sly. Now we'll have a feast . . . and it doesn't have feathers like those mynah birds. I'm sick and tired of feathers! Look, someone must have plucked this already!"

"Goats," said Farhad slowly, "don't have feathers."

"So they don't," said the tiger. "You're right. One forgets these things after living in captivity so long. I'll just go and fetch the other half—"

"Stop!" cried Farhad. "Nitish! Stop right there! You can't—"

But the tiger's black-and-white striped tail was already coiling away underneath a stall like a large snake in a hurry. Farhad sighed.

"I'll take the goat back," he said, and the butcher nodded.

"However you came by your unusual pet," he said, grinning, "you ought to train it better."

Farhad took the half goat by both legs and set off with it more or less the way that Nitish had come. It was one thing to make off with a jewel the size of a pigeon's egg, quite another to be caught with half a goat.

The goat was heavy and slippery, and Farhad was gasping with effort and annoyance. Only a moment—only the twinkling of an eye—had stood between him and the information he wanted.

The non-twinkling eye of a dead goat, more like, he

thought bitterly. And the goat wasn't giving away the where-abouts of the bloodstone. Farhad hadn't gone far with the carcass when he saw two men making their way through the crowd straight toward him.

"Over there!" cried an agitated little man with sparse hair, pointing to Farhad. "That's my half goat! There's the man the tiger belongs to!"

The second person coming Farhad's way was a tall Englishman. Much to Farhad's dismay, the Englishman was wearing a uniform with unpleasant associations: He was a policeman.

Farhad dropped the half goat's dirty legs and disappeared into the crowd. He was smaller and more agile than any Englishman. He knew that, so he slipped underneath a stall from which a row of dead sheep's heads stared at him.

He was planning to come out again on the other side and run, but he slipped on a piece of fat under the stall and fell.

Underneath an Indian butcher's stall is about the worst place in the world to fall. First, usually you'd rather not know what you're lying on. And second, your surroundings are generally so slippery that the chances of struggling to your feet again in a reasonable time are zero.

In a panic, Farhad tried to find a firm footing on the slip-pery surface beneath him. Then an arm suddenly grabbed him, and he was looking into the British police officer's red face. For a while they struggled grimly among the slimy stuff and the mud. But the other man was taller, stronger, and stood more firmly on his feet, so although Farhad was flailing around wildly, he was eventually dragged out from under the stall, with the help of the butcher it belonged to and the owner of the half goat.

"I've no idea," said the Englishman, setting Farhad down on his feet, "why this man is rambling on about tigers roaming free. But you've stolen his goods, no mistake."

Farhad twisted and turned in the policeman's grip. "I didn't!" he cried. "You heard for yourself! It was the white tiger! And I don't know the tiger at all! Never met him."

"Well, well," said the policeman, handing Farhad over to the owner of the goat and wiping his hands, with a look of disgust, on a cloth that one of the interested bystanders had given him. "So it's a *white* tiger into the bargain! Can it by any chance fly?"

"Something like that," muttered Farhad—quietly enough for the police officer not to hear him.

"This is a crazy country," said the Englishman. "I always said so. Well, I know one thing for sure, there's no white tiger around here." He nodded to the butcher. "Follow me and bring him along."

"Where to?" asked Farhad, trying to free himself one last time. But fighting had never been his strong suit. "Where are you taking me?"

"To our nice new jail, for a start," said the police officer, shaking his head and looking over his shoulder. "You can sit there and think how you're going to pay for that goat."

"No!" shouted Farhad. "You can't do this to me! I don't have the time! Krishna's daughter is waiting for me! I have to—"

"Krishna's daughter, is it?" asked the butcher, grinning. "Well, I never! Krishna's daughter is waiting for him. Poor girl. She'll just have to wait a little longer. And you can stop bellowing like that!"

With these words and a nasty smile, he stuffed a dirty cloth into Farhad's mouth. Farhad, who was a vegetarian like most Hindus, could taste the sheep's blood on the cloth, and he cursed Krishna and this whole journey from the bottom of his heart.

The cell where they put him was dark and stuffy. It had four bunk beds made of thin wood on each side of the cell, and a barred window looking out on the backyard.

"Well, not a bad view," said Farhad, going over to the window.

The only other occupant of the cell was sitting on his bed, watching Farhad.

"What's so good about the view?" he asked.

"It doesn't lure you out into freedom," Farhad explained. "I hate having a view of green fields when I'm stuck in jail."

"Do you end up in jail often?" asked the other man.

"Sure. All the time," replied Farhad, and he dropped on one of the other hard beds. His companion turned to the wall, apparently considering the conversation over.

For his part, Farhad looked at the man. A Muslim. He wore a dirty turban, a long robe, and a mustache artistically twisted up at the ends. Farhad had caught only a brief glimpse of those ends, but he had a feeling that there was something not quite right about them.

However, he could be just imagining it.

When he was sure the other man was asleep, he sat cross-legged on the narrow bed and took out the silver amulet. He opened the tiny catch and looked at the photo. And suddenly, to his surprise, he didn't feel so lonely. After all, the young girl in the photograph was in a dungeon herself, waiting somewhere to be set free. While he looked at the picture, he had a curious feeling that the sepia veil had been withdrawn slightly, like mist very gradually dispersing. It was still a blurry photo, but now Farhad could see the girl's features. How beautiful she was!

Well, Krishna's daughter would have to wait a little longer. But would her patience be rewarded in the end? Would he reach her in time, now that he had lost his mount?

Nitish heard the uproar in the meat market and crouched down under one of the many stalls with the second half of the slaughtered goat.

He listened to the excited butchers and their customers for a while, and then he figured it out: They had taken Farhad away. He quickly ate some of the goat and then set off in search of the prison that the people had been talking about. He felt slightly guilty for landing his hero behind bars. But he felt sure it wouldn't be hard to get him out again.

Unfortunately, it turned out to be very much harder than he had expected.

He approached the prison grounds through the main gate. Inside, everything was green. The British had planted a handsome lawn in front of the prison, and it was gleaming in the sun. A gravel path led straight across the grass to the double doors of the main entrance, and the tiger was about to pad along this path and scare the guards at the gate away when he flinched back. A jet of water from a hose had almost hit him.

He staggered back and sat down on the gravel. And then he saw them: They were on both sides of the lawn, three of them on each side, and they were holding long hoses and turning them regularly around in circles: six men smartly dressed in white, with fine red caps on their heads. Nitish shook himself in disbelief. The men's hoses were all connected to a pump in the middle of the lawn.

"Oh, well," said the tiger to himself. "You can't let a pump make you run, can you?"

He waited until the men were pointing their hoses another way, and then he set off along the gravel path for the second time.

But one of the men had seen him. He called something out to the others. The tiger didn't understand it, but presumably it was to do with him, because now they all looked his way. He snarled to scare them off, but they simply turned away again. If you had well-paying work in India in those days, you weren't going to let anything keep you from doing your job, not even a white tiger.

Nitish made another attempt to take the gravel path. It didn't work. At least one of the hoses was always spraying water on the path. Nitish tried to reach the main gate of the prison by skirting the lawn, but it was no use. He snarled furiously in frustration, and then gave up and sat down to think. The dust he had raised as he jumped about on the gravel had colored his coat gray, and after a while he heard a little girl saying, "Look, Mama! The British have put a stone tiger outside their prison!"

At first that frightened Nitish so much that he couldn't move. Had a drop of water fallen on him after all? Had he turned to stone? He squinted at the lawn sprinklers. No, they were far enough away.

And if he could move his eyes, he told himself, then he probably hadn't been turned to stone. As an experiment, he retracted his claws and then shot them out again. No, he hadn't turned to stone. A smile spread over his broad, black-and-white striped face. *Pretending* to be made of stone wasn't a bad idea, though. He'd bear it in mind for the future.

I'm made of stone, he told himself, chuckling quietly into his fur.

Evening came, and Farhad was standing at the tiny barred window again. The white tiger must be dozens of miles away by now. Someplace where no one threatened him with a waterskin anymore . . . Farhad must have left the wretched thing under the butcher's stall. He imagined Nitish catching one of the talkative mynah birds far from Gaya and eating it at his leisure under a half-dead tree. The tiger was lost once and for all. And now what? Would Krishna call him, Farhad, to account?

How much help could he expect from Krishna when it came to dealing with the British?

Not a lot, he guessed.

The Muslim with the handsome whiskers was already asleep on his bed, but Farhad couldn't sleep. He stared out at the dark backyard until his eyes hurt.

There was a waning crescent moon in the sky. Soon the moon would begin to wax again, eating its fill of light, and when it was round and full, Ravana's wedding would be held. Krishna's daughter would be doomed. Time was running away from Farhad, and suddenly he thought he saw something moving on the rooftops—something pale, as if the moon had come down from the sky and was now bounding from house to house.

The white shape stopped here and there, apparently thinking about its next leap before finally moving closer to Farhad. The maze of decrepit balconies and cornices on the buildings looked like a mouth of dangerous teeth, which the shadowy figure made its way across with great care—not an easy task.

And then Farhad saw the shadow's big paws and long tail.

"Nitish!" he whispered in amazement.

The tiger crouched between two roofs for a last mighty

leap—and then jumped down into the dirty yard, skirted two great mounds of rubble and garbage, and stole silently up to the barred window where Farhad was standing. The tiger's blue eyes glowed in the night, and his whiskers were quivering with effort.

"It's much easier to cross a city as complicated as this with a couple of big bounds," said the tiger's eyes, "than to find your way through its backyards."

"Why did you come?" Farhad asked.

The tiger gave him a look of scorn. "Did you think you were the only one with a great mission to carry out?"

"What has he promised you?"

"Who?" asked Nitish.

"You know who I mean. Our flute-playing friend—Krishna."

"Krishna?" The tiger uttered a soft, purring sound, like laughter. "Freedom. Freedom for the length of about ten human lives. It was an old promise. I've waited too long for it to be kept."

"Freedom? But you're free now."

"Freedom from my gifts," said Nitish. "When the princess returns to her father, I'll be a tiger like all the others again. I'll drink water, and take a long time to go anywhere, and swim across rivers."

"Help me, Nitish. I have to get free myself—free from these walls."

"That's why I'm here, you clever little thief, to ask you what I should do."

"Can't you chase the guards away from the great door?"

"Er . . . no." The tiger looked down at his paws, embarrassed. Then he looked Farhad in the eye again. "*Lawn sprinklers.*"

Farhad looked inquiringly at him.

"Well, what about it?" snarled Nitish in annoyance. "Don't you know what lawn sprinklers are? Men stand on that wretched green lawn with long water hoses, turning around in circles. And everything gets wet, everything: the grass, the gravel path, anyone passing by. Even now, at night, the grass is still wet from all that sprinkling, and the gravel is shining as if it had sucked up water like a sponge. What was I to do?"

"Don't upset yourself," whispered Farhad. "We'll just have to find some other way."

They said nothing for a while, and Farhad put his arm through the bars and touched the tiger's white coat. It felt soft and slightly damp with dew. That surprised Farhad, but he thought the dew probably wasn't wet enough to turn the tiger to stone.

"I just wanted to make sure you were really here," he said. "This whole story is getting rather outlandish, if you ask me, and it's better to find out in good time whether one's just dreaming. Because if I'm dreaming, the easiest way of getting out of here would be to wake up: no tiger, no Krishna, no prison."

Farhad sighed. "But it doesn't seem to be a dream."

"It isn't," he heard someone say in the darkness. "It's a damn real, solid prison."

Farhad spun around. The Muslim with the handsome whiskers was sitting upright and cross-legged on his bed, watching him.

"A mirror," he said.

"What?" asked Farhad, bewildered.

"We need a mirror," said the man. "Can your friend there outside the window get hold of a mirror?"

Farhad looked at Nitish. "Can you?"

"Of course," said Nitish boastfully.

"He'll do it," Farhad told the Muslim with the handsome whiskers, for the tiger's eyes spoke soundlessly, and the man couldn't read what Farhad had read in them.

Nitish turned and went away, leaping silently from wall to wall in the darkness.

When morning came, and the prisoners were given a plate of rice, the tiger hadn't yet returned.

The Muslim with the handsome whiskers ate his rice in silence, still watching Farhad. Farhad was watching him, too. They hadn't exchanged another word during the night. Farhad was waiting. Eventually the man would tell him what he planned to do with the mirror. As the sun climbed higher, and its rays somehow found their way through the bars and into the cell, Farhad watched the stranger with growing distrust.

Daylight had changed him. Yesterday the man had lain with his back to Farhad all day, but now he sat on the bed as he had sat last night, apparently thinking—and Farhad saw how the light revealed his skin.

It was brown as an Indian's, yet a paler color showed through in some places, as if the stranger had worn it out like an old coat. His turban had slipped slightly, and Farhad saw that just behind the ears his skin was almost white.

Farhad could also see his face more clearly by daylight, and his features seemed increasingly suspect. The man's eyes, hidden in the shadow of his turban most of the time, were a watery blue. Not the bright turquoise of the desert tribes, just blue like a cloudless sky.

While Farhad was wondering if his companion in the cell

was a master of disguise like himself, the man put his hand in his pocket and brought out a number of small objects which he placed on the bed. Farhad leaned forward.

"Incense sticks," the man said. "I've been here a few days. Long enough to do a little trading."

Farhad knew about the trade that went on in prisons. Their stout walls had often provided him with a place to sleep, and even when you were on the outside, it was sometimes worth visiting prisoners to do a little bartering . . .

"I couldn't get a mirror, though," the man went on.

"What are you planning?"

"We'll need the water they give us to drink and our clothes. Are you coming, too?"

"You bet."

"There'll be a lot of smoke and vapor, like in a temple," said the man, smiling. "All that vapor is very confusing. And maybe the straw of the mattresses will be burning, we'll have to watch out for that. There'll be panic. Fire! Wonderful, wonderful panic. The vapor will show us the way out. We just have to be fast enough."

"Suppose it doesn't work?"

"Then we're no worse off than before."

Farhad slowly nodded. "And what kind of business brings an Englishman like you to jail?" he asked.

The man twirled the ends of his mustache up a little more neatly still. "It *was* a business opportunity, in fact," he replied, "but I missed it. However, there'll be another. There always is." He looked searchingly at Farhad. "And I'm French, by the way, not English."

"You speak very good Hindi."

"I know. What's your trouble?"

"Time," said Farhad. "Lack of time."

"Time for what?"

Farhad smiled. "An opportunity for what?" he asked back.

The man smiled back. "I see we understand each other," he said. "Maybe we can work together."

"Not likely," said Farhad briefly. "That is to say," he added, "maybe if the price is right."

"*Un prix très haut.* A very high price indeed," said the Frenchman. "A price higher than any in the world. A jewel bigger than any gemstone you ever saw."

"Red."

"Yes, red as blood. You've heard of it?"

"In the marketplace," said Farhad vaguely. "I thought it was just a rumor."

"Well, I wasted my first chance to get my hands on that rumor," said the Frenchman, with a soft laugh. "You're going to be my second."

"I *am?*"

"Of course. I'll show you the house where the precious stone is kept, and you'll find out exactly where it is hidden inside. I can't show my face there anymore. Not even as a Frenchman. The owner's been warned that I change my appearance from time to time."

Farhad nodded. His heart was in his mouth, and he clenched one hand as hard as he could behind his back. To think that here, of all places, he had met the man who would lead him to the bloodstone!

Outwardly, Farhad Kamal showed none of his excitement; he acted calm, casual, doubtful. Almost indifferent.

"How am I to know you're telling the truth? How do I know this bloodstone really exists?"

The man put out his hand and showed Farhad a small, sore cut on its palm. "I held it in this hand," he whispered, looking around as if someone else might overhear him. "I was already at the door when they caught me. The stone has a sharp edge, and this is the mark it left on me so that I could find it again."

He ran a fingernail along the reddened wound, and a drop of blood oozed up in the middle of it.

"The bloodstone," whispered the Frenchman, and now his watery blue eyes were shining. "It raises blood wherever it goes."

Farhad instinctively shivered, and not because of the wound—he doubted whether it was genuine. He shivered because of the light in the Frenchman's eyes. They showed a kind of passion that struck him as dangerous. It was with the same kind of passion that the demon, Ravana's servant, was said to have pursued the stone for so long.

"They say that stone brings death," said Farhad. "They say a demon's after it. I am a devout Hindu. If I'm to help you in such a delicate affair, then the price must indeed be a good one."

The Frenchman seemed to be thinking. "We'll have it cut in two," he said at last. "Each of us will keep half the stone."

"Very well," said Farhad, who didn't believe a word of it. The man would be crazy to share a jewel like that with him, a gemstone as big as a pigeon's egg. "Where do I find it?"

"You must get into Mr. Edwin Parker's house," whispered the Frenchman, "and ask his daughter. She's a pretty, impressionable girl. A young fellow like you ought not to have any trouble with her. I'll be close by, so never feel you're unobserved. On the morning after we leave the prison, I'll be at the door of the house, and then we can discuss the rest of the deal."

The man placed his hands together and sketched a bow. "My name is Morbus," he said. "Morbus Menière."

"Matsya," said Farhad, also bowing.

Matsya was the god Vishnu's first incarnation in the form of a fish, and Farhad congratulated himself on his choice of name, for he was as slippery as a fish himself. He'd slip through the Frenchman's fingers as soon as they were outside.

"Here's to our harmonious cooperation in liberating the stone," he said. "May we work well together." And may the gods blind you and break your hands, he thought silently, so that you can never hold the stone again and admire its beauty. I need it whole and all for me, to bribe Ravana's servant.

Night had already fallen, and Farhad had been standing impatiently by the barred window for a long time when he saw the white outline again.

He breathed a sigh of relief.

Nitish was on his way.

As the tiger silently padded closer, Farhad saw that he was carrying something round and shining in his mouth. The sky was covered with clouds—the monsoon was on its way at last, though there was still no rain. Without a trace of light in the sky, it looked as if the white tiger had stolen the moon and was now carrying it carefully in his sharp and deadly teeth.

Farhad reached his hand through the bars again and took the small, round mirror.

"It wasn't easy," Nitish's eyes told him. "Finding something like that is a tough job. I searched the whole marketplace . . . at least ten times I pretended I was turned to stone, and I had to lie flat on the ground under the stalls another seven times so that no one would notice me."

"Stealing," replied Farhad, with a smile, "needs practice like any other art."

Nitish snorted.

"What will the mirror do?" he asked.

"It will kindle a fire," said Farhad.

The tiger put his head on one side. "There's fire asleep in that mirror?"

"It's sleeping very deeply," Farhad explained. "Wait for me on the lawn outside the gate tomorrow morning."

"Fine," said Nitish. "I'll pretend I've turned to stone again."

As morning came, the fire in the mirror woke.

Menière skillfully caught the first rays of the sun in it, and turned them on his collection of incense sticks until the incense began to smolder. Then he took off his cloak and set fire to that, too, and Farhad sighed and jettisoned his dhoti once again.

The Frenchman had bored holes in the straw mattresses,

and now he was stuffing them with incense sticks like a joint of meat for roasting. The heavy, sweet smoke that rose from the smoldering straw curled its blue way up the walls of the cell, and Farhad began to feel rather nervous at the sight. After all, they were locked in here, with no way of opening the cell door. And it could well be that no one even noticed the fire.

"Do you think—do you think this is really a good idea?" he asked. "We could still put it out."

Menière gave him a scornful glance. "Nonsense," he said. "I have the fire under control."

"You have?" asked Farhad. "I was just thinking . . . I mean, if the plan doesn't work—if no one comes—"

By now the small cell was full of dense, stifling smoke. Farhad coughed. Through the swathes of smoke he could see the Frenchman's face. It wore a strange grin.

"Well, then we'll burn to death," he said. Farhad was alarmed to hear the satisfaction in his voice. He ought to have taken a closer look at the Frenchman before letting himself in for this venture. Maybe there was something not quite right about the man's brain. Damn.

"I have certain objections to burning to death," he said in a calm voice, trying to suppress his coughs, "if you don't mind my saying so."

"Why?" asked Menière, laughing. "They say it's not a bad death. Better than wasting away slowly in jail. This is the only way we can get our hands on the bloodstone, boy. We have to take risks. And burning to death is an interesting kind of risk."

The Frenchman narrowed his eyes, sucked in the smoke, and blew it out into the air again in a ring, like a smoke ring from a cigar.

"I like fire," he explained. "It fascinates me. Doesn't it fascinate you, too?"

"No," said Farhad, shaken by a coughing fit. The mattresses couldn't even be seen through the smoke anymore.

He felt soot collecting in his lungs, and the sweet scent of incense rose to his head. Soon he was dizzy and had to lean against the wall. Menière pushed him down on the floor, where breathing was a little easier.

"Fascinating," he said. "Fascinating, don't you agree? But here on the floor, you have a little longer to . . ."

Farhad pushed the man aside. "You . . . you're out of your mind!" he gasped.

Groping his way through the smoke, Farhad tried to stamp out the fire. But the heat of the straw mattresses made him cry out with pain and give up the attempt.

As coughing shook him again, Farhad saw the Frenchman dancing in the middle of the fiery mist, dancing with the swathes of smoke. A lunatic. He'd agreed to go along with a lunatic's plan.

In his mind, Farhad uttered furious curses against the crazy Frenchman and his own stupidity. If he died in a smoky prison cell, there'd be no one to set the princess free . . .

Anyway, he didn't *want* to die. Crouched on the floor, under the dense white smoke that was growing even denser, Farhad Kamal was aware how much he really loved life. He put up a quick prayer to Krishna and the entire pantheon of gods, asking them to help him just this once . . .

The Frenchman was singing in a language that Farhad didn't know. Then he suddenly stopped, crouched down beside Farhad on the ground, and reached for his arm.

"*Now!*" he whispered. "Any moment now!"

"Any moment now what?" asked Farhad, fighting for breath.

"They're coming!" said Menière. "You're in luck, my timid friend!"

And then, through the crackling of the fire, Farhad himself heard steps coming down the corridor.

The next moment, the door opened, and a draft of air sent the flames shooting up from the smoldering straw. Through the glowing yellow shower of sparks, Farhad saw the horrified face of a uniformed guard.

"What in the name of all the gods is going on in here?" cried the guard. "Fire! Fire! Fi—"

Farhad tensed every muscle, gathered what little air was left in his lungs, and leaped. As he did so, he thought of the great bounds taken by the white tiger, and he brought the uniformed man down. Then he dived across the figure as it lay on the floor, and the next moment he was racing along the narrow corridor. Once he turned, and saw that the Frenchman was following. They must be a fine sight, thought Farhad: two filthy, naked figures, their skin blackened with soot—like a couple of demons. The smoke accompanied them, for Menière had snatched up one of the damp, smoldering pieces of cloth and was waving it like a banner as he ran. Didn't he feel it burning? Couldn't he feel pain at all?

Soon the corridors were full of the screams of the prisoners and their guards, everyone shouting *Fire! Fire!* Farhad and the Frenchman made good use of the chaos breaking out around them, slipping through the main doors into the open air. Soon they were running down the gravel path, past the stone statue of a tiger.

Once in the city, Farhad managed to shake off his companion, losing him quite quickly in the maze of old alleyways. Menière had told him enough. Farhad knew who had the bloodstone, and where to look for it. He didn't need the crazy Frenchman anymore, and naturally he wasn't going to keep his word and give him half the jewel. He would steal the stone himself and then return for Nitish.

But when he finally stood still, gasping for air, he had an uneasy feeling.

The other man wasn't to be tricked so easily.

Even if he was deranged.

From now on, Farhad would have to be careful.

THE TRUNK OF THE
SACRED BODHI TREE

I T WAS STILL EARLY MORNING, AND THE BIRDS in the garden were singing their dawn chorus when Eleanor Parker opened the door and took in the newspaper.

It was important to read a newspaper when you lived so far from home. She always read the news of the royal family first, then the recipes at the back of the paper, and then, if she had any time left after breakfast, the political news. Because Eleanor Parker was a modern English girl who took an intelligent interest in these things.

A girl of good family.

The house where the good family lived was on Gayasura

Street, in the quiet suburbs of the small city of Gaya, which was the best place for a good family.

Gayasura was the name of a sacred giant who, according to legend, had once lived where the city of Gaya now stood. It was said that the giant had more cleansing power in him than all the sacrificial sites of India put together.

Eleanor sometimes wished the giant were still alive, because he would probably also have more cleansing power than all the bars of English soap she used to wash the red dust of India out of her white dresses.

But most of the British didn't believe in legends, and they had renamed Gayasura Street, Queen Street.

Eleanor had arrived here a year ago with her father, an administrator high up in the civil service, and she loved the customs, the beliefs, and the way of life of the people of India, although she thought that those customs, beliefs, and the Indian way of life could have done with a little tidying up in general.

All the many religions in this chaotic country bewildered her.

She had once written home to a girlfriend in England that there were as many different religions in India as there were different kinds of rain in the British Isles.

There were the Hindus, and their alarmingly large

number of gods with alarmingly large numbers of arms; there were the Muslims, who flung themselves down on the ground to pray at the most inconvenient times; there were the Parsees, who gave their dead sky burial at the tops of towers around which flocks of vultures were always circling; there were the Sikhs, whose holy book had to be read aloud twenty-four hours a day; there were the Buddhists with their stoical calm; and finally the Christians, who had come to India from Portugal and the Netherlands long ago.

This morning Eleanor was to be struck with particular force by the general disorderliness of the country.

She had only just reached the part of the paper in which a member of the royal family was complaining of the state of Brighton Golf Course when the doorbell rang again.

"Father!" called Eleanor in a soft voice, to the rooms upstairs.

Edwin Parker would be somewhere up there with his papers and his morning coffee. Eleanor felt too curious to call any louder. She opened the door herself.

And shrank back.

Outside the door stood a young Indian with untidy hair and a large red-and-white mark on his forehead as a sign of blessing. He was clutching a simple staff in one hand and a wooden bowl in the other, and he held the bowl out to Eleanor with a shy smile. His thin brown body had white chalk marks on it, and he wore a silver chain and a red string with a sacred nut on it around his neck. He had another string around his waist.

"Please," he said in faltering English, "please, madam. We live on what people give us. I am on my travels. I've gone many miles. It is many more miles to the sacred place. Do you have a little rice for a poor monk?"

Eleanor quickly looked around. But the front gardens of the only other two British houses were empty.

Before that state of affairs could change, she quickly drew the begging monk into the house.

After all, the neighbors had very high moral standards. And the young monk was not just tousled and smeared with chalk. He had no clothes on at all.

Farhad saw that the eyes of the young woman at the door were as blue as the eyes of the tiger. But they were a different blue, the color of blue flowers in a field swaying in the wind.

He also saw that she was startled, and he was pleased. He had gone to a lot of trouble to find the chalk, and had resisted the temptation to get himself another dhoti. The string was uncomfortable and bit into his skin around the hipbones. For the first time in his life he felt slightly sorry for the monks who wandered the country with their begging bowls and staffs.

"Come with me," the young woman told him. She wasn't much more than a girl, but around the corners of her mouth there was an imperious expression.

She obviously liked to make decisions. Let her. Farhad thought of the Frenchman, who was no doubt lying low somewhere in Gaya, waiting to see what happened next. What *was* going to happen next?

"I'll give you something to eat," the young woman went on. "There's still something left over from what the servants cooked for their supper yesterday. You'll like it, it's very Indian." She shook with cheerful laughter. "So spicy and hot you feel you're breathing out fire after eating it. Where do you come from?"

"Far away," said Farhad, realizing to his own surprise that he was telling the truth. "Very far away. My feet are tired with all that walking. But it is the will of the gods."

The girl smiled, and Farhad knew what she felt about him and the will of the gods—mild amusement.

In the entrance hall, Farhad saw some small statues of Ganesh the elephant-headed god, Hanuman the monkey god, and Durga the avenger with her red tongue sticking out. And in the dark living room, as he saw when he glanced into it from the large entrance hall, Krishna stood on the piano, acting as a paperweight to keep the sheet music in place. In the shadow of the heavy, dark green velvet drapes, it seemed to Farhad as if the god were longing for the Indian sunlight.

Everything in the house seemed to be muted. It was as if someone had filtered the colors and sounds out of the Indian air before letting it into this place.

Eleanor led him to a spacious but also dimly lit kitchen, where he obediently sat down on a fine carved chair of black wood. Then, under the watchful gaze of her cornflower-blue eyes, he ate everything that Eleanor put before him: saffron rice; preserved chilies; flat, floury chapatis; little balls of chickpeas and sour white yogurt—he had seldom eaten so many delicious things. He refused only the meat.

"It's not pork," she said.

"I am not a Muslim," said Farhad, smiling. "I am Hindu. Most of us eat no meat. And I have eaten enough. Thank you."

His thanks were not a lie, either. He had come because of the bloodstone, but it would have been worth it for the meal alone. Perhaps that uncomfortable string wasn't such a bad idea after all.

"I thank you many times," said Farhad, "and now I will

128

go to somewhere to sleep. I walked all night, I am very tired. It seems hard to find a quiet place where a begging monk can sleep in this city . . ."

He was watching the Englishwoman closely as he spoke. She took the bait.

"I don't think my father would mind if you slept here," she said hesitantly. "We have plenty of empty rooms. I could have one made ready for you . . ."

"A shady place on the floor would be enough," said Farhad modestly, taking his staff and standing up. "But I had better leave."

"No, no!" cried the Englishwoman, waving her white arms, which were encased in a great deal of fabric. "Don't go! It'll be quieter here than in the streets outside! There's just one thing—well, yes. Before I introduce you to my father, you'd better put some clothes on."

Farhad felt a quiet sense of triumph.

A little later he was wearing a white shirt and a clean dhoti and facing Edwin Parker. It was a fine, dark blue dhoti, and Farhad wore it reaching down to his ankles so that Edwin Parker wouldn't look disapprovingly at his thin, scratched legs.

Edwin Parker looked over the rim of his glasses and nodded. "Rescuing someone again, I see," he said to his daughter.

"Oh, Father!" whispered Eleanor, glancing at Farhad. "Hush! He can hear you."

"Does he understand English?"

Eleanor nodded, and Farhad gave silent thanks to the British on the streets of Madurai who had unintentionally taught him over the years how to lure money out of their pockets in their own language.

"I'm going away for a few days tomorrow," said Edwin Parker, straightening his glasses. "You'll be on your own here with Aunt Barbara."

Inside, Farhad was jumping for joy.

"Yes, of course, Father."

"Mind you let him out into the street again when he wants to go," said Mr. Parker with a nod to Farhad, and turned back to his desk.

"Oh, Father! You act as though I was always shutting poor souls up here! He only wants somewhere to sleep for a single night!" protested Eleanor. "He's a monk on his travels, and ..."

"I'm not interested, Eleanor," said Mr. Parker over his shoulder, "in either your orphaned children's shoe sizes or this gentleman's profession. You know I love you more than anything in the world, but please don't overdo things."

With those words, he rang a little bell, and an elderly

Indian burst in so quickly that anyone could tell he had been listening at the door.

"Show our guest somewhere he can sleep," said Edwin Parker.

And those were the last words that Farhad would ever hear him say.

The next morning, Edwin Parker was gone, and because Aunt Barbara was sick in bed with poor circulation, over the next three days Eleanor had only Farhad for company.

It was decided quite naturally that he would stay. Eleanor let him protest a bit, and then she was pleased to have won him over.

"A little rest won't annoy your gods," she said, laughing. "Don't they go rushing about, too? The Christian god rests for a whole day every week!"

When Farhad woke after the first night, he ate breakfast with the three servants, among them the old Indian who had been listening at the door the day before. After that, Eleanor walked in the garden with him and told him about her orphans.

"I'm making them into brand-new people," she explained, her eyes shining. "You should just see how keen they are to learn to read and write! And I give them history and geography lessons, too. Once, before I came to India with Papa, I was going to be a history and geography teacher. Here, I don't even need a college training to teach people." She happily clapped her hands. "Isn't that wonderful? Only last week we were studying the course of the Thames . . ."

Farhad nodded politely, supposing that the Thames was some kind of ravine. Even Eleanor's orphan children knew better than that by now.

"Ah, children. Like jewels," he said dreamily. It was time to come to the point. "Like jewels, every one of them."

Eleanor gave him a strange look. "Yes . . . to be sure," she said.

Did she suspect something?

No. The next minute, she flung her arms up in the air as if to hug everything around her. "But then I decided to go to India with Papa. It's such a spiritual country!" she cried. "Especially here, close to Bodhgaya! I feel so inspired by Indian spirituality!"

Farhad had no idea what she was talking about, so he just nodded politely once more.

Then, to his alarm, she took his hands and pressed them warmly. "What luck," she whispered, "that you can stay a little longer! Perhaps you could teach me . . ."

"Of course, of course," he murmured, in his mind going

over what he knew about the holy men who wandered through India as begging monks. Not much, which was unfortunate. What did this blue-eyed girl want of him?

What did she want of India?

"You're wearing a beautiful necklace," he said, glancing at Eleanor's neck. It had a narrow silver chain around it, with a tiny yellow stone as a pendant. "What a pretty gem. It shines like the evening star. There's a story in our religion of a stone that shines as brightly as the sun. But no one knows where it . . ."

"I sometimes meditate, too," said Eleanor. "But I'm more inclined to Buddhism."

She looked at him for a long time, which didn't suit Farhad's plans.

"Perhaps," said Eleanor softly, "you could teach me Hindu meditation. I don't know very much about it yet, but I'm a quick learner."

"Hmm," said Farhad. Teach her Hindu meditation? What on earth did she mean? He felt increasingly bewildered, and tried hard to find some way he could bring the conversation around to the stone at last.

But before he could think up a really good idea, Aunt Barbara called Eleanor from inside the house. In spite of her poor circulation, she had remembered that Eleanor mustn't miss the art and literature lessons that she took from a lady neighbor with a liking for canned mint sauce.

Farhad was left alone in the garden. He sighed and sat down on a stone bench.

Beside the bench, in the shade of a dying rosebush, lay a large, gray stone statue. When Farhad looked more closely, he saw that it was the statue of a tiger, and he ran his forefinger over the surface of the broad head. His finger left a white trail in the gray dust.

"Aha," said Farhad. "I thought it was you!"

The stone tiger opened his eyes and looked at him.

"Of course it's me," he said. "Who else? Don't worry, I won't disappear. Not until we've rescued the princess."

Farhad sighed louder than ever. "I think I'm in a fix," he whispered, just in case Aunt Barbara's hearing wasn't as poor as her circulation. "If only I could find that wretched gemstone! And I can't make this girl Eleanor out."

"You can't?" asked Nitish, purring happily to himself.

Farhad gave him a sharp look. "What's that supposed to mean? Do *you* know what she wants?"

"It's a bit difficult to explain," replied the tiger. And Farhad could see that Nitish was teasing him. "It's better if you find out for yourself. I'll be close by, even if you don't always see me. But if you want your jewel you'd better do as she asks. Tell her something about the gods. Make it as hard as possible to understand."

"That," said Farhad, thinking of Krishna's impossible demands, "is something I won't find difficult."

That day, however, he was not to see Eleanor Parker again.

He fell asleep on the floor beside the bed he had been given, which was so soft that he was afraid of sinking right into it and stifling.

The British were odd in some ways. Until now Farhad had thought it was easy to predict what they'd do, but Eleanor had him lying awake for a long time, brooding.

He got up in the night and went quietly out into the hallway. Perhaps he would find the stone even without the help of the girl whose eyes were as blue as a flower. Perhaps it was simply lying in a drawer somewhere, or in a glass display case, and he had only to pick it up . . . After all, the most unlikely answers were often right . . . Farhad decided to mention this wise saying to Eleanor the next day.

He stole along the hall to the study, the room where he had met Eleanor's father, Edwin Parker, for the first and only time.

The slender crescent of the moon was shining its white light into the study, changing the dark furniture into strange, four-legged demons. *Another two weeks,* the moon silently reminded Farhad. He cursed that impatient heavenly body, and hastily opened drawer after drawer, closet after closet, but except for thick piles of paper, envelopes, and a few china figurines, he found nothing.

However, thought Farhad, Edwin Parker could have given his daughter the stone for her last birthday. The best reason for him not to keep it in his study was that he didn't own it himself anymore.

And it belonged to Eleanor instead.

He knew where her bedroom was from his exploration of the grand, high-ceilinged rooms that afternoon, but he hadn't ventured to search it while the servants were in the house.

Now they weren't around. But Eleanor was. Farhad was relieved to find that her door was not locked.

She was lying asleep in a big bed under a mosquito net. He listened to her regular breathing for a while, and then began to search the dressing table in the corner of the room. He found a great many things the use of which was a mystery to him. But no jewel.

He carefully pulled out the top drawer of the bureau. It squealed slightly, and Farhad froze in alarm. Eleanor sighed, turned over in her sleep, then went on breathing peacefully.

Relieved, Farhad put a hand into the drawer and groped around. He felt a good deal of silk and lace, and wondered whereabouts on their bodies Englishwomen wore these things. With a certain uneasiness, he realized that he didn't know much about Englishwomen at all.

There was no hard jewel hiding under the heaps of ribbons, straps, and softly rustling silk. Farhad closed the drawer again and went over to the bed once more to make sure Eleanor was still fast asleep.

He saw her face through the mosquito net as if it were behind a veil of mist. A pretty face, even under that veil. The rest of Eleanor Parker could be seen in outline under the covers—attractive curves scented with perfumed soap. Farhad closed his eyes and breathed in deeply.

At the same moment he heard a rustling sound, and then a sleepy, "Papa?"

In alarm, Farhad opened his eyes for a fraction of a second, but he immediately closed them again and stumbled a couple of steps backward.

He heard a sound like the mosquito net being drawn aside.

"It's the begging monk," said Eleanor's drowsy voice. "It's my monk. A sleepwalking monk. Who'd have thought it?"

She laughed softly, and Farhad felt her laughter running

all the way down his spine. The scent of perfumed soap was rather stronger now.

Then he felt her cool hand on his bare shoulder.

"Wake up!" whispered Eleanor, very close to his ear. "You lost your way in your sleep!"

Farhad opened his eyes and stared at her in bewilderment.

The moon shone brightly into Eleanor's bedroom. She was standing in front of him in a long white nightdress, smiling. Her hair fell around her face in disorder, and her nightdress had slipped slightly so that he could see one of her bare shoulders.

"Where—How—?" stammered Farhad.

"You ended up in my bedroom," whispered Eleanor, pushing him gently away. "You'd better go back to yours. If Aunt Barbara finds you here, there could be serious trouble."

"I ask . . . I humbly ask your pardon," he stammered. "I do walk in my sleep now and then . . . I can't explain it even to myself. Sometimes I find myself in quite a different street in the morning, but it's never happened indoors before . . ."

Eleanor placed her finger gently on his lips, and he felt his whole body turning warm.

He quickly turned and left her bedroom.

But that night Eleanor's bare shoulder made its way through his dreams, and not all his thoughts were of the bloodstone.

The next morning he sat cross-legged in the garden and tried to look as if he were meditating.

He'd calculated correctly.

Quite soon he heard footsteps, and Eleanor sat down beside him. He knew her by her fragrance, but he acted as if he hadn't even noticed her.

When he did look up briefly, he almost laughed, because she was sitting there looking so serious, with her legs crossed like his. Her eyes were closed, and she was frowning with concentration. She was trying so hard to meditate, too!

They hadn't been sitting like that for long when one of the servants came into the garden.

"I don't like to trouble you," he said, kneeling down in front of the two figures rapt in meditation, "but there's a man at the gate who wants to speak to the monk staying here. He says the monk's name is Matsya."

Eleanor and Farhad opened their eyes at the same time.

"Oh, is that your name?" she asked. "Matsya?"

Farhad, who had introduced himself only as a monk on his travels, looked surprised. "No," he said. "My name is Kurma."

Kurma was the next incarnation of the god Vishnu, the one directly after Matsya, so he'd taken another step forward. Kurma was a turtle, and he himself, Farhad thought, was as

139

good as a turtle at pulling his head in to make himself invisible when he wanted.

Now, for instance.

"Maybe it's a mistake. What does the man look like?" Farhad asked.

"Tall and lean," replied the servant with a slight bow. "He has fair hair and a French accent. He said his name was Menière."

"I don't know anyone of that name," said Farhad firmly. But he had a sinking feeling in the pit of his stomach. Menière wasn't going to be shaken off so easily. "Tell the man he's looking for his monk in the wrong house. Whoever Matsya may be, he must have gone somewhere else."

That afternoon, Eleanor finished her art and literature lessons remarkably quickly. She came back, smiling radiantly, and told Farhad they were going on a little outing together.

She knew he was a Hindu, she said, but would he mind visiting the holiest place in Buddhism with her?

Her blue eyes were pleading like a child's, and he spun out his hesitation for a little while.

"The gods will be angry with me," he said. "They must be wondering why I've put off continuing my journey so long."

"Oh, please!" cried Eleanor, clasping her hands. "You

must come! Bodhgaya is a very, very impressive place. The Bodhi tree is terribly old, and there are pilgrims everywhere, and . . . couldn't you tell your gods that you're doing it for me? Perhaps," she added, "perhaps I'll convert to Hinduism some day if you try very hard!"

And she smiled at him in a conspiratorial way, as if the gods were waiting right outside the door to ask Farhad for an explanation.

Which indeed, he thought, might well be true. "You're making very slow progress," he heard Krishna say in his mind. "Have you searched the other rooms? The cellars? The stone's not likely to be slumbering in Bodhgaya . . ."

Farhad pushed this uncomfortable thought away. Wasn't everything he did in this house ultimately done in the cause of finding the bloodstone?

"Very well," he said, "I'll go with you. But don't ask me to fasten a pilgrim's little flag to the Buddha's holy place."

They went in one of the many rickshaws that waited for customers around the marketplace, and Farhad felt strange. He had known many rickshaw men in Madurai, and had once helped one of them out for suitable payment, but he had never ridden in one himself. He kept looking around, but the Frenchman was nowhere to be seen.

141

To Farhad's great surprise, Bodhgaya consisted mainly of a tree. Everything else in the place had something to do with that tree: the temple, the tea stalls, the sellers of little cloth flags, even the only house. The man who guarded the tree by night lived there.

"They call it the Bodhi tree. And it was under that tree," explained Eleanor, raising her forefinger, "that Buddha found enlightenment."

"I may be a Hindu," said Farhad with a smile, "but even I knew that."

He held the gaze of those cornflower-blue eyes, and Eleanor murmured an apology.

Of course Farhad hadn't had any idea where and when and indeed why Buddha had found enlightenment. He didn't care, either. After all, Buddha had never yet helped him to earn his living.

Eleanor bought a little yellow flag and knelt down with it by the low, rectangular iron fence around the foot of the tree. Farhad looked at the gnarled roots of the tree, which were as thick as a man's arm. And he looked at Eleanor kneeling in front of them. From above, he could see the soft little hairs on the nape of her neck standing up.

He knelt down beside her and helped her to tie the little yellow flag to the fence with the others. Her knee touched his, and he felt the same warmth as last night. Eleanor looked at him. Her eyes were sparkling.

"Will you pick me a leaf?" she asked. "A leaf of the Bodhi tree? I'm not tall enough, and no one else will do it for me."

It struck Farhad that she was suddenly speaking to him as if this outing to Bodhgaya, or perhaps that strange encounter last night, had made them allies.

"I don't think it's allowed," whispered Farhad.

Eleanor pouted. "But you're a Hindu!" she whispered. "And a monk, as well! What's going to happen to *you* if you steal a leaf from a Buddhist tree?"

"We Hindus," replied Farhad, with all the dignity he could muster in the presence of Eleanor Parker and her left knee, "we Hindus respect other religions."

I can't afford trouble, he thought.

"Please," begged Eleanor. "No one will notice. Do you remember the jewel you were telling me about in the garden? The one that shines more brightly than the sun?"

Farhad pricked up his ears, but he said nothing.

"They say here that the leaves of the Bodhi tree shine more brightly than the sun, too. Who knows," she said dreamily, looking up at the ancient branches, "perhaps the jewel is quite close. Perhaps it's hanging in the Bodhi tree."

"What makes you think that?" asked Farhad. "Do you believe the stone really exists?"

She laughed. Then she moved a little closer to him, and he felt her breath on his cheek as she whispered, "I know it does. You'd be surprised. Just a single leaf!"

"Very well," said Farhad, standing up. "But promise to stop talking about Buddha after that."

Eleanor laughed once more and put out her hand to let Farhad help her up. Her fingers were pleasantly cool and prettily shaped.

Farhad looked around and waited until no one was watching them, and then swiftly reached up to the lowest branch of the tree and plucked a leaf.

He glanced around once more, but no one seemed to have noticed. However, Farhad now saw the stone statue of a large tiger at the entrance to the temple. He could have sworn it hadn't been there before. He and Eleanor walked a little way from the tree, as if they were just devout pilgrims, and passed quite close to the tiger.

Farhad saw the tiger open his eyes.

"Don't lose your way, Farhad Kamal," said Nitish's eyes.

"What are you doing here?" asked Farhad in annoyance.

"Did you say something?" asked Eleanor.

Farhad shook his head, but he looked at the tiger again,

reading his dangerous gaze. "Have you forgotten," asked the tiger, "that I can be everywhere? I am as fast as the clouds in the sky and the sand blowing in the wind. I'm watching you, Farhad. Don't forget, you're not really a monk. You're nothing. Just a dirty little trickster and thief. And you're here to steal something. Remember our task! I've chased your French friend away for now, but even without that problem we don't have much time."

Farhad was relieved to hear about the Frenchman, but he didn't want to know any more. He turned his eyes away, and if the tiger was still talking he couldn't hear him.

"Come on," whispered Eleanor. "Let's go!"

She took Farhad's hand again, and they made their way through the crowd of pilgrims together. Then they began to run like two high-spirited children. Farhad felt the hard, round leaf in one of his hands and Eleanor's fingers in the other, and his heart was singing like a bird that hasn't flown free for a very long time.

At the first bend in the road they stopped, breathless and laughing.

"Give me the leaf!" demanded Eleanor, and she tucked it down the neck of her dress. "No one's going to look for a stolen leaf there," she said, giggling. "Anyway, I'm going to be a Buddhist. Maybe quite soon."

"You are?" said Farhad. "And what will your father have to say about that?"

"Papa?" She looked thoughtful. "Do you think—" she asked at last, mischievously, "do you think I ought to tell him?"

In the night Farhad woke, feeling cold under the thin covers. Surprised, he rose and went to the window. There were no stars, and even the moon did not show its slender face: The sky was covered with clouds. A cool wind caressed Farhad's bare skin, whispering words of hope: The monsoon was on its way. The land was thirsty, and soon it would drink.

He remembered how, as a child, he had danced in the muddy streets with the other children when the rains came. And suddenly he saw Eleanor in his mind's eye, dancing in the mud with him. She flung her arms up in the air with a cry of joy, as she loved to do, and her dress was so wet with rain that it was almost transparent . . .

"I'm a sleepwalker," whispered Farhad, pushing the door of his little room open. "I can't help it if I roam the rooms at night."

This time Eleanor wasn't asleep when he entered her bedroom. She was waiting for him.

He took care to keep his eyes closed except for a little crack so that she would think his feet really were moving of their own accord while he himself was fast asleep.

Through the crack, Farhad saw a figure sitting up behind the misty mosquito net, and as he passed her bed he felt her hand on his shoulder—just like the night before.

"Kurma," she whispered, and he remembered the name he had chosen this time. "My begging monk. Where are you going?"

He blinked, and turned toward her voice.

"I'm sorry," he whispered. "I must have been walking in my sleep again."

She put out her hand and stroked the tousled hair back from his forehead. "Stay with me," she whispered.

147

He looked at her hair, loose over her shoulders, felt her hands on his face—and then he heard a warning snarl out in the garden, and turned his head, listening.

"That'll be the wild cats," whispered Eleanor. "The tom-cats fighting for their females."

"Do they do that?" asked Farhad.

But then she drew him down to her, and the next moment he found himself in the softness of a broad bed once more. This time he wasn't afraid of being smothered.

"Are you monks allowed to fight for women, too?" she

whispered, playing with the amulet around his neck. Gently but firmly Farhad removed her fingers from it.

"Fighting," he replied, having not the faintest idea how begging monks felt about women, "is not our weapon. Our weapon is knowledge."

He undid the buttons of her white nightdress and touched the skin under it, which seemed even whiter.

"Do you remember," she whispered, "what I was saying about meditation in the garden?"

Farhad nodded. He really didn't intend to discuss meditation with her just now.

"I said I didn't know much about it, but I'm a quick learner . . ." she whispered, stripping her nightdress off.

Farhad simply looked at her for some time.

"You're perfect," he whispered at last. "Perfect as the jewel I was telling you about . . ."

He chose the comparison at that moment only because it was the first thing to come into his head, and her answer surprised him all the more.

"It really does exist," she said. "It's mine."

"What?" he asked, hardly paying attention.

Then she laughed, and put her white arms around him. Farhad felt her desire, and he had no objection at all. Once he heard a distant growl outside the window, and he thought of the tiger as he tasted the scented soap on Eleanor's skin.

Nitish had known what she wanted all along. But at that moment Farhad didn't mind in the least about Nitish or even Krishna. Eleanor and he were the only two living creatures on earth. Time was lost somewhere in between them, and the mosquito net came away from its fastenings. Eleanor even did him the favor of keeping quiet for quite a long time.

When she lay in his arms at last, exhausted and perspiring, she blinked at him and said, with a tiny yawn, "The stone . . . I buried it. The night after that Muslim with the funny whiskers tried to steal it. No one will find it, not where it is now."

She laughed softly, and pressed close to Farhad, who was still trying to get his breath back. Her skin didn't smell of scented soap anymore, but of life itself. With a happy smile, she whispered proudly, "It's under the Bodhi tree."

Then she looked at him again and whispered, "Stay with me, my begging monk."

Seconds later she had fallen asleep in his arms.

Farhad looked at Eleanor's pretty face for a long time. He felt lethargic and tired, and for some reason a little melancholy.

Suppose I simply do stay here, he thought. Then what?

Eleanor didn't believe in reincarnation. Suppose he himself just jettisoned any belief in it, like throwing away a mango peel?

Suppose he wasn't reborn at all? Not as a Brahman, not as vermin. Never reborn as anything? Suppose he stayed here with Eleanor and began a new, entirely different life? He could become a Christian, or even a Buddhist if she insisted, and forget Krishna. Forget the threat. Forget his promise. Forget Nitish.

He closed his eyes and felt Eleanor's sleeping breath, and he wanted to rest at long, long last. Never to cheat anyone again. Never to steal. Never to disguise himself, but keep the same name.

He gently put Eleanor out of his arms, slipped silently off the bed and went to the window.

All was dark down in the garden. The monsoon clouds still refused to let light through.

Perhaps Nitish was down there.

Or perhaps he wasn't.

Farhad pressed his forehead to the cool glass pane.

Then something clinked quietly against the window. Farhad felt for the amulet that he was still wearing around his neck. He opened the delicate catch, knowing he wouldn't be able to see the inside of the locket in this darkness, not any more than he could see what was down in the parched garden as it waited for rain.

But to his surprise, a faint light surrounded the picture in its silver frame.

And again it looked clearer to him than the last time he opened the amulet. It was as if the princess's features had emerged further from behind a veil.

He had the uncomfortable feeling that her dark eyes were looking at him.

They were not at all like Eleanor's cornflower-blue eyes. They looked at him in a much graver, more grown-up way, and they radiated calm.

I am going to die, those eyes seemed to say. On the night when the demon king Ravana takes me away to his domain, I will die, for I cannot live without the light and the beauty and goodness of the world.

It's in your hands.

The princess's eyes did not plead, like Eleanor's blue eyes. They were too proud to plead.

Then Farhad—or Matsya, or Kurma—opened the window and climbed out, down the twining clematis into the darkness of the garden. His clothes, he felt sure, would come in useful for Eleanor's next visitor.

Nitish was waiting for him under the rosebush.

RAKA AND LALIT

Indian rain, heavy but rare,
like Indian coffee tastes strong.
Their fragrant aroma wafts through the air
to worlds of sweet, sad song.

Indian rain casts a magical spell,
bringing new life to birth.
It makes the trees grow, it makes the seeds swell,
it heals the thirsty earth.

Indian rain in an Indian town
in raging torrents will flow,
then it masters the floods that come pouring down,
telling them where they must go.
Is it a god or a demon wild?
You ask, I fear, in vain.
Who in the world can answer you, child?
Who knows the soul of the rain?

THE OIL IN THE LITTLE LAMP HAD BURNED low, and it was getting darker in the room. Lalit could hardly see the outline of the girl sitting on the windowsill in front of him with her legs drawn up.

Bewildered, he blinked at the night.

How long had she been telling her tale? An hour? Two hours? Three? Four?

"Look," said Raka softly. "Dawn is coming."

Lalit was alarmed. "If anyone finds out I've been here, they'll ask what I was doing all this time."

She laughed. "What would they think you'd been doing?"

she asked. "Surely they don't let men work in the harem unless they can't do anything to women—men who are naturally unable to love."

Lalit felt himself blushing, and was glad it was dark.

"Of course," he said quietly.

"Well—so what would they think you'd been doing here?" she asked. "Is talking forbidden?"

"Talking . . . ," murmured Lalit. He had a feeling that much more had happened. He was cold from that flight on the wings of the wind, exhausted after the adventure with the rats in the temple, he was still fighting for air in the narrow, smoke-filled prison corridors, he felt the warmth of Eleanor's bare skin. Nothing seemed to him what it had been at the beginning of this night anymore.

He had ridden with Farhad on a white tiger's back all the way from the south of the land to Gaya, he had tied a yellow flag to the fence around the Bodhi tree . . .

"What's going to happen next?" he whispered. "Will he find the bloodstone? Will the princess in the desert city be rescued before Ravana makes her his wife?"

Raka shrugged her slim shoulders. "Who knows?" she said.

"Tomorrow—will you go on with the story tomorrow?"

"If I'm still alive," she said, "yes, I'll go on with the story.

Come a little earlier than you did today. You need your sleep, too. You have to work in the morning."

"I'll come," said Lalit, and he slid off the windowsill.

He stopped at the door, and turned around again.

"Forgive me for asking," he said, "but, how does it happen that you're not a virgin anymore?"

"I'm afraid it's not a very romantic story," replied Raka, and she extinguished the lamp. "He promised to marry me," she said in the dark. "I thought he really wanted to. He was older than me, he lived just next door to us. We shared everything: the shade in the courtyard, the clothesline, our childhood games, everything. Then his parents chose a wife for him in a village far away, a distant cousin. The right caste, and mine was the wrong one. Mine wasn't too low, it was too high, and as you know that won't do, either. What's more, in spite of his high caste, my father never had so much as a peisa to give as my dowry. The man who had promised to marry me didn't object or stand up to his parents. He went away and married the other girl. Of course he knew he was leaving me with a problem. But at least I wasn't expecting a child, so he himself had nothing to fear."

"And now?" asked Lalit. "Where is he now?"

"Nowhere," replied Raka. "South of Nowhere. I never heard from him again."

Like Farhad, Raka slept on the floor beside a bed that was too soft for her, and like Farhad she slept poorly.

But for different reasons.

She tossed and turned for several hours, and at last she got up and went down to the maze of inner courtyards. A trillion tiny, invisible songbirds were chirping in the tendrils of the clematis on the walls. But to Raka their little voices sounded ominous, like a warning.

The day was blue. As blue as melancholy.

A vague sadness weighed down on it, and fell on Raka's slender shoulders.

Around noon she heard that the Rajah was still sick, and she waited for the relief of that news to make its way from her ears to her heart.

"So I will not die tonight," she whispered to the birds, stroking the green clematis leaves. "I have another night left to tell a story. But will that be enough? And what does it matter under which moon I cease to live?"

The doves cooed in their dovecote, and from a distance Raka saw Lalit the young eunuch feeding them. He enticed them out so quietly that Raka couldn't hear what he was saying, but they must be magical words, for the doves came to him like children going to their mother. They settled on his hands and shoulders, their silvery gray heads nestled against his throat, and spoke their own strange language to him.

She watched Lalit closely. Had anything about him changed since last night? Was his beauty a little less cold and statuesque? Was his smile less empty?

Raka wasn't sure.

How many nights did she have left to go on telling her story?

She turned and walked away past the fragrant rose-bushes.

The Rajah's handsome eunuch never guessed that she was telling him the tale of her own life.

Toward evening, Raka sat alone on the rim of the fountain, turning the little statue of the goddess Kali in her hands. Darkness had already settled on the courtyards and the walls, and the birds in the flowering branches had fallen silent. Only the water in the middle of the fountain still played, with its melodious rushing sound.

Raka saw the silhouettes of the other women behind the lighted windows.

She knew they thought she was crazy. That afternoon they had seen her climbing to the very top of the cashew tree, and they went to find the chief guard of the harem to bring her down.

When they came back with him the branches of the cashew tree were empty, and Raka was standing at her window watching them. She hadn't missed the spite in their shrill voices. How much less harmonious than the birds those voices were!

Raka had hoped to see the desert from the top of the cashew tree. But the tree had disappointed her. She'd try the water tower tomorrow.

"So here you are," said Lalit's quiet voice behind her, and she knew that he was sitting on the stone rim of the fountain, too.

"The desert will be purple now," said Raka. "It will just have changed color. The long shadows have merged with night, the camels are chewing the cud of their thoughts one last time before they go to sleep."

She turned to Lalit.

"I can see it," she said. "I can see it all, every detail. I didn't know before, but every moment of life in the desert beats in me like a second heart. Isn't that strange?"

Lalit nodded, and she could tell that he was still afraid of coming too close to her.

"I'm here," said Lalit. "A little earlier than yesterday, as

you said. I don't know if I'm allowed to listen to you, but . . ."
He turned a dove's feather, blown to him on the evening wind,
awkwardly in his fingers. "But I didn't ask anyone."

Raka smiled. "Good. What isn't forbidden is allowed."

"You must have heard that the Rajah is still sick with a
fever," said Lalit. "They say he was furious because the doctor
said he mustn't do anything but sleep. It seems he threw a
hand mirror at the doctor. He has a great many mirrors. He
likes to look at himself in them."

"A hand mirror?" asked Raka. "And what did the doctor
do then?"

"Slammed the door, I suppose," said Lalit, laughing
quietly. "He's known Ahmed Mudhi since the Rajah was a
spoiled boy."

Raka clung to the little statue of Kali, the goddess of rage,
but even Kali's rage would not prevail against the Rajah's.
Then she felt Lalit's hand on her shoulder.

"You're trembling," he said softly. "It's turned cool. The
monsoon will soon be here. Shall we go in?"

"That might be better, because no one will see us indoors,"
said Raka, rising to her feet. "But it's not the cold that makes
me tremble."

He followed her through the Rajah's magnificent halls
and up the stairs to her apartments.

"Don't tell anyone," she whispered, sitting down on the wide windowsill as she had the night before. "Don't tell anyone, but I'm afraid. The time will come when Ahmed Mudhi is better, and well enough to kill me. My pride is greater by day, but my fear is greater by night."

"You are very brave," said Lalit.

"No," said Raka, and she smiled. "I am afraid I'm not."

"Go on," he asked. "Did Farhad find the bloodstone under the Bodhi tree?"

"He's looking for it at this very moment," said Raka. And she began the second night's tale.

தண்ணீர்

Through water

A GREETING FROM THE MONSOON

THE BODHI TREE ROSE AGAINST THE NIGHT sky like a ghostly creature with countless outstretched arms, and hands full of leaves.

The man who kept watch over the Buddhists' holy place by night was asleep on a folding chair at the temple entrance.

"If he wakes up," Farhad whispered into Nitish's round white ear, "make sure he stays out of my way. But don't hurt him, understand? He's not half a goat, and we can do without any more trouble."

Nitish growled, but he obediently sat down beside the man on his folding chair.

"I don't eat temple watchmen," he said with his eyes, which shone like little oil lamps in the dark. "They taste of incense sticks."

Farhad suppressed a smile.

He stole over to the great trunk of the Bodhi tree, climbed over the knee-high iron fence, and crouched down to look at the ground. In spite of the darkness, the new little yellow flag caught his eye. He and Eleanor had placed it here only that afternoon. How long ago that suddenly seemed.

He thought of Eleanor's soft white arms, and how she would wake up alone. And for the first time in his life he felt genuinely sorry about something.

Then he thought of the picture of the princess in Krishna's silver amulet, and he began carefully feeling around on the ground. There! Wasn't that freshly dug soil, damper than the rest of the earth and not trodden down so firmly by time?

Eleanor had hidden the stone here only a few days ago . . . He shook his head, and began digging. The little Englishwoman was no fool.

How dry even this fresh soil was! It was time the rains came. Even the sacred Bodhi tree needed them.

Farhad's hands met something hard, and excitement shot through him like lightning. Was it the jewel? Then he brought an ordinary chunk of rock up out of the earth. He went on digging grimly, felt an angular brick and dug around it. He lifted stone after stone out of the ground, and ended up wondering if Eleanor had lied to him. Suppose she'd seen through him after all and lured him here on purpose? Suppose her father's servants suddenly turned up? He looked around anxiously.

But he saw nothing moving in the darkness. Only the white outline of the tiger sitting motionless beside the man asleep on his folding chair: a strange sight.

The brick was in Farhad's way. He dug it out so that he wouldn't keep hurting his fingers on it. Surprised to find how light it was, he examined it more closely.

Then his excitement returned. The brick wasn't a brick at all. Farhad was holding a little rectangular wooden box. The rough surface that his fingertips, feeling it blind, had taken for baked earth was really wood carved into countless delicate patterns.

Trembling with nerves, he opened the lid of the little box. And closed his eyes.

Then, cautiously, he squinted at the contents.

Yes, there it lay before him: the bloodstone.

The gem was the size of a pigeon's egg and roughly drop-shaped, just as the holy man on the mountain, the butcher, and the Frenchman had described it. Farhad smiled.

He put his hand out, meaning to run it carefully over the surface of the stone—and snatched it back with a cry. When he licked his palm it tasted of wet, fresh blood. The stone really did have a sharp edge that you didn't notice at first glance—like a fierce animal pretending to be friendly and then biting you unexpectedly.

Farhad held it carefully up to the moonlight that fell through the branches of the Bodhi tree. The moon was only half of itself. By the time it had disappeared entirely and then grown to its full size again, the stone in Farhad's hand must have reached its destination. The bloodstone absorbed the moonlight, and, instead of reflecting it back, seemed to hold it in its heart. It changed the white, milky radiance to a dangerous red mist, and the longer Farhad looked at it the uneasier he felt.

He heard the tiger's quiet, padding steps behind him, and turned. Nitish's blue eyes were fixed on the stone, and Farhad read in them exactly what he felt himself.

"It is beautiful," said the tiger's eyes. "But not good. No. Worse than not good: It is evil. Wrap it up in something. You ought not to look at it for so long."

Farhad nodded, and unfastened a dozen of the prayer flags from the fence around the Bodhi tree. He wrapped the stone in the little cloths, and tied them firmly in place over it. Then he tied the bundle to his upper arm with another cloth. Nitish looked warily at the strange bandage. "At least it is quiet now. I could hear it before. Its blood-red radiance sang in my ears like an old song. A song of demons. Not a pleasing sound to a tiger created by the gods."

Farhad laughed softly. Then he again buried the little box that had held the jewel among the roots of the tree.

When he looked up, the moon had moved some way farther across the sky. Deep black shadows were gathering among the branches of the ancient tree. All of a sudden he saw the tiger beside him nervously lashing his tail.

"There—there's something there," said his eyes. "Look. In the tree."

Farhad looked more closely. Nitish was right.

A figure was sitting in the black shadows. Now it rose and climbed down over the branches as if the tree were a wide staircase.

Farhad took a step back, and the tiger tried to hide behind him.

"Buddha," said Nitish's eyes uneasily, without a sound. "We dug at the foot of Buddha's sacred tree. Perhaps we ought not to have done that. It's dangerous to anger someone like Buddha . . ."

"You—you mean . . . ?" Farhad whispered.

He wasn't sure what to think of Buddha. The Buddhists said he had been an Enlightened One, *the* Enlightened One. The Hindus said Lord Buddha had been one of the incarnations of Vishnu. It was difficult to be sure about him, anyway.

The figure had now reached the lowest branch of the Bodhi tree. It jumped down from there to the ground. Farhad retreated even farther. He could have turned to run away, but if this really was a supernatural apparition and he had offended it, that wouldn't do him much good.

"Who are you?" asked the figure angrily. "Who dares to dig among the roots of the sacred tree by night?"

"We—we had our reasons," replied Farhad in a trembling voice. "It—It was necessary."

"It's forbidden!" said the figure roughly. "It has always been forbidden. You can read it on every notice put up here. I see I shall have to take you into custody."

Farhad heard a click, and suddenly there was a gun in the figure's hand.

Buddha, he thought, with a gun?

"You'd better keep a civil tongue in your head. I am the watchman on guard over this tree," said the figure. "My friend at the entrance is inclined to drop off to sleep, but my eyes are sharp and my ears are good . . ."

The man didn't guess that this was exactly the wrong thing to say.

Farhad turned to Nitish, who was still crouching on the ground behind him. Now the tiger rose and stretched. *A watchman*, Farhad read in Nitish's eyes. *Just an ordinary watchman!* And before the man knew what was happening, the tiger had leaped past Farhad and the watchman was lying full length on the ground, a huge white tiger's paw planted on his chest, pressing him down. The gun had fallen from his hand, and the horror in his eyes was plain to see in the light of the half moon.

"May Buddha bless your eyes and your ears," said Farhad quickly, "but now let us go. I am traveling in the name of Lord Krishna, and I need your clothes. We won't hurt you if you give us your shirt and lunghi."

Nitish removed his paw, but sat beside the man with his tiger teeth bared. The watchman stammered something about spirits and apparitions and took his clothes off, trembling. Farhad quickly slipped into them. Then he placed the palms of his hands together and bowed slightly.

"The gods will be grateful to you," he said. "And a time will come when you understand them."

With these words, he swung himself up on the tiger's back—with practice, he was getting better at it—and Nitish took a great leap over the temple, over the top of the ancient Bodhi tree, and over the watchman's house. Soon Bodhgaya lay behind them, and they were on their way westward, making straight for the desert of Thar.

Farhad kept looking around nervously, but the Frenchman wasn't behind them.

"Why would he be?" asked Nitish, turning his head to Farhad and looking at him with his shining eyes. "Do you expect him to hang from a cloud and fly with it? Do you expect him to sit on a grain of sand and be blown away on it? His steps are slow and heavy. But we go faster than rumor runs in

 168

cities. The next place between us and the desert is Varanasi, where the holy river Ganges carries the remains of your dead away. I was keeping my ears open in Gaya while you . . ."

"Yes, yes," said Farhad hastily. "And did your ears hear how far it is to Varanasi?"

"We will reach Varanasi in two days' time," Nitish said. "Two days at the most."

But he was very much mistaken.

For something broke over them that Farhad had known was coming all along, without understanding its significance.

The monsoon.

They hadn't been traveling for more than half a day before

Nitish raised his nose to the wind, looked around at Farhad, and said, with an anxious look in his eyes, "It's turned."

"What's turned?" asked Farhad, waking with a start. After his eventful night, he had fallen fast asleep on the tiger's back.

"The wind, my clever hero," replied Nitish.

Farhad growled with annoyance and caught himself sounding almost like the tiger. The longer we travel together, he thought, the more of each other's habits we catch. Will I start purring next?

They looked up at the sky together.

Nitish had stopped in the middle of a parched field. The soil was dry and cracked like the lips of someone with a fever.

The sky was promising to make the field better.

Mighty mountains of cloud towered high above the earth, piling on top of each other to form ever taller structures. They were a dark grayish blue and seemed to blot out the sun entirely.

"The monsoon," said Farhad. "It may start to rain any minute."

"Water," said Nitish.

Farhad felt the tiger's flanks trembling beneath him. Nitish swiftly glanced around, and Farhad sensed his panic.

169

"What are we going to do?" the blue eyes asked. There was a hunted look in them.

Farhad, too, felt despair spread slowly through him. He cast a look all around, searching for shelter. If the rain touched Nitish, Farhad would lose his mount forever. "Over there!" he cried at last. "Do you see those huts? That's the only way we can—"

A rumble of thunder snatched the rest of the sentence from his mouth to use for its own purposes, but the tiger had understood. When the next roll of thunder came, he was already bounding across the field that seemed to reach out to the sky in longing.

170

The poor dwellings beside the sandy road were little more than a collection of loose boards. Their roofs were thatched with palm fronds weighted down by stones, and Farhad desperately hoped they would keep the rain out.

"Hello?" he called, while Nitish still trembled beneath him. "Is anyone there? We're looking for shelter from the rain . . ." He had hardly finished what he was saying when two things happened swiftly. First, people of all sizes and ages came streaming out of the huts. There were several very old women, one very young and thin one, three men, and a milling throng of incredibly grubby children whose dirty faces looked up, wide-eyed, at the strange rider. They seemed to be wondering, very thoughtfully and seriously, why he was mounted on a tiger, and why the tiger was white.

The second thing to happen was at least as impressive: The first drop of rain fell.

It fell in the dust next to the white tiger's left forepaw, and Nitish leaped to one side in horror.

Then he took another leap, a more deliberate one this time, and landed inside one of the huts. Farhad lost his balance and rolled over in the dust.

He lay there looking up into a crowd of surprised faces.

"My tiger," he said, rubbing a bruised elbow, "my tiger is afraid of water."

"Yes," said the tallest of the men, with a kindly smile. "We noticed."

And then the monsoon arrived.

It struck with its full force, as the monsoon usually does.

The first drops were joined by countless others, and, seconds later, water was cascading from the clouds as if someone had turned the ocean upside down and emptied it over the earth.

The children ran out into the dusty square among the huts, rejoicing and flinging their arms in the air, and a moment later the adults followed them. The man with the kindly smile took Farhad's arm and held him close, and he danced with the strangers in the rain until he was wet through. He raised his face, opened his mouth, and let the water run down his throat. It washed the sweat and dust off his skin, it sank into every pore, and he felt like the parched earth of India itself. He absorbed the water and felt it giving him new strength.

He had found the jewel, he'd shaken off the Frenchman, he had brought the tiger to safety—and they still had time to reach the city in the middle of the desert. For a moment, he was utterly happy. Nothing could harm him.

He picked up one of the small children and whirled him through the wet air. The child shouted with glee as rain ran down his bare skin. Then the other children clustered around Farhad's legs, and he had to whirl them all through the air in turn. Finally he dropped into the mud, exhausted, and all the small children fell on him in a heap, laughing in the rain.

There lay Farhad in the mud, looking up at the sky and the great raindrops falling steadily from it, and he thought of the rice that would sprout green shoots now, the banana plants that would raise their limp leaves and bear more fruit. And he smiled.

It wasn't his rice, and they were not his banana plants, and he wondered why it made him so happy to think of them growing. He also wondered what he was doing, lying around in the mud with a crowd of small children who were total strangers.

It worried him.

This wasn't like him at all.

He sat up, shook the children off, and crawled into the hut to see how Nitish was doing.

The tiger was lying curled up small on a stack of full rice sacks. Right above him, the people who lived here had mended the roof with tarpaulin, and though this seemed to be the driest place for the tiger, he could hardly fit in the space between the sacks and the tarpaulin.

He must have squeezed himself in by force.

Farhad reached out his hand, and the tiger snarled and struck at him with a paw. He had shot out his flashing claws, but he took care not to touch Farhad with them. And not out of concern for Farhad, either.

"Don't come too close!" said Nitish. "You're wet!"

It sounded as if Farhad had an infectious disease.

"Oh," he said, dropping his hand. "Sorry. Are you all right there?"

"Never better." Nitish's eyes were furious. "Can't you see how comfortable I am? I can't think of anywhere I'd rather be than jammed on top of a sack of rice beneath a tarpaulin, like a lizard underneath a horse's hoof."

Farhad heard steps behind him, and the kindly man with the large hands said, "He *really* must be frightened of water."

173

He had a smile in his voice. "How do you come to be traveling with a white tiger who won't go out in the rain?"

"It's a long story," replied Farhad. "If we may stay until the rain stops, I'll tell it."

"Of course you may stay," said the man. "You see how simply we live here. The drought was long and terrible. Our fields are thirsty for rain, but our hearts are thirsty for stories. Come, sit down by the fire and tell us yours."

"You won't believe me, of course," said Farhad a little later, crossing his legs under him. The muddy children were scuffling for a place at his side, the women made strong black tea with watery milk, and the fragrance of cloves, cardamom, and fire filled the hut. Even the men were hanging on Farhad's lips as he put down his mug of tea and began.

"Long ago, when things were not as they are today, and the British hadn't yet come to the country, Krishna and a woman, who was a cowherd in a little village south of Nowhere, had a daughter. Although she grew up as an ordinary girl, she was as beautiful as starlight from the day she first drew breath. So you won't be surprised to hear that when Ravana the demon king happened to see her, he fell in love with her at once . . ."

It rained all day and all night, and Farhad went on and on with the story.

He took the liberty of embroidering it a little here and there, and painting its characters in brighter colors, but he was sure no one would mind that. When he went too far, he heard Nitish growl quietly in his corner, and then he toned the story down a bit.

He left out his reason for finding the amulet, his terror when the ruin on the mountain collapsed, and what had happened between him and Eleanor Parker. But isn't the whole art of storytelling knowing what to embroider and what to leave out?

When Farhad finally lay down in the dark on the floor of the hut later that night, close to the many others that it sheltered and listening to the sound of the rain, he was a hero for a moment.

He almost believed what he had said about himself. He had nearly forgotten that he was a thief and a trickster, and always had been . . .

Before he went to sleep, out of the corner his eye, he saw that the white tiger was sleeping, too. One of his paws hung down from the rice sacks, relaxed, and five thin cats were nestling against his big, warm body. A sixth lay curled up between his ears.

The tiger sighed in his sleep, and with a smile on his lips, Farhad slipped into wonderfully happy dreams.

The next morning, Farhad tied some old pieces of leather around the tiger's paws. The family had given them to him in return for his wonderful story. Nitish protested, but in the end he had to admit that he had no choice: They mustn't lose too much time.

"And what will happen next time it rains?" his blue eyes asked accusingly. "These leather rags protect me from water from underneath. But what about water from above?"

"We'll just have to find shelter again," said Farhad.

"Suppose the rain takes us by surprise?"

"We'll keep an eye on the wind and the clouds."

"And suppose it comes on too fast?"

"Well, what do *you* want us to do?" asked Farhad, annoyed. "Find a better idea and I'll be all for it."

Nitish growled and said no more.

They left the family with an uneasy feeling, and even the smallest of the children waved to them for a long time as they went away.

The white tiger's fear of water slowed him down. He kept putting his head back and scanning the sky anxiously for any sign of another sudden shower of rain.

And then Farhad would call out, "Careful, a tree!" Or,

"Watch out, you'll run into that oxcart!" and the tiger would swerve aside at the last moment. Even worse, he tried to skirt the larger puddles, because he was afraid that if he trod in one, water would splash up. So they were tracing a zigzag course, and Farhad wondered if they wouldn't have gone faster if he had carried the tiger.

As chance would have it, the next heavy rainfall caught them in a road where there were no buildings, only smooth, white walls on either side.

Farhad had been anxiously looking up at the sky himself all day, and when they turned into that little road on the outskirts of a small village, he could smell the next rain coming. He looked around nervously, but the walls to the right and left of them were smooth and straight, with no doors in them. Tall trees reached their branches to the sky above, looking like curious women standing at their windows.

The clouds gathered closer together in the sky and drew breath, ready to pour their contents out on the two travelers. Wind sent garbage driving down the road and swept the few first drops before it.

"Quick!" said Farhad. "We must find shelter! Jump over the wall!"

Nitish turned to him. "No," replied his blue eyes firmly.

177

"Why not?" cried Farhad, pointing to the sky. "Can't you see that? Can't you sense it? The rain has come back!"

"You're right, it has," replied Nitish. "But I can sense something else, too. The garden on the other side of this wall is the garden of a mosque."

"So?" asked Farhad, feeling more and more nervous. A drop had hit him on the forehead right between the eyes, like a divine warning.

"I can't shelter from rain in the garden of a mosque," Nitish explained uneasily. "Even if the leaves of its trees were thick enough to keep the water off. I'm a sacred Hindu tiger."

"Jump!" said Farhad. He tried to make his voice as stern as he could, but it sounded desperate instead.

Nitish had stopped, and was hesitating.

"Jump! You'll turn to stone!"

Farhad dug his heels into the tiger's flanks as if he were a stubborn horse.

The tiger growled. He scraped his paws over the dust in the road a few times.

Another big raindrop fell to the ground next to him, and he jumped aside.

The wind was rising. A palm leaf chased past them, and the blurred picture of the princess flashed into Farhad's mind. Would the rain soon be pattering down on the date palm under which she once sat dreaming? Perhaps the place south of Nowhere was quite close. Perhaps the palm leaf being carried past them by the wind came from that very tree.

He watched the leaf, and then the wind picked it up and blew it over the wall.

"Jump," whispered Farhad one last time.

Then Nitish finally crouched to spring, uttered a terrifying growl, and leaped over the wall in pursuit of the palm leaf.

On the other side, there were shrubs with red hibiscus flowers swaying on them. The palm leaf tumbled along a paved path in front of Nitish's paws, and the tiger seemed to have forgotten that he was on the sacred ground of Islam. He was chasing the palm leaf like a cat chasing a ball of crumpled paper. It blew against a metal double door. The two halves of the door were open just a crack.

179

Nitish leaped after the leaf, leaped through the door, and the aromatic darkness of a mosque enveloped them.

Outside, the heavens opened. Farhad heard the rain beating down on the garden with the force of the entire universe—on the hibiscus flowers, the wall, the road where they had been standing a moment ago.

He looked for the palm leaf, but it was nowhere to be seen.

Farhad breathed a sigh of relief.

Red-patterned carpets covered the floor between the columns of the little mosque, and large oil lamps hung from the ceiling here and there, in places apparently chosen at random. Their wicks glowed faintly.

There was no one in the mosque except the two of them.

"It looks nice and dry here," Farhad pointed out, pleased, and he glanced at the dome overhead. "And there's plenty of room. We can stay here for a while."

"I'm not so sure," said Nitish. Farhad watched as he began padding restlessly over the red carpets. He turned around in a circle by the wall several times, stopped here and there, sniffed, nervously lashed his long tail, and then went on pacing again.

Finally he came back to Farhad. His eyes were flickering.

"I'm more than a thousand years old," he said, with an anxious expression. "And I've spent almost my entire life in a Hindu temple. The Hindu gods made me. But Muslims don't believe in anything like me! I'll lose my power here!"

He sat down on the carpeted floor with his ears drooping.

"But it's raining," Farhad reminded him. "Would you rather turn to stone?"

Nitish snarled and began pacing up and down again. Every time he passed Farhad, he looked at him accusingly.

"I can already feel myself dissolving," he said. Farhad watched the powerful play of the tiger's muscles under his white coat. No one could look less likely to dissolve than Nitish.

Reassured, he lay down on the carpeted floor himself to get some sleep. The rain was pattering down on the dome of the mosque, and there was nothing else to do.

The cry of the muezzin woke him.

A small congregation of people had assembled in the mosque. A few more came in, and they all sat down to pray with their faces turned the same way. They looked wet, and Farhad concluded that it was still raining on the minaret and out in the streets.

He stood up and walked behind a column to watch the people praying. They were so deep in prayer that they had no time to notice him.

Looking around for Nitish, Farhad finally spotted the tiger in a shadowy corner of the mosque, where he was sitting motionless but very erect, staring into space.

Farhad went over to him, keeping behind the backs of the praying congregation, and tried to catch his eye. But the tiger just went on staring straight ahead.

Then a terrible thought came into Farhad's head. He looked up. Was there a hole in the roof somewhere? A hole that was letting the rain fall in? But no, the roof seemed to be perfectly watertight. What had happened?

"Nitish," whispered Farhad. "Nitish, can you hear me? You haven't turned to stone, have you?"

At last the tiger slowly moved his eyes and looked at Farhad.

"No," he said. "I haven't turned to stone. I'm dying."

The words that Farhad read in his eyes were soft and faint. He put his hand on the tiger's coat, but the great cat's body felt as warm and alive as ever.

"You're not dissolving and you're not dying," said Farhad. "Or if you are, at least I can't see any sign of it."

 "I can feel it," replied Nitish, turning his head feebly toward Farhad. "My last hour is near. And all because of this mosque."

But however bitterly Nitish complained, there was nothing Farhad could do. The rain from which they had taken shelter in the huts where the large family lived had been only a first, drowsy forerunner of the real monsoon. Now it was breaking in earnest, gathering all its violence and deluging the earth with rain.

Farhad and Nitish stayed in the mosque for the next two days, and no one noticed them in the shadows. Now and then, Farhad went out to find something to eat in the town as the monsoon poured down on it. He always looked up at the sky when he went out, hoping to see a gap in the clouds somewhere. But the rain went on and on with only a few brief pauses. The cool silver of Farhad's amulet lay on his chest and seemed to be ticking time away like a clock.

Perhaps it is raining in the desert, too, he thought. Perhaps the princess is sitting at her window, looking out through the veil of raindrops, and wondering if she will see the sun again before her wedding to the demon king. Sometimes Farhad contemplated leaving Nitish to his own devices and walking on through the rain by himself. But what chance did he have of going so many miles on foot before the next full moon? None, thought Farhad. And that was the bitter truth.

The tiger wasn't feeling well. Every time they heard the muezzin's cry, he merged even more with the shadows. His coat was losing its glossiness again, he was growing weaker and weaker. At first Farhad had told him he was just imagining it all, but finally he, too, began to feel seriously worried.

On the second day, stormy winds rose. Outside, the monsoon swept rain down the street in a frenzy of wind.

Fewer and fewer of the faithful came to the mosque to pray. Through the window, Farhad saw the storm snapping trees and blowing off parts of rooftops.

When Farhad opened the old double door of the mosque, there was a stream rushing along outside instead of a road.

Nitish sometimes went as far as the door with him, looked out, and uttered a pitiful meow like a small, sick cat. He wouldn't even touch the chicken that Farhad brought back for him.

"It looks as if it died of drowning," said the tiger's eyes.

"It *did* die of drowning," said Farhad. "I fished it out of the stream running down the road."

Nitish turned away.

"If you hadn't taken me away from the temple," he growled, "I wouldn't have all these anxieties. I wish I could be back on my island in the pool of water in Mysore."

"To spend all eternity there feeling bored?" asked Farhad angrily.

He was hungry, too, and his nerves were on edge. Rainy weather was not a good time for him. Like farmers, thieves generally reap their harvest in the open air.

"I'd rather be bored to death than die in a mosque, of all places," said the tiger faintly. Farhad felt too cross to talk to him any more that day.

On the morning of the third day, sunlight fell into the mosque through the crack between the two halves of the double door. Farhad sat up with a start and listened. No, he wasn't imagining it: The regular rhythm of raindrops falling had stopped.

"Nitish!" he whispered. "Wake up! The sun is shining!"

But the tiger did not react. All four of his legs were stretched out, and his closed eyelids were fluttering slightly. Farhad saw the tiger's ribcage rise and fall as he breathed in and out, but his breathing was shallow and fast.

He shook the great animal roughly.

"Nitish!" he cried. "Open your eyes again, damn you! Speak to me!"

But this time the tiger did not open his eyes.

Farhad sat beside him for a little while, saw the rays of the sun falling through the door, felt the silver of the amulet on his chest, and tried to come to a decision.

Finally he couldn't bear to sit still any longer, and he got to his feet and went out. The clouds had left behind a sky washed blue and full of birdsong. The monsoon might not be over yet, but at least it was stopping for a long break.

Farhad took deep breaths of air smelling of the rain that had just stopped, and with it he drew in the aroma of the earth now beginning to germinate and sprout. A tree peered over a wall, its buds green and inquisitive.

And the heart of the hero who wasn't a hero felt both light and heavy.

His way west to the desert lay clear before him, the storms were over. There was nothing to stop him now. And time was pressing—more than ever. The road ahead awaited his feet, the desert awaited his arrival.

But Nitish couldn't come, too. The decision that Farhad must make burned in his soul, and that surprised him.

He would have to leave the dying tiger behind.

He had no idea how he was going to reach the desert of Thar alone in time, but there was nothing else he could do. However, it wasn't just his fear of failure that burned in Farhad's soul. Beside it, like a small fire with an unsteady flame, something else burned, too. Something he didn't recognize. He swallowed a few times before he went back into the mosque to pat and stroke the magic white tiger for the last time.

Farhad entered the dimly lit mosque and walked across the soft carpets to the big white body now lying there so still. Had the tiger already breathed his last? Farhad slowed down, for he was afraid of finding Nitish dead.

When he was about halfway across the mosque, he heard the door squeal softly behind him. Farhad turned. A bearded old man in a long robe entered the place of prayer and bowed his head reverently.

Farhad nodded in greeting and then went on. But before

he could take more than a step or so the bearded Muslim called him back.

"Wait!" he said. His voice was frail and old. "Wait a moment, my son! I have something to ask you. I am a believer, but I don't come from these parts. Maybe you can help me to . . ."

Farhad stopped. "I don't come from these parts, either," he replied, but he waited courteously for the old man to come up with him. "I was only sheltering here from the storm. I—"

At that moment, something unexpected happened.

With a movement too fast for even the expert eyes of a master thief like Farhad Kamal to follow it, the bearded man reached into the pocket of his wide robe and took something out. Then Farhad felt the cold blade of a knife at his throat.

Astonished, he stared at the other man.

"I was going to ask you what became of our bargain," said the man, and now his voice didn't sound frail at all. It sounded young, strong—and familiar.

"I have the strange but distinct impression that you still owe me half a jewel," he went on. "You can imagine how glad I was to hear that a traveler with a white tiger had taken up residence in the mosque of this pretty little village. I assume that the pleasure is entirely yours, for it must be terrible to go around with an unpaid debt preying on your mind. Terrible. I'm really sorry for you. An unpaid debt can be deadly."

And the man increased the pressure of his knife. Farhad felt a drop of warm blood running down his throat. He had underestimated the congregation at their prayers: Of course they had seen him and Nitish. Damn.

"It's an honor to see you again," said Farhad. "I'd almost forgotten our bargain."

"That's what I thought," said the Frenchman in his disguise as a devout Muslim. He smiled slyly. Then, with pretended concern, he asked, "What's happened to your tiger? The people say he hardly moves. Is he sick?"

Farhad did not reply.

"Last time I met him," said the Frenchman, "he made it very clear to me that it would be better not to pick a quarrel with at least one of you."

He rolled back the sleeve of his striped robe, and Farhad saw long, red scratches on his arm left by the tiger's claws.

"And now look at him! What a difference!" said the Frenchman. "There he lies as if struck by lightning . . . A very tragic turn of events!"

At these last words, he grinned broadly and pressed the knife even deeper into Farhad's flesh.

"Give me the stone," he said, quietly and calmly. "Then I'll let you go."

"I don't have it!" replied Farhad, stepping back. The

Frenchman tripped him with a practiced movement of his legs, and they fell to the floor together. Now Farhad saw the knife flashing directly above him. Its edge was alarmingly sharp, and the sunlight reflecting on the blade made it shine.

"If that's the way you want it," said the Frenchman, ramming his knee into Farhad's stomach. He was better nourished than Farhad and thus heavier. "If that's the way you want it, I'll slit your face first and *then* search you. Personally, I am against bloodshed—particularly in a house of God. They say the blood of cheats and swindlers is harder to wash away than any other. But of course, it's up to you."

With a regretful smile, he raised the knife. Farhad reared up, saw the blade coming down toward him, and with a cry he twisted his head to one side.

But the blade never reached his face.

The air behind the Frenchman seemed to explode, and out of the corner of his eye Farhad saw the man flung aside. The knife flew out of his hand and landed without a sound on the soft, carpeted floor. And before Farhad could even think straight, he felt himself being grabbed by the shoulder and pulled up from the floor. To his immense surprise, he saw two bright blue eyes shining through all this sudden confusion, and those eyes said, clearly and distinctly, "Oh, would he just!"

"What?" asked Farhad, dazed, and he scrambled up.

Nitish stood before him, large and white and with an expression of fury.

"That damn European!" flashed his eyes. "What does he think he's doing?"

The damn European was lying on the floor behind Nitish, staring at the tiger as if he were a vision.

Nitish turned to him and uttered a deep, throaty tiger growl that seemed to crawl up the walls of the mosque and fill the place entirely, like the soundboard of a gigantic musical instrument. His growl echoed back from the ornate ceiling, it wound its way over the soft carpets like a dangerous snake, and Farhad shuddered. He had never heard the tiger growl

190

like that before.

Finally Nitish turned to Farhad again. "We ought to start moving," said his eyes. "We've been here far too long. Climb up, my hero."

Still dazed, Farhad nodded and climbed on the back of the tiger.

A moment later, Nitish was taking a great bound through the double doors of the mosque and out into the bright sunlight.

"What happened?" asked Farhad. "I thought you were dying. I thought you were really sick."

"*Of course* I was really sick," replied the tiger. "I came back

to my senses quite by chance when that . . . that whatever he
is came in and threatened you."

"By chance?"

"*Entirely* by chance."

Farhad played with the silver amulet from which the
princess gazed at him with her unfathomably dark eyes, and
he looked into the setting sun.

He had a sneaky feeling that all Nitish had needed was
something to distract him. Something to take his mind off
the idea that a mosque could make a sacred Hindu tiger sick.
If Farhad had had any medical training, he might well have
concluded that Nitish was the first religious hypochondriac
known to history, legend, and fable.

But instead, he stroked one of the white tiger's ears, lost
in thought. "Thank you," he whispered. "Thank you for
saving me."

Nitish turned his head to him again. "What was that you
said?" asked his eyes. "My hearing's badly affected . . ."

"I said," remarked Farhad in a louder voice, "we mustn't
lose any more time."

There was no rain that night or the next morning. The many
puddles slowly dried up, and the tiger took longer leaps
again.

With every passing hour, the desert moved from a great distance to a lesser distance away, and Varanasi, the sacred city on the Ganges, moved from a little way off to fairly close.

Everything would have been fine.

But then they came to the river Son.

Most of the time the Son was a more or less narrow trickle of water running along a deep, dry riverbed full of garbage and dead, decaying dogs. If you crossed the bridge over the Son in the town of Badarpur, you usually avoided looking down.

A little upstream from Badarpur, the women washed their clothes in the water of the little river, and the narrow trickle took on the colors of their saris, dyeing the dry riverbanks saffron yellow, ruby red, and sometimes ultramarine blue.

The bridge over the Son was old and was often in a state of disrepair. The British had never thought Badarpur or the Son, the bridge over it or the garbage in the riverbed, important enough for them to make real improvements to any of them.

When Farhad and Nitish came to the river, the Son had swollen with the sudden great rainfalls of the monsoon and was now a fast, turbulent torrent. And the bridge was gone. There was nothing left of it but one of its piers, all alone in the middle of the river.

Even the banks of the river had turned to shallow lakes,

and Nitish trod carefully in his leather socks. Water stood inches deep where rickshaws usually waited, and the rickshaws themselves shone as if freshly scrubbed after the rain. Their owners sat on the old, fabric-covered seats with their knees drawn up, drinking tea and skimming pebbles across the surface of the water.

Farhad looked at the rushing river with alarm.

"You'll have to jump it," he told Nitish at last. "There's no other way."

"I can't jump it," said Nitish. "The bank on that side is covered with water, just like the bank on this side. If I land there, I'll disturb the water, and it will be scared and fly up like the white egret in the paddy fields. Water is very stupid, and it scares easily."

Farhad nodded thoughtfully. The tiger was right; the water would splash up.

"Over there," said Nitish. "Someone's carrying a child across—look."

Farhad followed his gaze. Sure enough, a woman was wading through the water with a small child in her arms. The brown water had caught the hem of her sari and was washing it around her knees in a cloud of color. The water tugged and pulled with all its might, but the woman held on to the sari with her free hand and wouldn't let the water have it.

"The river is strong," said Nitish. "But it only comes up to her knees. So it will only come up to your knees, too. You could carry me."

"No, I couldn't,' said Farhad firmly. "Maybe you haven't noticed, but you're a little larger than a child. Even if I were a strong, brave hero, you'd be hanging off my shoulders on both sides and you'd get very, very wet."

"I could make myself really small," said Nitish.

Farhad laughed. "I have a better idea," he said, and he slipped off the tiger's back.

Then he made his way over to the rickshaws. Nitish gave a throaty growl and followed him very cautiously so as not to scare the water.

The rickshaw owners had been too interested in their tea and their game with the pebbles to notice the two of them, and didn't see them until they were very close.

Farhad saw the astonishment and horror in the many pairs of eyes, both old and young, when they looked at the white tiger. He chose one of the rickshaw owners who looked particularly frail—a thin boy—and went up to him.

"I need your rickshaw," he said very politely.

The boy stared at him wide-eyed, but bravely tried not to show his fear. "Where do you want to go?" he asked, in a voice that shook slightly.

"Across the river," replied Farhad. "You can have it back again on the opposite bank."

"I'm not pulling my rickshaw through the river," replied the boy. "The current's strong and the footing on the riverbed is bad. It will get stuck and tip over."

"You leave that to me," said Farhad. "I'll pull it across."

"How much will you pay me if I agree?" asked the boy.

"Pay?" Farhad frowned as if he had never heard the word before. "I think you misunderstood me. I don't want to *buy* your rickshaw. I just want to borrow it."

"That'll be twenty rupees," said the boy, folding his arms.

Farhad glanced at Nitish, and the tiger came a little closer to the rickshaw and the boy sitting in it. He sniffed the boy's bare feet, and made a face as if he were wondering what they tasted like.

The boy tried to shrink away, but his seat was too small.

"Your life is worth more than twenty rupees," said Farhad, and after scrutinizing the boy, he added, derisively, "About thirty, I'd say."

"Well, if anything happens to the rickshaw, you'll be sorry!" said the boy. His voice was shrill with fear. He climbed out of the rickshaw on the side where no white tiger was standing, and hastily took several steps back.

Farhad placed his hands together and bowed in thanks.

"I knew you were a sensible boy," he said.

Then he got in front of the rickshaw and pulled it to the riverbank.

"Get in," he told Nitish.

"What, me?"

"No," said Farhad, "one of the other twenty-six white tigers waiting to cross the river. Hurry up. We have no time to lose."

Nitish growled quietly and then climbed up on the well-worn seat of the rickshaw.

It wasn't easy to climb with the leather rags on his paws, and the seat was much too small. Farhad took a step back and looked at him.

The metal of the rickshaw, with its chased patterns, gleamed in the sunlight. Farhad noticed that there was a leaping tiger painted among the brightly colored peacocks of the pattern. But under the metal canopy sat a real tiger, trying desperately to stay put on the tiny seat without slipping off. Farhad suppressed his laughter and braced himself against the rickshaw harness. "Hold on tight," he said.

Then he dipped a foot in the river and, seconds later, the current was washing around him. Yes, it was strong.

The wheels of the rickshaw did indeed sink deeper and deeper into the soft mud of the riverbed. The Son swept torn-off branches, scraps of fabric, and bits and pieces of other things past Farhad as he doggedly pulled the rickshaw along. Sometimes he thought it would go no farther, but finally the rickshaw would free itself from the mud with such a violent jerk that he almost fell over. Each time that happened, he heard Nitish meow and snarl with fright. But there was no time for him to turn and look at his unusual passenger.

The other side of the river Son seemed to Farhad to be moving ever farther away, and his legs were shaking with his efforts. He closed his eyes and prayed to Krishna to give him strength. Perhaps the rushing of the swollen river drowned out Farhad's prayer, for Krishna sent no strength, and Farhad had to do his best to pull the protesting vehicle on by himself.

He was gasping and beginning to feel dizzy with the strain. The veins throbbed in his temples, and there was a taste on his tongue like blood, as if his heart were beating between his teeth. As he went on struggling against the silt and the current, he wondered why he had chosen that particular day to go to that particular villa in Madurai where the god had hidden the amulet in the pool. Why hadn't he kept his fingers off the glint of silver? Why . . .

There! It was only a few more steps to the other side of the river. With the last of his strength, Farhad tugged at the rickshaw frame and pulled it a little way up the bank. But the slope here was steeper than on the bank opposite. Farhad could go no farther, and he turned, exhausted, to look at Nitish.

"Wait," said the white tiger's eyes. "I think that's close enough."

Farhad felt Nitish climbing cautiously out of the rickshaw and jumping to the bank. But although he knew with his mind that the distribution of weight would change, his exhausted body wasn't ready for it. He went on pulling with all his might, and when there was less resistance all of a sudden, his feet slipped on the steep ground of the bank. He fell forward, slipped out of the harness holding him to the frame, and slid down the slope into the river. Although the water was only knee-deep, the current carried Farhad a little way on before he could get to his feet. And then, suddenly, it wasn't knee-deep any more. Just past the ford over which the woman had waded and he himself had pulled the rickshaw, the Son became surprisingly deep. Farhad's feet felt in vain for the riverbed.

His arms flailed out wildly, and he went under, came up again, swallowed water, and coughed.

And he became painfully aware that he couldn't swim.

Desperately, Farhad kicked out, swallowed yet more water, and went under again. The river was holding him firmly in its strong, wet arms, throwing garbage and flotsam at him. Farhad couldn't draw a breath. He wrestled with the Son as if it were a powerful demon, Ravana himself trying to keep the hero away. Death suddenly seemed closer than ever.

In a brief moment when his head was above the surface of the water, he saw more rain clouds gathering in the sky. This, thought Farhad, was the end of his journey.

Then, amidst the grayish brown, foaming, swirling, and filthy water, a picture in a silver frame came before his mind's eye: the picture of the princess, a little clearer still now. There was something like deep grief in her eyes.

Perhaps, thought Farhad, Nitish will manage to rescue her by himself. As his head came out of the pitiless torrent for the last time, he saw something else besides the rainy sky.

He saw a white shape with black stripes leaping toward him.

Right into the middle of the raging waters of the river Son.

A Little White Cow

Farhad felt something seize him and drag him in a direction that he thought was up.

Suddenly, there was air in his lungs and he greedily breathed it in.

He couldn't make out what had happened.

Something was pulling at him. He kept going under again, but now he was being firmly held close to the surface, and he was moving sideways and away from the current. A vague sense told him he was being carried to the bank.

But what was carrying him? Hadn't he seen a white figure jump into the river? Didn't he feel something like sharp teeth firmly dug into the collar of his shirt? No, all this was impossible.

Was he dreaming the never-ending dream of a drowned man?

Farhad saw the bank quite close now, between two waves full of yellowish brown foam, and at last he managed to turn slightly in the grip of his mysterious rescuer.

He looked into the blue eyes of the tiger.

The tiger's fur clung close to his body, smooth and wet. It was untidy around his ears and hung in dripping strands. Drops of water were falling from his whiskers, too, but he kept his mouth firmly closed on Farhad's shirt, paddling with all four paws. Somewhere behind Nitish his long black-and-white striped tail was swimming through the waves like a large and peculiar watersnake.

Nitish was wet. As wet as wet could be. But he definitely didn't look as if he had turned to stone. Farhad could make nothing of any of this, but the next moment he was being dragged up the muddy bank and deposited in the shallow water at the top of it like a piece of flotsam.

He spat out a little water, then lay there for a while, concentrating on breathing and letting the sky shine through his closed eyelids.

Then he opened his eyes.

Above him he saw a large white face with black stripes bending anxiously over him.

"Are you all right?" asked those anxious blue eyes, and this time they didn't look at all dangerous.

"Nitish," whispered the exhausted Farhad. "You—you're wet."

"That," said the tiger with dignity, "had not escaped my notice. But thank you for pointing it out."

"You didn't turn to stone," whispered Farhad, baffled.

"No," said Nitish's eyes. "Do you mind?"

Farhad shook his head in bewilderment. "I—I don't understand it," he said, cautiously sitting up.

"Nor do I," said Nitish. "It simply didn't happen."

"You—you mean you didn't know it wasn't going to happen, either?"

"Of course not," said the tiger. "Would I have let myself be shut up in a mosque for three days if I had?"

Farhad shook water out of his hair. "So you jumped into the river even though you were sure you'd turn to stone."

"Well, someone had to rescue you," murmured the tiger awkwardly, and he began cleaning himself. "To think of Krishna picking a hero who can't even swim! What *can* you do, if I may ask?"

Farhad coughed up some more water, and felt his left

upper arm. Yes, the bundle was still there. "Steal jewels," he replied.

Nitish snorted. Then he suddenly looked thoughtful. *"If the salty fluid of life touches me . . ."* he said, *". . . the crystal-clear blood of the earth, the drops of death—then I'll turn to stone.* What does it mean, Farhad? What's the salty fluid of life and the drops of death? And the crystal-clear blood of the earth? It doesn't seem to be water."

"Maybe sweat," murmured Farhad. "But if that was going to turn you to stone, you'd have been a rock long ago."

"What else could it be?"

"No idea," said Farhad truthfully. "I'm afraid we won't find out until something happens to tell us."

He climbed on the tiger's dripping back, and Nitish shook himself like a dog. Drops of water flew off him, and Farhad almost flew off with them, too.

They left the rickshaw stuck in the mud. The boy would fetch it sometime.

As they set off westward, where the desert awaited them, it began to rain again.

The tiger had taken the leather rags off his paws and ran soundlessly through the wet night.

They reached Varanasi soon after dawn. The chaotic life

of the city had begun at first light, when the first pilgrims came down to bathe in the river.

Varanasi was a city that had seen many builders and many destroyers, and had just as many names. The British called it Benares, because they hadn't listened properly when people told them what it was called. The Indians called it Kashi, when they spoke of it with particular respect: *City of Spiritual Light*. The god Shiva sometimes called it *my city*, because he had once lived there with his wife Parvati.

A time must have come, Farhad guessed as they walked through the crowded city, when Shiva withdrew to his holy mountain of Kailash because too many pilgrims had come to visit him.

Pilgrims thronged the ramshackle, winding streets of the Old Town in great crowds. They streamed through its narrow alleys, and where there were just too many of them jammed together, the arteries of the city became blocked with angry cursing people.

The white tiger simply merged with the crowd, and no one noticed him. Farhad and Nitish let the pilgrims sweep them along to the banks of the Ganges where it flowed in its broad bed, full of the waters of the monsoon. The river looked to Farhad as wide as a sea, and even Shiva himself couldn't have pulled a rickshaw through it.

"Let's rest a little by the ghats," said Nitish, and he yawned a white, saber-toothed tiger yawn. "I'm tired and I'd like to dry my coat in the sun. Look, the women have spread out their washing over there. I could lie down beside it."

"Be careful," said Farhad. "Mind they don't take you for a big white sari, roll you up, and carry you away."

The tiger yawned again, and lay down in the dust beside the washing on the first of the great flights of steps going down to the river, the Ram Ghat. Soon he looked like a large stone statue again, if slightly out of place.

Farhad was feeling tired, too, but there was great uneasiness in his heart. He couldn't say where that uneasiness came from or what it meant, but it kept him from just lying down in the dust beside Nitish. How much time had passed now? And above all: How much time was there left before the day of Ravana's demonic wedding?

The jewel was digging slightly into the flesh of his upper arm, reminding him that it was there. With the help of a purse of money that happened to come his way in the crush of the city streets, Farhad bought several triangular samosas filled with potato for his breakfast, and began pacing restlessly along the bank of Mother Ganga.

The ghats—flights of steps, each several yards broad and set at some distance apart—led down to the water. They were as full of pilgrims as garbage heaps are full of flies. Farhad's restlessness finally drove him into the river at the Dasashwamedh Ghat, both to wash in the holy water and to drink a little of it. But nothing would dispel the uneasiness.

A garland of orange marigolds floated past, followed by a little ship made of leaves with an oil-burning wick in the middle of it. Farhad watched the two offerings for some time as they bobbed along.

But something in the turmoil of noise and voices sounded wrong to his ears. Was it Mother Ganga asking him for an offering of flowers—a burning leaf-ship, alms given to one of the holy men on her banks? Or was it the weariness and tension of the last few days that he felt?

Then, quite suddenly, he knew, and he froze. Of course. That explained his anxiety. He'd had a premonition. How stupid he had been to stop here in the pilgrim city of Varanasi, of all places, the city of begging monks and bandits!

A few paces behind him, one of the long-haired, naked sadhus was pouring holy water over his head from a bronze can, chanting his prayers to the great goddess Ganga in a soft singsong voice. Farhad knew that voice. It had a barely audible European accent, although at first it was difficult to tell just what country the accent came from . . .

Cautiously, Farhad turned as he moved slowly away from

the praying sadhu. Yes, there he was. Even if he now had a voluminous head of hair and a quantity of sacred implements: Menière, the Frenchman he had met in prison and who had threatened him at the mosque. It was Menière, and Farhad still owed him half a jewel.

Farhad made himself go slowly through the water. If he tried to run, he'd scare the water, as Nitish would put it, and the talkative water would tell everyone he was running away.

He reached the bank, cursing in his heart.

Why was it so long since he'd changed his own appearance? He was at least the Frenchman's equal in the art of disguise; it would have been easy. Before setting out on this journey, Farhad hadn't looked the same for two weeks together, and now that disguise was really necessary, he looked the same every day. What was the matter with him?

He remembered how he'd rolled about in the mud with the dirty children in the first of the rainfalls, feeling glad to be just a single person. Perhaps he was sick. Black fever had very strange symptoms in the early stages. It sent many people crazy even before their urine turned dark . . .

When he had climbed the smooth steps of the ghat, he looked around.

The fake sadhu hadn't seen him. He was deep in conversation with another sadhu, and the idea that this other sadhu

207

might be as much of a fake as the first made Farhad laugh. Few things seemed improbable in a city like this.

Farhad set off back to the place where the tiger was drying off, stretched out by the washing. It was high time for them to move on.

He didn't yet know that Varanasi was in no hurry to let a pilgrim go once he has found his way to the city.

Farhad came to the Mir Ghat, where the gleaming, golden dome of a temple rose above the dilapidated buildings. He stopped at a stall where a little boy was selling kulfi: frozen watery milk flavored with cloves, cinnamon, and cardamom, sold on round, thin, fibrous sticks. As Farhad was wondering whether to buy some from the boy, a hand came gently down on his shoulder from behind.

 208

He spun around and cursed himself for the second time that day—this time for having lulled himself briefly into a sense of security.

"My dear friend," said the sadhu, placing his hands together in greeting and bowing slightly. "How greatly it gladdens my heart to meet you here in the luminous city of Shiva."

Two more holy men were standing behind him, both of them old and as crooked as the sticks on which they leaned. Grave-faced, they listened to the conversation.

"But what a state I find you in!" said Menière, in a tone of gentle reproof. "Just look at you. Weren't you once a monk like us? Deep in conversation with the gods, leading a strictly ascetic life?"

He tapped Farhad's chest with his forefinger. "And now I find you not in devout contemplation of the message of the gods, but in contemplation of a kulfi seller instead."

The little boy behind his gaudily painted handcart stared at the sadhus and Farhad with wide, curious eyes, and picked his nose.

"Once the two of us sought Enlightenment that shines brighter than the sun," said Menière sadly. "And now you seem to have turned away from Enlightenment entirely, my friend. Or have you already achieved it in some other way, I wonder . . ."

The two old sadhus were looking at Farhad just as expectantly as the little boy, and he took a step back. As far as he could see, Menière was unarmed. And obviously he dared not attack Farhad openly in front of the holy men. He knew the unwritten laws of India.

"I think there must be some mistake, venerable father," replied Farhad, sounding utterly confused. "I respect religion, and the gods determine my life as they do the lives of every living soul on earth. But I have never been a monk."

"A mistake?" asked Menière, looking thoughtful. Then his arm suddenly shot out, and he seized Farhad's wrist. "Show me your hands, my son," he said with a sweet undertone in his voice. A tone that, to Farhad's ears, suggested a revolting mixture of smoking resin and rotting mangoes. "Hands always tell the truth about a man."

With surprising strength, he turned the palms of Farhad's hands up. And for a moment, Farhad didn't realize what the Frenchman was up to.

But then he saw what Menière saw, and he understood.

The palm of Farhad's right hand bore a long, still-unhealed wound—a cut, exactly like the one the Frenchman had shown him on his own hand back in prison.

The mark of the bloodstone.

No one who touched it seemed to escape the jewel's sharp edge.

Farhad's eyes met the Frenchman's. He saw a flicker in them like the fire at the end of a lighted fuse, eating its way toward the explosive at the other end. He had seconds left. But what would happen when the fire reached the far end, and the explosive in Menière went off?

Farhad gave up pretending.

He tore his hands away, ducked under the Frenchman's arms as they reached for him, and began to run. The crowd of pilgrims were on their way back from the ghats; most of them had finished their morning prayers. Farhad slipped between them, forging himself a path with his elbows.

He heard no cries behind him, which was worrying. The sadhu ought to have been calling after him indignantly.

If he wasn't, it meant that Menière, too, had decided the show was over.

Menière, who was *not* a sadhu, was following him fast and silently.

Farhad wondered which of them was the stronger. He had never physically fought anyone, and he didn't intend to start now. That was not his way. It might have been a long time since he changed his appearance, but he was still by nature someone who ran away, dodged, and ducked. If necessary, he would, at the most, attack from behind, but he would never fight openly.

If only he could reach Nitish on the Ram Ghat in time . . .

But Farhad reached neither the Ram Ghat nor Nitish.

Before he had gone much farther, there was an incident that would bring about many startling changes.

A little white cow caused the incident, and seemed just as surprised about it as everyone else involved. Farhad spotted her by the Lalilath Ghat, where there was a particularly large crowd of pilgrims. Between the lower steps down to the river and the upper steps leading to the city, there was a garbage heap, and the little white cow was standing by it. She looked very hungry.

The cows of India are sacred, but that doesn't mean that anyone feeds them. They wander city streets, live on garbage, and after a while they starve to death in a very sacred way.

The garbage heap that this cow had found, however, seemed to belong to a pale gray bull. Farhad saw the little white cow lower her head and show the bull her curving horns. Farhad stopped for a moment and watched as the two animals charged one another. They were both so thin that you could count their ribs, but the strength with which they fought seemed uncontrollable.

Within seconds, everyone on the Lalilath Ghat had gathered to see the show. Farhad tried to get through, but by now the crowd was as solid as a stone wall.

He heard people placing bets on one animal or the other. At the same time, he heard the crash of horns as the two of them charged again after a pause.

Hemmed in, he stood there looking for the Frenchman. Yes, there he was, on the other side of the fast and furious fight. But he, too, obviously couldn't move an inch.

A strange feeling came over Farhad; it was as if the animals there on the steps were fighting out the deadly battle that ought to have been his and Menière's. They were fighting for a heap of garbage. He and Menière were fighting for a jewel.

Would that make any difference to whichever was the loser?

If the white cow wins, thought Farhad, the smaller, weaker, but more agile of the two, then I'll succeed in taking Ravana's servant the bloodstone and rescuing the princess. As he watched the battle going this way and that, it was like a mantra chanted in his head: *If the white cow wins . . . if the white cow wins . . .*

But it didn't turn out like that.

Arthur Burns had not had a good day.

For the last three days he had been a guest in the Rajah's palace near Benares, and this was his second failed hunting expedition. He had been bitten by mosquitoes by night and tormented by the heat of the day. The Indian water had given him diarrhea, and his fair skin was burned by the sun.

With expansive gestures, the Rajah had told them about all the game they would find in the local country: the tigers and gazelles, the great nilgai and the delicate four-horned antelopes, the pheasants, and a great many other large and handsome birds whose names Burns had never heard before.

He hadn't been in India very long, so he thought everything the Rajah said was gospel.

His two older companions had smiled and nodded politely. Only gradually did Burns understand their attitude.

The gazelles were faster than the wind and wilier than any English fox, and the tigers never showed up at all. The only thing Arthur Burns had shot was a tiny, black bird with a yellow beak and bright eyes. The surly cook had refused to prepare it, so on their second day, they had to eat the provisions the Rajah had given them for the hunt, as if they were children and he had sent them out to play.

Yet it was men like Arthur Burns who ruled British India.

He didn't know what had made the other two hunters choose the path running beside the river, where at this time of day you could get along about as fast as if you were moving through cold porridge.

Anyone might have thought they enjoyed the slow pace of the country.

When he had finally persuaded them to ride away from the bank of the Ganges and into the city, Burns found their path barricaded by two fighting cattle. None of the cowardly Indians seemed prepared to separate them.

Well, *he* was no cowardly Indian. He'd had enough trouble already today, and he wanted to get past. Now.

Burns exploded. "Out of the way there!" he cried. "Move aside!"

He ignored his two older countrymen, who were calling out to him, and soon the Indians did reluctantly move aside. Arthur looked with distaste at the unkempt, bearded sadhus among the crowd. Or were they Brahmans?

Of all those present, only the cattle, who had just parted horns again, ignored his arrival. Burns reined in his horse, raised his rifle, and took aim.

His shot echoed back from the old city walls and was multiplied many times in the air.

At the same time there was a scream. The pale gray bull fell to his knees and keeled over on his side. After the second shot, he lay still. The foam at his mouth had settled, and his life-blood poured red and fast from his breast.

Arthur Burns smiled, pleased with himself.

Had he just imagined the scream?

The little white cow stood there as if turned to stone, staring at her opponent. She still made no move to stand aside. Burns loaded his gun again.

He felt someone clinging to one of his feet, and saw a man with crooked, rotten teeth and the white sign of blessing on his forehead. The man called out something that Burns didn't understand. Angrily, he tried to free his foot.

215

Then he raised his rifle for the second time. The little white cow looked at him with surprise in her eyes, and a dark patch appeared on her white chest when the gun went off. She collapsed, and her gentle eyes cast Burns a final glance of immense astonishment. Then her back legs twitched for the last time. Burns put the safety catch on his gun and stowed it away, satisfied.

But strange to say: This time he really had heard a scream as his bullet met its mark. And then he noticed the silence. It was absolute. The entire crowd was silent. Dozens of dark eyes were turned on him. And now Burns sensed that something was wrong.

216 He tried to ride on along the road into the city, but the crowd of people, barely perceptibly, had closed in around him. His horse was prancing nervously in place. Uncertainly, he looked around for his companions, and then one of the Indians addressed him.

"The cow is a sacred animal," he said in excellent English. "A sacred animal may not be killed."

Although he had not spoken in a particularly loud voice, the words rang through the air in the silence as clearly as if they were written there. And when they had faded away, the crowd began to move. It swayed back and forth, came together again, and grew dangerous. Arms reached out for the Englishman. He dug his heels into his horse's flanks, and it whinnied out loud and tried to race forward. But hands were now pulling at Burns, and he lost his balance. Then he slipped out of the saddle. Now they let his horse through. He saw it racing away among all the people, while he himself landed on the ground.

"Help!" he cried as loud as he could. "Help!"

His voice broke in his panic.

The heads of the crowd bent over him as if they were all listening to the same large monster. And for the first time in his short life, Arthur Burns knew the fear of death.

Farhad saw the cow fall, and sensed the crowd drawing together.

Something in him flinched when the shot tore through the morning air. He heard the woman behind him cry out, and saw the blood trickling from the animal's breast.

If the little white cow wins, then I'll succeed in taking Ravana's servant the bloodstone and rescuing the princess.

Now the little white cow lay dead in the dust, but she hadn't really lost the battle. What did that mean?

He tried to move out of the throng of people, but he couldn't. He was carried along in the middle of the crowd to the place where it had swallowed up the Englishman. Farhad saw the other two Englishmen trying to get through on their horses. One of them fired a gun into the air, and a flock of white herons, startled, flew up in the bright blue sky above the crowd. The crowd had turned into an insatiable wild beast. It swallowed up the two older Englishmen, too. They simply disappeared in it. It was Kali, the avenging goddess with the skulls at her belt and her red tongue, and now that her power had been unleashed there was no holding back.

But someone—perhaps one of the Indian servants who had been with the Englishmen—must have managed to raise the alarm, for after a while, Farhad saw British police uniforms in the raging chaos. He saw their batons flail up and down, saw their horses' hooves flash, and more shots were fired.

Farhad's desire to run grew to infinite proportions, but he was still jammed among the excited pilgrims. And then, suddenly, a riderless horse appeared beside him. It must have belonged to one of the Englishmen, and Farhad swung himself up on the animal's back. He hadn't gone far before a sadhu managed to clamber up on the horse behind him. Turning, Farhad saw with horror that it was Menière.

A moment later, he was surrounded by police officers.

And Farhad suddenly realized that they thought *he* had dragged the horse's owner off its back.

Farther away in the crowd, he caught a glimpse of white

fur with black stripes—and then he felt a policeman's baton.
A moment later, all was dark around him.

When Farhad came to his senses, he was lying in a courtyard
surrounded by old walls, and the sun was burning down on
him. His head hurt and he felt dizzy. Carefully, he sat up and
looked around. He realized that his dhoti was torn and a
piece of its patterned hem had gone missing.

The courtyard was full of people who seemed to be in the
same sorry state. They were crowding into the shade by the
walls, sitting in the sun looking resigned, or lying curled up on
the ground. Many of them were pilgrims; some still held the
bronze cans in which they had taken water from the Ganges.
They all seemed to be waiting for something. All was very
quiet, with only the bees buzzing around the climbing plants
that grew up the walls. It was some time before Farhad saw
the three uniformed British officers standing stiff as statues
among the people and leaning on their guns.

"What are we waiting for?" he whispered to an old man
who was dozing beside him.

The old man gave a start, and looked him up and down.
"We thought you'd never wake again," he whispered, smiling.
"Good to see you're better. Though I'm afraid that won't do
any good."

"What are we waiting for?" Farhad repeated.

"For them to decide what they're going to do with us," the man replied. "They took away everyone they could lay their hands on, and the rest of the crowd ran off."

"What happened to the Englishmen?" asked Farhad.

The old man sighed. "One hears this and that," he said. "It seems that two of them are dead and the third badly injured. The British are making a great fuss about it."

Farhad nodded.

Then he let his gaze travel over the courtyard and found the Frenchman. He was leaning against a wall with his eyes closed. For a moment Farhad was alarmed, and he felt his left upper arm. But the bundle was still there. It felt slightly damp, and the arm hurt. The stone must have cut into him as he fell off the horse.

Before Farhad could think of a better way to hide the stone, another uniformed Englishman put his head around the doorway leading to the inner courtyard and inspected the prisoners. Farhad's pulse beat faster. What would the British do to them? If they had anything unpleasant in store for him, there was no way he could run off. Now of all times, thought Farhad, he could have used a white tiger able to leap high walls with a single magic bound. Where was Nitish? Would he ever see the tiger again?

The uniformed man brought Farhad's train of thought to an abrupt end.

"You!" he said, pointing to Menière. The men beside the Frenchman shook him, and he woke up. "Come along. And you!"

This time, to Farhad's surprise, the irate finger was pointing at him. He rose to his feet, staggering, and made his way across the courtyard through the bright light.

Beyond the doorway, it was so dark that at first Farhad stumbled forward like a blind man. Someone pushed him in the right direction, and he felt almost grateful. When his eyes were used to the dim light, he saw that they were going down a long, dark corridor. Four men escorted them, and Menière's eyes met Farhad's with a silent question in them.

"Do you have the stone?" he whispered.

Farhad shook his head. "Not here," he whispered back. "And it wouldn't do you any good anyway."

Menière shrugged his shoulders, and Farhad didn't like the way he was smiling.

A moment later they were standing opposite a desk in a bright room, and the door closed behind them. The four men in uniform stayed in the room. An Englishman who wasn't wearing a uniform sat at the desk in front of the window, looking at them.

"The fact of the matter is," said the man slowly, "that someone has to be held responsible for this business. It would be wrong," he added, cracking the joints of his long, thin fingers, "to give a whole courtyard full of people the punishment due to a murderer. Especially as there are many pilgrims among them. The Indians don't like that kind of thing. Nor, I may say, do we British."

He cracked the joints of his fingers again, and looked over his shoulder and out the window, as if he had to think about the solution to this problem. But Farhad was sure he had already made up his mind.

"Do you understand what I'm saying?" he asked.

Farhad and Menière nodded at the same time.

"Good," the man went on. "We caught you two riding one of the British officers' horses. No one can deny that. So we have decided that you are chiefly responsible for the uproar."

He put a hand out as if to stifle any objection. "This has nothing to do with what really happened. Perhaps you didn't have anything to do with it. Or perhaps you *were* the chief culprits. I don't know, and I don't want to know. The fact is that you will pay for what happened."

"What does that mean?" asked Farhad.

He felt no fear as he looked at the man at the desk, only

anger. His head hurt, and once again he was being prevented from traveling on. It was as if everything was conspiring against him. The moon in the sky was inexorably waxing, pushing time on ahead of its growing belly. Farhad had watched it these last few nights. They had hardly a dozen days left to find the desert of Thar.

"Two of us are dead," said the man, "and two of you will follow. Sometimes an example has to be made." He sighed. "The execution will be at sunrise tomorrow," he said.

One word came into Farhad's mind: Nitish.

Lord of the Right Way.

Would Nitish find a way to rescue him from the hands of British justice once more?

He heard the Frenchman clear his throat and then, to Farhad's astonishment, he said in crystal-clear English, with the same slight smile on his lips as ever, "I understand your reasoning, sir. But there's a problem."

Farhad saw Menière digging into the plain fabric bag that hung over his shoulder from a strap. His hand found something small, flat, and angular, and he put it on the desk in front of the Englishman.

And although, like most Indians, Farhad himself had never had anything of the kind, he recognized the gilded stamp on it at once: It was a passport.

"I'm as British as you are," he said. "See for yourself.
It's very inconvenient for me to say this with so many ears
listening. But I have my reasons for mingling with the people
as a sadhu, and it certainly would not be in the interests of the
British Crown for those reasons to be made public. Nor do
I think the Crown would be particularly pleased to find that
you had executed me to set an example."

The man behind the desk opened the passport. "Steal,"
he read in disbelief. "Mr. Subclavian Steal."

"Correct," said the Frenchman, who seemed not to be a
Frenchman after all. Farhad's bewilderment struggled with
his headache.

"I'd be grateful if you would let me go," said Mr. Steal
mildly, taking off the wig he was wearing. He had short,
sandy hair under it. Farhad wondered if there was another
hair color and another wig under the sandy hair. He wasn't
sure that Steal, or Menière, or whatever he was called was
really British at all.

The man behind the desk beckoned one of the others
over and whispered to him for a while.

"We'll enable you to leave this building without attracting
much attention," he said at last. "This is a very . . ." He cracked
his fingers again. "A very unfortunate misunderstanding."

"I agree with you entirely," said Steal.

Farhad saw the sky outside the window. It was wide and blue, washed clean by the monsoon.

Soon after that, he was pushed out into the dimly lit corridor again.

The night was long and sultry.

He was lying in a small room without a window, and the lock on his cell door was a lock of excellent quality.

Around midnight he unwrapped the cloths from his upper arm and felt for the bloodstone. To his horror, he found that the jewel had broken into four pieces. But then the horror he felt changed into a sudden idea. Four pieces. Wasn't that much better than only one? The plan all along had been to bribe a guard with the stone when it was in one piece. So why not bribe another guard with it now that there were four of them. It seemed only logical.

Farhad kicked up a fuss until one of the guards came. He put his mouth close to the bars over the door.

"If you smuggle me out," he whispered through the grating, "I can reward you royally. Do you have a light?"

The darkness gave way to a flickering circle of light as the man held his lantern up to the barred opening.

"What do you have there?" he asked suspiciously.

Farhad held one of the four parts of the jewel out to him

on the flat of his hand. It glittered and glowed deep red, like the sun setting over the Ganges.

The man looked at the stone for some time. He was young, with unruly fair hair, and a collection of ugly acne scars disfigured his cheeks.

His eyes were tired, and there was longing in them.

"Think of the green meadows of your native land," said Farhad. "I'm told they are very, very green. This stone could pay for your passage home."

But the young man shook his head.

"Glass," he said scornfully. "You really didn't have to wake me for a piece of colored glass."

"Glass?" hissed Farhad incredulously. "The sun of this country has blinded you! You are looking at one of the most famous jewels in India! Have you never heard of the *bloodstone?*"

The young man looked at Farhad almost with disappointment. "And how would someone like you get his hands on such a stone?" he asked.

Then he turned and disappeared down the corridor. The flap in front of the grating in the door dropped with a metallic click.

Farhad tied the pieces of the broken stone up in a bundle again, seething with fury at the guard's stupidity.

After a while his fury turned to a sense of helplessness. He couldn't sleep. His upper arm was throbbing with pain, and the thoughts in his head were throbbing, too.

There was still hope. One possibility was the tiger.

The other was Subclavian Steal, the Englishman with the strange first name. He and his greed for the bloodstone.

If neither of them turned up before dawn, Farhad was finished.

His heart was cold and empty, and he felt for the little silver amulet. When he opened it, the princess looked out at him, and once again she could be seen a little more clearly than before. Now he saw that she had tiny lines around her eyes, as if she had often laughed in the past. Suddenly he didn't feel so alone anymore.

The grave look in the princess's eyes filled his heart with warmth, and at last he fell asleep.

227

A Copy of Himself

D AY WAS BEGINNING TO DAWN, BUT FARHAD didn't notice.

He knew only when the door of his cell opened.

It was no use resisting. He let them lead him away with his hands bound, thinking fast and furiously.

Nitish, he thought. Nitish, I'm here. Come on. Come and help me.

Perhaps when he stepped out into the light, the tiger would leap toward him with one of his mighty bounds. The guards would run away in terror, Nitish would bite through the bonds tying Farhad's hands with his sharp teeth as if they were chicken bones, and then they would finally leave this city behind, traveling as fast as the clouds, as fast as the grains of sand in the desert wind.

A door was opened ahead of him, and Farhad blinked at the light.

But there was no tiger there.

Two guards pushed him across a gray backyard. A single, withered red rose grew in the middle of it among the garbage and refuse. At that moment, the sight of the rose seemed to Farhad infinitely sad, and his heart was heavier than ever.

The guards stopped for a moment and seemed to be listening.

"Hear that?" asked one of the two uniformed men. Farhad turned to him, and in the gray light of the backyard he recognized the young man with a longing for home in his eyes and a face scarred by acne.

He listened, too. There was a confused babble of murmuring voices somewhere beyond the yard.

"Those are the people who've come to watch the execution," said the young man, with an unpleasant grin.

Farhad cursed the moment when he had seen the longing for green meadows in the young man's eyes, and hated him with all his heart.

He was propelled through another doorway on the far side

of the yard, and the babble of voices grew louder. They were approaching the place where the crowd was waiting. Was it the same crowd that had pulled the Englishmen off their horses? If what the man at the desk had said was true, everyone but Farhad had been allowed to go free. And so now they were waiting to see someone pay the penalty in their place.

"We'll soon be there," said the acne-scarred young man.

He pushed the next door open, and Farhad's heart concentrated on calling Nitish.

But there was no tiger with dangerous, speaking blue eyes waiting on the other side of that door, either.

230 At first, when the man held the piece of fabric under Nitish's nose, the tiger meant to kill him. The fabric belonged to Farhad's dhoti. Or more precisely, it *had* belonged to Farhad's dhoti.

Where was Farhad? What had happened to him?

But Nitish didn't kill the man. Someone who came close to a white tiger so fearlessly probably had a good reason for it. Farhad had told the man about Nitish. That must be it, the tiger thought. Farhad had asked him to look for Nitish, and now the man had come to take him to Farhad.

Obviously the hero was in serious difficulties again. That was nothing new. Ever since Nitish had known Farhad

Kamal, the thief kept getting into serious difficulties. The few minor difficulties that Nitish himself had caused were hardly worth mentioning.

After his refreshing sleep by the riverbank, Nitish felt younger and stronger than he had for a long time. Now that he knew even water couldn't do him any harm, the whole world lay before him.

Farhad wouldn't wait for him in vain.

The man whom Nitish was following through the alleyways of the city wore a long, striped robe like an Arab, and had a full black beard. Nitish didn't like the smell of him. But when he himself had roamed Varanasi aimlessly, trying to find out where they had taken Farhad, this man had been the only person who hadn't run away from him.

Nitish was surprised to find that they were a little way outside the city now. The houses did not stand so close together here, and the streets were not so crowded. Soon they were positively deserted. Where had Farhad been taken?

"This way," said the man, making his way through a dense network of dried-up climbing plants. Now, after the rain, they were blooming with new buds.

A little later the man opened a shed door, and Nitish slipped in ahead of him. The inside of the shed was dimly lit.

He strained his eyes to make something out.

Bales of straw . . . Just bales of straw. Nothing else.

Nitish growled angrily. What did this mean?

He turned to the man in the long robe, but the man was gone.

Angrily, the tiger padded over to the door he had come through.

It was closed. He remembered that it opened to the outside, and pushed his large head against it. The door still wouldn't open.

Then Nitish began to understand.

He sat down in the middle of the shed and let out a howl of rage.

He'd been tricked.

No, there was no tiger waiting behind the door that the acne-scarred young man opened.

But no excited crowd was waiting for Farhad there, either.

The door led into a narrow side street, deserted except for an old man and his donkey making their way down it. Farhad stared at the street, stared at the old man, stared at the donkey and the bundle of vegetables on its back, and felt bewildered.

The second man gently pushed him through the doorway.

Then Farhad felt his hands being untied.

"What . . . ?" he began, confused.

His heart was trembling in mingled disbelief, relief, and fear. Was this narrow alley a trick to lure him into a strange new trap?

"You're in luck," said the second man. "We lost you on the way to the place of execution."

"Lost me?" asked Farhad.

"Well, you knocked us down and ran away, and now we have to search the building," said the young man who had claimed that the bloodstone was just glass.

Farhad remembered how the young man had taunted him with the sounds of the waiting mob, how he had enjoyed Farhad's fear.

"Don't look so horrified," said the other man, laughing. "My colleague here said something about colored glass. Well, we've been paid by someone with more to offer than glass."

"Who?" asked Farhad suspiciously.

"You don't need to know that," said the man. "Be grateful to him and get out. But make sure you go fast enough and far enough away. If they catch you again, they'll have more than two men guarding you, and then no one will be able to help you."

Farhad looked uncertainly around him.

Had the old man with the donkey really just been an old man taking his vegetables to market?

Farhad placed his hands together in a hasty gesture of thanks and bowed briefly.

His dislike of the acne-scarred young guard was still burning his tongue as he ran down the street. He turned several corners, until he felt reasonably safe in the maze of pathways and alleys.

Who knew if the pair of them had set their fellow guards after him as soon as they let him go? Once Farhad had thought *he* was the only wily trickster in the world—but ever since setting out on this strange journey he had found that other people were just as unpredictable.

234

The first thing Farhad did was to shed his old skin, like a snake, and slip into a new one.

He still had some money from the purse he had stolen. A few hours later, when he walked past a small mirror, it reflected a blond youth with a haircut like English turf and two broad scars under his left cheekbone, as if he were an enthusiastic fencer. The trousers Farhad had put on seemed to him unnecessarily uncomfortable, and he felt sorry for the English who wore these prisons of fabric even in the most tropical heat.

"There," Farhad told his reflection. "Now, my dear Steal, let's see which of us is the greater master of disguise."

And he set off in search of Nitish.

But the tiger might have been swallowed up by the Ganges. The fair-haired English boy into whose skin Farhad had slipped searched for hours, looking in vain for a patch of white fur, the blink of a blue eye, a striped tail moving swiftly through the air.

At first he thought he was simply looking in the wrong places. Finally he began to wonder seriously if something had happened to the tiger.

As afternoon approached, he turned back for the third time to the Ram Ghat, where he had last seen Nitish, lying in the sun beside the freshly washed saris yesterday morning. Farhad sat down on the remains of an old metal rail with several shirts hung over it to dry, watched the calm movement of the flowing water, and put his thoughts in order. Running his hand over the rough, rusty iron, he flinched. The original cut on his palm from the bloodstone was still sore. But he had flinched for another reason, too. There was something on the railing—something that didn't belong there.

Looking more closely, he saw a small piece of paper, folded many times. Someone had tied it to the railing with string. Farhad undid the knot, and as he did so, he felt a kind of presentiment.

The old railing was the only place nearby where you could tie anything. If he himself had wanted to leave information

for someone who was sure to come back to this place, he'd
have tied his message to this rusty railing . . .

A couple of sentences were written on the paper, but in
handwriting that Farhad couldn't read.

That was because he couldn't read at all—neither Tamil
nor Hindi letters, and certainly not the angular, chopped-up
words of the European languages.

He put the note in the pocket of his uncomfortable, tight-
fitting trousers, and set off to look for someone who could tell
him more.

"It's about a tiger," said the old man looking down in surprise
at Farhad.

He was sitting on a stack of brightly colored bales of fabric
in his tailor's shop, which like all the other shops was a good
yard higher than street level—just in case the monsoon burst
the riverbanks. Farhad stood in the narrow alleyway looking
up at the old man.

"That's what I thought," he said.

"A white tiger," added the man in a meaningful tone,
watching Farhad's reaction.

"That's what I thought," Farhad repeated. The man
looked disappointed.

"Read it aloud," Farhad urged him, clinking his money.

"I'm short of time. I have to reach the city in the middle of the desert of Thar and defeat the demon king before the next full moon."

The tailor looked at him over the top of his spectacles and seemed to be wondering if this strange European was quite right in the head. He sighed and read aloud:

> If you want to see the white tiger
> again, bring what I want to the
> Hanuman Ghat by tomorrow evening.
> I have moved into lodgings nearby.
> When I hear the howling of a dog
> followed the next moment by the cry
> of a mynah bird, I will come out
> on the steps. If you are not there by
> sunset tomorrow, it will be too late.
> Then the white tiger must die.
> By the way, you owe your life to me.
> —A Searcher

237

Farhad took the letter back and gave the tailor a few coins. "Thank you," he murmured thoughtfully.

"What does the message mean?" the man asked curiously.

"It's a secret code," replied Farhad. "Of course the tiger isn't really a tiger. And the Hanuman Ghat stands for something else, too. But I can't tell you anything more."

The old man nodded and grinned.

"A secret code," he repeated. "You're going to fight the demon king in the middle of the desert before the next full moon? Well, well."

Then he turned back to his sewing and pulled a red thread through the silk of a cushion cover.

Farhad had gone only a few yards from the tailor's workshop when someone tugged at his shirt. He turned around. A small and very dirty boy was standing there, looking at him wide-eyed.

"I heard all that!" he whispered. "You want to find your tiger, right? The tailor thinks you're crazy, or maybe that it's really a secret code or something. But I've seen your tiger."

"Where?" asked Farhad quickly.

"He passed me," said the boy, "very early this morning."

"What way did he go?"

"I'll tell you for a peisa."

Farhad took a coin out of his pocket. "He went west," said the boy, pointing. "He was following someone. An Englishman, like you. If you give me two rupees, I'll help you to search."

"That," muttered Farhad, annoyed, "was *not* an Englishman. He was a Frenchman. Maybe."

"For three rupees, I'll help you look for a Frenchman, too."

"Three rupees?"

"All right, one rupee and fifty peisas. Because it's you."

Farhad smiled. The little boy reminded him of himself at the same age. "Where are your parents?" he asked.

The boy shrugged his shoulders. "No idea. I never knew them."

"And what do you live on? Looking for tigers?"

The little boy nodded eagerly.

"Very well," said Farhad, digging into his pocket again and putting another coin in the child's sweaty, sticky hand. "If you find the tiger, you'll get two more."

"Three," said the little boy quickly. Farhad bit back his laughter.

Not that he really felt in the least like laughing. He had to find Nitish. He had to find him soon.

Farhad couldn't imagine that the Englishman really had the tiger in his power—such a dangerous animal as the white tiger wasn't to be caught in a mousetrap. On the other hand, suppose he was wrong there . . .

Of course he didn't intend simply to give the man Steal the bloodstone.

He and the little boy searched the city until darkness fell. They asked everyone they met about Nitish, and a few people did remember seeing the white tiger. But where he had gone, no one knew. At first Farhad's temper grew worse and worse. What did Nitish think he was doing, just disappearing? Then he became increasingly anxious. Suppose something had happened to him?

Finally Farhad bought a bag of vadais from a street vendor, little yellow balls of dough filled with onions and coriander leaves, and sat down on the bank of the Ganges to eat them.

The little boy sat down beside him like an expectant dog, and Farhad found himself sharing his food with the child.

The sun was just sinking beyond the river, leaving a pool of light on its waters. It reminded him of the glowing red of the bloodstone. His upper arm still hurt, but it was convenient, he thought, that the cloths tied around it were stained with dried, brownish blood: Now everyone would assume that the bandage was a real one.

The little boy lay down in the dust at Farhad's feet and looked up at the stars. The waxing moon hung among them, and once again it seemed to be ticking time away like a big, shining clock.

It was going to be difficult to get rid of this boy.

"We'll go on looking tomorrow," he said, yawning contentedly. "Then I'm sure to find your tiger, and you'll be very happy and give me a lot of money."

Farhad laughed, but by now he was entertaining serious doubts.

He lay down on his back beside the boy, and he, too, looked up at the stars. "When I was your age," he told the dirty little boy, "I'd have liked to earn money looking for people's tigers myself."

"Where was it, this place where no one lost a tiger?" asked the little boy. "Where did you live when you were my age?"

"Far, far away," replied Farhad. "In Madurai."

"Is it nice there?"

Farhad thought. "Yes," he said. "There's a big temple, and everything looks much greener than here. Sometimes the wind blows from the sea, bringing salty air with it. And in the streets, the women weave garlands of flowers for their hair. It smells sweeter there. It doesn't smell of fire so much."

He heard the love in his voice for his native city, and was surprised. Until now he'd not realized that he loved anything at all.

"Did you bring something from there? Is it what the man who stole the tiger and wrote the letter wants?" asked the little boy.

"No," said Farhad.

"What is it?"

Farhad was silent for a while. He didn't intend to tell the

little boy any more of his story. On the other hand, he could tell him a story so strange that he'd never believe it . . .

"I'll tell you a fairy tale," said Farhad, clearing his throat.

The little boy moved closer. He smelled of a mixture of the dirt in the streets where he lived, the coriander of the vadais, and the inescapable, spicy smoke of the city itself, the smoke of the dead brought from far and wide to have their ashes consigned to the river goddess Ganga.

"Once upon a time," Farhad began, "there was a princess. She was the daughter of Krishna, the god with the cowherd's flute . . ."

242

While he told the story, it was as if he were listening to someone else tell it. His spirit rose above the river and saw the big thief and the little one lying on the bank of the Ganges under the starlight, listening to words running through the night.

The tale of the hero who set off to rescue the beautiful princess from the clutches of Ravana now had a life of its own. It told itself more easily every time, and its words were scented with jasmine and tasted of dates from the palm under which the princess had been dreaming when the demon carried her away. And there was hope in them—a hope so improbable that a fairy tale was the only place for it: the hope of freedom. Freedom for the frightened, waiting princess, freedom for the hero whose cycle of birth and rebirth Krishna had promised to shorten if he bravely faced all that he had to do, freedom for the tiger who was white as snow and fast as the wind, but who wanted to be just an ordinary tiger someday. The radiance of the bloodstone shone out of Farhad's fairy tale like a light in the night, and while he listened to himself, the story seemed as unreal as if it were nothing but a fairy tale.

He hadn't reached the end yet when he heard the regular breathing of the little boy beside him, and soon after that Farhad himself fell asleep.

The white tiger padded through his dreams on silent paws.

He came to Farhad and sat on his chest, and Farhad felt his fur tickling his nose, and sneezed.

"You're sitting on the wound in my arm," said Farhad.

Nitish moved up a bit. "I'm waiting for you," he said. "This time it's *me* they've caught, not you. I'm waiting and waiting—and all you can do is talk about your arm!"

"The bloodstone . . . ," whispered Farhad. "It broke into four and cut me when I fell off the horse and landed on my arm."

"You can ransom me with the bloodstone," said Nitish.

"And then how am I to bribe Suryakanta, the demon king Ravana's servant?"

243

"Into four," said Nitish, and his eyes were gleaming. "Your stone broke into four."

"That's right," said Farhad, and then he added, "You mean . . . ?"

"Of course I do," replied the tiger, laying one of his big white paws on Farhad's arm. "Well?" he asked. "Do you feel that? Does it press down on your wound? I'll feel the same pain when the Englishman kills me."

"How can he kill you?" asked Farhad. "You're a sacred tiger, the work of the gods. You're more than a thousand years old and as swift as the clouds in the sky. How can you die?"

244

"I can die," said Nitish gravely. "I can die like any other living creature in the world. I won't do it of my own accord, and your English friend isn't likely to wait about until I do. He has a gun, Farhad." His blue eyes flashed like lightning, and his whiskers twitched nervously. "A gun full of bullets, a kind of long metal thing. All the British have them. Guns like to destroy tigers. They lick our mouths with their gunpowder tongues, their leaden teeth bite our hearts, their fiery claws gouge out our eyes. They shred our strong muscles and spit our own blood out on our coats. They dig around in our guts and plunge deep into our heads, where our most secret thoughts live. The guns of the British do all that and much more. Do you want to carry your bloodstone into the desert on foot while your English friend shoots me and feeds my remains to the vultures?"

"No," said Farhad, "of course not. Take your paw off my arm now, will you? I think the wound is bleeding again."

Farhad woke up drenched with sweat. The pain in his arm really was worse.

For a while Farhad just lay there, staring at the dark sky. The faint light of a few stars was making its way through the thick clouds, but only with difficulty.

Farhad realized that he was burning, and longed for something to cool him. The wound was beginning to poison his blood and make him sick.

"Nitish," he whispered to the morning air. "I will go to the Hanuman Ghat today, and bark like a dog, and imitate the cry of a mynah bird. I'll give the Englishman a piece of the bloodstone, and then we'll go on again, don't worry."

Farhad sat up and felt his arm. His fingers met something wet. It wasn't only in his dream that the wound had begun bleeding again. He carefully rolled down the bandage to look at it in the first light of dawn.

Also carefully, he felt for the pieces of the stone, which were still firmly wrapped up in the bandage . . . weren't they? *Where exactly* were they wrapped up in it?

Farhad's bleached blond eyebrows drew together in a frown, and he felt the bandage rather more urgently. Finally he took it right off his arm, spread out the little cloths and smoothed them. The marks on the bandage made it seem as if the stone itself had bled when it broke. Gritting his teeth, Farhad carefully felt the countless deep cuts in his arm. Perhaps the pieces of the stone had stuck to his blood and . . . No.

No, they weren't there.

All of a sudden Farhad was wide awake.

He looked around, thought for a moment, and realized that something else wasn't there either: the beggar boy. The beggar boy who, so he had thought, had fallen asleep long before he reached the bloodstone part of his story.

And he understood why the wound was bleeding, and why he had dreamed of the tiger pressing his paw down on it. The bandage had been unwrapped and then wrapped around it again.

Damn.

Farhad Kamal, master swindler and first-class confidence trickster, had been taken in by a younger version of himself.

Such a thing would never have happened to him before he set out on his journey.

Farhad leaped up.

He had only just had that dream. The boy couldn't have gone far yet.

Farhad saw the shadowy figure just before he reached the Manikarnika Ghat, where the smell of fire still hung in the air. The figure was small and agile, and it avoided the great burning ground, still faintly starlit, and black with the ashes of thousands upon thousands of the dead whose bodies had been burned there over the never-ending course of time.

Farhad smelled transience in the air, and a shudder ran down his back. A presentiment, as if something was about to happen to link him more closely to the Manikarnika Ghat. The reflected stars flickered on the surface of the nocturnal Ganges, and the night air seemed to him unusually cool.

Farhad shook himself and followed the figure.

They were both moving through the night as soundlessly as if they were no more than restless, disembodied spirits, and their pale shadows followed them in the starlight as if in a dream.

At the Mir Ghat, the little figure looked back and saw that he wasn't alone. He swiftly turned right, scurried up the steps of the ghat, and disappeared into the labyrinthine confusion of the city.

Farhad followed him.

The boy had an advantage in navigating the maze of alleyways, for this was *his* city. Farhad's own city, Madurai with its many temples, was far away, and he didn't know if he would ever see it again. While he followed the swift shadow of the little boy through the streets of Varanasi, he suddenly seemed to himself lost and homeless—as if he had been traveling for many years, and Madurai had ceased to exist a long time ago.

Keeping the boy in sight was hard work. Several times he thought he had lost him, but then he reappeared on a far corner, and Farhad sprinted in his direction. The boy led him deeper and deeper into the heart of the city, its most ancient center, where only beggars and the very old knew their way around. No strangers came here, and Farhad began to wonder if he would ever find his way out again.

Stray dogs were sleeping curled up together outside the low doors of houses, and here and there a white cow dozed, looking improbably bright in the starlight.

The figure ahead of him scurried into a narrow alley, but when Farhad entered it, there was no one to be seen. He waited for the boy to reappear somewhere, but the alley remained deserted. Only a row of closed doors looked coldly back at Farhad.

Was the boy behind one of those doors at this very

moment? Which one? He could hardly go rousing the entire street from sleep . . .

Had he better sit down on the ground and wait for the boy to come out again? But suppose he had gone through a back door into another alley, and was well away by now?

Farhad couldn't make up his mind.

The red light of dawn was showing in a narrow strip of sky above the alley, laboriously clawing its way higher. Soon the first pilgrims would be saying their morning prayers in the shallow water on the bank of the Ganges.

There was one place, Farhad thought, where the boy was sure to go: the Hanuman Ghat—the place where the Englishman was waiting. He had heard every word of the message that the tailor had read aloud to Farhad. And who would he sell the stone to if not the man who was obviously ready to give anything to own it?

Farhad turned back.

He would wait for the boy at the Hanuman Ghat.

But the city wasn't letting him go so quickly. He had been right to suspect that the maze of old streets and houses was like a giant mousetrap.

As the day slowly grew brighter, Farhad suspected that he was going around in circles. Had he seen that doorway before? Had he already come to this corner? Didn't he know that stunted tree growing out of the wall? Wasn't that the same old man sleeping in the street?

He shook him gently, and the old man opened two empty eyes and looked right through Farhad with his blind gaze.

"The river!" said Farhad urgently. "How do I get to the river?"

The old man closed his eyes again. "The Ganges!" cried Farhad in a louder voice. "I have to get to the Ganges. How do I find my way to Mother Ganga? What street must I take to reach the river?"

The old man reached out his hands to fend him off, and Farhad stopped shaking him. Then the old man fell into a high, mindless chant, rocking his torso back and forth, apparently oblivious of the world around him. Farhad let go of him and clenched his fists.

Why wasn't there anyone here he could ask?

He raced on, running up and down among the buildings like a hunted animal, getting more lost in the alleyways all the time. He'd never find his way out. He'd arrive too late. Very likely the boy had been back at the river for a long time now. Perhaps he was talking to Steal at this very minute. Perhaps he'd already been paid for the jewel. Perhaps Steal wouldn't be there when Farhad arrived. He'd have disappeared without trace, and Farhad would never even be able to find

Nitish again. His panic grew until it filled him entirely, and he stopped.

Farhad felt his heart beat painfully against his ribs, and he tried hard to breathe more slowly. He looked down the street, one of an infinite number of streets. There was a wall on one side, with cowpats looking like bricks set out to dry on it in neat and tidy rows: fodder for the city's insatiable fires.

But a few yards farther on, a grating was fixed into the masonry of the wall at knee height. Hesitantly, Farhad went over to it. Two small statues stood in a niche behind the grating.

Rice and fresh flower petals lay at their feet, the remains of the wicks of tiny lamps left as offerings were scattered on the floor, and a garland of dried marigolds hung on the grating, which was black with soot.

He had come upon one of the tiny temples hidden away in the most unexpected places in every city—and it didn't take him a moment to recognize the brightly painted statues that stood before him: The god playing the flute and the beautiful woman beside him were none other than Krishna and his wife Radha. Krishna had closed his eyes and was absorbed in his flute music. And Radha, the personification of the loving, adoring wife, stood at his side with her eyelids devoutly lowered.

Then Farhad did something he had never done before: He crouched down in the middle of the street to pray.

"I have nothing to offer you," he whispered through the grating. "Nothing at all. No flowers, no rice, no ghee lamp— not even a good idea. But I need your help. Couldn't you lead me out of these streets? How am I to set your daughter free if I'm left wandering in this maze forever? How am I to reach the city in the middle of the desert if I can't find the white tiger again? I know you want me to do all this by myself. But I'm not a hero."

Farhad didn't expect anything to happen. He was praying to calm his racing heart more than anything else. But suddenly the clay figure of the god opened his eyes. He took the flute out of his mouth. His lips, which were painted bright blue in his white face, parted. And he spoke.

"Farhad Kamal," he said, and his voice was the voice that had spoken to Farhad once before. In that voice he heard the wind whispering in the trees of Madurai, and the water rippling in the pool where he had seen the glint of silver in the lotus flower . . .

"Farhad Kamal," said Krishna, "you *are* a hero."

Every instinct in Farhad told him to move away from the little shrine, but he forced himself to stay crouching quietly in front of it.

"You see?" Krishna went on, and something like a smile appeared on his lips. "Last time we met you avoided me. You wailed like a child and wrung your hands. Now you hold my gaze. You have ridden with the wind, you have been through water. You will find the way again. Do not fear."

"But what am I to do?" cried Farhad desperately. "What am I to do to find it?"

"Climb up on high, hero," whispered Radha. "There you will see what you need to see."

"What?" whispered Farhad, bewildered. "How?"

But the two statues were standing rigid and still in their shrine again, eyes closed, deep in their silent devotions.

Had they ever moved?

Farhad found that he was clutching the grating with both hands. He let go of it and stood up.

Climb up on high . . . Hero . . .

He looked up to where bright dawn now stood in the sky.

And a moment later, he understood.

He ran down the street to the end of the wall, where he found a good place and jumped up on it like a cat. From there he climbed on to the next house and crossed its flat roof, until he came to a taller house . . . and then, at last, he saw what he wanted to see: Krishna had been right. The gleaming river lay just beyond the forest of houses, and praying pilgrims adorned its bank like the marigolds in ceremonial garlands.

Farhad's heart lifted again and sang like a little bird in his breast. He didn't climb down into the street. Ducking low, he raced at high speed over the houses, jumping from roof to roof, balancing on crumbling walls, once even getting across a small temple courtyard. And finally he reached the broad promenade along the bank of the Ganges.

There he dropped to the ground and was at the Hanuman Ghat before the pilgrims had finished their first prayer in the light of the day's young sun. He saw no one among them who looked like the Englishman, but that didn't mean anything.

Had he arrived too late?

On the left of the long flight of steps leading down into the water stood a dense conglomeration of houses. Subclavian Steal must have found lodgings somewhere there. Farhad felt desperation rise in him again, growing rampantly like a wild, poisonous plant. How was he ever to find Steal here?

He hid in the shadow of a ledge, under the branches of a bougainvillea that had come up, long ago, through a crack in the stones of the steps, and had then taken over the wall in front of the tumbledown houses.

Farhad kept watch on the steps through the purple flowers.

If the Englishman was an Englishman at the moment,

then it was still early morning for him, and presumably he was asleep. But who knew what he might have changed himself into by now? Anyway, no doubt he would turn up here sooner or later.

Merging into the bougainvillea, Farhad waited.

He did not wait in vain.

After a while, a thin, shadowy figure appeared on the flight of steps . . . but no, now, in the light of morning, it wasn't shadowy anymore. Farhad clearly recognized the boy with whom he had shared his supper and who had listened to him telling a fairy tale.

Now the little thief had come to collect the reward for the hero of the fairy tale.

Farhad clenched his fists behind his back.

For a moment he considered leaving the shelter of the climbing bougainvillea and taking the stone away from the little boy. But no. The nimble child would run away again, then look for another place to meet the Englishman, making it even more difficult for Farhad to find him.

So Farhad stayed in the shadows like a snake lying in wait. His opportunity would come.

The barking of a stray dog, the cry of a black-feathered, yellow-eyed mynah bird.

255

That was what the Englishman had written in his message, and those were the sounds heard that morning on the steps of the Hanuman Ghat, for the little thief was there, lured by the hope of money.

Only a few yards away, a tiny window opened in the wall above Farhad, and two doves that had been dozing on the narrow sill fluttered up in alarm.

The little boy tilted his head back and narrowed his eyes against the light of the brightness now growing in the sky.

"Who are you?" Farhad heard the Englishman ask. He was looking for *him*, his cellmate in prison, the begging monk, the rider of a fallen British official's horse, condemned to death and then set free—the white tiger's friend.

But all his observant bright eyes could see on the steps was a boy about ten or eleven years old.

"Here I am," said the child. And Farhad imagined the Englishman's astonishment. Was he wondering for a moment whether Farhad had actually succeeded in turning himself into a little boy?

"You?" asked Steal, and he opened the squealing shutter of the window a little further. "What do you want?"

"Come down," said the boy, "and you'll see. The dog has barked, the mynah bird has called. Didn't you hear it?"

"Yes . . . ," murmured the Englishman thoughtfully.

"Very well," he said at last. "I'll come down. But if you've woken me just to hear the sound of a mynah bird's call and nothing else, then may all the gods known to Kashi, the City of Light, have mercy on you."

Farhad saw the little boy shifting restlessly from foot to foot like a temple elephant in its chains. He himself still wasn't sure what to do. The Englishman was taking his time. Farhad's fingers itched. Should he . . . Shouldn't he . . .

He'd do it. Now, before Steal came out. He tensed his muscles as Nitish would have done under his white coat and prepared to spring.

Then the door opened, and Steal came out.

Farhad cursed himself for hesitating, and blended into the bougainvillea surrounding him once more.

"I've brought you something," said the little boy. "Something as red as blood and brighter than the sun. Can you guess what it is?"

"Indeed I can," growled Steal. "But where did you get it?"

"From someone who didn't keep a close enough watch on it," replied the boy. "If you want what I've brought you, you'll have to pay a good price. The riverbank down there is full of pilgrims. See them? Some of them are watching us. It wouldn't be a good idea to take something from me by force when I want to let you have it without any violence."

"That's not what I had in mind," replied Steal. "Money doesn't matter to me."

"It matters to me," said the boy, grinning.

"And money you will have," said the Englishman. "Any amount of it, for all I care. What matters to me," he said, lowering his voice to a whisper, although the pilgrims were certainly too far away to hear his words, "what matters to me is the stone. You do have it, am I right? Do you have it?"

The boy nodded.

As for Farhad in his hiding place, he wondered for the first time just why the man of many faces and those light, foreign eyes was pursuing the stone with such greed.

If money didn't matter to him, then he didn't want the stone to sell it. But what did he want it for? It was almost as though the bloodstone had some magical power of attraction that drew the Englishman to it, a magnetic force that it had exerted, ever since it came into being, on those whose hearts offered ground where its blood-red radiance could take root. To Farhad's surprise, he felt none of that magic himself. He just wanted to bring the stone to its journey's end, and then, he hoped, never to set eyes on it again.

"Where is it?" asked the Englishman, coming closer to the boy, who retreated down the steps.

"I can't show it to you," said the boy. "Not now. Not here."

Steal laughed. "I see. You can't show it to me, but I'm supposed to believe you have it, is that so?"

"There's nothing to be done about that at the moment," said the boy. "I had to bring the stone with me in a special, safe way. If its owner had caught me, he'd have taken it away from me again, right?" The boy looked mysterious. "Well, he wouldn't have found it. The stone is in an absolutely safe place. Give me your protection for a day or two, so that your friend can't get his hands on it. Then you'll have what you want."

As he spoke, Farhad could see the Englishman's features harden with distrust.

"And what's that supposed to mean?" he asked with growing anger. "A day or two and I'll have it? When, exactly?"

"I can't say," said the boy, feeling for the ground behind him with his feet as he moved another step down. The old flight of stone steps was slippery with dirt and moss and the slimy remains of the last downpour of the monsoon.

"You can't say?" Steal's voice became an angry growl, and he moved closer to the boy. "*Where is the stone?*" he hissed. "*Where is it?*"

"I can't say that either just now," replied the boy, grinning. "But it's in safe keeping." And he grinned even more broadly, proud and sure of victory.

259

Perhaps it was his grin that finally infuriated the Englishman. Perhaps it was Steal's disappointed hope of closing his fingers around the stone at that moment. Perhaps it was the stress and strain of the days in which he had lost track of Farhad and the stone, before they both arrived in Varanasi. Perhaps it was all these things together.

Anyway, Steal lost control.

He lunged at the boy, his large hands outstretched, a curse on his lips, and Farhad saw the confident grin disappear from the little boy's face and his eyes widen, like the eyes of a rabbit facing a cobra.

He jumped back, and the Englishman's hands closed on empty air.

But the boy seemed to have forgotten that he was still standing at the top of a flight of steps.

He landed on the edge of a step, stumbled for a moment, with both arms up in the air as if he were doing a strange dance, slipped on the smooth stone, tried to recover, and finally cried out as he lost his balance. The slippery stone beneath his feet was no help. He fell down the steps unchecked, rolling over and over at terrifying speed.

Farhad had never noticed before just how steep the Hanuman Ghat was.

The boy tumbled all the way down.

The people by the river had heard him scream, and they all saw him falling.

He landed at the feet of a pilgrim with an orange cloth around his hips. The pilgrim stared at him, wide-eyed. Even from above, Farhad saw the surprise in the man's gaze. It was reflected in the faces of all the other people down by the water.

The man bent over the boy and tried to help him to his feet. But then he stopped.

Farhad saw him put his hand in front of the boy's mouth and nose, and then he shook his head. There was no breath left in that slight body.

The hard stone steps of the Hanuman Ghat had ended his wretched life, to lead him to a new one.

If there was ever anything unlikely, thought Farhad, it was for someone to break his neck, out of the blue, on the steps of the Hanuman Ghat.

And if someone does break his neck on the steps of the Hanuman Ghat, it is very unlikely indeed for him to be the one and only person in the city who knows where a certain jewel is.

If the boy had fallen only a little farther, he would have ended up in the Ganges.

Those who died in the waters of the Ganges, so it was

said, went straight to Nirvana and redemption. Those whom the Ganges took to itself escaped the cycle of birth and reincarnation, life and suffering. All who felt their time coming went on pilgrimage to the Ganges, hoping to die in the river.

The beggar boy down there had very nearly succeeded.

Farhad was standing perfectly still all this time, hidden by the climbing bougainvillea, and he realized that he felt dizzy.

He had just lost contact with the bloodstone for the last time. He had seen the younger copy of himself die. It was a little too much all at once, even for a hardened master thief and small-time criminal.

And he asked himself what *that* meant.

A Light as Bright as the Sun

L IFE IN ITSELF ISN'T VALUED HIGHLY IN India, but even there it has its price.

Subclavian Steal saw the eyes of the people down by the river, and he was painfully aware that at this moment he was an Englishman.

He was even more painfully aware that two Englishmen had recently died at the hands of a furious Indian mob.

Slowly and calmly, he went down the steps of the Hanuman Ghat.

The boy's limp body lay there at a strangely distorted angle, and Steal knelt down beside it under the eyes of the pilgrims. Although he knew it was pointless, he checked once more that there was no life left in the boy. The pilgrims' eyes followed every move he made.

Steal looked up, and infinite pain and deep grief were reflected on his features, which were used to reflecting such things when he didn't really feel them inside him at all.

"He was my servant," said Subclavian Steal in a broken voice. Then it occurred to him that some of the people by the river might be natives of the city themselves, and would know the beggar boy from seeing him in the streets of Varanasi. And as they would also know that the tall stranger with the fair complexion was *not* usually to be seen in those streets, he quickly added, "Whenever I visited the City of Light in these last few years, he worked for me, and I was very fond of him. Poor child. He was a beggar and a thief, but he had a good heart."

Murmurs of distress surrounded him like a swarm of bees buzzing.

The bees might still sting, but they were prepared to believe him and confine themselves to buzzing. Good.

"His body will have to be burned," said the pilgrim at whose feet the boy had fallen. "That will take wood."

"The boy has no family," said another man. "I knew him. Someone will have to be found to pay for the wood. Even the cheapest wood doesn't come for free."

Subclavian Steal understood what they meant, and rose to his feet. Placing his hands together, he bowed slightly and said, "I am not of your faith, wise men. But I respect your customs. I will provide the wood and pay the priest to say prayers over the boy's body. You need not fear for his soul."

Once again there was a murmur of approval around him. And deep inside, where no one could see it, he breathed a sigh of relief.

Now there was just one question to be cleared up—and it was the most important question of all: Did the boy really have the bloodstone on him? Or had he somehow gotten the message left for Farhad, and thought he would try to extract money from Steal? Was the stone still in the hands of that young Indian trickster whose white tiger had gone missing?

265

From above, Farhad saw the Englishman crouching beside the boy's motionless body and talking to the onlookers. He soundlessly emerged from the bougainvillea and was soon mingling with the people by the river. He kept a little way to one side, for although he too was outwardly a European at the moment, Steal might recognize him if he was too far to the front of the crowd.

The Englishman picked the boy up in his arms as if he were his own dead son, and standing very straight and looking very composed, he strode away with him in the direction of the Manikarnika Ghat.

Some of the crowd followed, and Farhad joined them. A few people seemed to wonder why a British youth would be taking such an interest in the incident, but Farhad pretended not to understand much of what they said, and he just nodded and smiled.

The Brahmans at the Manikarnika Ghat were still busy with the ceremony being held for another corpse, accompanied by countless members of the dead man's family. He must have been one of those who have their bodies brought here from far away, thought Farhad, carried on a litter to Varanasi for their ashes to mingle with the waters of the sacred river.

The wood that this other dead body could afford smelled of perfume and expensive oils.

The varieties of timber used for pyres were of as many kinds as the castes and histories of the dead burned on them. People were burned on a pyre that was right for them and the depth of their purses. The wood used to burn poor people was light in color, fibrous, and dry as straw. It smelled of nothing but ashes.

When at last the priests could spare a moment, the Englishman chose wood under the stern gaze of the pilgrims, and spoke quietly to the officiating Brahman.

While the pyre was being built, Steal seemed to think he
was not being observed. And he was almost right. Those who
had come to the burning ground with him were now attracted
to the splendors of the other ceremony, watching with both
respect and envy in their eyes. They were gazing at the fine
clothes of the family standing around the fire and looking into
the flames, the richly decorated litter with yellow tongues of
flame now licking at it, the garlands of flowers around the
dead man's neck . . .

All this magnificence dazzled the crowd, and they forgot
the poor little body of the beggar boy. Only one man had not
forgotten him: the Englishman.

Farhad was crouching in the shadow of a stack of timber
and watching him like a cat. Steal had knelt down beside the
boy again and was desperately searching his clothes for the
bloodstone. He felt around inside the pockets of the ragged
shirt more and more impatiently, unwrapped the cloth that
the boy was wearing around his hips, searched every inch of
his bony body . . . and found nothing.

Farhad heard him curse quietly.

He heard himself curse, too, even more quietly.

Where had the boy hidden the four parts of the bloodstone? Were they lying safely concealed somewhere in the
maze of the Old Town, in a place where no one could ever find

them? What had the boy meant when he said he couldn't tell Steal exactly how long he would have to wait for the stone?

Had he pawned the thing after all? No thief in his right mind would do so. It just made no sense.

Finally one of the Brahmans beckoned the Englishman over, and he picked up the little beggar's body to lay it on the freshly built pyre. The boy seemed to weigh almost nothing. Farhad saw two other thin boys hanging around nearby, watching wide-eyed as the Brahman kindled the fire. The two of them stared, as if hypnotized, at the flames licking around the dead body.

Farhad wondered if they were friends of the dead boy.

Briefly, the flames shot up and began devouring the wood with a greedy crackling sound. They charred the boy's skin and caught his hair, and a little later the sweetish smell of smoldering flesh spread over the burning ground. For a moment it was so strong that Farhad's stomach heaved.

Steal stood beside the fire for a little longer, watching it begin to turn the boy into a black mass. Then he shook his head and disappeared into the turmoil of the city. Farhad stayed where he was.

If two people are looking for each other, he thought, it's no use for both of them to move around in circles. One of them must stand still and wait patiently for the other to come to him. The bloodstone and he had lost each other—and chasing after it hadn't been any help. So now he would wait. But he couldn't wait long.

He had until sunset. After that, Nitish would be lost. And with him any chance of reaching the demon king's palace in time. Where *was* the tiger? Where was the stone? Where was Krishna, who could have helped him?

Farhad's head felt heavy from lack of sleep the night before, and his eyes were closing.

The sun climbed higher above the river, higher and higher, its heat united with the heat of the fire into a single glowing ball, which rolled along an unbearably long track through the dreams of Farhad's half-sleeping mind.

269

When he opened his eyes again there were clouds in the sky. The monsoon season wasn't over yet. But the rain clouds had brought a flock of birds with them: large, dark birds with a slow and dignified way of moving. Vultures.

They gathered in the air above the two pyres waiting for the rain to fall. For rain would put the fires out early. Anything not entirely burned was thrown into the Ganges with the ashes, and the vultures were hoping to snatch a few fragments of it.

Farhad instinctively shook himself, and imagined them carrying away pieces of half-charred flesh in their beaks, triumphing over life . . .

He hoped the rain would keep them waiting a little longer.

But then he saw that the vultures weren't after the dead flesh. They were hunting something. Something small and inconspicuous. In surprise, Farhad watched the flight of a frightened bird being chased by the vultures. It was a pigeon, a silvery gray pigeon with shiny black button eyes.

Farhad had never seen a vulture chase another bird before. Vultures usually lie in wait; they are persistent creatures with plenty of time. But these vultures, Farhad thought, were clearly after the pigeon. And now he saw that it had a red ring around its foot: a breeder's mark.

He shaded his eyes with his hand and watched as the panic-stricken bird tried fluttering faster. It was fluttering straight toward him—him and the fire.

And not only did it have a red ring around its foot, there was a little roll of paper stuck in the ring. This was a carrier pigeon. Carrier pigeons, so he had heard, could tell exactly where they were going, and once they knew their destination, nothing in the world would keep them from reaching it. They would fly until they were exhausted; no ocean, no desert, no enemy front was too dangerous for them. A kind of obsession with carrying out their task was bred into them, and it had once been rumored that many breeders bewitched their birds instead of just raising them.

But this pigeon must have lost its way.

Farhad bent down, picked up a stone, and threw it.

"Go away!" he called. "Get out! It's not me you want!"

But the pigeon was not deterred. It kept flying straight to him, bringing the vultures after it like a living, dangerous train. He saw its eyes flash, and retreated toward the fire. He could feel the biting heat behind him.

And then Farhad realized: No, the pigeon had not lost its way.

It was heading for *him*.

He watched it tumbling through the air toward him, saw its separate gray and white feathers. Still the pigeon didn't slow down. The sharp beaks of the vultures gleamed above Farhad, and he put out his hands to offer the pigeon shelter from its black pursuers' claws.

But all he caught was the roll of paper on its foot. The red ring broke, and the pigeon flapped its wings wildly. It looked as if it were trying to brake its wild, crazy flight at the very last minute.

However, it was too late, and the little bird was too panic-stricken. Without a sound, the pigeon plunged past Farhad into the flames. He heard the greedy hiss of the fire as it consumed the bird. And he heard the pigeon's death cry.

He had never known before that such birds could cry

out as they died. He had only ever heard them cooing in the afternoon in rich people's gardens.

So he stood there confused and horrified by the fire, with the rolled-up letter in his hand, at a loss.

The vultures landed on the charred, burning ground in front of him and shook their feathers. The largest of them, which had wings as untidy and full of gaps as Farhad's thoughts, put its head on one side and stared at him. Farhad saw its eyes gleam, as if a little of the fire blazed in the vulture, too.

"Shoo!" said Farhad. "Get out! There's nothing for you vultures here!"

But he had the feeling that there *was* something, and he clutched the letter so tightly that his knuckles hurt.

Why would the vultures want this letter? Was he going crazy?

They opened their beaks in a hungry, angry croak, and Farhad felt as if they were trying to talk to him. *How small!* they seemed to be saying. *How small you are! How lost! They tell tales of a great hero, and we came to see him. But all we find is a thin young man losing his mind!*

Farhad heard the dead boy's hollow bones singing, heard his ribs crack and his skull burst in the heat—and Farhad's guts contracted, as if he were the one who must burn.

The tousled vulture flapped its huge, untidy wings as if it agreed. *One day you'll be lying on a pyre, too, motionless, lifeless, hopeless.* Farhad read what it was saying in the flapping of those wings. *You will be just like the boy behind you. And soon, my hero, soon!*

Farhad had to exert all his strength of mind to keep from retreating even farther.

"Who are you?" he whispered. "What do you want of me?"

Then an absurd idea came to him.

"Ravana," he whispered.

The largest of the vultures unexpectedly fluttered up, flew toward Farhad, and reached its claws out for the roll of paper that he was still clutching. Farhad cried out and defended himself. He struck out with both arms, saw an explosion of feathers and flashing eyes, and once again Farhad felt as if he could hear the bird whispering secret words to him.

A poor sort of hero, it seemed to whisper. *I can sense that you, too, will betray the one who sends you. You want to steal the princess's heart. You will pay for that. Wait until the fire is devouring you . . .*

Then the vulture suddenly stopped attacking Farhad and made its way up into the sky where the clouds were piling into ever higher mountains.

Farhad stood motionless, staring after it.

The other vultures flew up, too.

Farhad opened his fingers that were clutching the paper, and the letter slipped out of them and sailed into the flames. He spun around, saw the paper catch fire—and for a moment he thought he had lost it. Like a big, burning butterfly, the letter staggered helplessly through the air for a second or so, then Farhad reached for it, snatched it, and screamed. The fire had scorched his hand. He dropped the letter, trampled on it, and a little later he was smoothing out the charred and crumpled paper on his knees.

The words on it were still legible. But of course Farhad couldn't read.

He looked around. The two little boys were still crouching nearby. The other curious onlookers had gone away—except for a young woman he hadn't noticed before who was sitting on a stone and mending a piece of cloth. Now and then she glanced up at the sky anxiously, as if it were in her own interest for the two funeral fires to burn down to the very last remnants before the rain.

It was as if these stragglers had seen nothing of the dove and the vultures—or of how Farhad had jumped up and down on the burning letter like a big cat catching an insect.

Had his sun-singed brain simply imagined all that?

But no—he was holding the letter. The letter for which the pigeon had flown into the fire.

Farhad stood up and went hesitantly over to the young woman.

He tried to guess her caste. She looked neat and clean— neat and clean in the way of the very poor. He needn't feel afraid to speak to her.

"Excuse me," he said. "I have a letter . . ."

The woman looked up.

Sathia Ramia Prakash had not always sat by the Ganges mending cloth and staring at funeral pyres. As a child she had dreamed of seeing the world beyond the stuffy streets by the river.

There had been a time when she learned to read and write in a large garden, under the branches of a mimosa with feathery leaves. A better time, long, long ago. Her mother had worked in a rich man's house, and Sathia used to sit in the corner, wide-eyed and listening, when a private tutor came to teach the rich man's children.

So now, when the untidy young man before her held out a piece of paper, that memory suddenly returned. She saw the mimosa leaves and heard the children laughing. And she smiled.

"I have a letter," said the untidy young man. "And I can't read it. Is there anyone here on the ghat who can read?"

"I can," she replied, and observed his astonishment with pride.

Then she gently took the charred paper from his hand. Her eyes had forgotten with the years, but her heart remembered.

"*My dear hero,*" she read.

Farhad saw the young woman cast a quick glance at him.

"*My dear hero,*" she repeated. "*You know who I am.*"

No, thought Farhad. I've no idea.

"*Maybe you are surprised to hear from me at this late date.*"

What? Farhad thought.

"*But I have only just managed to find someone who can make sure that my message reaches you. A great many secret letters are passed in the shade of the gardens here. However, only now have I met the one who is master of these secrets.*"

Secrets? Gardens? Messages? Perhaps the letter really was for someone else. Nonsense, he thought. The pigeon . . .

"*It is all my fault,*" the woman read on. "*I see everything that is happening, and if you are harmed I will never forgive myself. But I cannot save you; it is you who can save me.*

I think of you daily, and wait with great longing. My longing is as great as the desert and as wide as the sky.

You were right to stay where you are. The bloodstone will find its way to you again. Unless it rains.

Be constant and fearless . . . I can't read the signature," said the woman. "It looks as if something has burned it."

Farhad took the letter from her sinewy hands and stared at it in silence.

Who was it who saw everything that was happening? Where were the gardens in which the master of secrets lived?

Who could know that the bloodstone would find its way to him again—unless it rained?

Not a drop was falling yet. The fire had half consumed the boy's body. Here and there his bones appeared through the bright flames, like the framework of a burning house.

"Did you see the vultures?" Farhad asked abruptly.

The young woman nodded.

He hesitated. "And did you . . . Did you hear them speak to me?"

She shook her head. "There's a proverb here in Varanasi," she said, smiling. "The vultures speak to those with something on their conscience."

Farhad said nothing.

He felt the weight of the words he had heard in the wing-beats of the vultures. Would he betray Krishna? Would he come to the same end as the beggar boy? And was he to blame for the boy's death?

He looked thoughtfully at the young woman, who had gone back to her sewing. She wasn't beautiful. Her nose was too long and slightly hooked, and one of her eyes strayed to the right as if it wanted to hide. But there was something open and friendly in her face that made him feel ashamed of himself for thinking of nothing but the jewel.

Farhad Kamal hadn't known that he *could* feel ashamed of himself.

"Did you know him?" he asked at last.

"Not really," she said. "No one knew him. But if anyone did know him just a little, then maybe it was me."

"When I was a child," said Farhad, "I was like him. I saw him fall. He fell down the steps."

"I know," said the woman gently. She spoke without any bitterness, as if it were inevitable for the boy to have fallen down the steps. And she was right: It was too late to do anything to stop it.

"Sometimes he came to see us," the woman went on. "When my husband wasn't at home. I used to give him something to eat."

"Why?" asked Farhad.

The woman shrugged her shoulders and glanced at the

two boys, who looked even smaller and dirtier than the dead child. "I feed them all."

She picked up her sewing things again and went on threading her needle through the fabric, as if her conversation with Farhad came second to her work.

"I don't understand," said Farhad. "You don't look as if you have much money. Why do you feed the children?"

"They once stole all our washing," said the woman. "Off the wall outside. They were trying to sell it to anyone who would buy it in the market. All kinds of things: saris, shirts . . ." She smiled again. "I'd gone to buy rice. Instead I bought our washing back. Since then I've fed them."

"But I don't understand," said Farhad again.

"You don't have to," said the woman. After a moment she added, "He came to see me not long ago. He was scared."

"What of?" asked Farhad, pretending innocence.

"I don't know. He knocked on our door, very softly, and I let him in. He was out of breath. He said someone was following him, and I must help him."

"Yes?" Farhad leaned closer to her. "Did he give you anything that he wanted you to hide?"

She looked at him in surprise, and then slowly shook her head. "No," she said. "Why?"

"Oh, I—I was just thinking. A thief being followed . . .

Well, he usually has something with him that the person following him wants back."

"I see," said the woman. "No, he just said he had to stay with me a moment and wait. Until whoever was after him had gone away. But then he climbed through the window into the yard and off over the wall. I couldn't persuade him to wait any longer. He said he had to see someone urgently, and it was important business." She smiled again. "He always had important business. Whenever he turned up. Sometimes he needed money, sometimes a place to hide—and he always said that if the important business worked out he'd be rich, and then he would buy me a blue sari with gold embroidery and I could walk through the streets in it looking beautiful."

"So he thought this business of his would make him rich."

"Very rich," said someone behind Farhad. "But I told him not to do it."

Farhad spun around.

The two dirty little boys were standing behind him.

"He had something terrible with him," whispered one of them.

"But he didn't believe it was terrible," the other whispered. Their large, dark eyes were even larger and darker with horror now. "We knew this was going to happen," said one of them.

"What did he have with him?" asked Farhad, although of course he knew.

The little boys looked around, and then one of them leaned forward and whispered, "The bloodstone."

"But there's no such thing," said Farhad. "It's only a rumor. It doesn't exist."

"Oh, yes, it does," said the second little boy. "We've seen it."

Farhad felt triumphant. "How large is it, then?" he asked.

"It was in four pieces," said the other little boy. "Rahul showed it to us. Just for a moment. He was in a hurry, but he wanted to show us how rich he was going to be. We told him it wasn't a good idea. There's a curse on the stone."

"But Rahul always said he didn't believe in gods and curses," added the second little boy, wiping his dripping nose with the back of his hand.

"And now he's dead," said the first boy.

"Do you know where the stone is?" asked Farhad.

The two little boys nodded. "But we wouldn't touch it. Not even if it was right here in front of us. Stealing is one thing. The gods are something else."

"Did he say he wanted to hide it with someone?" asked

the woman in alarm, and she added, very firmly, "I would *not* like to have a thing like that lying about my house. If he did leave it there somewhere, and I don't know about it . . ."

"He didn't leave it anywhere," said one of the little boys with a cunning grin. "Rahul sometimes showed off, but he wasn't stupid."

He cast a quick look around and then whispered, in conspiratorial tones, "He swallowed it."

Of course. Now it all made sense. The pieces of the stone had been small enough to be swallowed.

"I can't say exactly how long you'll have to wait . . . A day or two . . ."

Rahul hadn't known exactly when the stone would make its natural way out into the light of day again. Not a bad idea, Farhad had to admit. But very foolish, he thought a second later.

For clever as the beggar boy had been, he had made a deadly mistake. He had not, after all, died of a broken neck on the steps of the Hanuman Ghat. The sharp edges of the broken bloodstone had slit his guts open, making the boy bleed to death internally. The black irony of his fate was that the moment of his death coincided with the moment of his fall.

As Farhad's train of thought reached this point, the first raindrops fell.

A little later, water was pouring from the sky as fast as it always does in the monsoon. Farhad saw the two fires struggling with it. The members of the rich corpse's family pulled their saris and scarves over their heads, and some put up umbrellas.

The flames flickered, fought the water, and died down gradually, one by one.

Then the two pyres were nothing but two black mounds of ashes. No one was going to investigate what precisely was inside them.

The priests helped to take the remains to the river. They began with the rich man, and a sea of floating white flowers accompanied his clogged ashes down the sacred Ganges.

Then the priests set about shoveling the remains of the second pyre into the river. Farhad simply picked up one of their shovels and helped.

Feverishly, he turned over the charred remains of the wood and dug through what was left of the boy.

Narrowing his eyes, he searched the gray black ashes, sticky now with rain, with a nervous humming in his ears. He felt the eyes of the two little beggars and the woman watching his back.

But he had no time to think about them now.

If the broken stone found its way into the Ganges he would never see it again. He might be able to ride the wind, but he still couldn't swim. And even if he could, once the mud at the bottom of the Ganges swallowed something up, it lay buried in the river's unfathomable depths forever.

When all the ashes had been shoveled into the Ganges, every last little piece of charred wood, every small bone that hadn't burned, Farhad stood on the riverbank, breathing heavily.

"The skulls," said one of the Brahmans, looking at a dark shape floating down the river. "The skulls burn worst. There's always part of the skulls left. We ought to think about that. Maybe it means something."

So saying, he turned and walked away through the rain, with his shovel over his shoulder.

Farhad's sweat mingled with the rain on his skin. A handful of red flower petals floated past him, and he turned. There stood the woman with the slightly hooked nose, smiling for the last time that day.

Then she, too, left the burning ground.

The rich man's family had left long ago for someplace drier, and Farhad could see no sign of the two dirty little boys, either.

He stood all alone on the Manikarnika Ghat, with a shovel in his hand that didn't belong to him, and that he didn't even want to steal. What would he do with a shovel?

Somehow it made him sad to think that the wish to make off with it, however pointless, didn't flicker up in him even for a second.

He went back to all that remained of the pyre. Nothing but wood that hadn't been burned lay there now. The rain had colored it dark, and it would have to dry out for a long time before it could be used for the next corpse.

Farhad crouched down in the rain beside the pitiful, wet little heap and watched the Ganges soaking up the raindrops as it flowed, always in the same direction.

The rain brought evening on faster than usual, and slow, desolate dusk began to fall around Farhad.

He stacked up a few of the charred pieces of wood in a tower, like a child who doesn't know what to do. He put a large, dirty stone on top of the tower.

He noticed that the rain was making him cold. He sneezed and the tower fell over. The stone rolled aside. Its sooty, dirty surface had a mark on it.

A red streak.

Red as blood.

Farhad looked more closely.

Then he picked up the stone and rubbed it on the uncomfortable British trousers that he was still wearing. Under the soot, it glowed red in his fingers, and he cried out.

Something had cut his fingertips.

But the red wasn't his blood.

The stone itself was red.

Red and about the size of a pigeon's egg.

Farhad carefully cleaned it, and then looked at it in utter disbelief.

It was here.

The bloodstone, and it was a single stone again.

The fire—or death—or something else that no one would ever understand had fitted its pieces together once more.

The rain stopped, and the clouds moved away.

Farhad looked with satisfaction at the bandage that he had wrapped around his arm again, just to be on the safe side, and then he glanced up at the sky. He saw the sunset still glowing like the wick of a lamp, and then its light began to fade.

And he remembered the Englishman's message.

If you are not there by sunset tomorrow . . .

The sun sets fast in India.

Farhad leaped up and raced along the bank of the Ganges.

Minutes later all was dark around him. A fire glowed here and there in the darkness, that was all, and the enticing aroma of rice and curry rose to his nostrils. But he didn't stop.

The bark of a dog and the cry of a mynah bird. The words drummed in his heart as he ran. The bark of a dog and the cry of a mynah bird . . . A yellow-billed mynah bird. A yellow . . . A yellow . . .

Struggling for breath, he stopped.

The Hanuman Ghat lay there, unlit, black, and silent.

The bark of the dog and the cry of the mynah bird went unheard. No window opened anywhere in the towering building, no door squealed anywhere. No hasty feet ran down any of the steep old steps.

He had come too late.

Farhad looked frantically around, although there was nothing to be seen.

He had to find Nitish.

Toward evening, Nitish woke from a late-afternoon nap and saw light falling through the cracks in the shed walls. His mind was full of mingled hunger and impatience.

Impatience won the upper hand.

Why was nothing happening? Where was Farhad? Had he by any chance forgotten Nitish?

He couldn't have traveled on without him, could he?

No, impossible. That thin and slippery young man was much too weak and much too slow to undertake the long journey to the middle of the desert all alone.

Something must have happened that kept Farhad from finding him.

The tiger stood up, stretched, yawned, and began padding up and down inside the shed. He knew every bit of it—he had done nothing the day before but pace up and down between its walls.

They were too strong for him. He had tried to damage them by clawing at them and throwing his whole weight against them, but they hadn't budged. And now he had a long splinter in the pad of his left forepaw.

288

It had stopped raining very suddenly. And now Nitish saw the sun setting through a chink. Another day had passed, and still Farhad hadn't come to set him free. Wasn't he going to come at all? Nitish put his big head on one side, straining his ears.

He heard something. Footsteps. But they weren't Farhad's. They were coming closer and closer yet. They were deliberate and full of an anger that Nitish couldn't explain. Now they were stopping outside the shed door that had closed in such a sly and final way . . .

"Are you there, tiger?"

That was the man who had lured him here!

Nitish uttered a growl that came from the deep and angry pit of his stomach.

"Your hero never turned up," said the man outside. "Looks as if he preferred to make off with the bloodstone."

Nitish didn't believe that, and he forced his doubts away. Another growl helped him do it.

"Growl away, my boy," said the Englishman, "because that's the last thing you'll do. You're too dangerous to be set free."

Nitish heard a hissing sound. He didn't know what it meant.

Seconds later, a smell rose to his nostrils. It made him shake his head involuntarily and sneeze. The smell grew stronger, and then the wall cried out. The wall that had no feelings, the wall that he hadn't been able to hurt, cried out in pain and despair, and seemed to be writhing.

Bewildered, Nitish stepped back. Suddenly yellow tongues of flame were coming through the cracks between the boards.

The straw on the floor of the shed reached all the way to the wooden boards of the walls, and a moment later it was crackling in alarm. The fire was spreading and, to the tiger's horror, it was growing. It was here, there, and everywhere. He tried to tread on it, but it bit his paw. He withdrew the paw and licked it in confusion.

The fire was growing with every minute.

And there was no way of escaping it.

It was turning the wooden shed into a burning cage.

When Nitish realized that, he roared loud and long.

But no one seemed to hear him.

LALIT AND RAKA

The dance divine of Indian fire
is hotter, fiercer, stronger
than other flames; it burns up higher,
so mighty is its hunger.

Indian fire loves sandalwood,
and whispers tales of death
of many kinds—some bad, some good—
told when we last draw breath.

Indian fire on Indian nights
up to the stars goes flying,
kindling itself at lofty heights
beckoning home the dying,
as if the heavens themselves to breach,
in search of spheres beyond its reach.

FOR A WHILE THERE WAS SILENCE ON THE broad windowsill.

Outside, the night was silent.

It was late again, later than Lalit had thought, yet oddly enough he didn't feel tired.

He was not really back in a room in the Rajah's palace yet. He was still standing by the Hanuman Ghat in Varanasi, the City of Light, frantically wondering where to search for the tiger.

His mind slowly returned to the place where he actually was.

No, he wasn't Farhad, the hero traveling through India with the bloodstone in his hand and the princess's portrait around his neck.

He was Lalit the Beautiful, the little eunuch in Ahmed Mudhi's harem, whom no one took seriously. Who did what he was told. Who was obedient. Who served his master.

But since he had been immersed in Raka's story, a spark of rebellion had been kindled in his heart. Much had changed since the beginning of that story. He felt as if weeks had passed by and not just two nights.

Lalit met the glance of Raka's turquoise eyes as they looked searchingly at him, and he realized that she was an enchantress. She worked magic with her words.

293

A childlike, "And then what? What happened next?" was on the tip of Lalit's tongue, but he bit it back. He knew he would get no more answers tonight.

"Farhad is beginning to lose his heart," said Lalit at last. "That's it, isn't it? It's beginning to beat for the princess."

Raka raised an eyebrow. Her brows were fine and curved like the neck of a swan. "Do you think so?" she asked.

"Next time he opens the amulet," said Lalit, "the picture of the princess will be even clearer, am I right? Until at last he sees her perfectly distinctly in front of him."

"Maybe," said Raka.

Lalit let himself slip off the windowsill.

Raka jumped down from the sill, too. She jumped like a boy, and her eyes shone.

"Is the door to the inner courtyard open?" she asked in a whisper. "I want to breathe the night air. Who knows, I may never be able to breathe it again after tonight."

"The door is open," whispered Lalit, "but it's cool. You'll catch a cold . . ."

"Then I'll catch a cold," replied Raka, and she laughed softly. "What difference does it make whether I die with a cold or not?"

Lalit followed her as she ran down the narrow stairway, light of foot.

"I don't like to hear you say such things," he said.

Outside, Raka stood with her eyes closed for a moment. She breathed in deeply, as if she must lay in a stock of air for the long, long time when she wouldn't be able to feel it. The time between death and rebirth.

"Just in case you were thinking of climbing the wall again," said Lalit, "there are some guards outside it now. Ahmed Mudhi doesn't want to lose his desert treasure."

He realized how heartless these words sounded, and regretted them even as he spoke.

But Raka just laughed.

"One can understand Ahmed Mudhi," she said. "After all, he paid a high price for me."

She pulled the branch of a rosebush closer to her, and buried her nose deep in its flowers to breathe in their scent. "And you?" she asked. "Does he pay you to guard me, as well?"

"That," said Lalit stiffly, "is not among my tasks."

"Then why don't you go to bed? I promise not to climb the wall. I just want to walk in the night for a while."

Lalit felt the blood rise to his face.

"If you don't mind," he said quietly, "I'll stay outside for a while, too. I'm not tired. We could walk in the night together."

She nodded slowly.

"Come on," said Lalit. "I want to show you something."

And so he led Ahmed Mudhi's treasure through Ahmed Mudhi's gardens, where the wealth of flowers turned the various inner courtyards behind Ahmed Mudhi's walls into a sea of color by day, a place sheltered from the dusty, dirty, sandy world outside.

But the hand that Lalit held, as he sensed very clearly, did not belong to Ahmed Mudhi and never would. Even if the Rajah killed Raka in his fury, he could never possess her. She alone possessed herself.

At first he had thought that wasn't fitting for a woman.

Now he admired her for it.

295

His fingers burned where they touched hers, and though he imagined that he was sweating because of the hot desert wind, the wind blowing from the desert was actually cold.

Too much of Lalit had become Farhad; he, too, was falling in love. But there are never any good ways leading to the country called love. The roads there are all dangerous, uneven, winding, and poorly paved. And you can get lost only too easily on many of them.

The pair passed the dovecote, which was perched above them on a tall post like a strange plant growing in the garden.

Lalit stopped, placed a finger on his lips, and pointed up.

He saw Raka listening intently.

The cooing of the doves, a quiet sound, came from their dovecote.

"They're dreaming," he whispered. "Dreaming of freedom. Just like you."

"And you?" whispered Raka. "Don't you dream of freedom?"

Lalit was about to shake his head, but then he hesitated. Two days ago he *would* have shaken his head. He would have said freedom was dangerous. His place was here, behind these safe walls where he was always told what to do and what not to do. Where there was enough to eat and he was regularly paid for his work.

Life could quickly turn against you in freedom.

That was what he would have said two days ago. But now?

"Who knows?" he murmured, and he felt Raka's fingers holding his a little more firmly.

"Would you like to send a message?" he asked, pointing up again. "My doves can take one for you. Anywhere you want. I often send them to carry messages for the other women in the harem. Ahmed Mudhi has never told me not to. Though maybe that's just because he doesn't know."

"Well, who'd have thought it!" said Raka, and her eyes sparkled at him. "So you *do* do things that aren't entirely allowed? Apart from listening to me?"

"Only sending the doves with messages," replied Lalit shyly, avoiding her eyes. "And it wasn't my idea. The women asked me to do it."

"A pity," said Raka softly. "A pity it wasn't your idea."

"Well," said Lalit, "do you have a message for my doves to carry? There's not much else I can do for you. Only this."

Then Raka pressed his hand again and smiled up at him.

"No," she said. "But, thank you. I don't have any message. The message I did have I've sent already. I'm afraid I forgot to ask your permission."

He looked at her inquiringly.

"Your birds flew a long way to deliver it," Raka went on, "and I'm very grateful to them, because it was an important message."

"I—I don't understand," said Lalit. Having Raka so close confused him. The inside of her hand wasn't as smooth as he had expected, but rough as desert sand, and she smelled of the wind blowing over the dunes beyond the city walls: distant and spicy and a little disturbing.

"You don't understand?" she asked in surprise. "Don't you remember the letter that came for Farhad?"

"Well—yes," said Lalit slowly. "The letter was from the princess, right?"

"Right," replied Raka.

"So she's you," said Lalit, smiling.

They went on along the gravel paths of the Rajah's quiet gardens, surrounded by the nighttime fragrance of the white flowers that open their petals only in the dark.

"You're the princess waiting to be rescued. You're the girl waiting captured in the city in the middle of the desert, counting the hours until the hero comes. And Ahmed Mudhi is Ravana the demon king, pretending to be human. Only Ravana's coming wedding isn't quite the same."

"In a story," said Raka, "some things have to be different from real life. Otherwise it wouldn't be a story."

"*Stories are an excellent way of escape . . .*," said Lalit. "Yes, now I understand." He stopped beside a little pool of water and looked at Raka. "But it's not a true story," he said earnestly. "Farhad won't come to rescue you. Krishna isn't your father. Your father is somewhere in his village in the desert, happy because your husband paid him a good price. And your mother is like any desert woman cooking rice for her family in the heat of the day, looking after your younger brothers and sisters . . ."

He felt Raka's sand-rough fingers on his mouth. Her lips were quivering, and her eyes flashed angrily.

"Be quiet," she spat. "Be quiet, be quiet, be quiet. You don't understand at all. It doesn't matter what's true and what's a fairy tale. That's not what matters. The dividing lines aren't as straight and simple as you think. Just wait and see."

"Will I see Farhad appearing at the gate here to rescue you?" asked Lalit. His heart was suddenly full of infinite sadness.

She really did believe it. She had to believe it. If she hadn't made up this story, she'd have despaired.

"Wait and see," said Raka again, and she let go of his hand. She had been holding it all this time.

Lalit bit back his grief. There was no point in trying to make her see the truth.

"Look around you," he said. "This is what I wanted to

show you. I was walking through the courtyard last night and I saw it."

The little pool in front of them was covered with *kamal*, the lotus. Its large flowers floated on the smooth surface of the water, and its broad, round leaves lay like little rafts anchored deep below. The lotus flowers had closed their delicate faces when night came.

But one of them, almost in the middle of the pool, was fading slightly and couldn't fully close its petals, and some water had collected in them.

The moon was caught in the large drop on the lowest petal, and the drop of water concentrated the white moonlight and reflected it softly back. The drop shone like a silver ornament on the velvety surface of the pool.

A silver amulet lying in the middle of the flower.

Raka turned and nodded. "There," she said. "You already see how thin the dividing lines are."

"It's only water, of course," whispered Lalit.

"Did you wade into the middle of the pool to look?" asked Raka.

"No, but—"

"Well," said Raka, "as long as you *don't* do that, we can imagine it's the silver chain."

Then she looked at the windows on one side of the

courtyard, and he saw her become frightened. His eyes followed her gaze:

The Rajah's rooms lay there in the golden light of a little oil lamp. And behind those windows the Rajah himself was pacing up and down, impatiently, aimlessly, restlessly—like an animal in a cage.

"It's him," whispered Raka, "isn't it?"

Lalit nodded. "It looks as if he can't sleep."

"If he can walk up and down like that," Raka whispered, "then tomorrow he'll be well again. Well enough to convince the doctor that he can do more than just sleep."

She turned to Lalit, very suddenly, and put her arms around him like a small child seeking an adult's protection. "Hold me tight," she whispered. "Please, just for a moment. I'm afraid."

He put his arms around her slender body, not knowing if that was the way to put your arms around a girl. Somehow or other, someone had forgotten to teach him that.

He felt strangely clumsy, as if his arms belonged to someone else.

"I—I'm afraid, too," he whispered, and he had to clear his throat twice before his voice would obey him. "I'm afraid everything will be the same as before when you're gone. I wish you could stay."

301

"I wish I could stay, too," whispered Raka into his shirt. "It's not nice to think of suddenly not being here anymore."

They stood beside the pool for a long time while the Rajah paced up and down his rooms without looking out of the windows. Finally the light behind them went out. Presumably he had given up pacing and was going to sleep at last.

But the handsome eunuch and the Rajah's eighth wife still stood holding each other close.

Then something happened that Lalit couldn't explain to himself. Perhaps it was because of the night air.

When Raka tried to let go of him, he held her tightly, leaned a little way down to her, and then he kissed her.

Her lips were not like rose petals, not like silk and velvet, not like the tender colors of dawn over the desert, or like the breath of the evening wind.

Her lips were as rough as her hands, rough from the desert sand.

Lips like the storm that blinds you among the dunes, like the desert's unbearable heat, like the trunks of palm trees in the oases, like the blazing sun at noon, like the sky just before it darkens with the rain that so seldom comes.

Raka did not withdraw.

Lalit tasted all the colors of India in her mouth.

And he forgot the night, forgot Ahmed Mudhi up at his
window, forgot who he was—he, whose real name meant the
Right Time, forgot time itself.

The kiss in the Rajah's dark garden went on forever, or perhaps
only for a few seconds, or perhaps it had happened before,
long, long ago, and now it was only remembering itself.

The garden with all its leaves and flowers leaned eagerly
toward the couple to share that kiss, and even the shadows
of the night seemed to crowd more closely around the two
young people by the lotus pool. It was as if someone were
taking a large, sharp pair of scissors and cutting the kiss out
of reality. The laws of nature became small and unimportant,
forgetting their precise functions. The large flowers on the
surface of the pool all opened at the same time, even though
it was night, and the earth opened its pores and breathed out
an ancient, aromatic scent such as even the garden itself had
never known.

And Raka smiled in the middle of the endless kiss.

"It—it's like this," Lalit whispered at last, struggling for
air. "I—I'm here under false pretenses, too. I'm a cheat like
you. I didn't want to, but they said I had to do it . . ."

He let go of her and stepped back.

"I'd better warn you . . . ," he whispered.

Raka laughed, very, very quietly. "Warn me of what?" she whispered.

"It was my younger brother who was going to work in the harem," Lalit whispered. "Not me. But he fell sick just before he was to come here. After the Rajah had already seen him and given him the job. So they sent me instead. My family—they need the money I earn here. They need it badly. We—we look very like each other, my brother and I. But he's . . . And I'm not . . . I'm not a—"

He gave up and stopped talking.

Raka looked at him standing there in the moonlight, standing outside time by the pool of open lotus blossoms, and something in her contracted painfully.

How helplessly he was trying to explain himself.

She hardly knew him, but at that moment she loved him so much that it hurt. It hadn't been part of her plan to love him. But perhaps it was necessary for her to love just once. To love with all her heart and every pore of her skin and every hair on her head, before she looked into the inscrutable eyes of Death.

"Of course not," she whispered, putting her hand up to his face. "You're not a eunuch. That's what you wanted to warn me of, isn't it?"

He nodded.

"I'm not a virgin, Farhad's not a hero, you're not a eunuch," whispered Raka, laughing quietly again. "That makes all three of us tricksters!"

And then she drew him down into the lotus pool with her.

The pool was not deep. Its water lapped around the two nocturnal intruders in warm, lazy ripples. Raka sensed that Lalit wanted to say something, to protest, to explain that this was impossible, but he bit back the words, and she took his hands and guided them slowly and very carefully over the desert of her body.

"This . . . this is all new to me," whispered Lalit. "The desert. I've only known life in the city before . . . Behind its walls . . ."

"Shh," whispered Raka. "You'll scare the lotus blossoms."

Soon their clothes were floating among the flowers like a strange new variety of lotus leaves.

The aromatic fragrance in the garden was so strong now that it intoxicated them like a dense, soft opium cloud.

How good that this piece of time had been cut out of reality. How good that no one saw the two unlikely figures merging into one among the flowers.

If only the night lasted long enough, thought Raka. If only it lasted long enough perhaps they could turn into a lotus blossom, a single lotus blossom that would flower forever in this pool. And next morning Ahmed Mudhi and his seven other wives and all his guards and servants would wonder where the eunuch and the eighth wife in his harem had gone, and why there was suddenly such a big, beautiful flower in the pool . . .

But the moon, which was nearly full, ended its journey, and the Southern Cross moved sideways like a huge crab across the sky, and the night didn't last long enough.

The next morning, the pool lay there, empty and abandoned as it had been before.

There was only a forgotten scarf floating among the broad leaves of a lotus, a scarf with a golden brown pattern like the desert on its best days.

Around midday, Raka heard that the Rajah wanted to see her that night.

"When the full moon reaches the top of the date palm," said his chief guard. "Then I will come for you and take you to him. Do you understand?"

Raka nodded, and her knees were trembling, but no one could see that under her richly embroidered sari.

She spent the rest of the day having things done to her.

Being bathed, having her hair combed, being perfumed and dressed, being adorned with jewels, being painted with henna. She had to let it dry for hours with the palms of her hands raised to the sun. In short, being prepared for her wedding night with the Rajah. Her eyebrows were plucked, and every single hair on her legs was removed with fragrant beeswax as yellow as honey. Her fingernails and toenails were filed and painted with shiny, silvery lacquer, and her hair was plaited into elaborate braids and pinned up this way and that, until the maidservants were finally satisfied with the result.

Raka let it all be done to her without showing any reaction at all.

She heard the women whispering.

"How beautiful Ahmed Mudhi's eighth wife is! She grows lovelier every hour."

She felt their envious eyes burning as they rested on her skin, which had been scrubbed pink.

But their gaze soon lost its envious heat.

For what a poor creature Ahmed Mudhi's eighth wife was, after all. There seemed to be nothing whatsoever in her head. She had been seen on the water tower that morning. She must have climbed it like one of the black-faced monkeys, and now she didn't move a muscle as they made her into a work of art.

Every time one of the maidservants held a mirror up to her, the poor girl looked away, as if she didn't even know what a mirror was for.

Her head was empty, entirely empty, with nothing in it

but a few strange ideas that made her climb trees and water towers . . .

At last, exhausted, Raka sank into a chair in her room.

And she began to wait.

It would be midnight before the moon reached the top of the date palm. Long enough for her to finish telling Farhad's story.

Lalit came even earlier than before. He had slipped away from the kitchen.

"How beautiful you are," he said as he came through Raka's door.

"It's terrible," said Raka. "They'd have peeled away my skin and given me a new one if they could. They did all in their power to change me. But they didn't do it, because in my heart I am still Raka, the light of the full moon."

And she tried to hold her head as high as possible.

"Don't cry," said Lalit, and that made it almost impossible for her not to. "Perhaps your hero will come in time."

But she sensed that he didn't believe it.

"Who knows?" she said with a sniffle—a sound that didn't suit a mysterious beauty made fine for her wedding night with her husband.

Through Fire

ASHES

FARHAD STOOD IN THE DARKNESS, FEELING the seconds run through his fingers like a burning stream.

"Nitish!" he called into the gathering night. "Nitish! Where are you?"

Only the slow sound of Mother Ganga's indifferent waters replied.

"Tiger!" Farhad called, not expecting any answer. "Wise old white tiger! Which of the mouths of this miserable city has swallowed you up?"

Then he sat down on one of the steps, clasped his knees in his arms, and laid his head on them. There was nothing he could do.

A thin voice spoke out of the darkness, frail as old paper.

"Are you looking for a tiger?" asked the voice, shaking slightly. "A tiger swallowed up by the city?"

Farhad raised his head from his arms and looked around, searching for the speaker.

"Yes," he said. "I'm looking for a tiger. A white tiger who runs as fast as the clouds in the sky and the sand in the desert wind. Have you seen him?"

"Well, not exactly," replied the voice, which was a little closer now. "But I have an idea where he might be. It's strange . . ." The voice came closer yet, like a dancing, invisible spirit in the black night. "It's strange what may be found here in Varanasi."

310

Farhad rose, turned around in a circle a couple of times, and then at last he saw the owner of the shaky voice. He was a bent, shadowy figure carrying a tiny bright point of light—a kerosene lamp with the flame turned so low that it was nearly going out. And as he came closer, Farhad saw that the figure was at least as frail and shaky as the voice. The man must be so old that his years could hardly be counted, and his back was bent as if he had carried the whole firmament through the desert on it.

"Who are you?" asked Farhad, intrigued.

"Who are *you*?" asked the old man.

"My name is Varaha," said Farhad, for Varaha was the next incarnation of Vishnu after Kurma the turtle. In Varaha's body, the god Vishnu had appeared as a boar-headed figure who came to save the earth from a demon.

Although at this moment Farhad felt nothing like as strong and brave as boar-tusked Varaha.

"Ah, Varaha," said the old man in the darkness. "A fine name."

He turned the flame of his kerosene lamp higher so that he could see Farhad's face.

"You don't look like the bearer of a sacred name," he said. "In fact, forgive me, you look more British. Your hair is fair . . ."

"Camouflage," whispered Farhad. "Camouflage, all of it. But I don't need it anymore. My enemy has my best friend in his hands, so what use is camouflage to me now?"

The old man nodded. He himself wore a much-mended dhoti with a gray check pattern, and no shirt. "I need a shirt," he said. "Give me your shirt and I'll take you to your best friend."

"The white tiger?"

"Whether white or not, I can't say," replied the old man, and he laughed, showing the single tooth still left in his head.

"Tracks don't tell you a tiger's color."

"So you've seen his tracks?"

"I've seen the tracks of a tiger," the old man corrected him. "Some tiger or other. In the city, two days ago. But I can't tell you what kind of tiger it was, Varaha, dear friend. However, I was surprised, because it is most unusual for a tiger to come into the city."

Farhad took off his shirt and handed it to the old man, who stroked the fabric lovingly with his bony fingers.

"There's no time to lose," Farhad urged him. "Maybe the man who has the tiger in his hands has already harmed him. Hurry! Where did the tracks lead?"

"I must find the place where I first saw them before we start," said the old man. "Then we'll follow them. My lamp is faint and my eyes are old. But my tracking instinct won't let me down. It's found many tracks . . . for the British. When all that uproar was going on recently, I was out and about with the British. Guests of the Rajah from the palace beyond the bridge. 'Go with my guests, Muruganan,' the Rajah told me, 'and put them on the trail of the tiger in the undergrowth so that they can shoot at his stripes and enjoy the wonderful color of his coat . . .'"

Farhad hastily followed the old man up the steps into the city.

"But that day there were only old tracks outside the city," Muruganan went on, and in a side street he lowered the kerosene lamp until it was very close to the ground, and shook his head.

"Do you see them here?"

"No," said Farhad. "I don't see anything."

"There you are, then," said the old man, sounding pleased. "Old tracks. Anyone can see new tiger tracks. Only an old tracking instinct can find old tracks, only an old eye can see them."

The old man was following the tracks like a dog now, and Farhad understood why his back was so bent. After all the years he had spent following different kinds of tracks, he couldn't stand up straight anymore. Only what was on the ground mattered to him.

He followed the invisible tracks and Farhad followed him, through narrow alleys and across backyards, around sharp bends and over the remains of walls, until they had left the buildings of Varanasi behind.

"The English are blind when it comes to tracks," the old man said. "They see only what's obvious." He climbed over the ruined foundations of a house. With his bent back and his thin arms and legs, he looked like a large and surprisingly agile spider.

313

"I've read too many tracks in my life," he continued after a while. "I've read the tracks of the gods, too, and they were angry with me."

"Tracks . . . of the gods?" inquired Farhad, with a slight smile on his lips.

"Krishna's tracks, for instance," said Muruganan. He stopped beside a wall and turned to Farhad. "It was only the other day, in the city. I had no work to do and I felt curious. So I followed Krishna's tracks . . . and they led me to you, friend Varaha."

He thoughtfully nodded his head. "I'm wondering who you are," he said.

"I'm not sure myself," said Farhad, and he was telling the truth.

"Go around the wall," said the old man. "The tiger's tracks will end there."

When Farhad reached the end of the wall and went around it, the light blinded him.

It was a fierce, crackling light, and it took him a moment to understand what he was seeing.

The smell of burning wood rose to his nostrils. At first he thought of the funeral pyres by the Ganges, but then he saw the angular outline of the great blaze, and he cried out with alarm: It was a burning building, some kind of wooden shed.

He ran over the dry, fallow land to the structure as his heart fluttered wildly like a captured bird. *Nitish*, sang his heart. *Nitish, Nitish! Are you there? Are you in that world of flame—somewhere at its terrible, blazing center? How did this happen?*

And then he heard the tiger's cry.

The burning wood crackled out loud in the fire, the planks of the shed creaked and groaned, but above all that Farhad heard a plaintive, drawn-out cry—not like the roar of a huge, proud tiger, but the sound a little kitten makes when it has lost its mother.

"I'm coming!" he shouted to the fire. "I'm coming! I—"

At this point he had to cough, because the smoke was rising to his lungs, and he stopped shouting.

Instead, he fought his way through until he was close to the fire. A hot wind was blowing from it, trying to keep him away. But he ignored the wind. For somewhere beyond that heat was Nitish. Nitish who had saved him from the Frenchman's knife in the mosque. Nitish who had pulled him out of the river when he was close to drowning. Nitish who had shown him what it meant to be in someone's debt.

Farhad protected his face with his arms and looked for an opening so he could get into the shed. Its tall wooden walls were still standing. A piece of the burning roof fell; flames rained down on all sides, and Farhad heard the kitten crying again.

He needed something to knock a hole in the burning wall. It couldn't be very strong now. Hastily, he looked around. The one thing his streaming eyes could find was a piece of a beam that had fallen with part of the roof.

The beam wasn't burning anymore, but it was smoldering dangerously.

Farhad didn't think for long. To be honest, he didn't think at all. That's what marks out true heroes: They simply act with no thought for the consequences, and if what they do works, the world will sing the hero's praises later. Generally, however, the things they do prove fatal, and the heroes sink into the gray oblivion of unwritten stories, never to be seen again.

Farhad picked up the red, glowing beam in his bare hands, took aim, and swung it against the wall. The charred planks broke with a loud crash.

A moment later there was a large hole in the blazing cage of the shed.

It was only when he saw the hole that Farhad felt the burning heat on the palms of his hands.

He yelled so loud that the waves of flame in the shed shook, and he dropped the burning beam.

Then he leaped through the gaping black opening, right into the sea of flames. And if, at that moment, anyone had seen him, the onlooker would have thought he was a demon, wreathed in the yellowish-orange tongues of the fire flickering back and forth, his face and bare torso black with soot, his mouth distorted in another scream of rage and pain—and in the middle of that blackened face, his eyes were wide open.

"Tiger!" cried Farhad, fighting down his coughing. "Nitish! Lord of the Right Way! Here it is—this is the Right Way! Here's your way out into the world! Come on, come to me!"

The whimpering of the little kitten was coming closer through the chaos of the dancing flames.

Another piece of the roof came away from the charred beams and crashed to the floor a few feet from Farhad. He leaped aside, jumped over the ruins, and almost collided with a large, soft Something coming out of the darkness.

Now one of the walls keeled over and fell in. Farhad saw it slowly coming toward him and Nitish. And with a practiced movement, he swung himself up on the tiger's back and dug his heels into Nitish's sides as if he were a horse.

"Run!" he shouted. "Straight ahead! Duck down! Now, through the hole in the wall!"

He himself crouched low on the tiger's back, pressing his soot-smeared body flat against the tiger's, but still he felt a part of the wall graze him. There was a keen pain right above his head. His hair must have caught fire.

317

He clapped his burned hands to his head, saw the fire licking around him, and then, finally, saw it retreat. They were out in a field, he realized. They had left the shed behind. Farhad let himself drop off the tiger's back, and he rolled about in the new grass that had begun to grow in the monsoon.

He put out the fire on his head, but the next moment he saw the fire climb down the shed. Now it began eating its way forward across the field like a greedy caterpillar.

The fresh, damp, green monsoon grass wasn't fresh and damp enough to hold the fire back.

Farhad tried to stand up, but he couldn't. Something was the matter with his body. It wouldn't obey him as usual.

He wanted to crawl or roll away, but he couldn't manage that, either.

The fire was approaching Farhad like a beast of prey on the prowl. He closed his eyes and noticed that the heat had singed his eyelids, too.

Soon it would have the rest of him.

Fascinated, he listened.

So this was what it was like to lie in the fire.

This was how the dead felt when they were burned.

He felt no pain, only great exhaustion and a strange abstraction.

Would they sweep his remains into the Ganges?

He felt the flames around him now, and something took him in a strong grip—it must be Death, thought Farhad. He didn't struggle.

He felt his body dissolving and turning to ashes—first his toes, then his feet, his legs up to the knees, then his hips . . . He opened his eyes and saw that he was lying on a pyre beside the Ganges, right down by the river, very close to the flowing water of eternity. But beyond the fire, to his surprise, he saw Madurai—his own city.

He saw its streets and temples, heard the voices of its people, smelled the intoxicating fragrance of the fine white garlands of jasmine woven by the women in the flower market, so that the ladies who came to buy could twine them into the oily sheen of their beautiful dark hair. And at this point it occurred to Farhad that he might just be dreaming.

"That's right," said the Frenchman (or maybe the Englishman) from the prison. "And I'm not really British, either. I'm a Polish emigrant, and my name is Richardson Olszevsky . . ."

Nitish licked Farhad's hand, as he had done again and again over the last few days, and watched his face.

Farhad's face twitched. But he didn't pull his hand away.

Even when the tiger very cautiously nipped his arm with his teeth, he didn't move.

Nitish watched the woman with the hooked nose smooth out the damp cloth on Farhad's forehead, and thought she could have paid just a little more attention to him, Nitish, as well.

The fire had eaten so much: parts of his coat, the particularly beautiful fur at the tip of his tail, the whiskers around his mouth, and the especially sensitive tactile whiskers above his eyes.

Farhad, too, lay there like someone who has sacrificed all his hair to a temple. Someone making a new beginning.

"At least he's rid of his lice," said the woman with the hooked nose, and she smiled. "I'll bet he had a *lot* of them. Everyone who lives in the streets does. I know that from my little beggar boys . . ."

Nitish had been lying beside Farhad on the floor of the simple hut for three days now, watching his motionless master.

He had dragged him away from the field just before the fire reached him. He had taken his trouser leg in his teeth and hauled him a long, long way, until somewhere on the city outskirts he met the woman.

She had known what to do at once, and she set about doing it.

Somehow she seemed to know Farhad already.

When she had removed the half-charred bandage from his right arm, something rolled out: Nitish knew it at once. It shone bright and red in the light of the little fire in the hut, and he and the woman flinched away at the same time.

The bloodstone.

The woman didn't touch it.

She spread a cloth over it, and pushed it and the cloth under the shrine where her domestic altar stood. Now and then she cast a distrustful glance at the bundle under the shrine.

And although she seemed to hate the stone, she nursed Farhad and let Nitish sleep in her hut, though he more or less filled the whole place.

The woman's husband had been rather alarmed when he came home to find a gigantic white tiger on his floor.

But the woman, who understood a great deal without being told, explained that it had to be this way. There had to be a white tiger pacing up and down the hut, and there had to be an injured boy lying there.

"I don't know just what it is about the two of them," she had told her husband. "But look at the burn mark on his forehead, right between the eyebrows. The same mark that every woman in India paints on her forehead. The mark that the priests paint with colored powder on the foreheads of all who come to ask their advice. There's something special about our two guests. Something beyond the power of simple folk like us to imagine. Something sacred."

The man had shrugged his shoulders, looked suspiciously at the tiger, and growled that he didn't have the money to feed two more mouths.

But then the injured boy had begun talking in his fever. He had told a story—a strange, chaotic story. The woman and her husband couldn't get the order of events entirely straight. A story about a hero who met Lord Krishna by a lotus pool. A story about a white tiger and a princess and a demon king . . .

Confused, but wonderful. A fairy tale as colorful and adventurous as the dreams people dreamed in the little huts of Varanasi. And though it was a fairy tale, you could only wish it were the truth.

The man had eventually stopped grumbling. Although just sometimes, when Nitish was hungrily devouring yet another heaped plateful of rice and lentils, he had given the figure of Krishna on the domestic altar a reproachful look.

Nitish wasn't just hungry, he was anxious, too.

He watched the moon growing dangerously fuller night after night, and he felt time running out in the fur of his coat.

If he hadn't been a tiger, if he had owned a watch, and if he had been able to tell the time by it, he would have been looking at that watch every five minutes, impatiently scraping his claws over the mud floor of the hut.

There were only a few days left before the demon king Ravana married Krishna's daughter and took her away forever to his black realm, where she would become like him.

What a terrible idea! Nitish shook himself at the thought of it, and knocked a small table over. The young woman with the hooked nose sighed, and stood the table up again.

She, too, seemed to be anxious about the boy who had been lying so still on the thin ricestraw mat by the wall of her hut for the last three days. Unlike his large, four-footed companion, he took up hardly any more room than a shadow.

She had smeared ointment thickly on his hands, for their palms were black as coal. He had deep wounds all over his body, and they became inflamed and made him feverish, so that he sometimes shook like a demon.

She said many prayers to the little gods of her shrine during those days, asking them to call the boy back to life. But the gods seemed unable to make up their minds.

The woman had not dared to put ointment on the mark she had found on Farhad's forehead: It was right between

323

Farhad's eyes, in the place where the god Shiva has his third eye—the place where the priests paint the sign of blessing in the temple, and where Hindu women stick the sign of the Third Eye, the bindi, on their faces to protect them.

The woman with the hooked nose was sure that this wound the boy had suffered was sacred.

He was special, and even if he did carry the red jewel that she hated, she would nurse him until the gods made their decision.

Then she would either see him burned on a pyre, like Rahul—and in that case she would sink the jewel deep in the mud of the Ganges—or she would see him go away, and in that case she would keep the knowledge that she had been a part of his great, godlike adventure in her heart. Which was more, she thought, than most people could say of themselves.

Sometimes Nitish saw that Farhad was dreaming, his face twisted, his eyelids fluttering like restless butterflies. Then Nitish growled beside him to wake him. For he couldn't speak except with the dangerous blue of his eyes, and as long as Farhad was looking only inward the white tiger's words could not reach him.

But Farhad lay in a fever, dreaming chaotic dreams. In these dreams he was still sure he had died. Two thin priests shoveled the remains of his damp ashes into the Ganges under a rainy sky.

He felt the water accept him.

The priests did not watch him float away; they turned and made haste to get themselves safely indoors. But Farhad became one with the water.

Mother Ganga flowed softly around him, and even if no one had thrown flower petals after him, he felt greatly honored to sink into her waves. He dreamed of the demon king Ravana and his chief servant, Suryakanta, whose greedy eyes demanded the bloodstone. He dreamed of divine figures with many arms, and the holy mountain of Kailash. He dreamed himself back to the beginning of the world. He sank in the wide expanses of time, and drifted deep below the surface of reality for a long time. Now and then the princess appeared in his dreams.

Unfortunately she never stayed for long . . . And then Farhad was drifting alone through the flickering darkness again.

He had only seen her inside the little silver amulet, on a slightly blurred, yellowing photograph. Now, out of the photo, she was even more beautiful. How did she know that he was here, outside reality? Did she know everything that happened to him?

325

Once the princess reached out her hand to him, and opened her mouth to speak.

At that moment, he woke up.

"Farhad!" said Nitish's eyes, full of blue astonishment. Then they sparkled happily. "Farhad, it's you! You're back at last!"

"Back where?" asked Farhad, dazed. Cautiously, he turned his head and was surprised to find that he could do it. Still cautiously, he moved first his left and then his right arm.

That was surprisingly easy, too.

Then he looked at the palms of his hands and wondered what was wrong. They were hidden under thick bandages, and when he put them up to his face to take a closer look they smelled of a bittersweet ointment with an aroma that made him feel slightly sick.

"Nitish!" he whispered. "Old tiger! I thought I was dead. In my dream the rain put out my fire, and they scattered my ashes in the Ganges."

"Dreams!" said the tiger's eyes, and he grunted disapprovingly. "No one here scattered your ashes in the Ganges, and that's solely and entirely because I saved you. I was a hero. I dragged you out of the fire, and the fire was too slow to follow me. And then I found this wonderful place for us to stay."

Farhad smiled at the tiger's pride.

"Where am I?" he asked.

Then another face bent over him. A human one. He knew that face.

"You're in good hands," said the owner of the face. "Don't worry. I'll look after you until you're better again."

"You! It's you!" Farhad wanted to cry out, but his voice wouldn't let him produce more than a hoarse whisper, and a fit of coughing shook him.

"That's the soot," said the woman, nodding. "The soot in your lungs."

Farhad tried to get his thoughts in order. "How many days are there left?" he asked at last, slowly and cautiously, so as not to encounter the soot in his lungs again. "How many days until the next full moon?"

The woman with the slightly hooked nose thought about it.

"Four," she said.

Farhad sat up in a hurry, ignoring the painful throbbing in his head and his burning wounds. "Four days?" he whispered, horrified. "Nitish, we must set out at once! Only four days left, and the city waiting for us is in the middle of the desert of Thar . . ."

Nitish yawned and stretched luxuriously. When he

arched his back, it rose almost too high for the low, palm-thatched roof of the hut.

"We can leave this very minute if you like." It was as if the tiger's eyes were purring. "I was just waiting for you to come back. You weren't here, you see. Only your body was lying around. And I couldn't very well go off to the desert without you, could I?"

Farhad nodded, gritting his teeth as he tried to stand up.

The woman gently pressed him back down on the rice-straw mat.

"You can't set out for *anywhere*," she said firmly. "Your hands are charred like two logs of wood. Your body is marked by the fire. And you're still feverish. You're weak, you have no strength in you. You won't get three yards without falling down and lying where you fell forever."

Farhad looked at her, and pointed to the little silver amulet. She carefully opened it and bent over the picture of the princess. Even more veils of mist had moved away, and now it was quite clear except for one or two little patches.

"She's waiting," said Farhad earnestly. "She's waiting for me. If I don't get there at the right time, Ravana the demon king will take her away from this world forever."

The women thoughtfully pinched her slightly hooded nose. Perhaps, thought Farhad, she had been born with a perfectly straight nose, and had simply done too much thinking and pinching in the course of her life.

"You want to go to the desert?" she asked.

Farhad nodded.

"I met that Englishman," she said. "A few days ago . . . The one who's to blame for Rahul's death. A bad man. He's still looking for the . . ." She cast a swift glance around her. "Well, for the jewel. He asked me if I'd seen anyone who fit your description. I mean your description before you were in that fire."

She laughed softly and pinched her nose again.

"I didn't know where you were going. You didn't mention it when we met by the burning ground. So I sent the Englishman in what I thought was the wrong way. I said yes, I'd seen you, and you were on your way . . ."

She hesitated.

"On your way to the desert," she finished.

"Oh," said Farhad.

"The desert is large," said the woman, letting go of her nose. "And you can easily lose someone in the desert. It's hard to find anyone there. Certainly by chance."

"I wouldn't be so sure of that," replied Farhad, hauling himself up until he was standing on his tottering feet. The hut was swaying slightly around him.

"Where's the bloodstone?" he asked.

The woman put a finger to her lips. "Don't speak of it," she whispered. "It's bad enough that you must have it with you to rescue your princess!"

And she fished it out from under the shrine with her foot, and helped Farhad to tie it to his arm again. She took great care not to touch the stone herself.

"Thank you," said Farhad. "Thank you for all you've done for me. There's nothing I can give you in return except a story."

"I have that already," said the woman, and she smiled. "You've told it to me. The fever led your tongue the right way. May your feet carry you the right way, too. I will not forget either of you. Oh, and I have a gift," added the woman, handing Farhad a white shirt—much mended, but clean. "I think you'll need this. Perhaps we shall meet again in another life, and then you can tell me the end of your story."

Farhad nodded awkward thanks, then he climbed on the tiger's back, and at long, long last they left the lights of the city behind.

The woman stood in the narrow alley outside her small hut for some time, stroking the thin, hooked bridge of her nose thoughtfully.

"He doesn't even know," she murmured, "that he has the Third Eye burned into his forehead . . ."

At last she bent and slipped back into the hut, to carry on with her life of cooking rice and mending clothes . . . and waiting for the evenings when, from now on, she would tell the neighbors the amazing story of the hero and his white tiger over and over again.

ARRACK

FARHAD LAY ON THE TIGER'S BACK LIKE A dead man.

They had crossed Allahabad, where the three great rivers—Ganges, Yamuna, and Sarasvati—come together at the same thrice-holy place. With the clouds, they had passed the old, domed fortress of Gwalior. It looked down rather grimly on the city, now ruled by the British, and remembered its better days.

At sunset they came to Jaipur, the Pink City, with its houses glowing in the evening light. When Prince Albert visited some years earlier, he had the city painted royal red—

never stopping to think what the overall effect might be. The Prince Consort felt a little uncomfortable when he saw the results. No British man enjoys passing through a city that's been painted pink in his honor.

Now, however, the pink color of the city went well with the light of the setting sun, and Farhad's weary eyes surveyed it with a smile. But he was too exhausted to admire it at greater leisure.

His injuries hurt, and there was a throbbing in his hands as if the blood in his veins was telling him he had very little time left to reach the city in the middle of the desert. He hadn't taken off the bandages, although it was difficult to hold on to his mount while they were wrapped around his hands. Now he was afraid of what he would find under the thick layers of fabric.

When they reached the first houses of Jaipur, the sunset was already changing to darkness.

"Let's spend the night here," Farhad whispered in the tiger's white ear. "The desert begins beyond Jaipur, and neither of us knows it. It will be better to stand up to it by daylight."

Nitish's blue eyes inspected Farhad critically.

"You don't look," he said, "as if you were in any state to stand up to the desert *at all*."

"Well," said Farhad, with a faint grin, "I won't be standing up. You'll be carrying me on your back."

"That," said the tiger, "is what I was afraid of. It seems to be all I'm good for on this journey." He looked around him. "So just where in this city are we going to spend the night?"

"I don't know," said Farhad. "We need something to eat, too."

They had been traveling for a night and a day without once stopping for more than a short time. During one of their brief rests, Nitish had brought down an antelope in the deciduous forests of Gwalior, but he had left most of the carcass, because time, like the antelope's warm, red blood, was flowing inexorably away.

Farhad sat up on the tiger's back and looked around. The wide, straight streets of Jaipur lay around him like a geometrical pattern for a carpet.

"Oh, there's no strength left in me at all," he said, vexed. "Not even the strength to steal some food."

"I could—" the tiger began.

"No," said Farhad sternly. "You couldn't. May I remind you what happened when you tried to make off with half a goat on the sly?"

"Um . . . er . . . well," Nitish said, and fell silent.

He had slowed down, and was now trotting along the magnificent streets in the shelter of the tall buildings. The streets were wide and just right for grand parades, so it didn't surprise Farhad much to find their way soon blocked by such a procession.

Seen from behind, it consisted of a number of large gray bodies towering up in front of the tiger like massive, thundering dreams. They formed an impressive double row.

"Elephants," said Nitish in surprise. "Shall I just leap over them?"

"No. We might find something to eat here."

"I don't think," said Nitish firmly, "that eating elephants is very easy."

"But elephants seldom travel alone in this country. A procession of elephants could mean a festival, and a festival could mean a meal."

"All right," replied Nitish's eyes, "then I'll join the procession and pretend to be an elephant." He suited his pace to the huge animals and trotted along behind them, and in spite of his exhaustion and the burning and throbbing in his hands, Farhad couldn't help laughing. After a while, Nitish padded farther forward through the ranks of the elephants, and they began to trumpet uneasily.

In the faint starlight, Farhad saw that the elephants had

white patterns painted on them. They were works of art on the move, adorned with ornate lines, flowers, and good-luck signs. Each animal bore a rider enthroned on a richly decorated saddle. The men were looking straight ahead into the night, and didn't notice the strange new additions to the procession.

"Excuse me!" Farhad shouted up to one of them after a while. "What are you celebrating?"

The man turned his head and froze. He was swaying on the elephant's tall back, and for a moment Farhad feared he would lose his balance, but the rider caught himself. Now the other men were staring at Farhad and Nitish, too.

Evidently they couldn't believe their eyes. Here was a strange, soot-smeared boy among them, riding a white tiger. He had slipped into their ranks as silently as a ghost, and he was as improbable as an illusion conjured up by the night.

"We're celebrating the marriage of brave Barat Singh to Laila, daughter of the great merchant Kumar Sander Pratap," replied the man Farhad had spoken to.

"Ah, good," said Farhad, who had never heard the two names in his life, nor were they of the slightest interest to him. "Then we've found the right place."

"Where do you come from?" asked another of the elephant riders.

"Far, far away," replied Farhad. "We were sent to bring the happy couple greetings from the gods this evening."

"Who sends you?"

"Krishna sends us," replied Farhad, without a moment's hesitation. "And the wind of South India sends us," he went on, "the monsoon rains in Gaya send us, the river goddess Ganga and the sacred fire in Varanasi send us, and so do all the begging monks in the land."

"You're a good storyteller," cried one of the elephant riders. "Whoever has really sent you, you're welcome to Barat Singh's wedding feast! As the night wears on and sleep threatens, we'll be glad of your words."

"Won't your tiger hurt anyone?" asked another.

Nitish uttered a warning growl.

"Oh, no," Farhad made haste to say. "So long as no one provokes him, he'll keep his teeth and claws to himself. He's very hungry at the moment," he added in a meaningful tone. "Being hungry does sometimes provoke him. Quite a lot."

They followed the procession to a magnificently decorated wedding hall, which gleamed in the brightness of thousands of lamps and cast out light like a starry sky.

The room was full of long benches, and the long benches were full of dozens of people, and more and more kept pouring into the hall. Farhad had been to several weddings in his life, joining the crowd of guests unnoticed to eat a good meal, but this one was more magnificent than all the rest put together.

A man at the entrance inspected him with slight suspicion, and handed him a sweet-smelling new dhoti and a fresh shirt.

"You'd better wear these," said the doorman, with a rather sour smile.

Farhad obediently wound the dhoti around his waist, put on the shirt, and mingled with the crowd.

On the platform at the far end of the hall, Barat Singh, Laila Kumar, and a priest were performing rites of some kind that Farhad didn't understand, and in which he had never taken an interest anyway. The rites included a lot of rice, flowers, incense sticks, and sacred fire, and they would go on all night. What did interest Farhad, however, was the food.

You must know that at a Hindu wedding, the guests are constantly moving around, listening to the priests for a while, going away again, sleeping now and then—in short, they are a milling throng in which a white tiger can pass almost unnoticed.

Farhad didn't stay in the decorated hall for long. He discovered a side door, and in the courtyard to which it led he found what he was looking for: an unlimited amount of food. An equally unlimited number of wedding guests were sitting on the ground in long rows, using their fingers to roll fragrant white rice into little balls. The rice, arranged on green banana leaves, looked pretty as a picture.

Nitish had a whole mountain of chicken bones to chew on. The thin, hungry dogs waiting in the dust put their tails between their legs, surprised by the presence of this unusual competitor.

Farhad hadn't yet finished eating when a small hand touched his elbow. He jumped, because it was the elbow where the fire had left its teeth marks.

"What happened to your hands?" asked a very small voice, just the right size for the hand. Farhad glanced around in the faint light of the courtyard, and found himself looking into the large, dark eyes of a pointed face that was leaning toward him between two braids of hair. He guessed that the little girl was about eight or nine years old.

She wore a clean but much-mended punjabi, and was looking at him gravely.

"I got the brilliant idea of picking up a burning wooden beam," replied Farhad, with some bitterness.

"Why?" asked the little girl. It didn't sound like a child's question, but plain and down to earth, as if she were recording evidence.

"I had to get a friend out of a burning shed," Farhad replied.

The little girl nodded. "You need a fresh bandage," she said, taking Farhad's right hand. "Look at that! The old one is as dirty as if you'd wiped away all the dust between here and Varanasi with it."

"Hey, let go of me!"

But before Farhad could snatch his hand away, she had skillfully undone the old bandage, and was looking critically at his palm. She frowned in a very grown-up way, and if the sight of his own hand hadn't alarmed Farhad so much he would have laughed. His palm was scored with deep burn marks which weren't healing over, and the pus oozing from them had soaked the bandage.

"Neem leaves," said the little girl.

"What?"

"The leaves of the neem tree. That's what you want for your hands."

He looked at her distrustfully. "How do you know?"

"From my mother," said the little girl firmly. "She cured a lot of people in our neighborhood. The British gave her a job in their hospital, nursing people who were wounded, or sick with malaria. But the British didn't want to know about the neem tree, so their wounds don't heal, and when they get malaria they die."

"Could you maybe just fetch your mother, then?" asked

Farhad, rather vexed. Pain was throbbing in his veins, and at last he managed to get his hand away from the little girl.

"No, I couldn't," said the child, very firmly this time.

"Why not?" asked Farhad. He wished she'd just leave him in peace.

"Because she's been dead for two weeks," said the little girl. "Dead as a doornail."

"Oh. I'm sorry. What—what happened to her?"

The little girl examined him in an odd way, as if she were comparing him with someone else. "Promise to stay put while I tend your hands. There's a neem tree growing in the backyard here."

"Why should I promise?"

"So that I'll tell you why I'm bandaging your hands and why my mother isn't alive anymore."

Perplexed, Farhad watched her as she bustled off into the darkness of the long, narrow courtyard. This girl was like no child who had ever spoken to him before. And she talked in riddles.

He looked at Nitish for help, and saw that the tiger's blue eyes were sparkling with mischief. "So the great hero's afraid of a little girl," said his amused glance.

Farhad turned away in annoyance.

When the little girl came back, she was carrying a great

many tiny, round, dark green leaves in the hem of her punjabi. Farhad watched suspiciously as she undid the bandage from his other hand and dropped it in the dirt of the courtyard. Then she set to work, carefully tearing a strip off the shirt he had only just been given, placing the leaves on his wounds, and binding up his hands again.

"It was the fire," said the little girl. "Fire bit you, and it devoured my parents, too. Kerosene is very useful. You pour it over things and they go up in flames as soon as a spark touches them. My father was very angry with my mother, and the kerosene helped him to be angry. But it killed them both. I didn't see it. Sita saw it. She said it was very bright."

Farhad did not reply. The matter-of-fact way the little girl spoke sent a shudder down his back.

"It was because of another man," explained the little girl, pinning Farhad's new bandage in place. "One of the patients she was nursing in the hospital. He had burns on his hands, too. And my mother's neem leaves helped him. But then he followed her home and asked her questions. Questions about you."

Farhad almost jumped up into the air. "Me?"

"You ride a white tiger with blue eyes, don't you?"

He nodded and tried to forget the way his hands were throbbing and concentrate on the little girl's words.

"Then it must have been you the foreigner was looking for. A German. I didn't like him from the first. He wanted to know whether my mother had seen a young man with a white tiger in the British hospital. She shook her head and laughed. And my father heard her laughing heartily and saw the other man slip away. He was going out into the desert . . ."

"What did the foreigner look like?" asked Farhad. But then he dismissed his own question. "No, it doesn't matter. He looks different every time."

"Who is he?"

"I don't know," replied Farhad. "How strange. He's the one who's looking for me, and now it seems as if I'm following in his footprints."

At that moment, someone clapped him on the shoulder so powerfully that he jumped. There were still burns all over him.

Farhad looked up into the face of a tall woman in a pink sari. She had lips painted red, a broad nose, and a rather square chin—and she was offering him a bottle.

"Here," she said in a voice as deep and smoky as logs of wood crackling in the flames. "You look as if you could do with it. We saw the little girl here unwrapping your hands." The tall woman shook herself. "Arrack is good for pain."

Farhad gratefully put the bottle to his lips and looked at

343

her as he drank. Her bosom was surprisingly angular, and somehow seemed too far up. The arrack ran down Farhad's throat like liquid fire. But he knew the tall woman was right; it would help the pain. He handed the bottle back, and the woman drank from it, too, without moving a muscle of her face. Now he saw three more women standing behind her, also tall and curiously rough-mannered. The lips of all four women were painted red, and they had drawn black kohl around their eyes. The most striking thing about them, however, was their clothing. The saris of all four women were so gaudily colored that even at night in the courtyard it hurt to look at them by the faint light of the oil lamps. Bright green, blazing yellow, glaring purple stung Farhad's eyes. His head began to *boom* like a big drum. Perhaps it was pain, perhaps it was his exhaustion, perhaps it was the bewildering figures of the four huge women.

Before he could find out, he heard real drumming somewhere—drumming that didn't just exist in his tired head. A group of other instruments joined in, and the crowd formed a circle.

People began clapping and stamping their feet in time to the music—and then the huge women began to dance.

The circle of spectators cheered them on, and the garish saris swirled in the air like colorful clouds. Now Farhad saw the women's muscular legs, he saw how they threw their sinewy arms up and made secret signs in the air with their fingers. He was going to clap in time when he realized that the arrack bottle had found its way back to him.

He raised it to his lips and drank in great gulps.

The things going on at this wedding bemused him more and more. The odd little girl, the Englishman who had now turned into a German, the strange dancing women . . . and then there was the pain of his wounds, pulsing through his blood and slowing down his thoughts.

The arrack helped. It mingled with his bloodstream, and at last the pain was chased away. And suddenly he realized something about the dancing women.

He knew others like them in Madurai. *Of course.*

He knew them from weddings and *pujas*, ceremonies of blessing. They had gone to those, too. Yet they were outcasts, and no one came too close to them, because they weren't women at all.

Only their souls were feminine, but under the saris, the lipstick, and the false breasts were hidden the bodies of strong, grown men. Those who angered them were cast into misfortune by a glance from their kohl-rimmed eyes, brought to ruin by a word from their sharp tongues. But the men-women brought good luck to those who befriended them.

You will bring me luck, thought Farhad. I need some luck. Urgently.

At last the music died away, and the gaudy saris stopped swirling. Farhad saw that the arrack bottle was almost empty. He finished the last of it, and saw the dancers circling around him now.

"Stranger, you're a storyteller!" cried the one in bright green in a deep bass voice.

"We've been entertaining the crowd," said the one in bright yellow, "and now it's your turn, teller of tales! We want to hear a story!"

"Yes!" agreed the others. "Let's hear a story! Let him tell a tale!"

"It—it was a misunderstanding," stammered Farhad, looking at the floor, which was going up and down a bit. "I'm not really a storyteller."

"Of course you are!" cried the woman in bright yellow. "They've just this minute told us! Please!" she begged, giving Farhad a seductive look. "Tell us one of your tales!"

"Very well," said Farhad uncomfortably, rising to his feet.

He remembered telling his story: in Varanasi, on the bank of the Ganges. He had told it as if it were a fairy tale, and so absurd that no one could possibly believe it. But the beggar boy had understood every word when he told it, and had stolen the bloodstone from him that night.

Farhad sighed, for the men-women were shuffling their feet impatiently. Better not make them too impatient if luck was needed . . .

All right, he thought. I'll just alter a few things in it. No one will realize it's about *me*—that I'm the hero traveling all over India . . .

And so that night Farhad told his story once again, under the stars in the city of Jaipur on the edge of the desert. He cleared his throat, shook his head, stepped into the middle of the empty circle, and began.

He told them about the oasis with the date palm, and the green groves where little birds sang. He told them about the princess, and the greedy eyes of Ravana and his chief servant, Suryakanta. He spoke of the lotus pool where the hero found a silver amulet, he described his meeting with Lord Krishna, and his ride on the wings of the wind. He told them about the British prison and the rushing river in the monsoon rains.

He went on and on with his story, telling it as if it were happening all over again. The arrack made his head light and loosened his tongue.

Soon he didn't hear what he was saying anymore—the

347

words came out of his mouth by themselves, and he could neither control nor stop them.

Once he glanced at the little girl who had bandaged his hands, and he saw her put her finger to her lips. But his head wasn't clear enough for him to understand her sign.

He left his body and saw himself from above, standing in the middle of the crowd and telling his story. And he saw the people listening spellbound. It was as if they had forgotten that there was a wedding going on in the hall. They pressed forward to hear better, the old leaning on their sticks, the young sitting cross-legged on the ground, and it seemed as if Farhad's voice were carrying them away into a world full of adventures and marvels, just like the heroic sagas of the *Ramayana* and the *Mahabharata*, which are ever old and ever young.

A moment came when Farhad's mind discovered three men at the very back of the crowd listening in a different way, not like the others. They were richly dressed and had well-tended beards. Polished metal buttons shone on their coats, but their eyes shone even more brightly than their buttons. However, they didn't reflect the glow of the fairy tale. It was a greedy aura, like the light in a beast of prey's eyes just before it pounces.

Farhad's mind hovered in the air, wondering about them. But the world was still swaying and turning around him, and what with all this turning and swaying there wasn't much time to form a clear idea.

A moment later, Farhad's mind tumbled and fell.

All was black around him, and very quiet.

He woke because someone was shaking him.

"Hey there!" said a whisper in his ear. "Wake up!"

Someone else gently nipped his arm.

Farhad sat up abruptly, and wished he hadn't.

His head was echoing, and he felt terrible.

"What . . . what happened?" he whispered, bewildered.

The little girl who had bandaged his hands was sitting in front of him, the white tiger beside her.

349

"You drank half a bottle of arrack all by yourself. *That's* what happened," said the little girl.

"You were very drunk, great hero," added Nitish's blue eyes. "But now we're in a hurry. You can sleep off the rest of your hangover on my back."

"What?" asked Farhad. "Do we have to leave now? It's still night, and—"

He felt his stomach rebelling, and he scrambled to his feet in haste. Staggering, he climbed over a few sleeping bodies to throw up in a corner of the courtyard. For a moment the flavor of the arrack came back into his mouth very unpleasantly. But once he had emptied his stomach, he felt a little better. Except that the world was still turning in circles when he groped his way softly back to Nitish and the girl.

"You said a little too much in your story," the girl whispered. "There are ears here that listened to your words more closely than you may like. The ears of powerful men. They are lords of the desert of Thar, and they trade in what they find there."

"Find?" asked Farhad, dazed.

"Well, mostly they find it in travelers' baggage," said the girl.

"They're robbers," Nitish's eyes explained.

"They like trading in jewels best," the little girl went on. "And none of them has ever seen the bloodstone. As soon as they get a chance, they'll ask you, very politely, to let them have a glimpse of it."

"Oh, no," whispered Farhad. "What did I say?"

"You shouldn't have mentioned that the hero wears a silver amulet around his neck," said the little girl. "That was a mistake, hero."

"I thought I'd changed the story enough . . ."

"You did," Nitish's eyes flashed angrily. "Thank you very much indeed! You changed *me* into something else in your story, for instance."

"What was it?" asked Farhad. An uneasy feeling was spreading through him.

"A large green turtle," said the tiger indignantly.

"Oh, no," Farhad whispered again. "I'm really sorry! That was because—because I once introduced myself as Kurma. Vishnu's turtle incarnation. I didn't mean to hurt your feelings."

"You two don't want to lose any time," the little girl whispered. "The lords of the desert are asleep now. But tomorrow morning, the wedding of Barat Singh and the daughter of the great merchant Kumar Sander Pratap will be over. And then, if not before, they'll come looking for you."

Resigned, Farhad nodded, and with some difficulty he climbed on Nitish's back.

The thought of the Englishman—or was he a German?— flashed briefly into his mind. He, too, was looking for Farhad—and he, too, was on his way through the desert of Thar. The desert of Thar, he told himself, was a big place.

"Well?" asked Nitish's eyes as he turned around to his rider. "How does it feel, sitting on a wrinkled old turtle?"

Farhad knew there was no point in trying to soothe his feelings. And he felt too miserable to make the attempt.

"Thank you," he whispered to the little girl. "Thank you for everything."

"Say hello to the desert for me," the child replied. "And take care you don't lose your way there. The Thar is large and hungry, and it's swallowed up many travelers in its time. My sister Sita is there, too . . . ," she murmured finally. But the tiger was already crouching, ready to spring.

He sailed over the courtyard wall with a single bound, then leaped over the rooftops of the pink houses of Jaipur until they reached the open spaces beyond. So it was that Farhad and Nitish first came to the desert of Thar in the dark after all.

And Barat Singh completed the rites of his wedding to Laila, daughter of the great merchant Kumar Sander Pratap, without them.

It was a long and unhappy marriage. Laila bore Barat Singh seven daughters and not a single son, which grieved her so much that over the following years she grew to be five times her original size.

As for Barat Singh, he fled from the enormous woman in his bed to go into the desert, where he followed in her father's footsteps: He became just as successful a merchant as Kumar Sander. The jewel trade in particular made him rich, and as for the way he acquired jewels, he took after his father-in-law there, too.

But that was all many years later.

At Barat Singh's wedding, not even Barat Singh himself noticed that in the morning his bride's father was gone.

Gone—as anyone might already suspect—to do an extremely lucrative deal in jewels on the road between Jaipur and Jaisalmer.

Sand

THEY HADN'T BEEN ON THEIR WAY THROUGH
the desert for five minutes when Farhad felt a pang in
the back of his head. His head itself still ached, but now it was
as if the pain had gathered in one particular place.

And before another five minutes were up, he realized
that it wasn't the pain, it was the unpleasant feeling of being
watched. Farhad turned around.

Out there in the darkness, he could just see a black line
moving toward them.

He narrowed his eyes to get a better view. The line was

like a huge snake moving sideways through the sand. But it wasn't a snake.

"Nitish," said Farhad suddenly, in a harsh voice. "There are horsemen behind us. Maybe two dozen of them riding side by side. And they're gaining ground."

Nitish turned his head.

Together, he and Farhad watched the row divide. The horsemen rode off on both sides. "They want to encircle us," said Nitish's eyes, which caught and seemed to multiply what little light there was: They were two burning points in the night. "Well, just look at that," Farhad read in those burning pupils. "Those must be your friends, the bandits—the men you described the bloodstone to in such glowing colors."

But the bloodstone had only one color, the color of blood, and that, thought Farhad, was exactly the color that the men behind them liked best.

"Faster," he whispered. "You must run faster. How is it that you're not as fast as usual—as fast as the wind and as weightless as smoke?"

"The desert is trying to suck my paws down," replied Nitish angrily. "It makes them sink in. It's not fair. I'll get used to its unfairness in time, but it isn't easy."

Farhad looked nervously around at the men. Their horses were used to the soft sandy surface. They flew through the

355

night like black shooting stars. The net cast by the bandits was beginning to close in.

Then the air exploded behind them. Farhad ducked.

From the left, a second shot wounded the wings of the desert night.

Farhad heard someone call out, and he was almost sure it was the voice of Kumar Sander Pratap: the host at the wedding, the man whose food he had eaten and whose arrack he had drunk.

"They're only firing into the air," he whispered in the tiger's ear. His cheek was lying on the back of Nitish's neck now. "They're warning us."

The third shot came from right behind them.

As it echoed through the air, a star went out in the sky.

And the tiger took a great leap at the same time. A leap larger than any Farhad had known him to take before. Farhad clutched Nitish's coat to keep from losing his balance. The leap carried them a long way—carried them over the next dune out of range of the bandits, carried them away into the night, and once Nitish had his paws on the ground again he was able to go as fast as he had always gone before.

The night wind followed close on their heels like a dog, and when Farhad looked back once again, he could hardly make out the figures of the bandits in the distance.

"What—what happened?" he asked.

Nitish turned his great head while his paws flew on through the sand.

"The shock made my paws forget that the sand was sucking them in. That man Kumar Pratap—*he killed a star*," said the tiger, stunned. "An eternal, shining star. I've never been so scared in my life."

"I don't think the shot and the star . . . Well, stars sometimes do go out," said Farhad. "Entirely of their own accord. It was coincidence . . ."

Nitish snorted disapprovingly. "I'm not just any old tiger," he replied. "I'm a *sacred* tiger. The gods made me to run races with the wind. And you found me because it was my fate to carry you. Are you trying to tell *me* there's such a thing as coincidence in the world?"

Farhad didn't reply to that.

He thought of Krishna and wondered if he extinguished stars on purpose to scare sacred tigers.

The stars that were left showed Nitish and Farhad their way for the rest of the night—and they were glad of the starlight. The desert is like the sea. If your heart lives there, you don't need the stars. But if you are a stranger in the desert, your only chance is the luck to survive it.

Toward morning, Farhad nodded off to sleep again, and when he woke the sun had already come up quietly over the horizon.

Farhad yawned, and as yawning is infectious even in India and even to sacred tigers, the second time he and Nitish yawned in unison.

Farhad thought of the night that had passed: the bandits, the wedding, and his loose tongue.

"Are you really . . . are you still angry about that turtle?" he asked the white tiger cautiously.

"I don't remember any turtle," said Nitish. And then he asked, with a certain satisfaction, "How's your arrack hangover?"

"Wearing off," said Farhad. "But my head still isn't perfectly clear."

The night had been cool, but as soon as the yellow disk of the sun was up above the horizon, the heat became almost unbearable. There was nothing around them but the desert, endless as an ocean. They could see no sign of the robbers now, but there was nothing else in sight, either. Farhad tried in vain to see Nitish's tracks in the sand.

"You're still as fast as you were yesterday after that shock you had," he said.

"My paws are used to the sand now," explained the tiger.

"It was an enemy at first, now it's a friend. It knows it mustn't let me sink in. It's turned soft and friendly under the pads of my paws."

"I'm going to miss the way you talk about things as if they were all alive," said Farhad.

"They *are* alive!" Nitish told him, sounding rather injured. "Look at the sand rippling away in waves. Can't you hear the desert of Thar breathing? Didn't you hear the dunes wandering in the night?"

"No," said Farhad. "I think only a sacred tiger can hear the desert breathing and dunes wandering."

Satisfied, Nitish nodded and turned back to the living, breathing desert.

"I thought," said Farhad around midday, "that the desert would be full of oases. But I can't see a single one. It's all the same everywhere."

"It *is* full of oases," said Nitish. "You just have to look at it like this: Your head is full of ideas, my hero, but I can't see a single one of them."

The sun had already crossed a good part of the sky (which must have been a strain on it in such heat), when one of the desert's ideas reached Farhad and Nitish.

"There!" cried Farhad in excitement, pointing forward. "See those trees? See that green?"

His tongue was sticking to his gums like something that didn't belong to him, and his head ached with the heat. The shirt he had wound around it wasn't enough protection against the blazing sun. Cool streams and glittering fountains had been splashing through his overheated brain for some time, making him dizzy.

"Careful," said Nitish. "Not every oasis is a real oasis. They say some of them dissolve when you get there."

"This one won't dissolve," Farhad assured him. He had no strength left.

And this time the desert was kind.

It brought forth the shapes of huts and mud walls, with green treetops waving above them, and soon, with one last bound, the tiger landed in the middle of a shady orchard. Farhad slid off his back, felt the soil between the trees with his toes, and let a blissful sense of cool relief stream through him. Round yellow apricots grew on the trees. He breathed in their fragrance, and although there was no one keeping watch over them, he hesitated before stealing one. How little he would have thought about that in the old days!

Cool water ran from a pipe, trickling around the roots of the trees. Nitish dipped his pink tongue in the puddle left by the water. As for Farhad, he lay full length on the ground and drank and drank until he could drink no more.

He left the orchard reluctantly. He would have liked to lie down on the fragrant earth under the apricot trees and sleep for a long, long time—for days, months, years, until all his weakness was gone.

But Nitish urged him to go on. "You won't find your princess in an apricot orchard," he said, "and Krishna is impatiently waiting for us to finish our task at last. There's not much time. Come along, my hero."

"You just want to find a chicken somewhere," said Farhad.

"Yes, that, too," the tiger agreed.

He found his chicken straying among the gardens and orchards, and Farhad searched the green abundance of the oasis for a date palm where a princess might once have sat dreaming. But although the gardens were brimming over with green life, with fruit trees and vegetable beds, he didn't find a date palm.

He asked a woman who was busy repainting the complex pattern on the mud wall of a hut. Her fingertips were white with paint, her clothes had slipped down over her shoulders as she worked, and she smiled at the strangers without any shyness.

"You have a handsome tiger there," she said, putting out her hand to stroke him. Nitish stood still with surprise.

The desert women, thought Farhad, must be different

361

from all others. And his heart beat faster. If the princess came from anywhere, surely it was this place.

"We have no date palms here," said the woman, putting her untidy hair back from her forehead and laughing at the white mark she left there. "But where are you going if you need a date palm to help you get there?"

"That's not exactly it," said Farhad, smiling. "We're bound for the city in the middle of the desert."

"Jaisalmer," said the woman. "You still have two days' journey ahead of you. But there's no good road leading from here to Jaisalmer. Too many caravans go that way. Too many caravans with too much cloth, too much pepper, and too much silver. The robbers lying in wait will catch you easily. They are armed, and you are alone."

"Thank you," replied Farhad, "but we have one such encounter behind us already."

"Well," said the woman, and the corners of her mouth twitched with amusement, "I don't know how you escaped them, because few get away as intact as it seems you two did. But if you'd rather not repeat the experience, I'd advise you to join a caravan." She laughed. "A date palm may help you against the bandits if you know what to do with it. But as there are no date palms here . . ."

"Is there a caravan, then?" asked Farhad.

"There was a caravan here yesterday, and I don't think it's set off again yet. If you go ahead past those walls, you'll find it."

Farhad could still hear her merry laughter as he went in the direction she had pointed out.

Sure enough, at the end of the path he found a small pool, and a group of camels stood around this pool drinking, with their legs awkwardly spread and their long, swaying necks bent over the surface of the water.

Nitish growled, and the camels looked up. Their eyes were large and reproachful.

"We don't need this bunch to help us cross the last part of the desert," said Nitish's eyes with hostility.

"Calm down," said Farhad. "It's better this way. We escaped the bandits once, but who knows what might happen next time?"

Farhad asked for the leader of the caravan, and found him loading up his camel. He was an old man with a long white beard, and he gave Farhad a suspicious glance.

"Where have you sprung from so suddenly?" he asked. "Did you fall into this oasis from the sky?"

"More or less," said Farhad. "May my white tiger and I travel through the desert with you?"

The old man lashed his pack firmly into place. "And what will you pay me for taking you with us?"

"We don't have a peisa to our names," Farhad said, "but when we reach Jaisalmer, a story will be told of a hero who traveled right through the country on a mission for the gods. And if you give us the protection of your caravan, there'll be a wise old man with a handsome beard in the story. Everyone will say he had a good heart because he helped a stranger who had nothing with him but his courage and his fear. That story will be our payment to you."

"Your words are strange, my son," said the old man, and he looked more closely at Farhad. For a while his eyes lingered on the young man's forehead. Finally he nodded slowly.

"We ride on as soon as all the animals have drunk from the pool," he growled. "Join us if you really want to. We have enough rice to feed two more mouths, and Jaisalmer isn't far now. We'll be there when the moon is full."

With these words he turned away, as if he felt embarrassed to have shown such kindness to strangers. But Farhad's heart leaped up when he heard of the full moon.

They would arrive in time.

The caravan was made up of men whose faces told tales of the desert. Only one among them seemed to be as much of a stranger as Farhad himself.

He was a European with hair and a mustache the color

of sand when the sun shines on it at noon. Rumor in the caravan said that he was a spy, for this was the time when war was being planned in Europe, and you could never tell what Europeans in Asia really were and what they were just pretending to be.

The European rode at the front with the leader of the caravan, and at first Farhad took no special notice of him.

He had almost nodded off to sleep on the tiger's back when a small voice made him wake with a start.

"What happened to your hands?" it asked. Farhad knew that voice. The first time he had heard it, it had asked him exactly the same question.

He looked up at a heavily laden camel trotting along beside the tiger, and among the wooden crates and bales of cloth he saw something else, another small part of its freight: a little girl with her hair in long braids. He hadn't noticed her before. Farhad guessed that the girl was about eight or nine . . .

"How did *you* get here?" he asked in surprise.

"On the camel," replied the girl.

"Yes—but how did you manage to come so far in such a short time? The tiger I'm riding is fast as the clouds and can't be stopped any more than you can stop the wind, but a camel . . . ?"

"We've been traveling for many days," said the girl,

slightly bewildered. Then she repeated her question. "What happened to your hands?"

Farhad stretched them out and looked at them. "They're better," he said. "The neem leaves did them good. Thank you for bandaging them."

"Me? I didn't bandage your hands! I've never seen you before! I only asked because your hands shine so strangely. You probably can't see it yourself, but they shine from the inside."

Farhad's hands shone no more than the camel's feet. What had happened to the little girl from Jaipur? Had the desert robbed her of her wits?

"You really don't remember me?" he asked.

She examined him, and her eyes told him very clearly what she was thinking: Has the desert robbed this stranger of his wits?

"No," she said firmly.

A terrible thought occurred to Farhad. Whatever had happened to the girl's mind, she had reached this part of the desert of Thar ahead of him. Had he himself lost time somewhere?

Stranger things had happened on this journey already. He had talked to gods, he had ridden on the wind—why shouldn't he have mislaid time, too?

When the moon is full, the old man had said. *We'll be there when the moon is full.*

Had he just meant next time the moon was full?

Farhad felt fear coursing through his veins, and his throat was dry.

"It's an odd thing," said the girl, breaking into his thoughts. "Back then before we set off, I heard about someone else riding a white tiger."

"Who told you about him?" asked Farhad.

"A man who was looking for the white tiger and his rider. He said he'd caught the white tiger, but it escaped him, and he had to find the tiger and its rider. He wouldn't say any more."

"And who exactly was looking for us?" asked Farhad. Was the girl's memory coming back to her?

"A German," she said, just as Farhad had expected. "It's his fault that my parents died in a fire. They quarreled, and my father was very angry . . ."

"Kerosene," said Farhad.

"Yes. It was very bright."

"Just a moment." Farhad was racking his brains. Something about what she was saying sounded odd. Last time the little girl had said she wasn't there at the time of the fire . . .

"And you're sure we didn't meet in Jaipur?" he asked again.

"Jaipur?" The little girl shook her head. "You say you met me in Jaipur?"

Farhad nodded.

"Oh, that wasn't me," said the girl. "That must have been Chita. I'm Sita."

Of course, thought Farhad. That was it: *Sita saw it . . . She said the fire was very bright . . . And my sister Sita is in the desert, too . . .*

"We're twins," explained the girl, and Farhad knew he hadn't lost track of time, they were riding toward the right full moon, and a stone as heavy as the whole desert of Thar fell from his heart.

"Our relations in Jaipur couldn't feed both of us," said the little girl. "That's why they sent me away. We have a distant cousin in Jaisalmer. He works for a merchant who's so rich that he has eight wives. But the merchant thinks our cousin isn't really a man, so he's entrusted his eight wives to him. He can work with the maidservants in the harem, and he breathes in the fragrance of the eight wives and is surrounded by their beauty. I'm sure my cousin will be able to find me work in his master's house." She put out her hands and looked at them critically. "My hands are small," she said, "but they can work hard."

"This rich merchant," said Farhad, "does rumor say that he hasn't had his last wife very long?"

She nodded. "It's said that she comes from the desert."

Farhad smiled.

"There are other rumors about your rich merchant," he said. "Bad rumors. I know his story, and the rumors are true. You're not going to work for him."

"I'm not?" asked the little girl, looking at him suspiciously.

"No," Farhad heard his voice saying, and he was surprised at himself. "Chita healed my hands, and I can't let her sister end up in the household of a man like that merchant. I'll find you other work, a better job."

"Do you promise?" asked Sita, with distrust in her voice.

"I promise," said Farhad, and to his own amazement he meant it.

"Maybe," said Sita after a while, "it would be a good idea if you knew something. That man who was looking for you. The German. He's here with the caravan. When I found that out, I didn't want to come, but they made me."

That evening, the travelers sat around a large fire, and the old leader of the caravan made sure that the stranger and his tiger had rice to eat, too.

Nitish growled quietly.

"First camels, then rice," he said. "I preferred the elephants. I can't stand these camels. They kick with their big feet, and you have to jump out of the way, and then they give you injured looks as if you'd been trying to eat them."

Farhad laughed.

"Why are you laughing, friend?" someone next to him asked. "Let me share the joke with you."

The speaker had a heavy accent, and Farhad found that he was looking into the face of the blond European. The mustache on the man's upper lip quivered when he spoke.

"We haven't had the pleasure of being introduced yet," said the German, offering his hand. "Gasser. My name is Gasser. Erwin Gasser."

Farhad took the man's hand, although reluctantly. He had never understood the European custom of constantly shaking hands, and it was a great effort for him to touch the hand of this particular European.

"Vamana," he said. "My name is Vamana."

Vishnu had come to earth to live with men as the dwarf Vamana. And facing the tall German, Farhad felt like a dwarf. So far he had defeated him every time by means of wiliness and his nimble mind, never by strength. But of course the German wasn't a German, although Farhad still didn't know where he really came from. Even in Farhad's feverish dreams in Varanasi, he hadn't hesitated to change his nationality again. But whether he was really Menière, Steal, Olszevsky, or Gasser, he looked as if he had difficulty in eating his rice with the spoon that the leader of the caravan had given him. Europeans, everyone knew, couldn't eat with their hands, so it was better to give them cutlery. However, this man with the blond mustache seemed more used to eating with his hands than with a spoon.

Wherever he first came from, he must have been in India for a long, long time.

That night, Farhad slept close to the tiger, whose large, warm, breathing body protected him from the icy cold of the desert night.

It protected him from something else, too: Once or twice Farhad emerged from confused dreams and saw a shadow slinking around the outskirts of the camp among the sleeping people and the camels. The shadow was watching him. It was waiting for an opportunity to catch him alone.

And it looked at the sky with a smile. The opportunity wouldn't be long in coming.

"We're nearly there," Nitish said next morning. "Only a day's journey lies between us and the princess. What do you think of that, great hero?"

"I'm not thinking of it at all," replied Farhad. "A great deal can happen in a day."

And he was to be proved right.

Around midday, the sky ahead of them grew darker. Farhad was sitting on Nitish's back, deep in thought. It was as if the desert were equally deep in its own thoughts.

And the tiger seemed to be brooding, as well. The end of their journey lay ahead, and who knew what it might bring?

Farhad didn't notice the caravan becoming uneasy. He didn't notice the camels quickening their pace or Nitish and him falling a little behind. Only when the German spoke to him did he come out of his daydreams with a start.

"Good to speak to you alone for once," said Gasser from the back of the camel he had brought up beside them. "It's a nuisance to have the caravan around us all the time."

Farhad pretended to be concentrating entirely on the view of the desert. "What do you want?"

The German made a movement swift as a shadow, and something metal gleamed in his hand. It was a pistol, and its muzzle wasn't pointing at Farhad.

It was pointing at Nitish's white chest.

"Tell your tiger not to go racing ahead to catch up with the others," he said calmly. "He may be sacred in some way that I don't understand, but I wouldn't be so sure that he's immortal. No, if I were you I wouldn't put it to the test."

Farhad said nothing.

"Apart from that, of course you know what I want. It's getting tedious, having to tell you yet again: I want the bloodstone."

Farhad saw that the last camel in the caravan was one of those carrying heavy burdens. Perhaps it was the camel with the little girl on it. Or perhaps not.

He thought of shouting.

"Don't shout!" said Gasser, as if he had read Farhad's mind. "The caravan won't wait for you. It has worse things to worry about. Haven't you seen the sky?"

Farhad looked up. Dark gray veils covered the sun, and he couldn't see the horizon.

"What's the matter with the sky?" he growled. He realized that he sounded almost like Nitish.

"We're riding into a sandstorm. I've been watching the sky since last night. If you can read the desert, its storms tell you they're coming well in advance. And I can read the desert much better than that white-bearded old man." He sighed. "A shame about the caravan. All those bales of costly cloth! The silk, the dried chilies! Nothing will be left of them when the storm is over. It will mop them up like a sponge."

"How about you?" asked Farhad. "What are you going to do?"

"I have no quarrel with the sandstorm, and it has none with me. Long ago we came to a kind of agreement to leave one another alone."

Farhad asked himself whether the desert heat had also softened the wits of the German—or the Frenchman or the Englishman.

He heard a click as the man took the safety catch off his pistol.

"Get off your tiger," he ordered.

Farhad wondered what he could do. He came to the conclusion that he couldn't do anything.

Nitish stood there, and Farhad felt the great body tremble beneath him. The sacred tiger who ran as fast as the clouds was shaking with fear for his life. Farhad slid off his back and Gasser jumped nimbly down from his camel, still pointing the pistol.

The first gusts of wind were sweeping over the desert now, swirling up sand.

The German had been right: The storm was swiftly approaching.

"Give me the stone," said Gasser.

Farhad knew it was no good telling this man some fairy

tale. And he sensed that the German meant his threat in earnest. In deadly earnest. Slowly, he undid the bandage on his upper arm. The dried blood had stiffened the fabric, and it broke like thin wood. At last Farhad had the gleaming red jewel in his hand. He felt its cold, smooth surface for the last time—the edge of it cut into his fingers once more—and then he handed it to Gasser without another word.

The German's eyes were gleaming like the stone that now lay in the palm of his hand.

He looked at the red light shining out of it, and smiled. Farhad saw that the caravan had stopped some way ahead of them. The camels obediently bent their long legs and lay down, their bodies forming a fortress against the storm. Farhad wondered whether they had better try reaching that fortress before the storm broke. Then he saw a quick movement out of the corner of his eye, and felt cold metal against his temple.

"Tell your tiger," said Gasser, "that if he moves I shall shoot at once." He laughed softly. "But no, how could I have forgotten? He's a tiger, not a human being. He doesn't understand our language. So if he moves it's just your bad luck."

Nitish stood as if frozen to the spot.

"Good," said the German. "Then I have just a moment

left to explain that you're better off this way. Do you feel the wind?"

Farhad felt it. It was sharp on his skin, already sweeping up great waves in the sand of the desert.

"The wind is only a herald of the storm. When it breaks, you won't see anything anymore, or hear anything, or feel anything. The sand will force its way into your lungs and stifle you. It will cover your body and squeeze the life out of your heart. Death in a sandstorm is a terrible way to die. All the riders in the caravan will die that death. They are small and unimportant. A hero like you, however, shouldn't die so wretchedly. You have helped me, and I will help you: I'll kill you *quickly*, before the storm can do it painfully, persistently, slowly."

Farhad wanted to close his eyes.

But then he saw something racing toward them. Gasser saw it, too, and turned his head.

It was a camel without a rider, a beast of burden that had obviously lost its sense of direction and was now racing toward them in panic, trying to escape the coming storm. Only a few yards separated the great beast from them. Gasser's own camel was the first to swerve aside.

Then the camel was upon them, and Gasser swerved too—a split second too late.

The camel brushed past him, knocking him down. Farhad saw him fall, but only through a haze, for at that moment the storm broke. A wall of wind and sand came between Farhad and the rest of the world, blinding him. He put out his hand to the tiger and clung to his coat, so as not to lose him.

Very close to them, in the inferno of sand and wind, Gasser screamed.

Farhad thought he saw the storm pick him up and carry him away like a leaf, but he could have been mistaken.

What he certainly did see was the camel with its load running off into the desert. But on its back, among the crates and bales of cloth, Farhad could also make out a small figure with two long braids.

Then the storm enveloped them entirely.

STONE

THE STORM WAS LIKE A WALL OF SAND. Like a heavy blanket thrown over you, taking your breath away. Like a hail of shots. Like a fist slamming you down on the ground. Like a monster with a thousand rough, sandy tongues and a thousand strong, windy arms. Like mist and fire in one.

Like death.

But death held no terrors for Farhad now.

Farhad was acquainted with death.

He dug his fingers deep into the tiger's coat amid the chaos of swirling sand. They drew their heads down, ducked away from the gusts of wind and the ferocity of the sand, made themselves small and thin to offer the storm as little of a surface to attack as possible. But it was no use.

It descended on them, seized and shook them, trapped their feet in sand dunes that suddenly appeared from nowhere, whispered savage threats into their ears.

Farhad kept falling over, and Nitish dug his yellow tiger teeth into his shirt and hauled him back to his feet. Farhad couldn't see him—he couldn't see anything at all, but he felt the tiger beside him and shouted soundless defiance at the sandstorm.

Nothing and no one could defeat a hero and his white tiger. Did the storm think itself stronger than fear? Stronger than the wind, high above the green south of the country? Stronger than the rushing water of rivers pregnant with the monsoon? Stronger than the fire in the city of the dead?

Yes, it did think so, and it *was* stronger.

"We're never going to reach the caravan!" Farhad shouted into the wind. "But maybe we can reach Sita! She's all alone! She must be out there ahead of us somewhere..."

The storm flung handfuls of sand into his mouth and prevented him from speaking. But Nitish had understood. Together they set off more or less in the same direction as the little girl had been headed when she disappeared. Farhad trudged along beside the tiger, pressing close to his large body, which offered a little protection from the wind.

So they fought their way, side by side, through the crazy spectacle of the sandstorm. It not only took their sight away, it wouldn't let them breathe; it blew its own rough breath into their lungs and seemed about to smother them. Narrowing their eyes, they tried to find their way, but the sand made them feel they were blind.

They could get nowhere and find no one in the storm.

And a time came when they were both too exhausted to stand up to its violence any longer. Too exhausted to go on looking for anyone, Farhad let himself drop to the ground, and next moment he felt the tiger's big body lying beside him. The storm swept over them like an army of hostile horsemen, shapeless riders made of sand.

Farhad buried his head between Nitish's paws to escape the battering of the grains of sand. Yes, it was better that way. At last he could breathe again.

But then he realized that it wasn't better: The sand was beginning to cover them at an alarming pace.

This was the cruel death the German had meant: being smothered under the sand. Buried alive. Aware of your inevitable end, yet at the same time feeling the exhaustion that wouldn't let you get up to escape it.

Were they going to perish like this in the sand: the hero, his tiger, and the bloodstone?

Farhad groped for the silver amulet.

Help me, he begged in his mind. Help me, princess with the grave smile, princess who loves to sit and dream under date palms, princess who already knows all the stories of our journey in your heart.

Help me.

Nothing happened.

"Oh, my goodness," said Nitish. "I can see now."

"What?" gasped Farhad.

"I can see," replied Nitish. His eyes were glowing in the air above Farhad, clear and blue. "I was keeping them almost closed all this time," Nitish explained. "My eyes. Because I was afraid of the sand. I wasn't to know it works like *this*."

"You weren't to know what works how?" whispered Farhad wearily, spitting out another mouthful of sand.

"When I open my eyes, I can see through the sand. It's like looking through a slight mist," said Nitish. "Amazing. Would you like to have a go?"

"Out of the question," replied Farhad, smiling faintly. "Those are *your* eyes. You can't lend them to people."

"Oh," said Nitish. "So I can't. I forgot."

He raised himself slightly and moved his large white head.

Then he suddenly became restless and turned his blue gaze to Farhad again.

"I can see her!" said his eyes. "I can see her lying there! A little figure, half buried in the sand. It must be Sita! She's lost the camel . . ."

"Is she alive?" Farhad whispered hoarsely. "Is she moving?"

"I don't know," replied Nitish. "We'd have to find out. We must take her with us."

"Take her with us?" asked Farhad. "Take her where? Nothing can save us—nothing! It makes no difference whether a tiger and two human beings die together or separately in the desert!"

382

"Oh, I don't know about that," said Nitish. "After all, I'm a *sacred* tiger. And I have to admit that the longer we travel, the more I impress myself."

Then he smiled in triumph. "I can see a shape ahead," he said. "Something rectangular. I don't know what it is, but it's sure to be less windy on its lee side."

He took Farhad's shirt in his teeth, hauled him to his feet, and the storm attacked them again with all its might. But now they had a purpose. And even in a sandstorm, it's difficult to stop someone with a purpose.

Farhad didn't see Sita until he almost fell over her. Without Nitish's eyes, they would never have found her, even if she'd been only a few feet away. Her frail body was half covered with sand; she had curled up into a ball and buried her head in her thin arms.

"Sita!" he cried, but the storm rubbed out his voice like sandpaper. "Sita! Here we are! Can you hear me?"

He shook her frail shoulders, and at last the little body twitched. Sita raised her head slowly, and blinked at Farhad through the storm and a lot of tangled hair where her braids had come undone. She looked very tired, but when she recognized Farhad a smile came over her face.

He picked her up and laid her on Nitish's back, and Nitish braced himself against the sandstorm one last time.

383

A little later, they reached a wall. There was a second wall beyond it, and after that yet a third— and finally they found the way into a small room like a hole in the storm. Farhad lifted Sita off the tiger's back and dropped to the floor behind her.

He took a deep breath.

"A temple," said Nitish. "An old temple. Rather dilapidated, but good enough for shelter in a sandstorm."

Farhad looked around. The tiger was right. The little room was full of the remains of low columns, with the blurred faces of small stone gods looking out from them. The years had begun to wear their features smooth, which gave them a curiously enraptured expression, as if they were dreaming of another time, of the old days when great caravans still visited them regularly to ask their blessing.

Farhad spat out a large quantity of sand. Most of the desert of Thar seemed to be in his ears and nose, and it seemed to him amazing that there was still so much of it left outside. He looked at Sita. "I have to thank you," he said. "You saved my life."

"Of course," said the little girl quietly. She looked around her in the silence of the ruined temple. "Looks as if it's your turn now."

384

"My turn for what?"

"To save *my* life. Now that the caravan's gone, you must take me to Jaisalmer with you."

"Of course," Farhad heard himself say, as if echoing the girl.

"Oh, and I've brought you something," she said. "I saw it in the German's hand when I was riding toward you on my camel. Then I saw it fall into the sand. And then I found it again. I thought maybe you could use it."

She held out her hand, and there lay the bloodstone, shining as brightly as the sun and as red as the sky when the sun goes down. Farhad gasped for air.

"Here, take it!" There was a note of urgency in Sita's quiet, exhausted voice. "I don't want it. It tried to bite me with its sharp edge."

Farhad took the glittering jewel from her hand and stared at it in amazement.

"I always found it again myself before," he said. "But now it looks as if the stone has made its own way back to me for a change. Thank you," he added. "Thank you again, Sita."

"Never mind that. Just think about finding me work when we reach the city," said Sita. With these words she curled up at Farhad's side, and soon she was fast asleep.

He looked at her arms and her face, which were covered with red weals like his own. The storm drew no distinctions.

385

"Where do you think she lost the camel?" he said thoughtfully.

"Well, it was a good idea of hers not to bring it with her, anyway," said Nitish. "I don't like camels. And it wouldn't have fit into this room."

Farhad stroked the hair back from the little girl's forehead. "What am I going to do with her?"

He looked at the tiger's face, and you might have supposed Nitish was grinning.

"Looks as if a child actually ran to you," purred his eyes. "Who'd have thought it? A professional swindler and con man with no family of his own—and a child runs to him in the middle of the desert."

"Don't laugh," said Farhad. "We have a serious problem. I really did promise to find her work."

"I know. But you've never bothered about keeping your promises, my dear Farhad Kamal."

"No," said Farhad. "I remember. But that was long ago, and my memory is fading. I'm a different person now."

"Fine words," said Nitish's eyes. "Great words. Heroic words . . . So what are we going to do with the child?"

"Take her with us." Farhad sighed. "And as I can't stay in Jaisalmer where the demon king lives, I'll just have to take her on with me a little farther."

Something occurred to him. "Where will you go yourself when we've rescued the princess?"

The tiger's eyes were shining. "I'll go back south," he said. "It's good country for tigers there. And as you know, I'll be a tiger like any other then. I'm almost sorry to think of not being sacred anymore. But I shall have a wonderful time. I hope I'll turn yellow."

"I'm sure you will," said Farhad. "As yellow as the desert. You'll be the yellowest yellow tiger in the whole of south India." He smiled, but it was a sad smile. "I'll come and look for you in the south Indian forests someday," he said. "Later."

"You won't recognize me when I'm yellow. I'll look like all the other tigers. And I won't be able to talk to you anymore."

They fell silent for a while, and only the howling of the sandstorm accompanied their silence.

"Where will you go yourself, my hero?" Nitish asked at last.

Farhad sighed. "I'll miss not having you to make fun of me . . . I hope Krishna will give me a new shape so that I can escape Ravana's fury. As soon as he's done that, I'll go looking for the date palm under which the princess fell asleep. Perhaps we can find it again together, the princess and I—the place where there are green gardens and the hedges are full of songbirds. The place south of Nowhere. It must be one of the oases in this desert . . ."

"Nonsense," said Nitish. "South of Nowhere! Where's that supposed to be? I'm afraid the hero has fallen in love. Heroes in love always talk nonsense." He shook his head.

"Hmm," said Farhad. All the tiny wounds left on his face by the grains of sand were burning as if he had been in another fire—and he couldn't say if his face was turning red because he was blushing or because of those wounds.

"Aren't you going to contradict me?"

"Why would I?"

387

"Well, it wasn't part of Krishna's plan for you to fall in love with the princess."

"Not everything in the world can go the way a god plans it."

"He won't give her to you as your wife. Even if we manage to rescue her. You have no caste and she's the daughter of a god. You can never marry her."

"Not in this life, maybe," replied Farhad.

No sandstorm lasts forever, or to this day, at least, none has been known to last forever.

Even the sandstorm that had broken over our dubious hero and his white tiger in the desert of Thar felt tired in the end.

It slowly lost force, swept once more over the desert, saw that there was nothing left to see, nothing left to be covered up, and lost interest.

Farhad crawled out of the ruined temple and found himself in a completely smooth landscape.

It was as if someone had taken the side of a gigantic knife and run it over the desert, as if it were the gaudily colored icing of one of the huge rectangular cakes in the Madurai confectioners' displays—the cakes he had stared at as a child with such longing in his eyes.

"Nitish!" he cried. "The storm is over! We must hurry. The sun's already low in the sky."

Nitish grunted, opened an eye, and got up all of a sudden. "The desert is all smoothed out," he said in surprise. "Someone very large with a very flat bottom must have sat on it while we were asleep."

"The storm did it," said Farhad, but the tiger didn't seem convinced.

Farhad shook Sita's thin shoulder, and she moved in her sleep. As she did so she changed position slightly, and Farhad saw, to his horror, that the girl's clothes were stained dark red.

She opened her eyes.

"What . . . what happened?" she asked, dazed.

"I wish I knew," replied Farhad brusquely. He pushed aside Sita's torn punjabi, and the little girl flinched.

"Keep still," said Farhad. His mouth was dry. "You're bleeding. What have you done to yourself?"

"The camel—it fell in the storm, and I was underneath it . . ."

She said no more, and Farhad saw her eyes beginning to close again.

"Sita!" He shook her. "Tell me! What happened then?"

"Then . . . then I struggled up. But I'd fallen on something sharp. The camel was screaming and rolling about, and the sharp thing cut into my side. When I felt for it, it was the red stone I gave you—oh! Don't do that!"

Farhad was busy cleaning the wound with part of his shirt. It was a deep cut, and blood was still trickling steadily out of it.

"The bloodstone," he muttered to himself through his gritted teeth. "Always the bloodstone. How terrible it is that to do something good, I need something so evil and dangerous."

He tore off a rag from Sita's clothing, pressed it to the wound, and wrapped a strip torn from his own shirt around her waist like a broad belt. The blood took some time to seep through it, but a small red patch slowly formed on the bandage. Farhad cursed, tore more strips off his shirt, wrapped the bandages around her more tightly.

"There's no point in that," said Nitish's blue eyes, when he glanced the tiger's way. "Come on. The city can't be far off now. We'd better make sure we reach it, and you can get help for her there. I promise to hurry. I'll be even faster than the wind, even more agile than the rain . . ."

Farhad nodded, and climbed up on Nitish's broad back. Then he bent down to Sita, picked her up, and put her on the tiger in front of him.

"The blood was flowing out of her body like a waterfall all this time," murmured Farhad, "and we—we never noticed. *I* never noticed. I looked at the bloodstone, and I didn't notice . . ."

Nitish turned and looked him right in the eyes. "Stop that and concentrate on what lies ahead," he said. "What's done can't be undone, and it's no use thinking of it."

And then he pushed off from the ground with his powerful back paws and began crossing the smooth ocean of sand in great leaps and bounds.

This was Farhad's last journey on the back of the white tiger, and while the desert of Thar moved away below them, he told his own story for the last time.

He held Sita firmly in front of him with both arms to keep her from slipping off Nitish's back, for all the blood her little body had lost had made her sleepy.

And as there was nothing he could do for her, he told her his story. This time he didn't stop to think what he ought to mention and what was better left out.

He told her about the date palm south of Nowhere, and said they would soon go and look for it together. He told her about the wind in Madurai that had carried him on its wings, and the night when he and Nitish had crossed the pool in the temple. He told her about the prison and the men spraying the lawns with water (here Nitish growled quietly). He told her about the many transformations of the Frenchman—or the Englishman, or the German—he told her about the Bodhi tree and all its little colored flags. He told her about the holy Ganges and the fires where the dead were burned. And finally he told her how Chita had healed his hands with the leaves of the neem tree.

As the day wore on, and the tiger's shadow on the sand began to look like the shadow of a long-legged camel, the outline of the city showed on the horizon.

"Jaisalmer," said Farhad. "There it is. Look, Sita, see it rising from the middle of the desert of Thar. Soon, soon we'll be riding through the city gates . . ."

Sita didn't answer. She had fallen asleep with her head against Farhad's shoulder.

Nitish sped up. Now he was racing over the wide sandy surface like light itself, hurrying toward their destination. The solid brown walls of the city became clearer and clearer, its towers grew higher, its buildings larger—until Farhad could make out individual people on top of the city walls. And he saw the silhouette of a palm tree that grew in one of the courtyards of Jaisalmer standing out against the red evening sky. Perhaps, he thought, it was a date palm like the one under which the princess once sat.

"Wake up, Sita," whispered Farhad, shaking the little girl gently. "We're nearly there! We'll find someone in the city to tend your wound! And I'll go looking for the demon king's house, and give his servant the bloodstone in return for letting the princess go free. And everything will be all right, everything."

Sita still didn't move, and Farhad carefully raised her drowsy head from his shoulder. "Sita!" he repeated in a louder voice. "Wake up!"

But she didn't wake up.

Farhad felt for the pulse in her throat, and then he knew that Sita would never, never wake up again. No breath came from her mouth, and the heart in her narrow chest had stopped beating.

She had gone to sleep forever lying against his shoulder.

Only a few more bounds of the tiger now separated them from Jaisalmer, but it was too far for Sita. When had she left them? When he was telling her about the wings of the wind? The night in the temple? The roaring of the river? The shade under the Bodhi tree? He hoped with all his heart that she had gone while he was telling her about something good. Something for her little soul to cling to as

393

she went on her way into the empty space between this life and the next.

"Nitish," he said, and his voice didn't sound at all like a hero's. "Nitish, stop. Just for a moment."

The tiger slowed his flying pace and stopped. He turned to Farhad with his eyes full of questions.

Farhad struggled for a long time as he tried to answer them.

Finally he nodded toward the child in his arms. "Sita," he whispered, "has gone ahead of us. Leaving only her body here."

Then Nitish's eyes were silent, his nose twitched, and his whiskers bristled, rejecting Farhad's words.

394

"Are you sure?" he asked at last.

Farhad nodded.

"What shall we do with her?"

"I don't know," said Farhad. He was still holding Sita to keep her from slipping off Nitish's back, as if that made any difference now. "I really don't know."

He heard his voice failing him entirely, and then he noticed something else: His eyes were full of water. He couldn't help it, the water ran down over his dirty cheeks, scored as they were by the sandstorm, and its saltiness burned his wounds. It dripped off Sita's lifeless body and ran into the tiger's coat.

A monsoon had broken out inside Farhad Kamal, hero and trickster from the south. It had burst the barriers that had kept it back all his life, and now there was no holding it anymore.

He laid his head on the dead girl's tangled hair and wept and wept. His tears shook his whole body. He wept like a little child; he wept for Sita, for the caravan lying buried under the sand, for the beggar boy he had seen falling to his death in Varanasi, for the whole incomprehensible world.

But as the first of his tears reached the tiger's coat, a change came over Nitish. His white fur turned gray, his black stripes slowly faded, and the tiger's pink nose stopped twitching.

Farhad saw the desert through a veil of tears, and it was some time before he realized what was going on underneath him.

"Nitish," he said, mopping at his eyes, but they wouldn't stay dry. "Nitish, what's happening to you?"

"*The salty fluid of life . . . the crystal-clear blood of the earth*," replied the tiger's eyes, and there was astonishment in them. "That's what it is, Farhad. Tears."

"Tears?" Farhad was bewildered. He was still too full of the death of the child in his arms to understand.

"That's what we didn't know all this time!" replied Nitish. And now Farhad felt the tiger's back beneath him grow harder, as if he were bracing all his muscles at once. "I'm turning to stone, Farhad," said Nitish's eyes. They were not blue anymore but had turned a color between gray and brown.

"I was Nitish, Lord of the Right Way. I was Nitish for a long, long time—more than a thousand years. Now I will be Ninit, *Silence*."

"No!" cried Farhad, clutching the tiger's coat with one hand. But it didn't feel soft and furry anymore, it was harsh and rough as rock. "My tears have dried up! I—I'll never cry again, Nitish, I promise you! Stop it! Stop turning to stone! Don't leave me alone! I—I didn't want to turn you to stone! I—"

Then the tiger's eyes said what they had told him once before that day. "Stop that and concentrate on what lies ahead," they said. "What's done can't be undone, and it's no use thinking of it."

His eyes smiled one last time. "You can't stop it now, Farhad. Go on into the city in the middle of the desert. Go and rescue your princess. You'll need all your strength to do it on your own."

"Nitish—"

"I will think of you," said Nitish's eyes.

Then the light in them went out. Farhad stared at them, trying to wrest another message from them, but they were cold, hard stone.

He let himself slip off the tiger's back and looked at him.

The tiger had become a rock, and his outline was already blurring, as if he wanted to keep it a secret that he had once been a tiger.

However, Sita was still lying on his back.

She was lying there of her own accord, without sliding off, even though Farhad wasn't holding her anymore.

He took a step back, and then another—and then he turned and began to run. He ran until he couldn't run anymore. Only when the pain in his lungs was worse than the pain in his heart did he slow down.

And he began walking through the mild evening air of the desert of Thar to the city in the middle of it, Jaisalmer.

A single palm tree waved its fronds at him.

And although Farhad's heart was heavy, so heavy that he thought it was dragging him down into the sand, he went on.

For he was a hero, and he had a task to perform.

Twilight had come and gone, and the first lights were flickering in the city when Farhad reached its gates.

He walked slowly, but he did not stop.

Two British guards and two Indian guards were on watch at the gateway.

"Where do you come from?" they asked.

"Madurai," said Farhad. They shook their heads and laughed.

"What, did you come all this way on foot?"

"No," said Farhad. "I rode here on a white tiger, but he has turned to stone."

The guards laughed even louder.

"What's your name, lunatic?" asked one of the British guards.

Farhad thought for a moment, but then he changed his mind.

He wasn't a swindler and trickster anymore.

398

This was the end of his journey, and he was a hero.

"My name is Farhad," he replied, standing up a little straighter. "Farhad Kamal. Farhad meaning *Happiness*, and Kamal meaning *Lotus Blossom*. And I'm in a hurry."

Then they let him through—a lunatic who had probably lost his mind in the desert.

"Did you see the scar?" whispered one of the Indian guards to the other. "Burned deep into his forehead?"

"The Third Eye," whispered the second. "The sign of Shiva."

"Maybe it was your god Shiva who robbed him of his wits," said a third guard, one of the two British.

Farhad went along the broad, paved street that wound its way up into the city, and his steps faltered. He had to force himself not to stop.

When he reached the first large square, he could see over the city walls and down into the desert. His eyes searched it for a rock looking vaguely like a tiger, but velvety black enveloped the desert now, and there was no pair of shining blue dots in it anywhere.

The city was beautiful.

Its buildings were like pointed filigree towers, full of openwork walls and fine patterns. The fires of coffee and vadai sellers glowed in the streets, and the patterns on the buildings seemed to dance in their light.

Farhad placed his hand on a column that was part of a small temple, and when he looked more closely at the intertwining stone tendrils beside the column, he saw a tiny stone tiger.

The light was too dim for him to make out the figure riding on the tiger.

"Nitish," whispered Farhad. "I'll soon be outside the *haveli*, the fine house where Ravana the demon king is pretending that he's a merchant. But you aren't with me anymore, and I'm helpless without you. I saved your life in the fire, and then I took it from you with my tears. If only I could undo that!"

Then he felt as if he heard Nitish speaking inside his head.

Concentrate on what lies ahead. What's done can't be undone, and it's no use thinking of it.

And he moved out of the shadow of the temple and went back into the maze of streets to find someone who could show him the way.

An old woman was crouching beside the first fire he came to, stirring a large metal pot. A fragrant cloud with an aroma of cardamom, nutmeg, and cinnamon surrounded her, and she ladled a mug of tea out of her pot as Farhad approached.

"Chai, my friend," she called. "Tea for a stranger. Cheap and good. Chai, chai, chai!"

"I don't have a peisa to my name," said Farhad. "I can't pay for your tea. But I need the answer to a question far more urgently than tea."

"There are many answers," said the old woman. "And some of them are worth more than tea. It all depends on the question that your answer belongs to."

Farhad smiled. "The question is: Which is the house of the richest merchant in Jaisalmer?" he said.

"That's easy," replied the old women. "You've just come away from it. I was watching you."

"I thought it was a temple, with all those decorations and columns," said Farhad in surprise.

"Oh, it *is* a temple," the old woman told him, laughing. "A temple built by Ahmed Mudhi for himself! They say his bedroom is lined from floor to ceiling with mirrors so that he can adore himself better. He has seven green courtyards in his temple, and three fountains, and eight wives who are more beautiful than the gold on the roof of the famous golden temple of the Jains in Ajmer! He is certainly the richest merchant in Jaisalmer. Maybe the richest merchant in the whole desert of Thar."

"Where's the entrance of his house?"

"Not far from where I saw you standing, friend. Go around the corner and you'll see it. But what do you want there? Ahmed Mudhi won't be available to speak to anyone, certainly not you, and particularly not tonight. They say that he is to spend the night with his eighth wife for the first time, and she's the youngest and loveliest of them all. A wild girl who comes from the heart of the desert. Folk say she tried climbing over the only wall that stands between the Rajah's gardens and the street, and she very nearly made it, but . . ."

She clicked her tongue and shook her bald head regretfully.

"All the same, I have to go to Rav . . . to Ahmed Mudhi," said Farhad. "And I must hurry."

"Wait!" cried the old woman. "Not so hasty, my son! Let me warn you: There's something I don't like about that man Mudhi. Keep your feet from taking the wrong path! Ahmed Mudhi's house is very fine, but it's not a good place to go. They say its master is sometimes seen slinking around in secret by night, they say he changes himself into a demon with glowing eyes and a burning tongue . . ."

"They seem to say a lot," replied Farhad evasively, and he turned to go at last, but the old woman held him back by his sleeve.

"Here," she said. "Take this mug of tea. If your feet are intent on entering that house, at least strengthen yourself a little first. You look as if you could do with it."

When Farhad bent down to her to take the mug, she whistled through her teeth. "You bear the sign," she said.

"What sign?"

"The sign of the gods. On your forehead, between the eyes. It must be something special that brings you here."

Farhad put a hand to his forehead, and for the first time he felt the scar left by the fire. He nodded and drank his tea. Its spiciness left a warm, calm feeling in his veins.

Then he gave back the metal mug, and without a word he went to the house of Ahmed Mudhi.

Farhad went around the corner that the old woman had mentioned and found the entrance to Ahmed Mudhi's *haveli*.

It was a tall, handsome gateway, and two night watchmen stood there, guards leaning on British rifles and looking at Farhad. He felt for the bloodstone, which was sleeping again in the bandage on his upper arm. But now it seemed to him as if he felt an angry, impatient throbbing there. The bloodstone wanted to go free at last, it wanted to reach the one who would soon be its owner.

"I want to speak to the chief servant in this house," Farhad told the watchmen.

"Do you indeed?" said one of the men.

"Interesting," said the other.

"Where is he?" asked Farhad impatiently.

"I don't think he'll speak to you," said the first man. "Suryakanta is a fine gentleman. He doesn't talk to beggars. What do you want?"

"I'm not a beggar," said Farhad firmly. "I am bringing Suryakanta something he desires. He'll thank you for it if you help me to reach his presence."

"He's busy," said the other man. "If you really want to know, this is the wedding night of Ahmed Mudhi and his eighth wife. A willful creature. Stunningly beautiful, but prickly—like the roses in the Rajah's garden. And his chief servant is on guard outside her door to keep her from trying to run away again before it's time for her to go to her lord and master."

"What I have for Suryakanta is far more important. He will know how to value it," whispered Farhad mysteriously.

But the guards were not impressed.

"Give it to me, then," said one of them. "We can pass it on to him."

Farhad looked him scornfully up and down. "You don't think I'd entrust something so valuable to you, do you?"

"You don't have anything of any value at all," said the man, and he laughed. "Just look at you! Your shirt is in tatters, the cloth around your waist is fraying into single threads, and only the dirt covering you clothes your body, dear brother! Not even the hair on your head seems to want to grow! You're nothing but a mangy dog! We'll give you some water and a crust of bread, and then you can leave us in peace and try your luck somewhere else!"

"You don't understand!" cried Farhad desperately. "You don't understand at all! Tell Suryakanta I have the stone!"

"Stone? What stone?"

"The bloodstone," replied Farhad.

The guards said nothing for a while, and then they roared with laughter.

"Yes, you certainly look like it!" said the first man. "You look just like a young man who carries jewels about with him!"

"There's no such thing as the bloodstone, dear friend," said the second man softly, and he took a step closer to Farhad. "It's only a rumor, nothing more. A good trick for worming your way into someone's house, but others have thought up better tricks when they tried to gain access to Ahmed Mudhi's treasures. Now get out before we really lose our tempers."

Farhad tried to slip past them, but the second guard pushed him back with the butt of his rifle. He staggered.

"What's going on out there?" he heard a third man call from inside the house.

"There's someone here," the first guard called back, "who's just asking for trouble . . ."

At that Farhad turned and ran, under cover of darkness, along the alley and around another corner. He stopped, his heart thudding, beside a blank wall that had no windows and no decorations. The moon came out from behind clouds, and by its light Farhad saw the palm tree that had waved to him on the other side of the wall. He felt for the amulet at his breast and thought of the princess who was closer to him now

than ever before. Only a couple of walls separated them . . .
He listened to himself, listened to the voice of the amulet, and
heard the words of the old woman selling chai.

A wild girl, the old woman had said, *who comes from the heart
of the desert. She tried climbing over the only wall that stands between
the Rajah's gardens and the street, and she very nearly made it, but . . .*

Of course. The princess was telling him what to do. It
was as if *she* had sent the woman selling tea to him. He just
had to find the wall, the only wall between the garden and the
outside world . . . But wasn't he standing by that very wall? He
examined it more closely. No, there wasn't a single window in
it, and the palm tree seemed to him too close for there to be
any rooms between it and the wall.

His feet found the uneven places in the baked mud of
the wall as if by themselves, and his fingers found the right
handholds so easily that he almost felt as if he were flying up
the wall instead of climbing it. For his heart, his heart was
singing with the princess's own, and both hearts knew that
the time for him to rescue her had come. The time they had
been waiting for through a whole book.

When Farhad was sitting astride the wall, he felt for the
stone once again.

Yes, it was there, all was as it should be.

He was ready to face Suryakanta.

Below him lay the gardens in the light of the full moon. He heard the cooing of the dreaming doves in their dovecote, he saw the surface of the pool of water with the fountain at its center, sleeping now, and he breathed in the fragrance of the white flowers that open only in the dark to let moths drink their nectar.

The light of an oil lamp was still flickering in one of the windows facing the wall, high above him. It gleamed with a bright and silvery flame, as if the light were reflected from dozens of mirrors. Farhad saw a figure standing on the balcony outside this window. At first he took fright. Then he saw that the figure wasn't looking at him, but down into the garden.

Ravana.

Or Ahmed Mudhi.

He was still alone. He hadn't carried the princess off to his dark domain yet. Farhad was not too late.

He took a deep breath and swung both legs over the wall. Then he began climbing down the thick old branches of the climbing plants on it, which were as entangled and intricately intertwined as life itself.

That night, a single servant was stationed in the first of Ahmed Mudhi's seven gardens, the garden where the most beautiful of his three fountains danced in the air by day.

It was improbable that the crazy girl would try to run away again, but one has to be prepared even for the improbable.

The servant stood at the foot of the date palm, leaning on the tree and looking up at its fronds, which seemed to be reaching for the full moon. He stayed leaning there for some time, wondering when the Rajah would finally summon his eighth and most beautiful wife.

He was tired; he wanted to leave the rustling, restless nocturnal garden and lie down on his mat. He thought the garden was eerie. They said demons haunted it, and the servant was a superstitious man. When he looked away from the top of the date palm and glanced at the wall, he thought at first that his eyes were deceiving him. Or was it just the wind blowing through the desert and its cities by night, stirring the bougainvillea leaves?

He looked again. No, someone was climbing down the wall.

That someone had turned his back to the servant to get a better hold on the climbing plants.

Ahmed Mudhi's servant didn't hesitate.

He raised his gun—a fine weapon that he polished every day; his master had bought it from the British—and he took aim and fired.

He had good eyes, and he hit his target.

Farhad had almost reached the ground and was thinking of jumping when he heard the gun go off. At the same time he felt something bury itself in his back just below his left shoulder blade. A fierce pain went through him, and his hands let go of the climbing plants.

When he landed on the soft earth, the pain had gone away. Farhad knew it was still there, but he didn't feel it anymore. Everything was going around and around in an unreal way. He put his hand to his chest and felt something wet.

The bullet must have gone right through his back and come out at the front.

It hadn't hit his heart, because his heart belonged to the princess.

But the blood was pulsing as it poured out of him—just as it had poured out of Sita, only a thousand times faster.

He heard voices in the garden, closed his eyes, and tried to lie quite still. The voices came closer, bent over him, and one of them said, "An excellent shot."

"Thank you."

"He'd already tried getting through the front gate on some feeble pretext. I wonder what he wanted here, on this of all nights?"

"Maybe he was trying to steal that crazy beauty away . . ."

The voices laughed, and moved away again.

"We'll deal with him in the morning," was all Farhad heard before the voices died away entirely, and the garden was quiet. It was a little while before the leaves found the courage to rustle again, or the trees to murmur and whisper.

Farhad saw their branches swaying above him in the wind. And he looked up at the trunk of the palm tree. Yes, it was a date palm. A date palm like the one under which the princess had once sat dreaming, so very long ago.

Had his journey really lasted only a month? It was as if a lifetime had passed since he found the amulet in the lotus pool in Madurai. He felt his strength draining out of him. Gasping with the effort, he groped for the amulet and pressed it to the wound in his breast.

He still didn't feel the pain.

And suddenly Farhad remembered what the wise old man on the mountain had told him. *You will go through fire, through water, and through air on the wind. But Death stands at the end of the way.*

"Princess," he whispered. "Princess whose name I don't know! Stand by me once more. I am so close . . . so close . . ."

He heard her answer in his reeling head. And for the first time he didn't just sense the words, he heard her voice quite clearly. It was beautiful, but not soft and yielding. It was rough like the desert sand.

"My own strength is at an end, too," said the princess. "It was a long journey we made together. Death chooses its own time. I cannot avert it. All I can do is . . ." She seemed to hesitate, and then she whispered, "All I can do is delay it for a little while. Perhaps only for minutes, perhaps for an hour . . ."

"So I can lie here a little longer," replied Farhad, with a strange sense of happiness in his heart. "I can lie here and think of you."

"I will weep for you," said the princess.

Then the amulet slipped out of Farhad's fingers, his head fell to one side, and a great, overwhelming weariness came over him. He closed his eyes, and for the last time in his life he breathed in the scent of the white nocturnal flowers.

LALIT AND LAGAN

Indian love is always taboo,
and smells of cardamom.
It tastes of chili, of spices, too.
Come, it says softly, come.

Indian love is red as rage
and deep, deep blue as sorrow.
It is not easy, it is not kind,
it may not see tomorrow.

In Indian gardens, Indian love
rustles like leaves in the wind.
And should two lovers in that grove
be both of the same mind,
the wind will have this tale to tell
of longing, grief, and death:
They loved not wisely but too well
they loved to their last breath.

R AKA SAID NO MORE, AND FOR A WHILE silence hung in the room like the last, clear note of a long, wild piece of music.

"But that—that's terrible!" Lalit whispered. "Is he really dead?"

"I'm afraid so," said Raka. "Or do you see any hero around here trying to rescue me?" she added bitterly.

Instinctively Lalit glanced around and realized how pointless it was. There was nothing in the room but the shadows of night lurking in the corners. And Raka. And himself.

Oh, no, he thought. No. I'm no hero. I can't rescue anyone.

How would I do it, anyway? How would I set about it?

He shook his head.

The moon hadn't reached the top of the date palm in the garden yet.

It was sailing in the sky, full and white, and it seemed to hesitate. But even the moon must obey the laws of the universe, and the laws of the universe commanded it to move on.

Lalit rose from the windowsill, went over to Raka, and took her in his arms.

414

She didn't look at him. She was looking out at the moon.

"I love you," said Lalit.

"Tomorrow," replied Raka quietly, "you won't love me anymore. You can only love the living. And tomorrow I'll be dead. Dead and still as the stone of this window seat. Ahmed Mudhi's fury tonight will leave no warmth in me."

"I'll love you all the same," said Lalit. "You may go, but you will leave your story behind. I'll tell it and retell it, and it will go on its travels—it will travel all over India, like Farhad. And as long as people tell that story there'll be a part of you left in it, living on."

"Fine words," said Raka.

At that, Lalit fell silent, and he kissed her one last time. He didn't need any words for that.

They looked out into the night together.

Down in the bushes, where the white flowers shone like little patches of light in the dark, the black wind was rustling. Or was it the wind?

"You did invent him, didn't you?" whispered Lalit. "Your hero. He doesn't really exist?"

"Of course I invented him," Raka whispered back.

"I have to admit, I felt a little jealous now and then."

Then he realized how stupid and selfish that sounded. Raka was going to face Death that night, and he was jealous of a hero she had invented.

But he couldn't do anything about the feeling.

The wind rustled again, very gently, very softly, and it sent the moon moving across the sky a little closer to the date palm.

"Go away now," Raka whispered. "Go and sleep. I would like to spend my last hour before I face the Rajah alone."

She slipped out of Lalit's embrace like a fish.

So he turned and left her.

But he knew he would not sleep that night.

அன்பு

Through love

AMONG THE ROSE THORNS

HE LAY AWAKE FOR A LONG TIME, FOR AN eternity, staring at the darkness in his small room.

His heart was burning in him because the girl he loved was going to die.

And there was nothing he could do about it.

As usual, everyone else was stronger than him. He had learned to serve, to obey, to avoid trouble, and no one had ever taught him to rebel. Because there was no point in it, he told himself. Because rebels always lost out in the end. For the first time Raka's flashing eyes had made him doubt the truth of that, but his doubts were small and new, and hadn't had enough time to develop inside his head.

He closed his eyes, and sleep came to him at last.

Then that sound came in the darkness.

It was as if someone were trying to open the tiny window through which the garden could see into Lalit's room. He lay perfectly still and listened. There! There it was again. Something landed heavily on the floor beside Lalit's window. Or no, not something, but *someone*—because now he heard soft, stealthy footsteps. They stopped beside the mat he was sleeping on, and the stranger must be bending down to him, for he felt his breath in the cool night air.

Breath that came irregularly, as if it hurt whoever was there to breathe at all.

Lalit blinked.

At first he felt afraid when he looked into the stranger's face. He had never set eyes on that face before, yet he knew it as well as his own.

The stranger was thin, and wore a ragged shirt that had once been white. He had three days' growth of stubble, his hair grew in small tufts on his head, countless tiny red weals marked his face in the pale moonlight, and between his eyes—just where the priests of every temple left their mark of blessing—there was a burn scar.

Lalit sat up and stared at him.

"Farhad!" he whispered.

Farhad put a finger to his lips.

Then he took Lalit's hand and placed something in it.

Lalit felt that his hand was bleeding. His fingers closed around something hard and cold, with a bright, glowing red light that streamed out through them.

And he woke, bathed in sweat.

Gasping for air, he sat up and looked around him, his eyes wide open.

No, there was no one here. No hero in ragged clothes. No jewel in his hand. He'd been dreaming.

He lay back again and breathed deeply. Judging by the position of the moon outside the little window, he hadn't been asleep for long. The top of the date palm was still waiting for its round, white visitor.

A dream. Only a dream.

"There's no Farhad and no bloodstone," Lalit whispered to himself.

But suppose there was? Suppose the dream had been trying to tell him something?

And suddenly it was as if he heard a voice in his head speaking loud and clear. Perhaps it had been there all the time and he had simply been ignoring it.

"No, the hero didn't climb in through your window," said the voice. "For once in your life you have to do *something* for yourself."

Then Lalit felt ashamed of his own thoughts, and he stood up and made his way quietly through the dark corridors of Ahmed Mudhi's large house to go and look for a hero in Ahmed Mudhi's garden. Perhaps it was all nonsense. Indeed, that was more than likely.

But what did he have to lose?

And how much more would he lose if he *didn't* obey the call of his dream and the dream had been right?

The garden was as beautiful as on the night when Raka drew him down to her in the lotus pool. The memory of that night sang on in the fragrant flowers and the rustling leaves, the cooing of the doves and Lalit's secret footsteps on the gravel path.

He found the only outside wall of the Rajah's seven gardens without any difficulty. Ever since Raka had tried climbing over it—before he even knew her—he had looked at it again and again, thinking of the strange girl's courage.

A hedge of white roses grew beneath the wall. It was a thick, dark hedge, and Lalit couldn't see through it. He hadn't brought a lamp with him, because what he was doing was not just crazy but also forbidden. No one must find him searching the garden for an imaginary hero who had come to steal away the Rajah's eighth wife.

Lalit went down on all fours and made his way through the dense, prickly foliage. The thorns left burning scratches on his arms and face, and he had to grit his teeth not to cry out. But he thought of Farhad and all the wounds that Raka's hero had suffered to rescue his princess, and he felt ashamed again.

The light of the moon didn't reach as far as the ground. It got caught in the thorns of the roses before it reached the foot of the wall, which lay in absolute darkness.

The scent of earth reached Lalit's nostrils—and suddenly it was mingled with another smell: the smell of sweat and blood and fear. Lalit's hand met a warm, yielding body. He flinched back, and listened.

Yes, someone was breathing there in the darkness.

This was crazy. This couldn't be happening. Lalit had come to find someone here, but he hadn't expected that anyone actually *would* be there.

He felt his head reeling.

"Who are you?" came a whisper out of the darkness. It was the voice from Lalit's dream.

"I am Lalit," he whispered back. "And you—are you—are you really . . . ?"

"I am Farhad," whispered the voice whose face he couldn't see. "But you don't look to me like Lalit. You look to me . . ." The voice died away, and Farhad coughed, a gurgling sound. "The blood," he whispered, "it's found its way into my lungs, damn it."

"Who do you think I am?" asked Lalit.

"You look to me like Lagan, the man who comes at the Right Time."

"How strange," said Lalit, or Lagan. "How strange, because that's the very name I had at birth, before anyone gave me this nickname."

"Are you a friend?" asked Farhad. "A friend of the princess?"

"Yes, I am. She told me about you."

"About me?"

"Yes. About the wind and the water, and the fire, too. And Nitish, the white tiger with blue eyes who turned to stone outside the city walls."

"If you know all that then it must be true, and you're a friend. Give me your hand," said Farhad.

Lagan felt for the other man's hand and found it, wet with the blood that was still pouring out of his breast. Next moment he felt something cold biting his fingers. He grasped it all the same. It was about the size of a pigeon's egg, and although he could see nothing else in the pitch darkness under the roses, he did see a faint red glow shining through the cracks between his fingers.

"The bloodstone," he whispered.

"Give it . . . Give it to Suryakanta, the demon king's first and chief servant," whispered Farhad, and he coughed again. "And get him to give you the keys to the whole harem in return. The keys to the doors of all the halls and corridors and the key of the gate. He'll let you have them. He's still in love with the bloodstone. I've seen his greedy desire for it."

"Seen it? But—did you ever meet him? I can't remember . . ."

Farhad didn't seem to have heard his question.

"The princess," he whispered, and there was an urgency in his voice that was not to be denied. "Please—tell me about her!"

"You'll soon see her yourself . . ."

"No," said Farhad, struggling for air. His breath came with a rattling sound. "No, I won't. It's not my own strength still keeping me alive. It's only the strength of her despair. Tell me, Lagan. Tell me what she's like!"

So Lagan leaned right down to the body of the stranger who seemed so familiar to him, and the blood from the cut on his hand mingled with the blood of the hero from Madurai.

"She is beautiful," he whispered. "Much more beautiful than in the picture in your amulet. But there's nothing soft and yielding about her beauty. She is wild as the desert, brave as a tiger, lonely as the sun, and timorous as the rain. Her heart is full of stories, and that's where you came from. And she'll make sure your story ends well. I know she will do that."

"Then—then everything's all right," whispered Farhad.

Lagan listened to the darkness for a while longer, but he heard no more breathing in it. He felt for the body under the rosebushes, and the body lay very, very still. Lagan felt a lump in his throat, and he wanted to weep, but he had no time for tears.

However, when he crawled out of the hedge with the bloodstone in his hand, he realized that his jealousy had disappeared entirely.

There were many, many lives, and perhaps Farhad had been right: One day Raka would be his wife. In a life where she was a real princess. That was what tellers of fairy tales demanded.

As he ran back along the gravel paths with the bloodstone in his bleeding hand, a question formed in Lagan's head. It wasn't the question of whether Ahmed Mudhi's chief servant was called Suryakanta. In this night and this story, he was.

The boundaries were blurring.

It was the question of whether he might not just strike Lagan down and take the jewel from him. What was he going to do when he found Suryakanta? How was he to approach him?

He was so deeply immersed in this problem that at first he didn't notice the figure standing in the middle of the gravel path in the middle of the garden—right in the very middle of it, under the date palm.

The figure was strong and stocky, like a watchdog, and it was looking Lagan's way.

He noticed it when he stepped on the tip of its shadow.

 424 Only then did he stop and look up from the path.

"What are you doing out in the garden at this time of night, little eunuch Lalit?" asked the Rajah's first and chief servant. "You'll catch a cold, you'll sneeze and cough and spoil your fine, handsome face!"

Lagan—or Lalit—did not reply for a moment. The moon lit up the coarse, pockmarked face of the man before him a little more clearly than he would have wished. The muscles played on the man's upper arms like kittens stretching in their basket.

Lagan considered thinking up an excuse. Or turning and running away.

But then he stood up a little straighter and found, to his surprise, that he was half a head taller than Mudhi's chief servant.

"I'd like to offer you a deal," he said calmly. He was amazed to hear just how calmly he spoke.

The man tilted his broad head to one side and inspected him like a fighting cock sizing up his rival. "I'm listening," he said.

"You're supposed to be taking the Rajah's eighth wife to him tonight, isn't that right?"

"Yes. And I can't stand about the garden here forever listening to a handsome eunuch's idle chatter."

"You will not take her to him," said Lagan. "If you give me the keys to the harem instead—all the keys—then what I have in my hand is yours."

"And what might that be?" asked Suryakanta. Lagan had begun calling him by that name in his mind. Then he leaned his broad torso forward and stared at Lagan's hand, and Lagan saw greed flash in his eyes.

A faint red glow was shining through the fingers of Lagan's closed fist.

Now, he thought, he will pounce on me with his bunched muscles and his greedy little eyes, and it will all be over . . . But he had to take the chance. There was no other option.

"The bloodstone," he whispered, opening his fingers.

To his surprise, Suryakanta stood where he was. He blinked and stared, and stared and blinked, and at last he said, "I've had it in my hands so often. And every time I was outwitted."

"By the stone?"

"No, not by the stone." Suryakanta smiled. It was not an attractive sight, but suddenly Lagan suspected that this new face was only one of many at the man's disposal.

"Not by the stone. By the strange youth who rode the white tiger . . . I don't know his real name. Any more than he knew mine."

"He brought the stone for you."

"For me?" Suryakanta's small eyes showed astonishment. "He really brought it all that long way for me . . . ?"

"For the price," said Lagan, "of the princess."

"That," said the man, "is the first good deal we've done in our acquaintanceship, that strange young man and I. With the stone in my hands, I needn't be anyone's guard or servant anymore, not even chief servant over all the others."

He reached into his pocket and then, to Lagan's great surprise, handed him a large bunch of keys without any more questions. "The one with most wards is the key to the great gate," he said. "I'll send all the servants to bed. Give me the stone now."

Lagan hesitated. "How do I know that it's really the right key?"

"You'll have to trust me. Trust is important. He could have explained that to you."

"He did explain it," said Lagan softly. "One way or another."

Then he gave Suryakanta the bloodstone.

For the first time, the stone left no cut. It fit into the palm of Suryakanta's hand like a child into its mother's lap, and Lagan knew that all was well.

Suryakanta went into the house first, to send the servants and guards under his command to bed. "The only one I can't command is the Rajah's 'private guard,'" he said with a grin that distorted his face in an ugly grimace.

427

"Private guard?"

"He keeps a silver rifle in his bedroom," said Suryakanta. "He sometimes suffers slightly from persecution mania. And I must say I'm beginning to understand him. But in any case, Ahmed Mudhi is a very fine shot."

Before he disappeared down one of the corridors, he turned once more. "What do *I* care for the Rajah's eighth wife, where she goes or who she goes with?" he said as if in passing.

"Who is she?" asked Lagan warily.

"She's a princess," replied Suryakanta, giving his ugly grin again. "If the rumors are to be believed. And not just any princess. Even if another man brought her up, I've heard folk whisper that she is the god Krishna's daughter."

With these words, he finally turned and marched away to give the last order he would ever give in the house of Ahmed Mudhi—or Ravana?—before he left it forever.

Lagan's feet flew down the corridor.

They were flying to Raka the storyteller, the princess, happy as they had never been before.

His heart was singing, and he felt as if his body were weightless.

All the same, his breath was coming short as he reached her door. He had prepared himself to knock. He had thought what he would say: *I've come for you*, he was going to say. *The desert is yours again.*

Wonderful words.

And this time they were true.

But the door was open. The bedroom beyond it was empty.

He saw the moon through the window where he had sat for long hours, listening to Raka's magical words. It had just reached the top of the date palm.

But Raka was not there.

And her statues of the gods were gone, too.

Lagan turned where he stood, and then he saw one of the bright little figures on the soft carpet of the corridor. He bent to pick it up: It was Krishna.

A little farther on he found Kali, the goddess of anger.

And a little way farther still lay Ganesh, the elephant-headed god of good fortune.

The figures made a trail, and he followed it: a trail of hope, the very last hope that someone might follow the owner of the little statues.

He smiled. She hadn't given up, not to the last.

The trail was leading toward Ahmed Mudhi's rooms.

No, she hadn't given up, but she had known that with so many guards in the house, trying to escape was pointless. She had gone of her own free will, as the moon had commanded her. Of her own free will, before the chief of those guards came for her. Of her own free will, to preserve her dignity.

She had gone to meet her fate all alone.

Lagan snorted angrily. The willful creature! If only she'd waited just a little longer, one tiny moment more.

Without a sound, he opened the door a crack and saw the ballet being danced by the two bodies and their shadows on the wall. And he smelled the fragrance of the flowers that always floated in great bowls of water in the Rajah's rooms—lotus flowers. Their scent mingled with the scent of desire.

For a moment, Lagan stood there quite still, unable to move.

He saw the bodies intertwining before him as if there were only one creature moving there, a god with a large number of arms and legs. But only the stronger half of the being dictated the rhythm of this nocturnal spectacle.

The soft silken cushions muffled the sounds of movement, and all Lagan heard was Ahmed Mudhi's breathing, heavy and excited. It filled the room like a bad taste filling your mouth.

Not a sound came from Raka's throat.

Lagan knew she was giving herself to the Rajah only because she had no choice. All the same, his heart contracted with jealousy.

Sheer rage went through him like a newly sharpened knife. Rage against Ahmed Mudhi, who could have anything, anything he liked; who could bring a new toy home from the desert and throw away a life when the whim took him; who was obeyed by everyone, including himself, Lalit the Beautiful One, whom no one took seriously.

But he was not Lalit now, the name that the harem women

had given him. He was far from being Lalit. He had changed that night. Or rather, Raka had changed him.

He was Lagan, the name he had been born with. Lagan— the man who chooses the right time.

And the right time had come.

Ahmed Mudhi might indeed be a fine shot, but he would never succeed in snatching up his rifle.

Lagan shut the door carefully as he turned, went back along the corridor, and ran down the stairs—faster than he had ever run before.

Outside, the doves were cooing in their sleep. They had cooed their way through a whole book.

Although they didn't know it, they were waiting for their master.

431

"Safia," said the Rajah, "come here to me! What a beautiful name you have! Safia the Virtuous. Don't be afraid. I've waited for you so long, my beauty! I was sick for a long, long time, sick with fever and sick with longing. All my life!"

Raka was determined that the Rajah would not break through her silence.

She wasn't going to tell him that the name Safia, *Virtue*, didn't suit her. She wasn't going to tell him that she was afraid not of him but of death. And even when he discovered that he had been cheated, and hadn't bought a virgin, she would say nothing.

"Come, Safia, sit here. The silken cushions in my bedroom are softer than anything else. Only my arms are softer . . ."

Ahmed Mudhi was not an ugly man, but the thick hair covering his arms and chest reminded Raka of the monkeys who had stolen Farhad's amulet at the beginning of his journey.

She felt him drawing her down into the alarmingly yielding world of his silken cushions. She felt she would drown in them. How different it had been diving down under the water of the lotus pool!

When she felt the Rajah's lips on her skin she tried to imagine he was Lalit. She did not succeed. The Rajah's lips were confident and demanding as he took possession of his property.

Lalit, thought Raka, had abandoned her.

She had told the story of her life for three whole nights, to show him that he could save her. That he only had to summon up the courage to do it. She had invented a hero so that he would be a hero, too.

But she had failed.

What was more, she had fallen in love with him a little herself, and that was a double failure: She had meant to be the strong one, the one who made the rules.

The one who made sure that *he* would fall in love with *her*.

She had wanted to be strong.

Now she needed the very last of her strength to keep silent as Ahmed Mudhi buried her slender body under his, and tried to unite himself with her by force.

Long after the moon had passed the top of the date palm, the Rajah was gazing at his eighth wife, satisfied and out of breath.

The light of the only kerosene lamp that had been lit was refracted a hundred times over by the mirrors lining the room. Like strangely shimmering, trembling silver, it fell on the Rajah's great bed. A bed of pale silk.

Ahmed Mudhi's eyes wandered lazily over the bed, in search of the blood that would be the evidence of his new wife's purity.

They didn't find it.

Raka opened her eyes, which she had kept tightly closed until now, and saw his face change. He had been cheated. He had been dishonored, fooled, tricked. *He*, the most powerful merchant of Jaisalmer, perhaps the most powerful merchant in the whole desert of Thar.

Ahmed Mudhi opened his mouth in a roar of helpless rage.

433

Under the Date Palm

AKA SAW AHMED MUDHI'S HANDS REACHING
for her. They aimed to close around her neck, and she
flinched back. But Ahmed Mudhi was quick and strong. She
held her arms over her face to protect it, although she knew
nothing would be any use. The next moment, the Rajah was
upon her, gasping furiously.

But at that moment she heard something else—something
strange.

A cooing, and the fluttering of wings.

Something made a sharp little sound, as if the window
left ajar with the fine mosquito net over it were opening, and

then the fluttering was everywhere. It grew louder and louder, and finally filled the room entirely.

Raka took her arms away from her face.

Ahmed Mudhi was still sitting on the bed in front of her, naked and breathing heavily, but he had turned and was staring. The whole room was full of doves.

They were flying back and forth between the walls, disoriented, crashing into the glass of the mirrors, reeling through the air, recovering themselves again—and still more and more came fluttering in through the room's only window.

Raka saw the doves and thought: Lalit.

He's here. He's somewhere here.

The doves didn't come of their own accord. He called them.

So he's done it after all, she thought. He's changed. He has conquered his obedience and his fear.

And she smiled.

Ahmed Mudhi jumped off the bed, waving his arms frantically about to shoo the birds away. But that only added to their panic and confusion.

"Get away!" cried the Rajah. "Get out of here! Get away this minute!"

The doves had interrupted him in mid-rage, and he looked more confused than angry now.

Raka saw him trying unsuccessfully to chase the doves out of the window and at the same time protect his face from their claws as they tried to find a perch—anywhere, even on Ahmed Mudhi. The shadows of the birds sailed across the walls, and the shadows and reflections and wings created a scene of such chaos that soon even Raka couldn't make anything out in it.

She rose from the bed, groped her way along the wall, and tried to remember just where the door was among all the chests, shelves, little tables, and mirrors. She was dizzy with fear and agitation, and her hands trembled uncontrollably as they felt their way.

Could she reach the door unnoticed while Ahmed Mudhi was fighting off the doves?

She avoided one of the birds, stumbled over a silk cushion lying on the floor, and knocked a small lamp over as she fell. The crash made Ahmed Mudhi spin around.

She saw him coming toward her through the chaos of wings.

"Was that you?" he shouted. "Did you summon the doves? *My* doves! How did you manage to let them out while you were in here? What are you? A demon? A goddess? Whatever you are, you don't mock me like that . . ."

This time, when he rushed at her, Raka saw a shadow behind him.

The shadowy figure came through the window. He must have climbed up the twining plants outside and over the balcony rail.

Ahmed Mudhi seized Raka by the wrist and pulled her up. His rage was back again, his confusion had left him.

"You wait," he whispered, drawing her to him. "You needn't think I'm going to let a few birds take my mind off you . . ." And this time his hands did reach her neck. They closed around it and tightened.

Then the shadowy figure came up behind Ahmed Mudhi. The doves gathered around him.

They flew to him like children to their mother, anxious, helpless, looking for protection, and fluttered above his head like a living turban. Some of the doves settled on the shadow's shoulders, others perched on his head—and the shadow let them do as they pleased.

He was attracting all the doves in the room like a magnet. But since he was standing right next to the Rajah, that dense, seething confusion of wings and beaks surrounded Ahmed Mudhi and Raka as well.

As she struggled for air, she thought she heard the shadow speaking to his doves, murmuring secret words that could hardly be heard through the fluttering and cooing. But the doves heard them. They fell on Ahmed Mudhi's hands and began pecking them with their beaks. Some of their pecks caught Raka, too, and she felt warm blood running down her throat, but she welcomed it like a friend.

The Rajah cried out and let go of her—and then Raka felt a hand in hers.

She let it draw her away—away through the fluttering confusion, away through the darkness in which the single lighted lamp had now fallen and gone out, away from Ahmed Mudhi's bedroom—accompanied by a cloud of gray wings and ringed necks that broke through the doorway with them.

And so this story ends as it began.

In chaos.

In India.

438

The corridors down which they ran were empty, and their footsteps echoed.

The Rajah didn't follow them. Presumably he had lit the lamp again and was examining the injuries to his hands by the light, wondering if the wounds were deep enough to leave scars on his well-tended skin.

Or perhaps he was calling his servants, who didn't hear him because Suryakanta had given them time off to get a good night's sleep.

Perhaps he was just sitting on the bed among the silken cushions, wondering exactly what had happened.

The doves found a window, and their master sent them out into the garden. They seemed to hesitate before flying away, but they obeyed him.

And their master led Raka on. The two of them didn't stop until they reached the foot of the last narrow stairway. Gasping for breath, they looked at one another.

The full moon fell through a small window, and by its light Raka saw that Lalit's face had changed. It was difficult to say just how.

But his features were no longer those of a handsome boy. His face was a man's face.

He looked at Raka's throat.

"It's not bad," she said. "The bleeding has stopped already, Lalit. It's not the artery."

He breathed out slowly, sighing with relief.

"There's been too much blood in this story already," he said. "And I am Lagan."

She smiled. "Of course. I ought to have known."

"I didn't know myself. Until a little while ago. Come on."

"The main gate is locked," said Raka. "It's still locked."

Lagan smiled. "The keys are in my pocket," he said. "We made a deal, Suryakanta and I."

"A deal?"

"Yes. He has his bloodstone now. *He* was the Frenchman, imagine that! And the Englishman, and the Pole, and the German."

She drew her eyebrows together. "Really?"

"And I met Farhad. In the garden."

"Yes," she said. "Yes, I thought so. Is he . . . Is he . . . ?"

Lagan took her firmly in his arms. "He is dead," he whispered. "But he died happy, very, very happy. I told him about you, and how strong and brave you are . . ."

"You're a liar," whispered Raka, and Lagan's shirt was damp with her tears. She couldn't say whether she was weeping for Farhad, or with relief because she was still alive, or because Lalit had found the courage to be Lagan, or for all those things at once.

"Let's go!" whispered Lagan.

"Wait," she asked, and loosed herself from his embrace. "I want to go into the garden and say good-bye to him."

Lagan opened the door to the garden, and Raka went out into it one last time. The fragrance of the nocturnal flowers mingled with the moonlight, weaving invisible fabric to clothe her naked body.

But a woman was standing on the gravel path, holding the reins of a horse that was almost white.

"I'm glad you've come," she said. "I was waiting. I thought you'd need a horse to ride."

Raka knew the woman. She was the Rajah's seventh wife, and Raka had always thought she despised her as much as the others did.

"How did you know . . . ?" she began.

But the woman put a finger to her lips. "I was listening," she whispered. "Forgive me, but I couldn't help it. I listened to your story, too, from the beginning to the end. That's why I got up in secret tonight and fetched a horse from the stables, and that's why I've opened the gate to the street for you."

Raka put her hands on the woman's shoulders. "Thank you," she whispered. "Thank you for everything. But before we leave there's something I still have to do. There's a hero lying here in the rose hedge."

"I've seen him," replied the woman. "But he didn't look like a hero. He was thin and untidy, dirty, and all over weals."

"He *is* a hero," said Raka.

"Anyway, he isn't there anymore," the woman told them. "There's no one in the rose hedge."

"No one?"

"No one at all. I heard the doves fly up, and then I knew it was time to bring the horse from the stables. But while I was doing that, I thought I heard the notes of a cowherd's flute playing very softly. And from the stable window I saw a figure go to the rose hedge. I could have been mistaken. I'm not a Hindu; I don't know about such things. But the figure looked remarkably like the pictures of Lord Krishna. I left the horse standing here for a moment and looked in the hedge—just before you came out. And there was nothing there but birds and the thorns of the roses."

Then Lagan climbed on the horse and lifted Raka up with him, and he whispered, "He came for him. Krishna came for him. He will keep his promise. Farhad Kamal's next life will be a better one."

And Raka nodded.

For a moment she thought of setting the horse to jump the wall, as Nitish would have done. But this was not a fairy tale. So they rode away through the gate that Ahmed Mudhi's seventh wife had opened for them.

She waved good-bye, and Raka knew that she would retell Farhad's story. Farhad was dead, but he was immortal. His adventures would live on forever in the minds of the people of Jaisalmer.

Outside the city, the sun rose.

The city gates had just been opened, and the watchmen were still half asleep. None of them felt like stopping the two riders on the fine horse that was almost white, although they were a little surprised to see that the woman was wearing a man's shirt.

She seemed to be entirely naked underneath it: naked and perfect.

The watchmen quickly looked away, and busied themselves with the stiff chains of the gate.

"Look," said Lagan. "See how red the sky is above the desert."

"Look," said Raka. "See how red the desert is beneath the sky. Red as blood. But there'll be no more blood in this story."

And then she pointed to a rock as they were riding past it.

"It looks a little like a tiger," she said.

Lagan nodded. "Yes, a little like a tiger."

The End of the Song

"WHERE ARE WE RIDING?" ASKED RAKA. Lagan breathed into her tangled hair. "Does it matter?" he asked.

"No," she said. "Just so long as we get far enough away from anyone looking for us."

"They won't be looking for us," said Lagan. "Ahmed Mudhi will have the sense to keep quiet about what happened. He's a powerful man, and he has a reputation to preserve."

Raka leaned against him.

"How strange," she said. "It's as if we'd changed places.

Now I'm the one who's weak and has doubts, and you're driving my doubts away. But I'm glad of that. I'm worn out. I can't be strong and reasonable anymore. Tell me," she asked, "tell me what happens after the end of my story."

"Oh, that's quickly told," replied Lagan, and he too felt glad that for once they had changed places. "The story is still an Indian story, and everything in India is in a state of constant change. Gods transform themselves; so do human beings. Rice grows from tiny grains in the fields and turns to proud green blades. Even the streams are transformed into rushing rivers in the monsoon. On the morning when the princess let a rider on a horse that was almost white carry her away, another transformation took place.

445

"For the soul of the tiger, which had slept in the stone all night, unable to decide what to do, woke again. And when the princess passed the rock where it lay, the tiger's soul rose from the stone like the goddess Lakshmi rising from the lotus blossom.

"Then it was wafted south by a gentle wind until it came to a great jungle where many tigers had always lived.

"The soul found the body of a young, strong tiger lying on its side in a clearing. Flies were already beginning to gather on it. A British hunting party had shot the tiger in the early hours of the morning and left the carcass there, meaning to come back for it later. The tiger's soul had already gone out of it, so the soul that had come with the wind happily entered the body.

"The flies were surprised when the dead tiger rose to his feet and disappeared into the jungle with a single powerful leap. But the members of the British hunting party were even more surprised when they came back and found their tiger gone.

"Many years later, as the tiger was roaming the forest, he came upon a little girl who seemed to him familiar. She was sitting under the only neem tree in the entire jungle, and she had two long braids of hair.

"The tiger sat down beside the little girl, who didn't seem at all afraid of him. Perhaps," Lagan concluded, "she was remembering an earlier life."

Lagan smiled and looked at Raka, and Raka said, "That's wonderful. But look—look ahead of us. There's the first oasis we'll come to on our way. I remember it, and it's beautiful. Let's rest there."

They sat down side by side in the shade of a date palm. Someone had pitched a tent with brightly colored tassels at that very place.

A nervous young man was pacing up and down outside

the tent, and a woman could be heard crying out inside. Several servants were busy preparing breakfast over a fire in the open air.

The young man beckoned Raka and Lagan over to the fire. He was far too agitated even to notice anything odd about the way Raka was dressed.

"Come and eat with us," he invited them. "Maybe you'll bring me luck. My wife is having a baby, and it's her first . . . We didn't reach the city in time."

At that moment, the woman in the tent cried out once more, and Raka clung to Lagan's arm as if she herself had to bear the labor pains.

Then an old woman came out of the tent carrying a tiny bundle in her arms. The bundle was red as a lobster, and just now extremely dissatisfied with the world that it had entered. It cried and reached thin arms into the air, and Raka leaned forward to see the baby better.

The young man clumsily took the child from the old woman. "Oh, look," he whispered. "I have a son. Just as I said, you've brought me luck."

"He has the sign on his forehead, my lord," the old woman said. "Right between the eyebrows. The sign of the gods. It looks almost like a burn mark . . . by Krishna, you are holding a very special child in your arms!"

"What should we call him?" asked the young man.

"She said," murmured the old woman, pointing to the hastily pitched tent behind her, "she said he was to be called Kalki, after the tenth incarnation of Vishnu. The rider on the white horse with the glittering sword. The one for whom the world is still waiting, the one who will finally destroy evil."

Raka and Lagan looked at each other.

And smiled.

Thanks

I WOULD LIKE TO THANK DANIEL FOR twice rescuing my computer when it was on the point of death.

Thanks, too, to Greifswald University Bookshop, for the sticky tape.

Thanks to Senthil for explaining the difference between green gods and blue gods, and to Navarathanam for trying to explain the difference between the three different letters *l* and the four different letters *n* in the Tamil language.

Thanks to a certain café in Aurich for a very long extension cord going right out into the sunlight.

Thanks to the friends sharing an apartment on the Rue Stephenson, Paris; for electricity; to Carolin, for strong coffee; and to my editor, for her strong nerves.

And I'd like to ask the German Railroads to install more electric outlets.

ANTONIA MICHAELIS was born in Kiel, Germany, in 1979 and spent her early years in a village by the Baltic Sea with her pleasantly eccentric parents and a variety of cats. A year teaching in southern India after school gave her a case of wanderlust, sending her to Peru, Ghana, Syria, and the British Isles. Antonia has studied medicine and currently lives in a small village in northern Germany, enjoying the perks and pitfalls of small-town life. Her work has been translated into a dozen languages.

ANTHEA BELL is a freelance translator from German and French, specializing in fiction. Her translations for young people include books by Cornelia Funke and René Goscinny. She has won a number of translation awards in the U.K., the United States, and Europe.

This book was designed by Maria T. Middleton and art directed by Chad W. Beckerman. The text is set in 13-point Adobe Jenson, an old-style typeface designed by the fifteenth-century French printer Nicolas Jenson. Redrawn in the 1990s by type designer Robert Slimbach, Adobe Jenson remains a highly legible face with a distinct caligraphic character.

Enjoy this sneak peek at Antonia Michaelis's new novel

DRAGONS
OF DARKNESS

AVAILABLE JANUARY 2010

"Who . . . Who are you?" gasped Christopher. "*Where* are you?"

"My name is Jumar," a voice replied out of the air. "And I would have thought that you just figured out where I am. Hold out your hand."

Christopher hesitated. What would he feel if he obeyed? Scales, fur, claws, teeth? This was a nightmare. It couldn't be real.

"Hold out your hand," the voice repeated rather impatiently. It seemed used to being obeyed.

Christopher felt another hand taking his and guiding it, and next moment his fingers felt skin, hair . . . a face.

"You see?" asked the voice. It was a silly question, because of course Christopher didn't see anything. "I'm just like you. Only no one can see me."

"Why . . . Why not?"

The voice sighed. "No one knows. I was born this way. It has its good points and its bad points. And by the way, I'm the son of the king."

"Oh," said Christopher blankly. "Uh, which king?"

"Well, *the* king!" cried the voice. "Where on earth have you come from if you don't know who the king is?"

"I've come from my room at home," replied Christopher truthfully. "Just now I was sitting on my bed, and then I was here in the jungle."

"You're crazy," said the voice. "But never mind that, so long as you help me. I fell into a trap, a kind of iron thing. I've no idea what kind of animals they catch in it. You'll have to bend the spring open . . . here, can you feel it? It's turned invisible because it's touching my skin. That's one of the other annoying things that happen."

The hand guided Christopher's fingers over rough, rusty iron, and he touched something wet: blood. Christopher flinched back.

"I can't see any blood," he said.

"Oh, great," said Jumar. "You can't see it because it's invisible, right? If you'd pull at this, then I'll pull the other side . . ."

They pulled together at the iron jaws of the trap, working hard, struggling for air together, and finally Christopher felt the pieces of iron moving, inch by inch. "It . . . It's working!" gasped Jumar. "Go on! Go on!"

Christopher narrowed his eyes, gritted his teeth, and pulled as hard as he could. He imagined it was his brother, Arne, in this trap.

He braced his legs against the ground and tugged. "Wait," he heard Jumar whispering. "This should do it. A little more . . ."

Christopher felt the bloodstained skin brush against him.

"Now let go," said Jumar. "But carefully, because it will snap shut again."

Christopher obediently withdrew his fingers, and something in front of him gave a metallic click. The next moment, an iron trap was lying on the leaf-strewn ground. When he cautiously touched the interlocking teeth, he felt blood sticking to them—invisible blood. And now he saw the shoe lying beside it. But as soon as he had spotted the shoe, it, too, dissolved into nothing. Nothing was left of it but the soft sound of a buckle closing.

His invisible acquaintance had put the shoe back on again.

"Please," said Christopher. "Please explain—does everything you touch become invisible?"

"Only some inanimate objects," replied Jumar. "Water, for instance, stays the way it was before. Earth and rock, too. It's a question of trial and error. If I walked barefoot, I suppose the dead leaves on the ground here would disappear. But the path would stay where it is. Anyway, I usually wear gloves so that the things I pick up won't vanish. But gloves aren't very practical when you're doing up your shoes."

"Interesting," said Christopher.

"Do me a favor," said Jumar, "just don't say that word for a while."

Half an hour later, they were sitting on a rock beside the path together, looking down into the valley through which a river clad in bright blue wound its way.

Actually, Christopher was sitting there on his own. But a voice beside him was telling him an incredible story.

A story about a sleeping woman and a garden under a gigantic glass dome, about dragons who lived in the mountains and ate colors, about a dying servant and a king who had forgotten his country. It would have been a fairy tale if there hadn't been airplanes in it, and doctors, and the crown prince's computer courses, and military tanks.

"So, now tell me something about you," said the voice without a name. "I still don't know anything about you. How did you get here?"

You don't know anything about me because you do all the talking yourself, thought Christopher. "My name is Christopher," he said rather stiffly.

"And how did you get here, Cri . . . Cisto . . . Krisho?" asked Jumar.

"Christopher," Christopher put him right, giving himself time to think what to say next.

"Crishnofer. What are you doing here?"

I have no idea, Christopher thought.

He said, "I think I've come looking for my brother, Arne. He's nineteen, and he came to Nepal to work in an orphanage. He does things like that. Everyone likes him."

"Where is he now?"

Christopher sighed. "No one knows for certain," he said. "They think the Maoists have kidnapped him. But no one's sure. He wanted to go walking on his own in the Annapurna region . . . and he didn't come back."

Jumar said nothing for a while. In fact, he said nothing for so long that Christopher began to doubt whether he was real. Perhaps he himself was sitting alone on this rock above this outrageously bright blue river . . .

He put out his hand—and felt another hand take it.

"I'm on my way," said Jumar, "to find the insurgents' camp. And you're on your way to find your brother. So maybe that will be the same thing. Why don't we travel together?"

Christopher smiled. "Did anyone say we wouldn't be traveling together? I mean, obviously this is a dream, and I'll soon wake up, but while I'm dreaming, I might as well dream along with you."

That was well phrased, Christopher thought, and it was a pity none of the girls from school had heard him—those girls who always used to spend their days waiting to hear Arne talk so smartly.

The path became steeper, and there were some large stone steps along it. At first, Jumar went ahead, but Christopher kept bumping into him. Being invisible really wasn't so helpful for them.

So Christopher led the way. He heard Jumar's heavy breathing behind him, and sometimes the crack of a twig under his sandals. When the path ran level, they talked to each other. As long as Christopher didn't turn toward where Jumar was walking, he could imagine he was on the road with a perfectly normal human being. That felt better than talking to a voice that came out of thin air.

"Where is this insurgents' camp?" asked Christopher. "Do you know the way there? How far is it?"

"Oh, we'll find the way," said Jumar. "I don't know exactly where it is, of course, and maybe it isn't easy to find. But it's somewhere here in these mountains."

"Ah," said Christopher. "Then it can only be a matter of weeks before we get there."

Maybe it was just as well that he didn't know how true that was.

"Tell me," said Jumar later, "how come you look so . . . well, so normal? Didn't you say you came from the Netherlands or Sweden or somewhere like that?"

"Germany," said Christopher.

"Same thing," said Jumar. "Why aren't you tall and fair-haired?"

"Oh, for goodness' sake! Not all Germans are blond and drink beer in front of the TV set around the clock!"

"But you look like the people here," Jumar insisted. "I've often stood at the window watching the tourists crossing Durbar Square. And I've seen lots of your movies. The actors in them are tall and hearty and they move around as elegantly as elephants."

"Oh, really? What about me?"

"You move perfectly normally, I'd say. You're the right height and size, and your face isn't peculiar. It's the right kind of shape,"

Christopher sighed. "Where I come from, they don't see it that way. I had this grandmother, you see. She came from Nepal."

"Is that why you speak our language?"

"*Your* language?" Up to this point Christopher hadn't given it a thought. Was he really speaking Nepali? It felt to him like German.

"It must be something to do with the dream," he muttered, rather confused. "That's all. This is just a dream. I mean, you do sometimes suddenly speak foreign languages in your dreams. It's about time morning came and I woke up."

But morning never came, and the strange workings of Christopher's dream were to grow darker and more disturbing for a long time, while the whirlpool of events into which they dragged him kept refusing to let the light of an ordinary ray of sun come into his bedroom and wake him.

Far from it. The dream that wasn't a dream grew wilder all the time.

After they had been climbing for an eternity, the huge trees, draped in climbing plants, gave way to the view of a high plateau, and a pale green ocean of rice fields stretched out before their eyes. They saw the brown roofs of a village in the distance. A breath of wind passed over the rice plants, and when the blades bowed under the touch of its soft fingers, it was as if the surface of an unusually green sea were rippling. Christopher stopped and listened. He heard the trickling of water, and then there was another sound in the air. He wondered if it was just the wind in the branches of trees in the jungle.

Jumar saw him listening. "What you hear is the irrigation of the fields," he said. "The rice stands in water, and the water runs along channels from field to field. I learned about the system in one of my lessons—"

Christopher put a finger to his lips. "That's not it," he whispered. "Can you hear that other noise? In the air above us?"

"The wind," said Jumar dismissively, his voice wandering past Christopher, out of the forest, and into the paddy fields. "Or the cicadas. You worry too much. Come on! There's a village ahead, and maybe we'll find something to eat there. I'm starving."

Christopher hesitated. The sound in the air seemed to have come closer now. It was like a tiny, angry whisper, a soft rustling, an alarming crackle secretly stealing nearer. In the green of the paddy fields, he saw individual workers who looked like brightly colored dots. Now they, too, straightened up to listen. There was a hissing and fluttering in the air, as if a flock of birds were coming—a huge flock of birds, hundreds of them, thousands . . .

The wind was stronger now, and all the tiny voices of the forest had fallen silent.

Christopher looked up. There was something like a vague outline high above the treetops that cast a shadow over him. Was it some vast creature moving up there?

Seconds later, he saw the people in the fields begin to run. They were scattering along the narrow paths between the paddy fields and moving toward the village that Christopher had seen in the distance. They stumbled, fell, and struggled up again, and when one of the women in a red blouse turned around, he thought he saw horror on her face like a mask, distorted and terrifying.

Somewhere inside him, a cold hand closed around his guts.

"Jumar!" called Christopher. "Where are you? Come back!"

But he didn't wait for the answer. He sprinted off, going up the path leading out of the forest, collided with an invisible body, and hauled it back into the shelter of the trees.

Gasping for breath, he stood among the leafy arms of the undergrowth and, with Jumar beside him, stared out at the green expanse of the fields until his eyes were burning. And his heart was also burning, burning with fear. Fear of the unknown.

And then they saw the shadow on the green surface of the fields. It was moving over them like a gigantic fish, and the blades of rice seemed to shiver at the shadow's touch. Christopher looked up at the sky, but it wasn't blue anymore. Something was blocking it. At first it looked like a colorful cloud, but the cloud had a shape. It had a head and two enormous wings, it had claws and a lashing tail, and now it seemed to be denser than before. It was a dragon.

A dragon like those Jumar had described.

A dragon soaring down from the mountain peaks on brightly colored wings.

A dragon on its way to destroy.

It shimmered as it wound its way through the wind, flew in a curve above the fields, and swiped at the air with huge, flashing claws as if to tear it apart.

"So they do exist," whispered Jumar.

Christopher nodded. The dragons did exist, and here, only a few feet away from him, one of them was displaying its full, gorgeous splendor.

"How beautiful it is," whispered Christopher in surprise. "So beautiful!"

For hidden in the depths of the human mind lies the conviction that everything bad is ugly and everything good is beautiful, and probably no one will ever find out why we think that way.

The dragon swept over the high plateau and away, and then

came down, bending its slender head and graceful neck toward the rice, as if it were about to graze an outsized meadow.

"What . . . What's it doing?" asked Christopher.

"Eating the colors," replied Jumar in a whisper. "Watch!"

And Jumar was right. When the shimmering dragon slowly passed over the fields, it left a black-and-white trail behind it. It was as if everything it touched changed into a clipping from an old-fashioned newspaper printed on cheap, coarse newsprint. The light reflecting off the blades of rice gave way to a dirty pale gray, and the brown wood of the wet irrigation pipes, which had reflected rainbow-colored sunlight here and there only a moment ago, turned to dull black.

"Where are the people?" asked Christopher. "All the people who were in the fields?"

However hard he strained his eyes, he couldn't see the red blouse worn by the woman who had run away, and there was no sign of the other workers in the paddies, either.

"Perhaps they reached their village in time," whispered Jumar. Everything in Christopher wanted to believe it, but he knew Jumar was wrong. Something had happened to the people, too.

But what?

"And that's not all," old Tapa had warned Jumar. That was how Jumar told the story anyway. There was something else you had to know about the dragons, something apart from the fact that they ate colors. Something, he thought, to do with human beings.

The dragon was taking its time. Now and then it raised its head, swung its long neck back and forth, and looked at its surroundings.

Its eyes were almost the scariest thing about it. They weren't there. Where it ought to have had eyeballs with pupils and an irises, there were only dark holes in its head. Everything about it was brightly colored and beautiful, except for those eyes. And yet it seemed to see extremely well. It was as if there were no bottom to the depths of those eyes, as if they went on forever, and everything the dragon saw with them had to disappear into them.

They radiated a sense of suction, and when Christopher saw those eyes, even from a distance, he felt as if he were standing on the edge of an abyss that threatened to swallow him up. He felt for Jumar's hand.

"Do you think it can see us?" he whispered.

"I don't know," Jumar whispered back.

Christopher took a step back, farther into the safety of the trees. Then another step. At the third step, he stepped on a dry twig that broke with a snap. If only the birds had been singing as usual—the thousands upon thousands of birds with their thousands upon thousands of melodies. If only the leaves had been rustling—all those thousands upon thousands of different kinds of leaves. If only the tiny creatures living on the forest floor had been scurrying about as usual with faint scrabbling sounds. Then no one would have heard the twig snap. But the forest was silent. The birds had stopped singing, not one of them raised its voice in song; the leaves were not rustling; the tiny forest creatures were keeping still in their hiding places. A deathly silence had fallen in the evergreen forest.

And in that silence, the snap of the tiny dry twig sounded like a gong. Christopher froze, and he felt the fear of Jumar's hand in his own. The dragon raised its head.

It swung its neck once in an arc, searching the outskirts of the forest. Christopher dared not breathe. He saw the dragon's dark, empty eyes scan across the undergrowth like searchlights, though no light came from them. Instead, they seemed to absorb the light. After an eternity of watching and listening, the dragon began to move. Its movement on the ground was as wonderfully elegant as its flight in the air. It was as if it were flowing through the swaying blades of rice, beautiful and almost weightless. It hardly crushed a single rice plant with its spotless, shimmering, scaly paws. And those spotless paws with their immaculate claws carried the dragon to the outskirts of the forest. There were just two thoughts that repeated in Christopher's mind: Run away. Stay put. Run away. Stay put.

Running away would be noisy. Staying put would be quiet. Running away would be active. Staying put would be passive. Running away would be an attempt to do something—a pointless attempt. Staying put would be pointless, and he wouldn't even have tried anything. He felt Jumar pulling at his hand.

Then the dragon stopped just before it reached the forest.

And Christopher felt that it was looking at him.

Perhaps its empty eyes could see through his. Perhaps they could see right through him and read his thoughts. Perhaps they saw his fear as a bright, pulsating energy. Perhaps they saw his heart beating and the blood pumping violently through his veins. Perhaps they could see the possibility of his death within the next few seconds there.

Christopher's mouth was dry and his throat was burning. He wanted to look away from the dragon. He wanted to close his eyes, but he couldn't. The black void had attached itself to him by suction.

After another eternity, the dragon bent its head as if nodding—a greeting?—but it was probably just an involuntary movement of the long, flexible neck. Then it turned suddenly and sank its dragon jaws back into what remained of the green in the paddy field, and it went back to grazing on colors.

Only when Jumar's grasp relaxed did Christopher notice how hard the prince had been clutching his hand. Fear gradually evaporated through every pore in his body, leaving a tingling, empty feeling behind. He would have liked to drop into a chair, but there wasn't any chair around—and anyway, it was better to go on standing perfectly still for a while.

And so they stayed there for a long, long time, in the shadow of gigantic jungle leaves: two timid little animals who didn't dare to move out of hiding. Christopher could feel Jumar's body close to his, and he didn't know which of them was responsible for the trembling.

At last, the dragon spread its wings, with a rustling sound like millions of tiny pieces of tissue paper, cast a final look around from the fathomless depths of its black eyes, and hunched its long neck down like a heron's. It was greener now than before.

The claws pushing off from the ground left no marks behind. Christopher watched the dragon rising into the blue sky, soaring higher and higher, and somehow seeming to lose density in a way he couldn't explain.

Finally, it was only a tiny green dot in the afternoon light, green as the paddy fields whose color it had eaten. And then that dot disappeared to the northeast, where the highest peaks of the Himalayas rose, waiting with their frozen, snow-capped summits incredibly far away.

The mountain peaks were waiting for the dragon's return, and for something else, too. But that was only a rumor.

Keep reading! If you liked this book, check out these other titles.

Dragons of Darkness
by Antonia Michaelis
978-0-8109-4074-1 · $18.95 hardcover

Escape the Mask
by David Ward
978-0-8109-7990-1 · $6.95 paperback

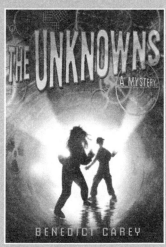

The Unknowns: A Mystery
by Benedict Carey
978-0-8109-7991-8 · $16.95 hardcover

Keep reading! If you liked this book, check out these other titles.

Fell
by David Clement-Davies
978-0-8109-7266-7 · $8.95 paperback

The Lighthouse Land
by Adrian McKinty
978-0-8109-9361-7 · $7.95 paperback

The Hunter's Moon
by O.R. Melling
978-0-8109-9214-6 · $8.95 paperback